343
Yvonne

The Major New Bestseller of
Love, Ambition, and Success by
NEAL TRAVIS

Author of

CASTLES

AND

PALACES

Other Avon Books by
Neal Travis

CASTLES
PALACES

Mansions

NEAL TRAVIS

AVON
PUBLISHERS OF BARD, CAMELOT, DISCUS AND FLARE BOOKS

AVON BOOKS
A division of
The Hearst Corporation
1790 Broadway
New York, New York 10019

Copyright © 1984 by Neal Travis
Published by arrangement with the author
Library of Congress Catalog Card Number: 84-91097
ISBN: 0-380-88419-4

First Avon Printing, August, 1984

For Tolly

Mansions

BOOK
ONE

Chapter
One

Even his name conjured a faraway world, exotic, rich. Angie listened, rapt, but as he spoke, part of her mind drifted into that world where handsome, powerful men like Richard Mansion directed destinies. She stole a glance at the eager faces alongside her in the lecture hall. All were awed by their proximity to greatness. All, she suspected, were sure this was as close to power as they would ever get.

Richard Mansion, though used to adulation, was still excited by it. That was why he made time for speeches, speeches to college groups or anyone else who wanted to hear his wisdom. He was spreading the word, showing the flag, reaffirming all that had made America—and the Mansion dynasty—great. And, besides, he loved a worshipful audience. Young men of great fortune often do.

She was sitting in the seventh row of the auditorium, and by moving just a little to the left of his podium, he could see straight up her tartan skirt. She had fine legs, long and slim and brown, stretching from white sandals up to a neat vee of white panties. He let his gaze settle on the panties as he went on speaking to the Florida college class. He didn't need to refer to notes, and he knew his topic thoroughly. He had given the same address to dozens of groups in recent months, and it was a message he believed in totally.

"This year's is the first election in which television will be the dominant medium," he said. "Through television, the American public will decide which man is worthy of the great office. If Nixon and Kennedy agree to debate on live television, all of us will be able to make an excellent decision, because you cannot lie to the camera."

She crossed her legs and pulled her skirt down over her knees. The view was gone. Had he not been in full oratorical flight by then, he would have sighed.

"I am confident Richard Nixon will emerge with distinction under the unrelenting eye of the television camera," he said, then smiled. "My political bias is showing. I do believe our vice-president is the man to lead us into the new decade, the man to stand up for us through the many challenges ahead."

His gaze left the covered knees and roamed upward, exploring her body. He stopped at her face, momentarily forgetting what he was saying. It was the most beautiful face he had ever seen. Young, but already perfectly formed. An oval face with a high forehead, long slim nose, strong, slightly squared jaw. Her dark red hair was tied back in a ponytail, accenting the high cheekbones. The eyes that gazed into his were dark green and flecked with gold. The perfect face, he thought. It would be too much to hope she had a lovely voice to match. Reluctantly, he

4

broke their eye contact and brought himself back to his audience.

"Whatever the outcome of the election," he said, "television will play a vital role, just as it does in our daily lives. Television is the greatest force for knowledge, for communication, ever to enter society. My family and I are extremely proud to be in the forefront of the television industry. We call ourselves The Family Network because we are dedicated to the American values of home and family, of good Christian standards. There will be no compromising our strict morals, not while a member of the Mansion family heads the network. Our competitors can go for the fast buck with cheap, pandering programs. The Mansions will never do that."

He studied her slowly. She was so much more than pretty. About nineteen or twenty, she stood out in the sea of bland young faces. So beautiful, the face so full of character. Their eyes met again and held for a few seconds, until she modestly dropped her gaze.

"In the Mansion family newspaper and radio interests, too, we reject sensationalism. The appeal to base desires used by many of our competitors is not the Mansion way. Television can be the greatest force for good society has ever known. Like my father, who founded our network, I am committed to defending and spreading the moral code that makes our country what it is.

"And so I say to you"—he glanced at her and then away—"the journalism students of this college, consider careers in television. Our industry needs bright, serious young people if it is to prosper as a force for good, and help keep America strong and free." He smiled again. "My brother, who runs our newspaper division, would hate me for saying this, but I believe

television news will quickly overtake newspapers as
the primary news source. Television is where the
great careers of journalism will be made now. Television is the future of the news media, and it is young
people like you who will be in the vanguard.''

He nodded to his audience and took a step back.

Angie Waring joined in the loud applause as Richard Mansion finished speaking. He seemed again to
be looking right at her and she felt herself blush. It
was a silly thought. The dashing young heir to the
Mansion empire would not have noticed her, not in
that crowd. But she was thrilled to be so close to Mansion. He represented a world she desperately—probably futilely—desired.

She pushed her way through the throng of students. She was on the hospitality committee and
wanted to get to the dean's office as quickly as possible: maybe she would get to speak to Mansion.

"God, he's impressive!" Marty Akerman said as
they hurried down the hall. It was almost unheard of
for anything to impress Marty, a senior who had already cultivated a journalist's cynicism. "He's right,
you know. Newspapers are yesterday's news. The future is television.''

Jane Whiting overheard and said hotly, "TV's just
a money machine, pumping out enough pap to separate the commercials. Television is information for
people who move their lips when they read. Mansion's a charlatan. But I'll give you one thing. He's
damn good-looking. He can audition me anytime.''
She gave Angie a wicked grin. "I saw you and the
great man eyeing each other," she said. "Lucky Jeff
wasn't there.''

Angie blushed. "Don't be silly, Jane," she said.
"I'm sure Mr. Mansion doesn't flirt with college kids.

And I agree with Marty. I think he was introducing the future."

"I bet I know what Mr. Mansion would like to introduce you to," Jane said, and she and Marty laughed.

Angie, taller than most of her classmates, found herself eye to eye with Richard Mansion as they met in the dean's office at the reception. He smiled right at her. She was shocked and flattered. The editor of the college paper introduced them, and Mansion held her hand a moment longer than necessary.

"Angie Waring," he repeated. "What a pretty name."

He stayed close to her as they toured the college newsroom, the campus radio station and, finally, the television studio.

Mansion whistled in admiration.

"You young people are very lucky," he said. "This must be the best-equipped journalism department outside of Columbia." He rested his hand on the single video monitor. "And who," he said, "is your anchorman?"

Marty Akerman pushed Angie forward.

"Angie is, sir," Marty said. "She's our star. We think we're real advanced, having a girl as the anchor. She's real good, though. And the camera loves her face."

Mansion looked at Angie seriously and nodded.

"I'd like to see you in action, Angie. You and the whole team. How about doing a quick newscast for me?"

Taken by surprise, they were all very nervous as they hurried to set up the shot. Richard Mansion was going to judge their work. It made them clumsy: light standards tottered, cables got twisted around desks, the camera dolly jammed. But finally they were ready and Angie slid into the newsreader's chair.

Her hands were shaking as she clutched the sheaf of hastily gathered campus announcements. She watched the floor manager counting off the final five seconds on his fingers. The red light over the camera lens came on and the director cued her, and for one dreadful moment Angie thought her voice had gone. Then she ordered herself to take control and it all came together for her. She breezed through the mundane announcements of pep rallies, class displays, and dire warnings from the administration about dress codes. She looked right into the camera, into a space behind the lens, stroking that space with her eyes and her voice, as if addressing an old, intimate friend.

And as her confidence surged she decided to take a risk. She laid down the papers and smiled into the camera.

"We have a very special guest here in the studio today," she said. "He's Richard Mansion, of whom you have all certainly heard. Mr. Mansion took the time to drive up here from Miami, where he's running his network's local station, to talk to our journalism school. It was such an interesting talk, we would like to share some of it with the rest of the student body. I wonder, Mr. Mansion, if you would mind coming down here."

There was a buzz of anticipation from the floor crew. No one ever did anything spontaneous in that studio. They were all too much in awe of the medium to depart from a script. But young Bob Talbot, the director, ushered Richard Mansion into the studio, found a chair for him beside Angie, and placed the single mike between them. It was time to roll the camera again.

She never let her nervousness show, just buried it and concentrated on the task before her. It was often like this when she was broadcasting: her natural shyness and reserve vanished entirely. Giving the camera her profile, she turned to her guest and smiled.

"Thank you, Richard Mansion, for agreeing to share some of your expert opinions with us. In your talk today you said you thought Nixon would win in November. Can you expand on that please?"

Mansion looked knowing, bemused. He had only seen this a few times before: the transformation of a personality when the camera was rolling. This kid was coming on like a professional. And she had the face and the voice to carry it off.

"Angie," he said smoothly, "it doesn't take a crystal ball to see Nixon winning. All the polls, particularly in the real America, have him way ahead. And the vast experience he has gained as vice-president means he knows how to cope with the pressures of a presidential campaign."

"Granted," Angie said, "but a lot of people, particularly young people, find John Kennedy much more appealing. A romantic figure, I suppose."

"I'll concede that," he chuckled. "And dyed-in-the-wool Nixon supporters thank God teenagers can't vote. But even all the Kennedy charisma can't obscure the facts. Dick Nixon is a statesman. He's perfectly groomed for the most awesome task in the Free World. Oh, sure, a few pointy-heads will never forgive him for flushing out Reds. But those are people outside the mainstream, and I don't think their votes will matter much."

"And you think television will be decisive?" Angie

asked. "You think Nixon should debate Kennedy on live television?"

"I think it will clinch the election for Mr. Nixon," Mansion said confidently. "When people see the two men head to head, the American public will choose experience and dignity over wealth and charisma."

The director gave her the signal to close the show. Their tape was running out.

"Our guest today has been Richard Mansion," Angie said into the camera. "Thank you, sir, for your valuable time and insights."

As they cut the lights Angie felt herself begin to tremble all over. Her palms were damp, and when she stood up her knees almost gave out. How could she have been so . . . so challenging to a distinguished guest? She'd made a fool of herself.

Mansion tucked his hand under her elbow and steered her off the studio floor, as if he knew how unsteady she was.

"Could I have a run-through of the tape?" he asked Bob Talbot. "Your interviewer here had me so involved I don't know what I said."

She stood in the crowded control booth watching their brief interview on the monitor. Everyone held his breath, waiting to see what Mansion thought.

"It's very good, Angie," he said when the tape was finished. "Very professional." He took her hand, felt how wet it was. "Congratulations. I guess you're nervous, but you concealed it from the camera. And you look just great on the screen. I think you've got a real future in television. You do want a career in television, don't you? How old are you?"

"Twenty, Mr. Mansion," she said. "And, well, we know what we do here is nothing like the real thing.

When I graduate, I guess I'll try for a job on the local paper.''

"That would be a terrible waste of talent," Mansion said wryly. "Angie, I've introduced summer intern programs at our station, and I think you'd benefit from a few months at our Miami station. Since I'm there for a while, building the place up, I could take you under my wing. I've been in this business quite a while now, and I don't recall when I've seen more natural talent."

The others had drawn back as far as they could in the small control booth, but they all heard. There was a collective gasp.

"I don't know if I could . . . I've never . . ."

"It's just for the summer," Mansion said. "Just to see if you've got what it takes. You might not even like us. There are some crazy people in this business." He took out his wallet and handed her his card. "Call my secretary next week. She'll go over all the details with you and find you a nice safe place to stay, that kind of thing. If your parents want to talk to me about it, I'll be happy to reassure them."

Mansion left then with Dean Semmler, the dean bestowing a proud smile on Angie. The others clustered around her, pleased and excited, as if they were all going to share in her big break.

Jeff was waiting for her in the parking lot, his big frame slumped against his car. He drew himself upright and hugged her as she reached him.

"Did you get detention for talking in class?" He grinned. "I was only going to wait another hour."

"I'm sorry, Jeff." She smiled as he held open the door for her. "It was because of Mr. Mansion. Let's

11

drive over to the beach and I'll tell you what happened."

She studied him as he drove. Dear sweet Jeff Tyrell. Big and fair and handsome, and so in love with her. And she loved Jeff, too, loved his patience, his calm. He depended on her, yet gave her strength. They were almost engaged, would be engaged at the end of summer. Marriage a year later, a baby the year after that. It was all mapped out, just as it was for many college juniors. She wanted to be a good wife and mother, and work for the paper while Jeff built his career as an agricultural scientist. It was the way they'd planned things.

He parked in a grove of palm trees above their favorite beach, and she began to tell him about her triumph. He listened eagerly until she came to the last part.

"You're not going to accept, are you?" he said. "It would destroy our whole summer."

"I don't know, Jeff," she said. For the first time that day, she began feeling miserable. "It's such a wonderful chance. Working with professionals in a big-city television newsroom."

"And what if you got to like it?" he challenged. "What if you wanted to stay in Miami and be a TV star? What would happen to us? You know I couldn't stand life in a big city."

"No one's going to make me a star," Angie laughed. "It's just a summer job. The experience might come in handy, somewhere."

"But it will ruin our summer, Angie." His stubborn streak was in control now. "This summer's our last chance to be kids. After that it's going to be marriage and babies and responsibilities. A whole lifetime of being grown up."

She looked at him sharply. "It almost sounds like you don't want to get married, Jeff," she said. "You make it seem like life ends with the first baby."

He kissed her. He searched for the words to make her understand his uneasy feeling that she was contemplating something dangerous.

"I do love you so, Angie," he mumbled into her hair. "And I want so much to be married to you. I'm afraid of losing you. You're so beautiful. And talented. I've never gotten used to the idea that you're willing to settle for me. I'm scared you'll go away and find somebody else."

The anger in her disappeared. Poor Jeff. She would make it all right. She kissed him, parting her lips and feeling his eager tongue.

"I think it's something I've got to do," she said when they came apart. "But there is nothing for you to fear. I love you. I'll just go to Miami and get this whole career thing out of my system all at once."

He looked so sad that she moved against him and took his hand and placed it under her blouse. She let her own hand rest on the bulge in his khaki slacks.

"Don't," he whispered. "It only makes it worse. You don't know what it's like, holding back all the time. I know you're right to stop us from going all the way, but it's so hard for me. I feel like I'm going to explode."

In that moment she knew what she had to do. It would reassure him, comfort him.

"No more waiting, Jeff," she said. "Not now, not if I'm going away for a while. Tonight, no more waiting."

He was flustered. "You mean . . . you and I are going to . . . ?"

"Yes," she said. "It will be my promise that I'm

coming back to you." She was calm. "Pick me up after dinner. And," she said, turning her head away, "you better bring something. I mean, we don't want to start all our responsibilities right now, do we?"

She remained calm as he drove her home. She had made her decision and now she wouldn't have to worry about him. But she could sense an electric tension in Jeff. He could hardly speak. She just hoped she wouldn't disappoint him.

Chapter
Two

"You're late, dear," her mother said. "But dinner's going to be late, too. I drove a hundred miles out along the swamps trying to find people to register. I'm starting to think there isn't a Democrat anywhere in this godforsaken state. And the rest all sign themselves X and vote for whoever the ward boss tells 'em to."

"It's Nixon country, Mom," Angie said. "We had a man speak to us today who—"

"I can't talk now," her mother said. She was searching through the kitchen cupboards, trying to put dinner together.

May Waring didn't think fate had meant for her to end up a housewife in Lantana, Florida. So she tried to keep involved in "good works." The result was that her housekeeping was a haphazard affair at best.

"You want me to help?" Angie asked, regarding her harried mother with real affection. She knew May Waring wasn't cut out to be a homebody.

"No, dear, I'll find something," her mother said.

"How did you get home from school? Didn't Jeff drive you?"

"Yes, and he waited until after our speaker had finished with us," Angie said. "But he just dropped me off. He didn't want to come in. He thinks you don't like him."

"Nonsense," May Waring said. "You know my only objection is I think you're far too young to be so serious. Jeff's a good boy, but I want you to see something of the world before you settle down. Don't get trapped in a place like this, for God's sake."

"Actually, something happened today that should make you happy," Angie said. "Mr. Mansion thinks I might—"

"Please, dear," her mother said. "Tell me over dinner." She took a frozen chicken from the big refrigerator. "Do you think if I ran hot water on this it would thaw pretty soon?"

Angie went out to the big screened porch where her father was working on his third or fourth drink. He needed at least four to recover from his job as senior editor of the *American Clarion*.

Harley Waring waved his drink at Angie.

"You want to hear what that crazy bastard has done?" he called. She didn't really, but she knew her father took a grim pleasure in relating the exploits of his publisher. A tyrant, Joe MacDonald ran his scandal sheet from the quiet confines of West Palm Beach. His newspaper made a great deal of money.

Harley Waring had the dubious honor of being the longest-surviving journalist on the *Clarion*. Virtually everyone on the paper was miserable. Everyone had come to the paper for the high salary. Most wished they were anywhere else.

"He decided to reorganize the office again," her father said. "Some management expert convinced him everything should be color-coded. So the staff has been split into four teams—the Red Team, Yellow, Blue, and Green. And everything they write has to be done on their own team's color paper, so Joe will know which team's producing the most copy."

"Well," Angie said carefully, "I suppose it might be one way of keeping track."

"Angie," her father said patiently, "printers won't set copy on anything but white paper. The colored stuff is too hard to read. And the boss is color-blind. He won't admit it, but he is. So he's *still* got no idea who's writing what. Can you believe this?"

She went to the bar and fixed herself a Coke.

"Don't you ever think of just quitting, Daddy?" she asked gently. "You could move back north, get another job on a regular newspaper. I now how sick it makes you, working there. It's a rag."

"That rag has been damned good to all of us," her father snapped. "You think we'd have a house like this, two cars in the garage, you in college, if I were still a rewrite man in Boston? I'm making three times the money. So Joe's a little crazy. And the people who read the *Clarion* are morons. It doesn't matter. The newspaper trade's had it anyway, so I might as well keep us all in comfort."

"That's something I wanted to talk to you about, Daddy," Angie said. "Today, at school, we had Richard Mansion—you know, the Mansion family network?—speak to us. And he said what you're saying, that newspapers are finished and television's the future."

"He's not far wrong," Harley Waring said. "Although most of the people I see on television never would have gotten a job on any of my old papers. Pret-

17

ty faces and capped teeth." He fixed himself another drink and settled back in his deck chair.

"Well," Angie said, "Mr. Mansion had us run through a TV show for him. I was the anchor. He was kind of impressed with my work, and he's offered me a summer internship at his station in Miami."

"No!" her father shouted. "No! Damn your mother for putting ideas in your head. I never should have agreed to that stupid journalism course. I'm not having you in this rotten business." He was out of his chair, storming up and down the porch, gesturing with his drink.

"I should have sent you to secretarial school." He turned toward the interior of the house. "May!" he yelled. "Come out here!"

Her mother emerged from the kitchen, wiping her hands on her apron, not at all perturbed by her husband's outburst.

"If you're going to yell at me, Harley," she said, "you can get me a drink first. Gin and tonic. Dinner is going to be a disaster."

He calmed down a little and got her a drink, then started in.

"I warned you something like this was going to happen. Our daughter has been listening to some con artist who wants to turn her into a TV journalist. My daughter isn't going into a business as rotten as this one is."

"Hush, Harley," his wife said, "and let Angie tell me. Your ranting won't clear my head." She smiled at Angie. "Tell me what happened, dear."

Angie ran through the exciting events, and her mother beamed as the story came out.

"It's wonderful!" May Waring said. "A chance for

you to see something of the real world, to get away from Lantana for a while."

"What in hell's wrong with Lantana?" Harley demanded. "It's been good to you. Where else could you swan around all day, doing good works? Where else could you live like a queen? This place has been great for us."

Her mother's good humor vanished in an instant. "I'll tell you where else we could be, Harley," she said. "We could still be in Boston, or New York, or any real city . . . and I could still be a reporter, proud of my trade and doing well at it. That night you came home and said you were dragging us all off to Florida was the saddest time of my life. I was just starting to make it on the *Globe*. They thought I was good. And I loved it. But you wanted money, and so all these years you've been doing a job you *despise*. And I've been vegetating and miserable. So if Angie has one chance of getting *out*, I want her to take it. You sold your talent for money, Harley, and look where it's gotten us."

Her mother was very near tears, and Angie just wanted them to stop.

"Please," she said. "It's only a summer job. It won't lead to anything, I'm sure it won't. And, anyway, I don't want it to. Just a few months in the city, and then I'll come home and marry Jeff."

"It'll change your life if you take this job," her father said flatly. "You get journalism in your blood, you'll never get it out."

"Harley," his wife said sharply, "she *has* journalism in her blood. Through you, no matter how bitter you are about it now. And through me, no matter how long it's been since I was dragged away from it. Angie can't help it. She has our talent."

"I never dragged you," he said, pleading. "I did what was right for all of us. Did you want to raise Angie in a walk-up in Boston? When a decent life came along I took it. I gripe about the *Clarion* because it's not a real paper. No one there is ever going to win a Pulitzer, but I've given you all the comfort and security I could. Is that so awful?"

"I know, Harley," May said wearily. "I know you were just doing what you thought was best for your family. But won't you agree to Angie testing the water? Let her go to Miami for the summer. She needs a chance. You and I had that much, at least."

"Journalism is no place for a young girl," he said. "It's filled with drunks and deadbeats and failures."

"I was a journalist when you married me, Harley."

"Oh, but I got you out of it as soon as I could," he said, as if that alone proved his point. "There's no need for Angie to be around that kind of life." He turned to his daughter. "Anyway," he said, "Jeff's not going to put up with this. He's not the kind of boy to stand aside and let you waltz off to Miami and God-knows-what-all for the summer."

"It's got nothing to do with what Jeff wants," her mother cried. "We've got the poor child married off already. Jeff's just a boyfriend, nothing more."

"I've told Jeff about it, Daddy," Angie said hastily. "He's thrilled for me. He wants me to get all the experience I can. And he understands it's only for the summer. I wish you would understand that, too. You, Mom, you're reading far too much into this. It's only a summer internship. And, Daddy, you mustn't be so afraid for me. I'm not running away to join the circus or something. This experience could help me get a good job here, after Jeff and I are married. Because I intend to work. I'm not going to be *only* a housewife.''

''Like her mother,'' her mother said boldly. She wasn't hurt, and Angie knew it. ''Only a housewife isn't enough, Harley.''

Her father stared down at the floor for a few moments. No one spoke.

''Okay,'' he said after a while. ''If you're set on this, I guess there's no point in trying to stop you. Please, though, promise me you won't get too involved. Just have fun for the summer and that's all. I don't want you to get hurt. Be careful, okay?'' he said gruffly. She nodded.

At eight o'clock, not a minute early or a minute late, Jeff picked her up. Without a word beyond ''hi,'' they headed for Boynton Beach. There were cars among the palm trees, parked as discreetly as possible so as not to be looking in on one another. Still Angie felt exposed and wished Jeff had suggested a motel. But she knew the idea would shock him.

There was an awkwardness between them as they embraced. Jeff didn't seem to know where to put his hands. It was like their first date. Finally, she felt his hands move under her sweater. She shivered as he touched her bare stomach and worked up to her bra. She reached around and unhooked her bra, kissing him hard. His hand caressed her nipples.

She was doing this just for him, she told herself, but she felt a glow building inside her anyhow. At last she was going to find out what the mystery was all about.

He began stroking her thigh and she parted her legs. He moved up to touch her through her panties. This was as far as they had ever let themselves go. Excitement mounting in her, she moved her hand into his lap and felt him stiff and strong through his jeans. He moaned and she squeezed him and he quickly unbuckled his pants.

She reached inside his underwear and took him out and began to stroke him. It seemed so big and she wondered how it would feel. Maybe it would hurt. She knew so little. But then, her friends knew as little as she did.

His hand moved inside her panties and she felt her own wetness and wanted it to happen now. She pulled up her sweater and he put his lips to her breast. Her hand was moving faster and faster on his shaft, in rhythm with his hand on her. She felt it building in both of them, and then Jeff suddenly pushed her hand away from him.

"Don't," he whispered. "You'll make me come too soon."

Her skirt was around her waist and she lifted her hips as he pulled her panties down to her ankles. He struggled with his jeans, pushing them down to his knees. Then, as she lay back on the seat, her head hard against the door, he came to her. There was so little room and the gearshift pressed against her thigh, but somehow Jeff got between her legs and entered her. There was no pain, just the sensation of expanding to take him. She pushed herself forward to get more of him and suddenly he was all inside her. It felt good, even better when the two of them began moving in unison.

"Stop, stop," he whispered urgently. "I haven't got anything on."

She held him, still moving her body, not wanting to stop. But he pulled himself away. She lay there, wanting, listening to him fumble. She heard paper ripping and more fumbling and a few moments later Jeff was back between her legs.

But this time there was a barrier between them, the artificial touch of the condom. It was nothing like the earlier sensation of flesh together, and it was all spoiled for Angie. The excitement went and her passion with it.

She became an observer, watching Jeff heaving and panting and then convulsing. When the shuddering in his body had stopped, he withdrew from her at once. She didn't know enough to pretend an orgasm and he didn't know enough to realize she hadn't had one.

He went back to his side of the car and tugged up his jeans, and there was nothing for her to do but pull up her panties, fasten her bra, and rearrange her skirt and sweater.

Jeff put his arm around her and kissed her on the cheek, very gently.

"That was wonderful," he said, "more wonderful than I ever thought it would be. I'm glad we waited. Oh, Angie, I love you. Thank you. I'll never let you down."

Her stomach started rumbling and she began to giggle.

"What are you laughing at?" he asked, hurt, suspicious.

"Nothing, darling," she said. "It was wonderful. It's just I didn't have time for dinner and my stomach's complaining. Do you think we could drive over to Frank's for a hamburger?"

As he drove she thought about all of it . . . the exciting, mysterious beginning . . . and the terrible disappointment. Maybe if they had gone to that motel instead, it might have been different.

"I love you, Angie," he said as they drove up the coast road, the ocean crashing on one side of them, boats moored in the canal on the other. "I don't want to ever do anything to hurt you. What we did tonight was dangerous. I almost got carried away. So did you. I don't think we should do it again until we're married." He was staring hard at the oncoming head-lights. "Is that okay with you?"

"Yes, Jeff," she said, knowing of nothing else she could say. "I think you're right. We'll wait until—until all the circumstances are perfect."

He glanced at her and she reached out and patted his cheek.

"It won't be long," she said. "The summer will fly past."

Chapter
Three

"It's a good newsroom—and a happy one," Susan Jarratt said. "No egotists and no infighting. Ted Buchanan sees to that. He's the news director and came down here about two years ago. Before that he was a hotshot New York newspaperman, but he's made the change real well. You couldn't have gotten a better place to do an internship."

"I'm so nervous about it," Angie said. "Meeting all those people tomorrow. I've never even had a job before and I'm scared I'm going to make a fool of myself. I'm starting to think I shouldn't have come here."

"You'll love it," Susan said. She was a tall, dark girl, twenty-five, who had volunteered to share her Miami apartment with Angie for the summer. Angie felt like an intruder, but Susan put her at ease by saying she needed a roommate. She was the youngest and lowest-paid reporter at the station.

Susan had shown her around Miami during the weekend—not the tourist areas, but the beats she would have to cover, the police precinct houses, courts, hospitals, and city offices. And she'd taken her into the rapidly growing area known as Little Havana. It was a revelation to Angie, all those Cuban exiles packed together and bringing their exotic island life with them. It scared her a little and fascinated her, too.

Now the girls were sprawled on the floor of Susan's apartment, eating pizza, drinking soda, and waiting for Channel 9's main Sunday-night news show.

"Oh, God," groaned Susan as the news logo faded from the screen. "David Button's doing the show tonight. He's such a pain. I'll bet he messes up the piece I did for 'Sunday Magazine.' "

They watched the show for a while. Angie refrained from saying she thought Button was handling it all right. The show was better than anything they did on the fledgling West Palm Beach channel, but she didn't want to sound like a hick.

When Susan's piece, a short one about a school for the handicapped, came on, Angie sat transfixed.

"Just a Sunday filler," Susan said airily as the piece ended. She turned off the set. "It's hard to fill a half hour on Sunday nights."

"But it was great," Angie said. "You looked so professional, so . . . in charge. It's kind of unreal."

Susan smiled at Angie. "It is a strange sensation at first," she said. "People recognize you on the street. It can go to your head. You start to think you know a hell of a lot more than you really do, that you're really important. But soon you come back to earth—like when you're covering some awful accident in the middle of a cold wet night out on the freeway."

"I don't think I'd ever come back to earth," Angie

said. "It's only coming to me now what television really means, how powerful it is."

Angie couldn't sleep all night. She was tense and afraid—but deep down, she was thrilled.

She walked into the newsroom with Susan and felt, surprisingly, as if she had come home. The cluttered desks, the wire service machines clicking out a continual stream of news, the wall clocks showing times all over the world. It didn't seem alien. It was as if she belonged there.

Ted Buchanan made her feel at home, too. He was about thirty, tall and skinny and rumpled. He wore a checked shirt and jeans and his dark brown curly hair was unfashionably long. He had sharp, dark blue eyes and he wore thick horn-rimmed spectacles that kept slipping down his thin nose and he looked nothing like the well-groomed reporters in his newsroom.

"Hey, it's great to have you aboard," he said, coming around his desk and extending his hand. "If you're here for work experience, you couldn't have picked a better place. We're so short-staffed you're liable to be on camera within a couple of days."

"I've got no experience at all, Mr. Buchanan," she said hastily. "Not at *any*thing. I'm going to be in everybody's way. If I could just make coffee or something . . . hide someplace where I can't mess anyone up."

"It's Ted," he said. "And don't worry, Angie. They're a nice bunch of people here and they'll all help you. No one expects you to be a hotshot right away. You're here to learn and we're here to teach you." He laughed. "Not that there's a hell of a lot to learn about this business. It's still seat-of-the-pants stuff. Look at me," he said mockingly. "Two years ago I was an ink-stained newspaperman. Now I'm supposed to know all about videocams and telecine and OBs and booms and lights and— I'll let you in on a secret. I don't really know all that stuff. I rely on the technicians. All you really have to know is a good story and how to tell it simply. And you have to look right to the home viewer. You certainly look right. Come on," he said, "I'll introduce you to the folks and find a desk."

There were a dozen reporters, most of them in their late twenties, and very hyper. They welcomed her warmly but there was no time for talk: already the newsroom was in high gear, everyone working toward the deadline, eight hours away. Angie was awed by their dedication, envious of their devotion. Ted fixed her a desk next to Susan Jarratt and suggested she spend the day reading the previous week's news scripts and trying to understand what was going on around her. She was reading when a figure loomed over her desk. She looked up.

"Hi," he said, "I'm David Button and you're the new intern. Angie, right?"

"Yes," she said, wondering whether she ought to stand. "Angie Waring."

"If you need any help, call on me," Button said, glancing around the newsroom with contempt. "Don't ask any of this crowd for guidance. They're all wet behind the ears."

"Well, David," Susan said, looking up from her typewriter. "You're so much *older* than the rest of us, aren't you?" She turned to Angie. "David goes all the way back to the days of steam radio. Isn't he well preserved? You'd never guess he's wearing a toupee."

Angie laughed, and was sorry when Button glared at them.

"You'll all still be down here in the boondocks writing dull stories about this dreary place when I'm anchoring the network news in New York," he said. Then, to Angie, he said nastily, "Maybe you'll make it out of here to someplace better. I hear you're Richard Mansion's latest. But don't count on anything." He stalked off.

"He's such an asshole," Susan said. "And a vicious gossip, too. What did he mean about you and Richard Mansion?"

Angie explained how she and Mansion had met.

Susan whistled. "That's quite a break for you," she said. "Mansion's a very big deal indeed. He'll take over the whole network from his father one of these days. You could go a long way." She glanced at Angie. "Just be careful. Mansion has a reputation."

"But," Angie said, "it's nothing like that. And it's only a summer job. He's probably forgotten I'm even here."

Susan went back to typing, saying, "Anyway, he's up north at the family compound in Newport for the next month, so we won't see him for a while."

That night, after the seven o'clock news had aired with only the usual technical hitches, Ted came out of his office and called to the half dozen of them still in the newsroom to join him at the bar down the street.

"I've got a date," Susan said. "But you go, Angie. The Crawdaddy's our second newsroom. It's all shop-talk, and you might learn something. And the crowd from the *Miami Herald* hang out there, too, so you'll hear the endless arguments about which journalism is legitimate, print or TV."

Angie worried the bar might ask her for proof of age, but she was swept in with Ted and the Channel 9 crowd. It was evident that television people were the

Crawdaddy's prized customers. There were three big booths set aside for them, and she found herself wedged in between Ted Buchanan and Rory Bates, a young black reporter. She listened to what the others ordered and said she'd have a beer, like Ted.

"So how was your first day?" Ted asked her above the shouting and banter at their table. "Could you make any sense of it? The newsroom's an insane asylum, but we always seem to get the show done."

"I was impressed," she said shyly. "Everyone is so professional, and they seem to love their jobs. It must be a joy to work at something you're proud of. My father . . ." She trailed off, embarrassed. She knew she ought not to talk about herself among these sophisticated people.

"What does your father do?" Ted asked.

"He's senior editor at the *American Clarion,*" she said. "And he hates it. He's trapped there by the money. So, when I saw you all enjoying what you do, I felt so sorry for Daddy."

"Yeah," Ted sighed. "We've all heard horror stories about the *Clarion.* I feel sorry for your old man." He drank his beer. "I've been in love with journalism all my life, never wanted to do anything else. Newspapers were my first passion, of course. I was dubious about going into TV but, you know, it's just the same spirit—on my side of the camera, anyway. I'm not so sure about some of the anchors, the ones who're only pretty faces and nothing more."

"So you're happy?" Angie asked. "You don't want to go back to newspapers?"

He grinned and shrugged. "For now I'm happy," he said. "I'll wait and see how television develops. Right now a lot of our news is pretty shallow. If you can't explain the story in thirty seconds, don't. I miss the chance to do real work, to explore the issues. In TV we're still governed by whether or not a subject's pictorial, which isn't appropriate a lot of the time."

The bar was filling up. Some of their people left the booth and were replaced by reporters from the *Herald*, coming off their shift. The newspaper journalists were easy to distinguish from their television counterparts. They were rougher, more cynical, older. They were proud of their craft and not at all in awe of the better-paid, slick television crowd. The truth was, they looked more dignified and smarter than the television journalists. She stole a glance at Ted: even with her limited experience, she knew he belonged with the print journalists. It wasn't just that he was as rumpled and cynical as the *Herald* men. He also had that extra depth, and the same eagerness to talk an issue right through.

"It's getting late," Ted said after a couple of hours and a lot of beers. "How are you getting home, Angie?"

"A cab, I guess," she said. "It's not far."

"I'll drop you off," Ted offered.

He called his good-nights as she trailed behind him out of the bar. They strolled back to the Channel 9 parking lot. It was a warm, still evening and the stars hung low in the blue-black sky.

"You want to have dinner with me?" he asked. "I'd appreciate the company. I'm getting sick of eating alone every night in a greasy spoon."

"I'd love to," she said, genuinely pleased. "Susan's on a date, and I don't think there's much to eat in the apartment."

They drove to Little Havana and again Angie was intrigued by the sounds and smells. Ted parked his car on the street, beckoned to a little Cuban boy sitting on a stoop, and took five dollars from his wallet. He ripped the note in half, gave one portion to the boy, and stuck the other in his pocket.

He said something to the boy in Spanish and guided her down the street to a tiny storefront restaurant. The proprietor, a fat, swarthy man, came trotting out of the kitchen to embrace Ted and usher them to a corner table. A jug of margaritas appeared before them, and Ted and the owner discussed the night's menu, speaking rapid Spanish.

"What's wrong?" Ted asked when his friend went back to the kitchen.

"I'm sorry if I look kind of stunned. All this," she said, waving her hand around the restaurant, "and the way you got that boy to take care of your car, and today in the newsroom . . . it's all so different. I feel like such a hick."

"You're no hick, Angie," he said. "You're just a very sweet young kid. That's nothing to be ashamed of. It's the greatest time of your life. Everything's ahead of you." He smiled wryly. "I remember when I was your age."

She laughed. "It wasn't that long ago," she said.

"It seems like it was," Ted said, a little too seriously.

The food came and Angie enjoyed the new tastes. She had two margaritas and liked the warm buzz. She felt, for the first time in her life, grown-up and confident. Ted ate very little and drank quite a lot and she worried for him, so thin and looking so vulnerable. But she was reassured by his quiet confidence, his frankness, his willingness to say whatever he wanted to.

He talked a lot during dinner. Later, she would realize he had taught her a lot. He explained easily and simply what television was about and what it wasn't about. He counseled her to listen and learn, but to be herself and not get talked out of anything she cared about.

"Angie, you have the right look for TV but, more than that, you've got a wonderful freshness about you, an innocence that comes across strongly," he said. "Just don't get all hard and smartass, like so many television people. The camera can always tell. It shows insincerity, and your innocence is your calling card."

She listened, never once interrupting.

"Hey," Ted said suddenly, looking at his watch. "I better get you home."

He drove her to her apartment building, saw her to the door, and waved good night. Angie felt a deep sense of unexpected disappointment. She wouldn't have minded at all if Ted had wanted to stop somewhere and neck. And then she laughed aloud in the apartment lobby. She was just a kid to him. He was her boss, for heaven's sake. He had been kind to her and that was all. Men like Ted Buchanan didn't neck with college girls.

She let herself into the apartment and found Susan lying on the couch in her robe, watching the late movie.

"How did you manage to tap into Miami's sparkling social life so soon?" Susan said. "I've been here three years and I haven't found anything worth staying out for past eleven P.M. Where have you been?"

"Ted took me to dinner after we all went down to that bar," Angie said. She sounded very sophisticated to herself. "It was a lovely night. He's a nice man."

33

Susan nodded. "He is. If Ted takes you under his wing, you'll be okay. A lot of guys in his position, young and good-looking and the boss of a bunch of very ambitious people, would take advantage of the situation. But not Ted. He's a good friend to all of us and a great editor. But that's where it stops."

Angie sat down beside Susan. "What do you mean?"

"Poor Ted," Susan said, shaking her head. "We all learned his story from someone at the *Herald*, someone who'd known him in New York. You go make us some tea while I straighten this slum. Then I'll tell you the story."

When Angie returned with the steaming mugs, Susan was back on the couch, the television off.

"What happened was," she said, "Ted married young, a girl he'd gone through college with. Everyone who knew them said they were about as in love as a couple could be. They had a few great years with Ted doing better and better at the *New York Times.* Then they found out why his wife was so sickly. She had some kind of anemia and it was getting worse. The doctors said another New York winter would probably kill her.

"So Ted applied for the Channel 9 job down here," Susan said. "I guess he hated to leave New York and his job, but he figured Rosa would get well here. She might have, too. But Rosa tried too hard to become an instant Florida girl. She'd never even seen surf before, and had to learn how to swim. About the end of their first month here they were on the beach up at Boynton one Sunday afternoon. Rosa went into the surf, a rip got her and . . ." She shrugged. "I guess she didn't know how to handle it. She was swept out to sea and they didn't recover the body until two days later."

Angie's hands shook. "The poor man. No wonder he looks so lonely."

"Yes," Susan said, nodding. "He is lonely. A lot of girls at the station, including yours truly, have tried to ease him out of it. But Ted doesn't seem to want to forget Rosa, or he isn't capable of loving anyone anymore. He's always just the best friend anyone could have and there's nothing he wants of you in return. You're in good hands, kid. Be nice to Ted, now. We're all in love with him."

Over the next few weeks Angie saw a lot of Ted Buchanan, both in the newsroom, where he took a close interest in her work, and after work. They often ended the day eating together since most of the other reporters had husbands, wives, or dates. It was a funny relationship, she thought. He treated her like a kid sister, or a favorite apprentice. He liked having her tag along with him and was constantly teaching her the business.

It was a confusing, exciting time for Angie. Her confidence in her own ability grew daily. She was guided through every phase of television reporting and began to think she could, someday, be a newscaster. But she was guilty and anxious about poor Jeff, waiting for her. There were many missed phone calls because she was working and just couldn't take the time to call back. When he did get through, he often sounded querulous.

"I'm sorry, Jeff," she told him late one night. "I know I always seem to be working, but we all are here. We're short-staffed and it's such a big city to cover."

"You talk like you think you belong there," Jeff

said bitterly. "Don't forget, it's only a summer job and you're only an intern. You're coming back to me in a few weeks."

"Of course I am," she said, though she was stung. "It's just that while I'm here I feel I should learn as much as I can. Jeff, please try and understand. I miss you and I love you and I'll be back with you soon. But this *is* a chance and I don't want to blow it. Why, Ted says—"

"Ted, Ted, Ted," he snapped. "You're always talking about Ted. What's going on with him?"

"You wouldn't understand," she said angrily. "You couldn't begin to understand a man like Ted Buchanan. He's the kindest man I've ever met. And he's so good at his job. He's teaching me so much."

"And what am I?" snarled Jeff. "The boy you left behind? I knew this was going to happen when you went to Miami. I never should have let you."

"You don't own me, Jeff," she said. "It's not up to you or anyone else to 'let' me do something." She was close to tears. She didn't want them to fight, didn't want anything to intrude on her wonderful summer.

"No," he said softly, "I don't own you. I just love you, that's all. It tears me apart to have you so far away, so many new influences around you. I'm scared, Angie, and that's the truth. I'm scared I'm going to lose you."

"I know," she said honestly. "I'm scared, too. But not of anything happening to us. Just scared you won't understand what it is I'm trying to do. Please, be patient."

"I'll try," he said. "But I've got to see you. How about if I drive down next weekend, get there on Fri-

day night?'' He dropped his voice. "Could we . . .
stay together?''

She didn't really want him to come. Sure, she
missed him, but somehow she wanted to keep this
part of her life all to herself. It wasn't for Jeff. Yet she
could hardly tell him so.

"Yes, please come,'' she said. "I think you can
probably stay here. Susan sometimes stays over at a
boyfriend's place. And Friday there's a party a couple
of guys in the newsroom are giving. In fact, we'd better meet there because I'll be working late.'' She gave
him the address, they told each other how much in
love they were, and she said good night.

Susan came out of the bedroom, where she'd politely taken herself so Angie could talk freely.

"I couldn't help hearing a little,'' Susan said. "It's
hard for a boyfriend to understand how much we like
our work, isn't it? I've lost more guys that way.''

"I don't know what to do, Susan,'' Angie admitted, exasperated and glad to be able to show it. "I
love Jeff, but I just want this summer to myself. I love
being at Channel 9. After that, I go back and settle
down and marry Jeff. Is one summer too much to
want, just for yourself?''

Susan looked at her keenly. "What's this 'one summer' nonsense?'' she demanded. "You're going to
make it in this business. I'm envious as hell. They're
going to offer you a permanent job, nothing surer,
Angie. Don't even think about going back home and
settling down forever. Christ, you're only twenty,
Angie. Don't throw away your life so soon.''

"I'm not throwing away my life,'' she said hotly.
"You sound like my mother. Love and marriage and a
family is important to me. This is fun, sure, but it's
not real life.''

"We'll see about 'real life,' " Susan said wryly.
"Try to keep an open mind for a while. You've been
given a great chance, one most people would kill for.
Don't throw it away. You don't know what you want,
not yet."

"I know what I want," Angie said stubbornly, and
Susan didn't argue.

That night, Angie got up and went to the window
that looked across the city. Traffic still flowed on the
freeway and farther out there were the lights of small
craft on the water. It was so different from the quiet
streets of home. But, she admitted, this city and
Channel 9 were starting to feel like home.

Chapter
Four

"You've drawn me for the day," Rory Bates told her when she went into the newsroom that Friday morning. "We're doing an airport interview at five o'clock. Won't be all that exciting for you, I'm afraid. I've got to interview Martin Luther King when he arrives."

"Who's that?" she asked.

"Actually, it's Martin Luther King, *Junior*," Rory said. "He's big in civil rights for us black folks. It won't entertain you much, watching the channel's token nigger interview the liberals' token nigger, but that's your assignment for today."

She flinched at the ugly word. It set Rory apart from the rest of them, and she had come to think of the station as a team. Rory's blackness just hadn't registered with her, not till that moment.

He understood her discomfort and said, "It's okay, honey. I was only kidding. Actually, television's one of the few areas where blacks aren't employed just as tokens. They have to have blacks on staff, even in Florida, because damn near half the audience is black and they want to see someone like them on the screen now and then. All your fine liberal newspapers up north, go find out how many blacks they've got writing for them." He shook his head. "Ten, fifteen years from now, there'll be black anchors all over the networks. And I aim to be one." He put his feet up on his desk and grinned at her. "Hell, there might even be a *woman* anchor someday."

She grinned back. He certainly was outspoken. She enjoyed working with Rory that day. They covered a couple of stories in the black sections of town, a bar holdup and a domestic hostage crisis that fizzled.

"Stick close to me," he whispered to her as they were setting up for a shot. "No telling how inflamed these people may get, seeing a cute white girl like you with me."

She glanced around, scared, then blushed scarlet as she heard Rory's whooping laugh. She punched him in the arm, hard.

They drove out to Miami International and waited until the Reverend King arrived and was ushered into the media room. It was a brief and uneventful news conference. A couple of the print journalists wanted to know if he was in Florida just to stir up trouble, but King handled them with humor and grace. When the print people were finished, Rory got to ask Reverend King some questions. Angie was impressed by King's dignity and pride. Rory had dropped his cynicism and seemed almost in awe of the man. It all reminded her yet again how little she knew of the real world.

Finally they killed the lights and began to pack up their equipment.

"We're damn late," Rory said to her. "I'd better rush the film back in a cab and leave you guys to bring all the gear back in the truck. You'll be okay here?"

"Sure," Angie said. "I'll see you back in the news-room."

She offered to help the crew but they waved her away, so she slumped in a chair and waited for them to get the cumbersome recording equipment back in its boxes. Jeff was arriving later that night and she tried to get excited. She planned to be so good to him. After the party they'd go home to the empty apart-ment and just be themselves. It would all be great, like it had been before this job. And they would sleep together in a real bed, and surely lovemaking would be better than it had been that first time.

Sirens whooped and alarm bells were stridently summoning the airport personnel. One of the Chan-nel 9 crew ran to the window and drew back the cur-tains.

"Great!" he shouted to the others. "Emergency on the runway. Open the boxes and let's get rolling!"

The soundman found a telephone in the corner and called the control tower. He listened and hung up, then called, "It's a big one! An Electra out of Tampa started to land at the military strip up the road. When he realized he was in the wrong place he pulled her up, but he's ripped off his landing wheels and he's going to have to do a belly landing."

"Shit!" said the cameraman. "You better call the channel and have them send a reporter down here."

"No time," the soundman answered. "The plane's coming in right now. Let's just get the pictures and the sound and they can dub over in the studio. What a break for us! Everyone else has left."

"You've got to have someone in front of the camera while we wait," Angie said, standing up. "I'm here and I'll do it."

They looked at her for a second, then the camera-

41

man shrugged. "Okay," he said. "Just don't get in the way when the fireworks start."

They raced out onto the tarmac, dragging sound and light cables. Emergency vehicles were screaming around the airport's perimeter. Fire trucks, ambulances and Federal Aviation Administration cars began lining up along the strip where the crippled plane would crash-land. While the crew set up, Angie dashed across to the tower and talked her way in.

A frantic flight controller gave her the airplane's port of origin, its operator—a charter in Tampa—and the number of people on board. Twenty-eight passengers and a crew of four.

Angie ran back to the Channel 9 crew, checked her hair and makeup in a pocket mirror, picked up the microphone, and said she was ready. At the signal, she said, "The lives of thirty-two people are at stake here at Miami Airport." She felt herself calm, yet charged up. "A severely crippled Lockheed Electra, operated by Tampa Air Services, will attempt to crash-land here within the next fifteen minutes. By the time you see this report tonight on Channel 9, you will know whether the result had been triumph . . . or tragedy. We are bringing you the drama exclusively. I'm Angie Waring, and this is Channel 9 News."

The cameraman signaled out.

"Great," he called to her. "Just great."

"Okay," Angie called back. She was completely in control of the situation and the crew all realized it. They were willing to take direction from her. "What we do now," she said, "is roll again and film right through to the end. Take the camera off me as soon as the plane comes into view, and don't move it again. Stay with the plane."

For the next five minutes, Angie talked. She pointed

out the emergency vehicles and managed to grab a quick interview with a harried FAA official. Once she decided what to do or say she never questioned herself.

At last the plane came into view. It made one long, low pass by the control tower and the cameraman zoomed in on the obscene tangle of the damaged undercarriage. Then the plane swung around and slowly began its approach to the runway.

Angie dropped her voice, almost whispering as she spoke into the mike.

"This is the moment we've all been dreading," she said. "The moment when all the skills of the pilot and the ground crew will be tested in a way no one ever wanted them to be tested. There are thirty-two people on board. We're praying."

She let the camera tell the story as the plane came down and down until it struck the ground with a terrible screech of metal and showering of sparks. A vicious tongue of flame raced along the wing facing Angie and the crew.

"Fire!" Angie cried. "Fire!"

Fire trucks were spraying huge clouds of foam onto the plane even before it stopped lurching along the concrete. The emergency exits swung open and people came tumbling out, the plane so close to the ground they just fell from the exits and began running from the plane.

"I'm counting them," Angie said into her mike. "Twelve, seventeen, twenty-five. There are still seven people in there, as far as I know. Wait! Here! Here's five, six more. Just one person to go."

A blue-uniformed figure jumped through the exit and sprinted across the runway, right toward Angie and her crew.

"It's the pilot!" Angie cried. "The last person off. They're all safe. All safe! It's a miracle!"

The pilot stopped a few yards away from them and sank down on the ground, head in hands, his shoulders heaving. The camera was focused in on him for a long time, and then panned to the foam-covered plane. The final shot was of the knot of passengers being ushered into the terminal building.

Angie glanced at her watch. No time for interviews if they were going to make the seven o'clock news. She glanced regretfully at the pilot, then signaled the cameraman that she wanted him back on her.

"All thirty-two people have walked away from a near tragedy. This is Angie Waring, at Miami International, for Channel 9 News."

Then it was time to sprint back through the terminal to their station wagon, throw the equipment inside, and spin out of the parking lot. Bert, the soundman, gave a whoop of joy.

"Look!" he yelled. "The competition's just arriving now!" He honked the horn and jabbed two fingers in the air at the Channel 7 car, which was screeching through the parking lot.

"A complete scoop!" Bert shouted to Angie and the cameraman. "Bonus time for all of us. How lucky can you get?"

Angie didn't feel lucky. She felt drained, beginning to realize how close those people had come to dying in a flaming wreck. She started to shake and then she burst into tears.

Eddie, the cameraman, reached back to her from the front seat and squeezed her knee.

"I know," he said. "It shakes you up to be so close to death. But you were just great. No one could have done it better."

She was still pale and nervous when they reached the station, fifteen minutes before airtime. Ted was waiting out front.

"Did you get it?" he demanded.

"You bet," Eddie said. "Every lovely moment of it. And all to ourselves. There wasn't another crew within miles."

They started jogging up the stairs, Ted in the lead. "You're sure it's okay?" he insisted. "I'm going to have to put it on without a chance to see it. It needs a voice-over, right? You didn't have anyone there."

"We had Angie, boss," Bert said. "She did it better than a pro."

Ted looked startled. He hesitated for just a second, then said, "It leads the seven o'clock."

The newsroom was packed but silent as the 9 News logo came up on the big screen on the back wall.

And then Angie was standing there before them, professional, appropriately emotional, taking them through the harrowing episode at the airport. It ran twenty minutes, and it was everything an on-the-spot news report should be. She felt herself trembling as the drama unfolded and she was relieved when it ended.

"The pilot," Ted rasped at the end. "Why in hell didn't you interview the sobbing pilot?"

And then he burst into laughter and hugged Angie.

"You're wonderful!" he shouted. "We'll get an award for this, for sure. That's one of the best pieces of reporting I ever saw."

They all crowded around to congratulate her.

"You pushed my Martin Luther King out," Rory complained. "And scooped me on my own turf. Good for you, kid. It was a classic."

Ted arranged with programming for a repeat of

their exclusive at 10:00 P.M. and ordered promos for the event to be shown throughout the evening. Then he came over to Angie again and looked at her closely.

"You look beat," he said. "Better come into my office. I've got a bottle I keep there for special occasions."

He sat her down and poured the brandy, then took one himself and toasted her.

"Watch out for delayed reaction," he said. "You go on a big news story like that, it hits you later. You suddenly realize how close you were. It's scary. You did a hell of a job, Angie. We're all proud of you."

"Ted," she said. "The guys made it all so easy for me. I just did it without thinking very much. It was kind of weird, as if it wasn't me talking to the camera."

"I know," he said. "Some of the best work comes out of that kind of situation. You let your instincts take over. Thank God you've got the right instincts for news."

The brandy warmed her and the trembling stopped. She was worn out.

"Thank God it's Friday," she said. "I could sleep all weekend." And then she remembered. "Jeff! Jeff's coming down for the weekend. I forgot. I'm meeting him at the party. No rest for the weary."

Ted took her to her apartment to change, then took her to the party.

"About Jeff," Ted said as they drove to Dan Peeble's house. "Try and keep your options open for a while. You're very young. And you have a great future. Don't get married yet."

The party was in full swing when they arrived, everyone buoyant because of the big news break they had scored. They all crowded around Angie, teasing her, proud for her. In all the excitement it was a full five minutes before she noticed Jeff was already there. He was sitting in a far corner, talking to no one, looking awkward. She pushed through the crowd to him.

"It's great to see you," she cried, and he stood up. She kissed him on the cheek. "I've missed you so. Sorry about all the fuss just then, but something big happened to me today." She began to tell him about her scoop but he didn't seem to be listening, or he didn't understand.

"How long do we have to stay here?" he whispered. "I want to get away somewhere on our own."

"We'll have to stay awhile, Jeff," she said. "These are my friends and the guys worked so hard to make this party a success. Please, just an hour or so."

He shrugged. "Okay. Then I better go get myself a few drinks. There's no one here I can talk to, and you're so popular I'm not going to get any time with you."

She frowned as he headed for the bar in Dan's kitchen. But she'd make it up to him later.

In the excitement of the evening, she actually forgot about Jeff. Everyone was so happy for her. She felt she was one of the team at last, and that was how they treated her. In the warm, crowded room, surrounded by her colleagues, she was at home.

They cut off the music at 10:00 P.M. and turned on the TV to savor their scoop again. As the piece ended there was a happy hubbub of self-congratulation, and Ted impulsively kissed Angie on both cheeks.

Suddenly, there was Jeff, standing in front of them, red-faced and shouting.

"Leave my girl alone!" he yelled, pushing Ted in

the chest. "You people . . . you're all rotten. Leave her alone!"

He made a grab for Angie, gripping her arm.

"Come on," he said, "we're getting away from here."

"Take it easy, kid," Ted said, stepping forward between the two of them. Jeff had to break his grip. "Don't get excited."

All Jeff's frustration erupted then, and he sent a long, looping punch in Ted's direction. Ted ducked under the punch easily, willing to placate the raging young man.

"Look . . ." he started to speak, and he didn't see Jeff's other fist coming up. All the breath was knocked from his body as Jeff's fist sank into his midriff.

Angie saw Ted double over. Stop it, she screamed to herself, someone stop it! But, like her, they were all immobilized. She shut her eyes before the next blow fell, and heard a sickening chop of flesh on flesh, then heard a body hit the floor close to her. She opened her eyes.

Jeff was stretched out on the floor, unconscious, a dribble of blood starting at the corner of his mouth. Ted was standing away from him, rubbing his hands and looking embarrassed.

"Holy shit!" Rory whispered. "I never saw such a fast reaction. The old one-two and the challenger is down for the count. Age triumphs over youth."

She moved away slowly, not knowing where to look. She was so ashamed for herself, so sad for Jeff. As the others stood looking down at Jeff, she moved to the kitchen, found some ice, and wrapped it in a towel. She went back to Jeff, who was moving a little, and tried to minister to his rapidly swelling jaw. She wanted to cry as she dabbed at the ugly little line of blood. He opened his eyes and looked at her blankly. Then he focused, shoved himself up on one elbow, and pushed away from her. Without looking at any of them, he scrambled to his feet and ran from the apartment.

"Get up, Angie," Ted said gently, taking her arm. "It's all okay, no damage done."

She cried then, sobbing uncontrollably. The rest of the party diplomatically resumed talking and someone turned the record player on. Ted guided her out of the room and onto the terrace. He didn't try to stop her from crying, just silently handed her his handkerchief, rested his arms on the wall, and gazed out into the night sky.

Finally she had control of herself.

"I'm so sorry, Ted," she began. "I've ruined the party for everyone. I never should have brought Jeff here. I just forgot for a while what kids Jeff and I are. We don't belong with grown ups."

He laughed quietly.

"The 'grown-ups' have been known to take a swing at one another when they're drinking, Angie," he said. "It's no big deal. I didn't want to hurt the boy, though. It's not his fault he's insanely jealous of you. A lot of guys would be."

"But he could have hurt *you*," Angie said. "Jeff's such a big, strong guy. And he's young, and you—"

"And I'm over the hill, weedy, wrung out," Ted said, bantering. For just a second she thought she detected bitterness, or sadness, in his voice.

"I'll have you know," he continued, "that old and fossilized though I may be, a long time ago—nine years, if you must know—I was an intercollegiate welterweight champion. No strength but fast reactions."

He looked down at her and grinned. "Want me to bring you a drink, or are you ready to go back and face the others?"

"I just want to go home," she said. "I'm so ashamed. And I should find Jeff. He must be feeling terrible."

"Leave him alone for a while," Ted advised. "He'll want to nurse his pride by himself. You just sit there and I'll go get us some wine."

It was good to let the warm night air soothe her, to postpone the time when she would have to face the others. Only minutes before they'd been saluting her, but she realized she was just an interloper, a kid playing at being an adult. The best thing she could do would be to resign, go home to Lantana, and make up with Jeff.

"I suppose you're thinking of quitting," Ted said, reappearing with two wineglasses.

"That's always our first reaction, cut and run when we think we've made a fool of ourselves. Don't, though. A silly little incident like this doesn't mean a thing," he said. "The only thing that does count is what kind of person you are, and how well you do what you've decided to do. And today, Angie, you were simply magnificent."

She shook her head sadly. "That awful scene made me forget all about the story. And I was so proud of myself. Why did something crazy have to come along and spoil it?"

"It sometimes happens that way," Ted said. "Fate is always waiting to give us a backhander"—he looked at her, then finished—"just when you think you've got it knocked."

"Thanks for talking to me, Ted," she said, standing up. "Thank you for everything you've done for me." And then, without thinking about it, she kissed him.

He held her close to him after their lips parted and it felt good and warm and comforting. She was sorry when he gently took her hands and moved them from his shoulders.

"You'll be all right," he said. His voice was husky. "I'd take you home, but I don't think I should. It wouldn't be . . . right."

She looked up at him and nodded. He knew best. But she was sorry. She wanted comfort and reassurance tonight, and something else, something she could not describe to herself. But it had to do with Ted.

She got her things together, said good night to them all, and went out to wait for her cab.

Jeff was sitting on the curb across the street, his head between his knees. He looked up when she appeared.

"Angie," he said, lurching to his feet. "Angie, I'm sorry." He was moving toward her, across the street. He held out his hands to her, palms up, beseeching. "Please say you're not mad at me."

She stood there looking at him. The bruised, swollen jaw, the red-rimmed eyes, the total defeat that weighed down his strong young body. She opened her arms as he came to her and they clutched each other there in the dark street. His breath came in sobs and she found herself stroking his cheek.

"It's all right, Jeff," she said. "It's all right. Let's go home now."

Jeff drove her back to the apartment and, in silence, followed her into the elevator and up to the apartment. She took him to the bathroom and gently undressed him and guided him into the shower, then left him there and went into her room. She was so glad Susan was out of the apartment.

Jeff came into the bedroom wrapped in a towel. He looked a little better, but still sheepish.

"Get into bed," she said. "I'll go brush my teeth. Rest. You need it." It was, of course, Angie who needed rest, but tonight she was the one who had to be strong. She felt quite wise and old and wondered if this was always the way youth vanished—suddenly.

He was almost asleep when she returned from the bathroom and she slipped into bed beside him. His big young body felt warm and she was glad she was not alone. He held her gently to him as he fell asleep. He was no longer the hard-edged, athletic Jeff she had always known. He had been beaten and humiliated, and in his shame he had turned to her. She felt protective of him, all the more so because she understood that they were changing. She could no longer be just Jeff's girl, or his wife. She was more than that. But she loved him, Angie told herself as she fell asleep. She loved him.

It was the perfect pink Miami dawn when she opened her eyes, but she just wanted to sleep. She felt tired and strung out. Jeff was against her, strong and hard, and he had hiked up her gown and was squeezing her breasts.

"Take it easy," she muttered, then worried that she had snapped at him. She turned her head and kissed him. Sleep was still so close, so seductive. She felt him pressing harder and harder against her. She opened her legs to his large hands. His mouth was on her breast and it was nice. If only he would go a little slower.

She felt him swing his body over her and she took

his full weight. If he would just wait a little while . . . but already he was forcing himself into her. She wasn't ready for him and he was hurting her. But she knew she had to let him. He was trying to reclaim her for himself, and she had to give him that chance.

He moved inside her and seemed to grow bigger with every thrust. She concentrated on relaxing and soon the pain lessened.

"Aren't you using anything?" she whispered, then remembered how frustrated she'd been when he had used something.

"No," he whispered urgently. "Nothing. I want this to be all the way." He pushed harder into her and his body bucked and strained. And then he came in her, spurting and spending himself, crying out in triumph or despair.

She felt the flood inside her. It was not unpleasant. If he'd given her more time, woken her, brought her along gently, she might have enjoyed it. As it was, she had done her duty to Jeff and she would not complain. She felt him going limp and sliding out of her, and she was fully awake. She didn't want it to end before it had really begun for her, but Jeff rolled off her and lay on his back, hands behind his head. In the pink light coming through the thin drapes she could see him smiling.

"You're mine now, really mine," he said. And he closed his eyes.

Later she felt dampness between her legs and reached down and touched herself. She almost laughed, because either she had really lost her virginity this time or she was starting her period. And she had no idea which she preferred.

* * *

She and Jeff went out to lunch at a downtown hotel. They talked about their friends and his job prospects, about surfing and cars and their families. They said nothing about the night before, about either his conduct at the party or what had happened in bed.

But Jeff's attitude toward her had changed subtly. He was attentive but he was also cocky, as if, by possessing her, he had also conquered her. It was not an attitude she liked, but she could understand why he was acting that way.

When he dropped her at the apartment, beeped his horn, and turned the car north for the drive back to Lantana, she stayed on the sidewalk for several minutes, watching the car disappear.

She knew she wasn't sure anymore. Not at all sure who she was, what she wanted to be, or whom she wanted to be with. She had given herself to Jeff and he loved her and she loved him.

And she still had six weeks to go at Channel 9.

Chapter
Five

The newsroom was humming with nervous excitement. Everyone was just a little better dressed than usual. Even Rory was wearing a tie.

"Mansion's back in town," Susan told her. "Which means he'll know all about your big scoop. You're getting all the breaks."

But when Richard Mansion did appear around noon he hurried past them all, straight into Ted Buchanan's office. When he emerged with Ted half an hour later Ted tried to get the boss to speak to his staff, but Mansion was impatient to get away and he didn't acknowledge Angie or anyone else.

"He doesn't look too happy," Susan remarked as she watched him leave. "I hope he's not on another of his morality-in-programming kicks. The last one cost us five points in the ratings." She got herself and Angie coffee. "Mansion's convinced the great American public wants to see only wholesome shows and happy news. I did a piece once on the home life of a stripper and almost got canned for it. And he's always after Ted to cover more moral crusaders and do-gooders. But as soon as the ratings slip he lets us go back to doing what sells.''

Angie ate a sandwich at her desk and was alone in the newsroom when Ted returned. He waved for her to follow him into his office.

"Sit down," he said. "Mr. Mansion's seen the clip of your Friday night effort and he was quite impressed. I suggested we hire you at the end of your internship."

She was flustered. It was what she wanted to hear, what she dreaded hearing. Now she would have to make the choice between Jeff and the job.

"He's not sure, yet," Ted said. "He thinks you might still be a bit young. I told him you were ready, but he wants to think about it. And he says he wants to get to know you before he decides." Ted gazed out of the window. "So he's going to talk to you over dinner tomorrow night. He'll send his car to pick you up at your apartment around eight. Are you free?"

"Of course," she said. It would never have occurred to her to refuse Mr. Mansion.

"Look, Angie," Ted said. "Mansion has . . . a reputation, as they say. He's rich, young, and appealing. For all his preaching about morality, he's supposed to be a swinger. Maybe it's all just gossip, but, well . . ." He was embarrassed. "But just remember, he's a sophisticated guy and you haven't met many like him. Be careful." He tried to make a joke of it. "I wouldn't want anything bad to happen to my star reporter."

The big black Lincoln was outside her building when Angie emerged just before eight. She had spent an hour worrying over her wardrobe and settled on a light blue gingham dress. It wasn't very sophisticated but it was the best she had.

The uniformed chauffeur held the door open for her and she sank into the plush velvet of the big limousine. Mansion wasn't there. She opened the oak cocktail cabinet and carefully touched the crystal decanters, the freshly filled silver ice bucket, the row of gleaming glasses.

The voice, right in her ear, startled her.

"I'm sorry, ma'am," the voice said. "I should have asked you if you'd like a drink. But if you would care to fix yourself one . . ."

It was the chauffeur, of course, speaking through a voice tube from his closed-off compartment. Angie laughed.

"No, thank you," she said, not knowing where to direct her voice. "I was just admiring all the things. It's such a beautiful car."

"We'll be in Coral Gables in fifteen minutes," the chauffeur said.

They swept into the driveway of The Arcadia in exactly fifteen minutes. She'd always heard it was the most expensive restaurant in Florida and it looked it. A big pink stucco building, surrounded by magnificent palms laced with tiny lights, and fountains playing on the broad lawns. A red-jacketed boy had the limousine door open the instant the car stopped.

She scrambled out of the back and stood for a moment looking up the flight of white marble steps. She prayed she wouldn't make any mistakes. She gave a little shrug, smiled thanks to the attendant, and started up the stairs.

Inside it was all plush and crystal chandeliers, acres of white starched linen and gleaming silver. And, she saw with a sinking heart, men were in black or white dinner jackets and the women in long gowns. Her little gingham looked pathetically out of place.

It certainly did to the maître d', who advanced on her with an expression of deep suspicion.

"Yes?" he said, scarcely bothering to conceal his contempt.

"Mr. Mansion, Richard Mansion," Angie said. "I'm having dinner with him."

The change was remarkable. Suddenly this superior being was fawning over her, bowing and murmuring his delight in serving her.

She held her head high as they threaded their way through the tables to a banquette overlooking the ocean. She felt she was being sneered at by all the rich, bejeweled women, but she was damned if she would feel inferior. She was quaking inside but she wouldn't let it show.

She approached the table and Richard Mansion rose to greet her. He wasn't wearing a tuxedo. He looked young and elegant in a white linen suit, which showed off his tan.

"Miss Waring. Angie." He smiled at her. "How good of you to come. I hope I didn't inconvenience you." He waited until she was settled. "Some wine?" He nodded to the hovering wine waiter, who filled Angie's glass. "It must seem irregular, us meeting like this, but I do it all the time," Mansion said. "For one thing, I'm very busy. For another, I think it's preferable to make interviews like this as relaxed as possible." He looked around the room. "Have you been here before?" he asked. "It's really quite good—for Florida."

"No," Angie said, "but I've heard about it. She was at a loss for words and sipped her wine. She stole a glance at the ice bucket and noted the label. "A lovely champagne," she said. "Tattinger, isn't it?"

"Very good, my dear. You have a well-developed palate. So many young people can't tell one wine from another." He drained his own glass and it was instantly refilled. Another waiter approached and presented them with menus. "Would you like me to order for us both?" he asked. "I know it by heart."

"Please," she said.

She listened as he ordered stone crabs, salad, and prime rib of beef and nodded when he suggested the beef should be rare. He called for the wine list again and ordered two bottles, an Italian white and a French red.

He grew more garrulous, drinking most of the wine himself, and she began to suspect he was more than a little drunk. At least it meant she had to do very little talking.

"I'm just damn glad I'm the oldest in the family," he told her at one point. "I got first choice of which branch of the empire I wanted to move into, so of course I grabbed the network. Television is going to take over this country, change it forever. Vast fortunes are going to be made. It's where the real media power will be. Money and power: an unbeatable combination." He drained the last of the Burgundy in his glass and signaled for another bottle.

"My kid brother, Lyle, had to settle for the newspaper division. I think he'd have picked it, anyway, even if I hadn't beaten him out of television." His voice held a sneer. "Lyle's a real wimp. He still thinks newspapers have a future, and all he's doing is draining away my profits. You just wait until the old man goes and I get control. I'll get rid of Lyle's toys.

God knows, I've always had to do his thinking for him. Just like the rest of my family.''

She looked up, startled. Should he be talking like that in front of a stranger? He looked at her and shrugged.

"My family," he said, "is not at all like the facade we present to the world. I've got all the Mansion genes. Alex, my father, is a tough old bird. He built the empire all on his own. I bet you didn't know he was a bootlegger during Prohibition. We keep *that* out of the family biographies. My late mother wasn't a strong person—she had no ambition, no stomach for the rough things you have to do if you're going to succeed. Lyle's the same. And my sisters—my God! Who knows where they came from! They've been through five husbands between the two of them. They're both lushes; they contribute nothing. I am carrying this whole family on my shoulders.''

Angie wondered what was expected of her. She kept nodding in sympathy, feeling so awkward. Mansion's rantings were both embarrassing and bewildering. Could this be *the* Mansion family he was talking about? The Mansions were the all-American success story, the close, proud family that had founded a dynasty and ran it using good Christian values. The Mansions were lauded as the epitome of private enterprise and public-spiritedness. And there she was, hearing the ugly side from the scion of the family!

"I guess I shouldn't be telling you all this," he said, but there was no apology in his voice. His eyes were glazed but his voice was still firm and clear. "But I just think someone your age should know things aren't always as they're presented. Nothing is as it seems. We have to fight against the cancers that attack our society, the forces aiming to tear down all we stand for." He took a generous draft of wine. "My own marriage," he said bitterly, "my own marriage was a symbol of the awful times in which we live."

He seemed to expect her to say something, but she was out of her depth, embarrassed, and didn't want to hear all this.

"My marriage," he said, "was a dreadful example of what has gone wrong with this country. Father rushed me into it, a union with the daughter of our fiercest competitor. We liked each other enough, I thought, and we came from similar backgrounds. But there was something wrong with the girl, a basic flaw in her character. She was . . . how should I put it? . . . she was soft. She gave me a son and then she proceeded to turn the boy into a version of herself. I was revolted."

He was drinking cognac by then, two doubles while Angie sipped her coffee.

"It became a marriage in name only," he said. "And then I became suspicious of her and hired a firm of very discreet private investigators, the best in Boston. They caught her at last, in bed with another young woman. She had no defense. I took custody of the boy and removed her from my life."

"I'm, uh, very sorry," Angie said carefully. "It must have been a terrible time for you. But at least you have your son."

"Yes," Mansion said. "I have the child. He's six now and I've got him in a good school, where all the damage his mother did is being undone. He's making out well—they wrote me the other day that he'd beaten up another kid. He'll go to Choate and Harvard and I'll make a real Mansion out of him." He nodded.

Soon he had exhausted the subject of his family and talked about Channel 9.

"I'll spend another year down here, getting the place right," he said. "And then I'll take over our whole network. Dad's getting on, even though he won't admit it. And the old man knows I'm already better than he is. He'll step down for me." He called for the check. "When that time comes, I want to have a lot of my own people in place. We are going to do it right. You're only a child, but from what I saw yesterday, and from what Buchanan tells me, you have a chance at making it. I suppose we'd better work out a deal, put you on staff awhile."

It was her chance to refuse, to say it had all been fun and excellent experience but she was going home to Jeff. But she said nothing, just nodded and thanked him for the lovely evening.

He signed the check and escorted her to the car and they swept back down the highway, through the dark tropical night. He was silent. He mixed a couple of drinks for himself from the bar and didn't mind that she refused. It was as if he had lost interest in her. When they arrived at her apartment, he didn't get out of the limo, just waved vaguely as the chauffeur held the door open for her. She looked at Mansion hesitantly, and decided to say only a brief final thank-you. She walked to her apartment lobby alone.

Later, in bed, Angie ran through the evening again and again. There was something badly wrong with Richard Mansion. People didn't unburden themselves to strangers like that. On the other hand, the man seemed desperately lonely. Maybe he just had no one to talk to.

"How did you get on with the boss?" Ted asked her the next evening. They were the last two people in the newsroom, it being Angie's turn to be "late stop," the reporter who stuck around in case something big broke.

"Okay, I think," she said. "He said he'd work something out about a permanent job." She fussed with some papers on her desk. "Actually, I wish he wouldn't," she blurted. "I can't take it, Ted. I promised Jeff this would be just for the summer. I guess I've just been . . . wasting your time, though I never thought of it that way. I hope you won't be angry with me when I leave."

"You haven't wasted our time, Angie," he said gently. "It's been fun having you around and you've more than earned your keep." He looked at his watch. "There's no need to hang on any longer tonight," he said. "Just one piece of advice, though: I'm sorry we're not going to be able to keep you, if you stick to your promise. But there are a few weeks left and anything can happen. Don't mention this to the others. Just let it ride for now."

She nodded, grateful for his suggestion. She didn't want anything to mar her final weeks at the station.

Three weeks later, on a Saturday morning, Susan woke her for a phone call.

"It's Mr. Mansion," she said. "Wow!"

Richard Mansion was crisp and businesslike.

"I've got a sailing party arranged for today," he said. "And one of the girls has suddenly dropped out. It's a chance for you to see another side of Florida life, if you can make it. I'll have the car pick you up in an hour. It's casual. Wear jeans, bring a swimsuit and sneakers."

"I'd love to come," she stammered. "But . . ."

"The car will be there in an hour." He hung up.

They were ready to sail when she arrived at Key Biscayne, and Mansion handed her a glass of champagne as the crew cast off. He introduced her to the others in the party.

"Bud and Ruth Colville, Jim Sanford, Gloria Welles," he said, with no special attempt at friendliness. "Angie Waring is working for me at the station. She's going to be a big television star." It was as though he were discussing the weather.

The others were nice to her but Angie sensed they were not impressed by her paltry credentials. They were part of the smart young Palm Beach set featured regularly in the social columns of the papers. After a couple of glasses of champagne in the hot sun, she overcame her shyness and talked with them.

The talk was exclusively polo and parties, and Angie was pleased she held her own. Exposure to the real world had paid off in social grace.

Just before lunch she excused herself and wandered around the yacht. It was a magnificent craft, scooting along under full sail. One of the crew took time out from trimming the sails to show her the belowdecks layout.

"It's a great old ketch," he told her happily. "Not many wooden boats like her still around. It costs a fortune to keep them up, but it's worth it. You don't get space and comfort like this on the new boats."

He showed her the teak-paneled dining room where a white-jacketed steward was setting the lunch table. Mansion's stateroom held a huge, incongruous round bed. There were four other, smaller, staterooms.

"Eighty-five feet overall," her guide said. "A crew of four plus a chef and two stewards. You could sail her around the world tomorrow. It's a real pity Mr.

Mansion can't spare more time to be aboard. I guess he doesn't get to spend more than three weeks a year here."

Angie joined the party again and soon they all went below for lunch. It was simple and delicious: chilled fresh shrimp, raw tuna marinated in lime juice, Caesar salad, fruit and cheese. She drank a little wine and relaxed, listening to the other guests' happy chatter.

After lunch they were allocated staterooms to nap or change into bathing suits to sun themselves on deck. Angie sat beside Gloria Welles in a deck chair on the afterdeck and let herself grow drowsy in the hot sun.

"So you're Richard's latest," Gloria remarked. "My, he's picking them younger all the time."

Angie opened her eyes and stared at Gloria, who gave Angie a broad wink. "Quite a catch, our Richard," Gloria said.

"It's not like that," Angie said stiffly. "I just work for him. This is only the third time I've even met him." It seemed so shocking, the thought that Richard Mansion would be interested in her.

She dozed some, waking when a cloud crossed the sun. She was relieved that Gloria was gone. She sat up, wondering where they were. It was late afternoon and she thought they should be heading home, but the land was still on her right, so they were still heading south. She shivered and wrapped herself in a towel. She could hear the clink of glasses and laughter forward on the main deck.

Angie went below to the stateroom, slipped out of her swimsuit, and got back into her jeans and sweater. Warm now, and relaxed from her nap, she went back up the companionway to the group on the main deck. Obviously, they had been drinking solidly. All were bright-eyed and gay. She asked the steward for a Coke and settled on the edge of the circle.

"You sure you don't want to join us, Richard?" Bud Colville was saying. "The party will be a hoot. He's an old bore but that new wife of his seems determined to spend a good chunk of his fortune before he finds out what she is."

"And what is she, Bud?" Gloria asked, feigning innocence. "Just what could the latest Mrs. MacDonnell be that her husband wouldn't approve of?"

"Oh, just ask the gardener, the pool boy, the children's nurse, or anybody else what she is," Colville said. They all laughed.

The boat changed course, the engine came on, and the crew set to work getting the sails down. She could see the Keys ahead of them and, as they got closer, a big black Rolls waiting on the dock. The boat came gently alongside the dock and a gangplank was run out.

It was only when they all said goodbye to her and Mansion that Angie realized she was expected to stay aboard. She panicked.

"I don't understand," she said to him. "I thought we were just going for the day. I didn't bring . . ."

"Don't worry about it," he said. "You'll find everything you need in your stateroom. I thought it would be a good experience for you, to cruise slowly back through the night. You'll be home in time for Sunday breakfast."

She didn't like it at all, but there was nothing she could do about it. The Rolls had already left the dock, and the crew was getting ready to put to sea again.

"Why don't you go below and have a shower and put on something warmer before dinner?" he said.

"You'll find shirts and slickers and things in your cabin."

Her bathroom was stocked with expensive soaps, lotions, and perfumes, and Angie took a hot shower, washing away the salt and taking the sting out of the slight sunburn she'd gotten. She stepped out of the shower and wrapped herself in a huge fluffy towel and took another from the stack to dry her hair. She opened a toothbrush from a box of a dozen but ignored the wide range of lipsticks and powders.

Back in her stateroom, opening drawers and closets, she found everything she could need. Crew shirts of the softest cotton, each embroidered with the name of the yacht, *Invicta*. Crisp white cotton ducks in several sizes. Underwear, new in plastic pouches from Saks. Mansion was certainly prepared for surprise guests! She laughed and began to luxuriate in the elegant room. So much luxury, so much casual wealth. Just for tonight, she would pretend she belonged here.

Angie finished drying her hair and tied it back in a fluffy ponytail. She selected a dark blue shirt and a pair of white ducks. She didn't bother putting her own bra back on: the shirt was soft and loose and covered her amply. Finally she took out a big warm sweater embossed with the yacht's name and knotted it around her shoulders. She examined herself in the full-length mirror and decided she looked very nice.

"Lovely," Mansion said when she came into the main saloon. He was sprawled out in a big captain's chair but he rose to greet her. "You look delightful. Maybe I should start employing an all-girl crew and dress them just like that." He pressed a button and a steward appeared. "What will you have to drink, my dear?" Mansion asked. "A martini?"

She'd never had a martini, but it sounded good and this was a night for new experiences. She nodded, wishing she felt easier with him.

It wasn't a big drink and it tasted vile, but it looked so good, the olive glowing in the crystal liquid, beads of moisture coursing down the fine thin glass. It was ice-cold and she drank it all, shuddering a little. Mansion poured her another from the silver shaker and she didn't object.

They sat there for three quarters of an hour, the handsome saloon warm and glowing in the light of three antique oil lamps. Mansion smoked a cigar and chatted easily about the cruises he had taken in the yacht, about wild weather and dangerous days sailing out of the family compound at Newport, Rhode Island.

"No danger down here in these waters, though," he said. "It's going to be a very smooth sail home."

Smooth it was. Angie sat listening to the sighing of the sails and the gentle lap of water. Inside her body was a warm glow, and in her head, lightness.

"You know something, Mr. Mansion?" she said. "I think everyone should live like this." And she giggled.

She noticed him look at her and smile. And soon it was time to go in to dinner.

There was wine and a cold soup, veal and fresh asparagus. She stopped drinking. The boat seemed to be rocking more and her skull felt tight. She didn't want to admit she was ill—it was so juvenile—but she was afraid of what would happen if she didn't speak up.

"I'm sorry, Mr. Mansion," she finally gasped. "I don't feel well. I've never been to sea before." His face swam before her.

"I can fix that," he laughed. "Sit there and I'll go get you a pill. It will make everything smooth in a second."

He returned with a small white pill and filled her glass with mineral water.

"Get that down and you'll be okay," he said. She was grateful that he wasn't offended.

She swallowed with difficulty but he turned out to be right. Within minutes the nausea had gone and was replaced by exhilaration. She felt better, wonderfully better. Still floating, but that didn't matter. She was sharp and clever, terribly bright. She even took another glass of champagne, then another. She laughed a lot. So did he.

And after that she didn't know much, just the vague impression of someone leading her from the table and toward bed. She was in a vast, soft space and all she wanted was sleep. But there were hands that wouldn't let her sleep, hands all over her body.

"Please, no," she heard herself whimper from far away. "Please don't. Please leave me alone."

There was no fight in her. Her arms and legs would not function, and only a small portion of her mind seemed to know what was happening to her. Naked, she shivered. Then there was weight on her, a body holding her down. It brought pain.

He was huge and impatient and several times the savage hammering at her defenseless body brought her into full consciousness. She could bear it if she lay still, but this seemed to enrage him, and so for a while she floated out of her body to somewhere above, where she looked down at the grotesque sight of Richard Mansion plundering her.

She gagged when he forced himself into her mouth and she forced her head away, but he slapped her again and again. She stopped herself from turning away. All she wanted was for it to be over.

It hurt enough for her to cry out when he turned her over and entered her from behind, but he stifled her screaming by forcing her face down into the pillow.

Finally the ordeal ended. She sensed his rage and frustration at her lack of response and was careful to feign unconsciousness. Still dazed, she let herself be bundled roughly back into her own cabin. When he was gone, she passed out.

"Good morning, miss." The steward was gently touching her shoulder. She opened her eyes. "I banged on your door for ages," the young man said. "I've got your breakfast."

He had set a tray on the small table on the other side of the cabin, and as he busied himself removing silver covers from the dishes, Angie glanced down at herself. She was covered with a sheet, and wondered whether the steward had done that. It hardly mattered. Her whole body ached and burned and she wondered whether she could move.

"It's eleven o'clock," the steward said cheerily. "Mr. Mansion went ashore an hour ago. He said you'd probably want to sleep late. He's sent the car back to drive you home when you're ready."

"Thank you," she said, her lips so swollen she could hardly speak. She remembered all the slaps and wondered if her face was bruised. "Thank you," she said as the steward left her cabin. Could he see? Did he know?

She edged herself out of bed, pain at every movement. The clothes she'd been wearing at dinner were tossed in a bundle in the corner. She staggered past the breakfast tray to the bathroom and threw up.

Angie stood under the shower for ten minutes, the hot water sluicing away some of the agony in her body, but none of the anguish in her mind. She didn't want to think about what had happened, not yet, but guilt and rage kept intruding. Had she contributed, somehow, to the terrible things he had done to her? Was it partially her fault? No, she told herself fiercely. No. The only thing she had done wrong was to come aboard this luxury yacht, obeying an order from the man who employed her. But shouldn't she have been wiser? Shouldn't she have anticipated the risk?

She willed herself not to break down, to hold herself together long enough to get out of this place and back home. She dried herself carefully and, at last, she looked at her body. There were bruises emerging around her thighs and breasts but no marks on her face, at least not yet. She stared at herself in the mirror and thought her eyes had changed the most.

In the cabin she found her own clothes and threw them on. They felt used, like her, but they were her own. Her throat was dry and she reached for the orange juice on the tray, then pulled her hand away. She wanted nothing that was his.

She went up on deck and the sun blinded her. She stumbled as she hurried down the gangway. The big black car was there but she skirted around it and hurried up the dock away from anyone who might know her shame.

She found a cab and stared straight ahead all the way back to the apartment, ignoring the driver's cheerful comments on the beauty of the morning.

Susan wasn't there. She'd left a note saying she'd be back that evening. Angie packed quickly then picked up the telephone.

"Mom," she said, "I'm coming home today. I'll be

on the bus this afternoon. Can you pick me up from the station when I call?''

''What's wrong, Angie?'' her mother demanded. ''Has something happened?''

''Nothing's happened! Nothing!'' she snapped. ''It's just that Daddy and Jeff were right. I'm not cut out for a career, so I'm coming home.'' And then she was crying into the telephone.

''Dear,'' her mother said gently. ''It can't be as bad as all that. Stay where you are and I'll drive right down and we'll talk. And then if you still want to quit, throw away this wonderful opportunity, I'll bring you back here.''

Her mother rang the apartment door an hour later and Angie fell into her arms. She cried again and her mother waited, asking no questions. She went into the kitchen and made them coffee and sat down across from Angie and studied her.

''Baby,'' she said. ''Something's hurt you very much. Will you tell me?''

''I can't,'' Angie said. ''I just want to go home.''

''Sure,'' her mother said. ''We'll all be so happy to have you back. And Jeff's missed you so. Have you called him to tell him you're coming?''

Angie shook her head.

''I don't want to see Jeff, not for a while at least,'' she said. ''I don't want to see anyone.''

Her mother glanced at her sharply and Angie realized she knew at least something of what had happened to her.

''Okay,'' she said, ''there's no need to see anyone for a while. Just come home and rest. But what about Mr. Buchanan? Have you told him you're leaving? I thought you were very close to him.'' Again that keen glance. Was it Ted Buchanan who had done something to her?

"Oh, God," Angie said. "I must leave a note for Ted. He's been so good to me and I'm letting him down. Will you wait while I write him something? Susan can deliver it in the morning."

She dashed off a single page to Ted, telling him she had to go home unexpectedly, thanking him for all he had taught her and the friendship he had given her, apologizing for letting him down. She sealed the envelope as if she were sealing a portion of her life.

The days at home ran together for Angie. She lay in the sun by the pool and kept her mind closed. Her mother was gentle and understanding, never pressing her, gently dissuading Jeff from coming around.

Angie did take one call from Ted Buchanan during the first week. He was hurt and bewildered.

"I can't understand you, running out like that," he said. "Something must have happened."

"I'm sorry, Ted," she said. "It just all got to be too much. I'm not cut out for life in a newsroom."

"Bullshit," he said. "Something happened and I know it. Because when I told Mansion you'd gone he just nodded and said something about you being too young for the job. Did you have some kind of trouble with Mansion?"

"No, Ted," she insisted. "No trouble. I just wanted to come home."

He pleaded with her to change her mind, to keep in touch with him, to let him know what she decided to do. If she wanted to work somewhere else, he would give her a recommendation and introductions.

She thanked him again, satisfied none of his suspicions, and hung up.

Eventually she did see Jeff. She told him she was simply drained by the whole experience of working at Channel 9 and asked him to be patient, to leave her alone to rest. He was hurt and surly but there was nothing he could do about it.

Angie was left alone to drift through the dying days of summer. In a few weeks she knew for certain. She went to her mother.

"I'm pregnant," she said. "I'm overdue and I've always been regular."

Her mother showed no surprise.

"Is it Jeff?" she asked, and Angie shook her head. "Then what do you want to do about it?"

"What can I do?" Angie asked.

"Do you want to keep the baby?" her mother asked.

"No," she said harshly.

"I'll make some inquiries," her mother said. "Don't worry too much, dear." She put her arms around Angie. "You'll come through all right. But I think you owe it to Jeff to talk to him."

Angie nodded. "Poor Jeff," she sighed.

She called him and asked him to pick her up at home that night. He sounded pathetically grateful that she was willing to see him, and he drove to their usual spot above the beach. Jeff turned off the engine and gazed out to sea.

"Angie," he said, "I'm sorry about how I've acted. That drunken scene I created in Miami, being jealous of you working at the TV station. I've been selfish and acted like a kid. I don't blame you cutting me off like you have been. But if you'll just give me another chance I'll make up for everything."

She felt tears welling. Poor Jeff. She wished she

didn't have to hurt him. But it was all out of her control now.

"Jeff," she said gently, reaching for his hand. "Jeff, I'm pregnant."

His hand stiffened under hers. Then he turned to her.

"But that's . . . wonderful," he said. "We can get married right away. Sure, it'll be a struggle, but we'll make it."

"No, Jeff," she said. "The baby's not yours. I'm not going to go through with it."

It was as if she had stabbed him. He stared at her and even in the evening light she could see his face had gone deathly pale.

"How could you?" he said. "How could it not be mine? You said you loved me."

"I did and I do, Jeff," she said. "If you want to know all about it, I'll tell you. It's a horrible, awful story."

But he didn't understand what she was getting at, and she made no further attempt to tell him what had happened to her.

"Miami changed you," he said bitterly. "You're too good for me now. Big-city ideas. You're a slut." And then he began to cry and there was nothing she could do anymore to ease his grief and anger and bewilderment.

They drove home in silence and did not say goodbye.

She hurt like hell, but there was the feeling, too, that not as much had been lost between her and Jeff as she liked to believe. If she pretended, for just a second, that the horror hadn't happened, that they were still going to marry and everything was what it had been . . . she knew she was lying. She wouldn't have married Jeff. They wouldn't have had the life they'd talked about. None of that was ever going to happen, she told herself. It ought to have made her feel a little less beaten, but it didn't. As soon as she understood that she and Jeff had never been meant to happen, she saw too vividly what that meant for Jeff.

It was as if the rape had happened to him, the tragedy had been Jeff's, not hers. She was coming out of a long dark tunnel. He was just going in.

Her father came to her the next evening.

"Your mother told me about your condition," he said. "Who is responsible?" He wasn't angry with her. It was more like he had suffered a blow. "You're just a kid, Angie," he said. "It's not your fault. I suppose it was this Ted Buchanan you were always talking about. Is he the one who took advantage of you? I've got to know."

She shook her head. She was so tired, so confused.

"No, Daddy," she said. "It wasn't Ted. He was just the best friend I ever had."

"Who, then? Who did this to you?" he insisted. "I don't want to bully you but I'm going to find out."

In that moment, she gave up.

"It was Mr. Mansion, Richard Mansion," she said, the words tumbling out. "I guess it was my fault. I was so naïve. I just didn't . . . didn't know anything."

Her father put his arms around her and hugged her tight. She could feel the anger in him and she was glad she hadn't told him the whole awful story.

"The bastard!" her father said. "He was your employer. He's a rich man, a big shot. And you were just a kid. Damn him!"

In the next few days Angie was more worried for

her father than herself. He brooded around the house, barely containing his anger.

Her mother handled the abortion, but it was not easy to arrange. No reputable doctor would even discuss it. Finally, she got the name of a man in a little town out in the swamps. She and Angie drove there early one morning.

Angie felt as though she weren't there. She waited in the front room of the little house while her mother talked with the doctor, whose name they never learned. His face wore the flush of a heavy drinker and his hands shook a little, but the bedroom where Angie was taken was clean and the doctor's instruments shining.

The operation was not too physically painful. It was her mind that hurt her—a sense of loss, of waste. She knew she was doing the right thing, but that did nothing to ease her. She was allowing her body to be violated all over again, just as Richard Mansion had violated her.

There was a sudden, sharp pain, more intense than any that had gone before, and Angie cried out. The sound brought her mother running in from the waiting room.

"It's okay," the man said. "It's all over. You rest awhile and you'll be able to go home in an hour," he told Angie. Then, speaking to both of them, he said, "There is one complication. I don't think the girl will be able to have children now. I'm sorry, but there's always that risk when you do this procedure under less than ideal conditions. Actually, it may not be a bad thing. The girl's pelvic structure is small. Childbirth would have been very difficult for her anyhow."

On the drive home, Angie glanced at her mother and saw the trickle of tears on her cheeks.

She spent a week lying in the sun, waiting for her body to heal. Gradually, by refusing to let herself think about any of it, she began to feel again.

When the special delivery letter arrived, the first thing that fluttered from the envelope was a check. Five thousand dollars? Yes. The accompanying letter, from Channel 9's accounts office, said the sum was for accrued overtime.

"Mom?" she said, showing her the check and letter. "They don't pay overtime to interns. And even if they did, I never could have earned this much."

Her mother frowned.

"Conscience money, I guess," she said. "Mansion's conscience money. I didn't want to tell you, but your father called Mansion last week. He told him what he thought of him and what had happened to you. I didn't want him to, but there was no stopping him. Your poor father. He feels so ineffectual. There's nothing he can do to make up for what happened to you, so he lashed out at Mansion. This," she said, holding the check between thumb and forefinger as if it were hot, "this must be the result. I think you should just tear it up. We don't want that man's money."

"No," Angie said evenly. "I'm not going to tear it up. I'll use his damned money to get me a car, get me north, and set up in a new job. I called Ted the other day, and he can get me a job on the *Washington Tribune* even though I still have a year of college left. I don't care about finishing, and I don't want to stay here. I'll use Mr. Mansion's conscience money—and someday I'll fling it back in his face."

Chapter
Six

"A great way to spend a twenty-first birthday," Angie muttered as she huddled deeper into her leather coat. The rain was threatening to turn into snow and it sheeted down on the two of them, standing under the streetlamp. They seemed to be the only people stupid enough to be out in the streets of Georgetown on that bitter night. The soft lights in the surrounding mansions mocked them, promising wine and food and laughter for those smart enough to be inside.

"Whose twenty-first birthday?" her photographer, Rolly Watkins, asked. "Not yours?"

Angie nodded.

"Well, congratulations," he said. "I thought you were older. Let's hope Ricky-boy does the right thing tonight and gives us both a present. Christ, I hate stakeouts."

"Yeah," Angie said. "It's time we came up with a good scoop. But I don't think tonight will give us one. There's no way the attorney general's going to come waltzing out of that house with a blonde on his arm."

"You sure keep secrets, Angie," Rolly said. "I thought you were twenty-five, with years in this business behind you. Hell, as soon as we're through with tonight's exercise in futility I'll buy you a drink to celebrate."

"We'll both need a cask of brandy to thaw out," she said. "But I'd appreciate it if you didn't broadcast my age around the newsroom. That just slipped out. When I came up here, I had to lie about my age and invent some experience or they would have stuck me on general assignment. Fortunately, I had a friend who was willing to lie a little about my background."

"You carried it off okay," he said. "There isn't a tougher reporter on the *Tribune*." He meant it as a compliment.

"Thanks," she said, then nudged him with her elbow. "Get ready for action." The outside lights in the handsome brownstone across from them had come on. She and Rolly moved toward the house and pressed against a gap in the privet hedge. They were only feet away from the big white front door and even closer to the black limousine in the driveway.

She stiffened with excitement as the door swung open. There were three people standing in the foyer, saying their farewells. There was a tall older couple, the man in a dinner jacket and the woman in a long gown. The fair, tousle-haired young man wearing a dark suit was preparing to leave them. He was alone. There was no sign of the movie star.

"Damn!" Angie muttered. Rolly tucked his camera back under his coat. There had been so many days and nights like this staking out the movers and shakers in Washington, trying for that compromising picture and damaging story that had become the stock-in-trade of their newspaper.

Her voice must have carried, because suddenly the attorney general bounded down the steps and across the drive to where they stood.

"How're my shadows tonight?" he demanded. He was laughing, his white teeth gleaming in the lamplight. "I thought this weather would keep even the *Tribune* team indoors. Sorry I haven't got anything to make your night worthwhile." He seemed genuinely to see the funny side of the hunt. It was as close as Angie had been to him and she felt the magnetism of the man. It made her, just for a second, ashamed of the keyhole journalism they were practicing. But, hell, gossip and sensation were the only things keeping her paper afloat. Respectable people read the other paper, but a lot of them also folded a copy of the *Tribune* into it, for fun.

The attorney general was in no hurry to get in out of the rain. He moved closer to them.

"I've seen you before, haven't I?" he said. "Angie Waring. I read your column. Great stuff! But you won't get me in it." He laughed. "God, I wish I was up to all the things you guys have me doing. All I really get to do is work, boring work. It's my little brother you should be chasing. He has all the fun in our family." He winked at Angie. "Come around and see me sometime and I'll tell you a few cabinet secrets." He jumped into the limousine and it slid off into the night.

"Another bad tip," Rolly grumbled. "Go call Newton and tell him we missed out again, then we'll get a drink. I don't know what I'm doing on this beat. I should have stayed in sports."

She went to the telephone down the street while Rolly got their car.

Jack Newton, the city editor, was disappointed but not surprised.

"Not to worry, Angie," he said. "Sooner or later we'll get the story. Meantime, your column for tomorrow looks okay so I guess you can call it a night."

"Thanks, Jack," she said. "I'm bushed and I think I caught a cold standing out in the rain all evening. But—"

"But you'll be here tomorrow bright and early to start on the next column," he said. "Because if you're not, there are a dozen eager reporters waiting to take over the column for you."

She hung up and got in the car with Rolly. Newton was right. If she let up for an instant, if she lost her touch, if she missed a big story—she wasn't going to let any of those things happen.

Washington! Hustle City! She knew from the start that there wasn't much to back up the charge people got from the city: little of substance happened anyplace in Washington. But there was the attitude: this is where it all goes down. She liked the attitude. It helped make her job easier and it got her through bouts of awful homesickness. Whenever she talked to her parents on the phone, she sounded so vibrant, so thrilled about everything in her life, that even she believed herself.

In fact, Washington had no cohesive feeling, didn't seem like one city at all. There were the very wealthy: one hardly ever saw them. There were the very poor: they were everywhere. And there were people like her, people with jobs and places to go and things to do: there were as many of her as there were poor people. What, Angie wondered, did everybody *do* here? Even counting all the bureaucracies and everything that fed them—restaurants and apartment buildings and taxis—it seemed impossible that there should be so many people tied to one city.

Rolly broke into her reverie.

"You spent your birthday standing in the rain," he marveled. "You're just a kid and you should be out having a good time. But all you do is work. You've got no friends at the paper, no social life that anyone knows about. You're a real oddball, Angie."

She shrugged.

"Work's important to me, Rolly," she said. "I'm willing to give up a lot to get the success I want. I've no choice, anyway. A job like this, you can't have a private life. There isn't any time."

"I know," he said. "My job is so demanding my wife left. I guess we're both oddballs."

She and Rolly had a couple of brandies, and then she drove carefully through the wet darkness to her apartment and wearily climbed the three flights of stairs. She let herself into the apartment and was pleased to see lights on in the living room. She felt like talking to someone and her roommate was a good listener.

But it wasn't Greer waiting for her. A tall figure untangled itself from the couch, the dark curly hair, the rumpled clothes. She ran across the room and flung herself into his arms.

"Ted, Ted," she cried. "There's no one I'd rather see. And tonight especially." She held both his hands in hers and looked up at him. "But what are you doing here?"

He grinned. "Your roomie is very trusting, or else I don't look dangerous. Anyway, she let me in. She's gone to bed. I was in New York at a convention, and I happened to know from your personnel records what day this is." He glanced at his watch. "What day it *was,* I mean." He kissed her lightly. "Happy birthday yesterday."

She slowly released his hands and stood looking at him. It felt so good to be with him, to remember when her life had been so full of warmth. Looking at him, she began to remember the glow.

"I've thought about you so often," she said. "I should have written, I know, but there never seems to be a minute. The paper—"

"I know," he said. "I talk to Jack Newton from time to time and he tells me what a great job you're doing."

"Thanks to you," she said, smiling. "And thanks for telling some lies about my experience."

"I was never worried about your bringing it off, Angie," Ted said. "All you needed was a break. You're a natural."

She reached out to touch him, then stopped herself.

"I don't know if there's anything to drink," she said hastily. "Greer and I really only use the place to sleep in. But there might be something in the kitchen."

"Actually there are a couple of bottles of champagne and a cake in the icebox," he said. "I brought them from New York. I'm afraid the cake got a bit crushed on the plane."

She was almost overwhelmed. They drank the champagne in the glow of the radiator. For the first time since she'd come to Washington, for the first time since that awful night on Mansion's boat, Angie was relaxed and happy, thoroughly happy. They talked about the Miami newsroom, their friends, the column she was writing for the *Tribune.*

"I'm sorry I just ran out on you like that," Angie

said hesitantly. He had been kind enough not to bring
it up, so she felt she had to. "I didn't want to go at all,
after all you did for me. But I just couldn't . . . take
the pressure anymore."

He held up a hand.

"Don't talk about it if you don't want to, Angie,"
he said. "I've got a hunch about what happened to
you. But it doesn't matter now, not really. Water under the bridge. It worked out for the best. Look at you
now."

She cried, tears from deep within her, tears she
couldn't stop. He held her gently and waited.

"Look at me now!" she sobbed. "A minor success
on a failing newspaper; a cold, hard, calculating
gossipmonger who doesn't have a friend in the world
and doesn't want one."

"You've got me," he said gently. "And you're
young and beautiful and you have a life to make."

"I feel like the best of my life has already gone,"
she said. "One day you're a child, the next a
grown-up struggling to make it."

"It's not that bad," Ted said, hugging her. He
stroked her hair. "You're just tired tonight." He separated from her. "I'd better let you get to bed. And
I've got to get to my hotel."

She sat looking at him for a while.

"Why don't you stay here, Ted?" she asked.
"Greer is a sound sleeper and . . . I want you to stay
with me."

He went to the door and got his coat from the rack.

"There's nothing I'd rather do, Angie," he said.
"But the time's not right. You're still hurting from
whatever happened, so you've thrown yourself into
your work. It's probably the best thing for you right
now. At this stage, I'd just be someone for you to

cling to on a cold dark night.'' He gave her a smile. ''And I want to be more than that. Much more than that.''

He opened the door and she got up from the couch and crossed to him.

''Okay, Ted,'' she said. She kissed him quickly. ''Thanks for the visit, for thinking of my birthday. Let's not wait so long between visits now. I've loved seeing you.''

She stood at the window and watched him standing on the curb in the rain. The street was deserted and he looked desolate, his collar pulled up against the cold. She opened the window and the cold rushed in.

''Ted, Ted,'' she called. ''Come back.''

The rain was streaming from his hair when he appeared at the door, and she got him a towel.

''You'll never get a cab on a night like this,'' she said as he huddled close to the radiator. She felt awkwardness begin between them and wondered if she ought to make up a bed on the sofa. She damned well didn't want to do that.

''Come to bed now,'' she whispered, taking his hand. He followed her down the hall, tiptoeing past the bedroom of the sleeping Greer and into Angie's tiny room at the back of the apartment.

They undressed silently in the faint light and crawled into her single bed. They were both cold and huddled close, their bodies warming almost at once.

Ted was shy at first, but then the desire in him took over and he embraced her with true passion. She held herself back, but when Ted kissed her and then let his lips stray to her nipples, she responded fully. The warmth spread through her body. His hands explored her gently, not forcing, never hurrying. Their touching went on and on, and at last Angie found true desire, a desire overwhelming everything else.

She felt his body enveloping her, shielding her, and she guided him into her. The feel of him deep inside her was a flame that warmed but did not burn. She moved against him fast and hard, all reservations lost in joy. She felt a tide rising in her, washing over her until she heard herself cry out. The tide swept over her again and again and washed through her to him. Ted's body convulsed and she savored the sensation of him pulsating inside her.

They clung together after, Angie loving the feel of him, limp and vulnerable now, against her. His mouth was close to her ear and she drifted into sleep listening to his soft murmurings of love.

She got up early the next morning, while he was still asleep, and sat at the kitchen table with her coffee. She looked out across the street, examining the trees lining the sidewalk, and thought about her and Ted. He made her happy. She liked him. She could probably love him. And then she thought about Jeff and their plans, all those plans that had seemed inviolate and were wrecked before they could start much of anything. She thought about her job, then, and the sturdy protection work had given her, protection from feeling sorry for Jeff, from being too homesick, from wanting what she couldn't have.

She kept on thinking about work, and when Ted joined her in the kitchen for coffee, she had put him in a place where she could manage him, a part of the back of her mind where she could keep him at bay whenever she wanted to.

"I could probably swing it to stay here a few days," Ted said as he sipped coffee at the table in the tiny kitchen. "I'd really like to stay here with you awhile.

Maybe we could take off somewhere together." He ducked his head shyly. "I don't want to lose you again, Angie."

"Ted," she said gently, "don't stay on. We've both got our jobs to do, and maybe . . ." She stroked his hair. "You've been so good for me. But I want to finish what I started here, and if I get deeply involved with someone wonderful, I'll never do what I want to do." It sounded selfish but she knew what she meant: she had come so far and at such a cost that she would not be diverted.

He seemed really to understand, and he didn't look hurt. It was eerie. Had he known all along what she would say?

"Angie," he said, smiling at her, "go get 'em, kid. You're going to be the best there is."

And he left, just like that.

Her lovely day seemed to fall apart when Jack Newton summoned her to his glass-walled cubicle. She waited until he looked up and beckoned her inside.

"Christ!" he said, waving proofs at her in exasperation. "You'd think an editorial writer could explain the civil rights situation in six hundred words, wouldn't you? But they pussyfoot around, taking both sides of the issue. If we're going to win readers from the goddamned opposition, we've got to be outspoken, not worry about being fair." He ran his hand across his bald head, leaving a smudge of ink. "You're a Southern cracker, aren't you, Angie? But even you could make a better case for Negro rights than this jackass. Anyway, that's not what I wanted to see you about. I'm taking you off the 'Intimate Washington' column."

Her heart sank. Just because she hadn't snared the

attorney general last night? Her column was one of the few features in the *Tribune* that got talked about.

"Newt," she began, "that's unfair. I've been working around the clock on that column and we've broken some good stories and—"

"I know, honey," he said. "It's because you've done such a good job I'm going to expand your horizons. I'm going to put Nick Carson on the column, now that you've got it going so well, and you're going to have most of page two every day, to do a kind of profile thing. A real good interview of someone the others can't get to. Or a nice bitchy send-up of the city at its pretentious worst. Or a guide to who's who in this week's pecking order. You know the kind of thing I'm looking for."

"I know darned well what you're looking for," she said. "You want me to be another Mary Hickson. You want me to challenge the biggest star the *Post*'s got."

"And why not?" he said smugly. "You're ready for it. Hickson's over the hill. Or I should say, under Capitol Hill." He put his hands over his belly, rocked back in his chair, and laughed heartily. "Get it? Under the Hill. Old Hickson wouldn't get entree to the Maryland Dog Show if she weren't screwing half of Congress."

"Very funny, Newt," Angie said. "I don't care how Hickson got where she is. The point is, she's there. Anyone who matters in Washington talks to Hickson before they talk to anyone else. I've had a couple of run-ins with her already. Can you imagine the doors she's going to close for me the minute she sees me being put up as her competitor?"

"That's what I like about the situation," Newton said, still chuckling. "It's creative tension. It'll bring out the best in both of you. And you'll win, Angie. You're younger and prettier and smarter than Hickson."

"Never mind prettier, Newt," she said. "I'm never going to employ the horizontal interviewing technique." Then she smiled. "It'll be fun to go up against her," she admitted. "She's had the field to herself far too long. But I'm not sure I can do it. She's an awfully powerful woman."

"Angie," he said, serious now, "I wouldn't put you in the firing line if I weren't confident. It's my ass, too. We can't afford any failures here. You'll carry it off."

"Okay," she sighed. "When do I start?"

"Now," he said, "but take the rest of the week to get your first couple of pieces ready. I don't want to send you into battle unprepared."

Back at her desk the momentary confidence Angie had felt evaporated entirely. This was what having a by-line came down to. You were on your own, and only as good as yesterday's article. Mary Hickson was formidable competition. She had held sway at the *Post* for five years and had the ear of every important congressman, cabinet secretary and White House official, plus all the society hostesses in the city.

She looked through her engagement book before turning it over to Nick Carson. There were a couple of parties she would still attend, even if she would be seeking a different kind of story. The Iranian ambassador was having another of his big parties that night. Probably all very predictable, but the mountains of caviar always pulled a high-level crowd. And lunch with Ken Beckworth at Sans Souci today. She'd keep that one for herself, too. Beckworth was only a third-term congressman from New York but he was starting to be noticed and he wanted to get to know her better. He could be useful.

Useful, Angie admitted to herself, was the way she approached everyone. Were they useful to her work or not? It wasn't a quality she liked in herself but she had been forced to develop that kind of view. She was in a tough game and all by herself. She would never be taken advantage of again.

Congressman Beckworth was at the table when the maître d' ushered her in. She was enough of a celebrity to get the full Sans Souci treatment, and she did. Ken Beckworth rose from the table and shook hands formally. He was about her height, conservatively dressed in a dark suit, carefully groomed, blond and blue-eyed, a model Wasp type. He ordered drinks for them both with that marked air of authority that meant he had worked hard to acquire it. Men to the manor born did not, she knew, have to impress the waiter.

They fenced through shrimp cocktails and steaks, and then he said bluntly, "It's a tricky job you've got, Angie, catching people in the act and listening at doors." She set him straight, taking more pleasure in his look of respect than she knew she should. "I'm not in the gossip business any longer, Ken. I'm about to begin my own column, page two, to say what I like. Interviews, profiles, hatchet jobs—whatever. So you don't have to look around the restaurant to see if you can still salvage your lunch hour."

The blue eyes flashed at her and he showed his fine white teeth.

"You've learned the power game very fast, little Angie," he said. "I figured you'd go a long way in this town. So you're going up against Hickson. It's time that bitch had some competition."

"That's funny," Angie said. "I heard you and Mary were very close for a while. Didn't she do a very sympathetic profile of you last year? Said you were vice-presidential material."

He shrugged. "In my line of business you have to be nice to everyone. But Mary's gotten to the point where she thinks she's a major power broker. Anyway, I'm pleased with your news. A little gossip column is one thing, but what you've got now, that's power. If you need any help lining up interviews, call me."

The waiter came and they both ordered steaks.

"If you need an escort, or an entree to the kind of parties where they don't want press coverage, I'm available," he said. "I get to most of the exclusive things in town, being young, single, and considered a future heavy hitter." This was said without boasting, just an acceptance of things as they were.

"What's in it for you?" Angie asked. She had been around long enough to know no one did anything for nothing. "Why would a heavy hitter bother with a fledgling columnist?"

"Oh, there'll be a time when you'll be able to do me a favor," he said. "And your owner in New York has backed me before. His paper here may be going down the tubes, but he's still got a lot of clout in New York City." He looked at her with open admiration. "And you're a lovely woman, Angie. Life wasn't meant to be all work, you know. We're both free, white, and over twenty-one. I'd like to see you."

"I don't socialize, Ken," she said. "No time. But there's no reason why we can't be friends while treading the political mill."

"More than friends, I hope," he said smoothly. He nodded to the waiter to bring them coffee. "This is a lonely town when you're setting out to make your name. People like us should stick together.''

She thought about that. People like us? Had she become a person like Ken Beckworth, hungry for power and personal success, a user? She supposed she had, but she preferred not to go into any deep self-examination just then. She just wanted to secure her own place in the scheme of things. Later there would be time to examine herself.

''This new column,'' Beckworth was saying. ''At least it will get you off those ridiculous stakeouts, all that gumshoe stuff. Hanging around in the rain trying to catch the attorney general with his pants down? You can leave that to the *American Clarion*.''

''How do you know about that?'' she asked, stunned and trying not to show it.

He looked around the restaurant and bent forward toward her, whispering conspiratorially.

''There are . . . people . . . watching that whole damned family all the time,'' he said. ''Professional watchers, who know what they're doing. They've got huge files on all of them, stuff that would curl your hair. When the time is right, we'll pull the rug out from under them all, the arrogant goddamn clan with their dubious money and their chic ideas.''

''Oh, come on now,'' she said. ''They might seem a little unconventional after the last administration, but they seem like good people.''

He scowled.

''I hate them,'' he said. ''Phonies, parading their left-wing views when they were born with silver spoons in their mouths. And claiming people like me represent the ruling classes! Christ, I worked my way through law school sweating two jobs, took on hopeless elections for the party, clawed my way to where I am now. No rich daddy buying elections for me. I got here because powerful people saw I had what was needed and backed me. I don't have anyone's fortune behind me. I'm out there on a limb: if I don't deliver what I promise, I'm through in politics. Of course I hate those privileged bastards. Hypocrites."

The speech invoked more passion than she had thought Beckworth capable of. It intrigued her. This was not the cool, calculating congressman everyone thought he was. He could be useful.

"So who've you got watching them?" she asked lightly. "Your own private eyes? Or the FBI?"

He glared at her.

"You'd better be careful what you say, Angie. Don't joke about this. One of these days the shit is going to hit the fan and when it does we'll remember who our friends are and who the enemies are." He called for the check and refused to split it. He relaxed, resuming the role of sardonic insider, the man who would show her the ropes.

"It's been fun," he said before they parted. "I really would like to see more of you, Angie. Not just professionally."

She watched him drive away.

The Iranian embassy glowed white in the spotlights. The formally dressed crowd hurried up the steps under umbrellas held by guards. Angie attached herself to a pair of undersecretaries so she wouldn't have to make her entry unaccompanied.

She had been right. The promise of unlimited caviar and the finest wines had brought out the A list.

She wasn't interested in the slow-moving receiving line, so she slipped away to check out the guests and the ornate embassy. Everything she had heard about the place was true. The representative of the Peacock Throne had spared no expense—the vast interior of the embassy glowed pink and gold; spotlights picked out art treasures and precious stones placed in wall alcoves. Gold plate gleamed everywhere.

"A thief would have a ball," Nick Carson said at her elbow. "Except the guards would cut off his hands. They're all SAVAK men, you know." He pointed out some of the grim-faced, dark-suited men around the room. "Toughest secret police in the world," he said. "Fantastically loyal to the shah."

"I'm glad you told me," she laughed. "There was a diamond under glass in one of the rooms that really tempted me." She took a glass of champagne from a silent footman. "Sorry you got landed with the column on such short notice, Nick," she said. "I only heard about it today myself."

"Oh, that's okay," he said. "Newt tipped me about all this a week ago, so I've already had a chance to gather some stuff for a couple of columns."

She shook her head in resignation. It had all been decided a week ago but Newt hadn't bothered telling her. That was all she was to the paper, just property to be moved here or there. She wondered how she could feel so loyal to the damned place.

There was a commotion in the foyer and flashbulbs exploded. The attorney general, grinning his boyish grin and ducking his head, was pushing his way through the crowd of photographers. The reaction around Angie was mixed. Some of the older women, the established matrons, clucked in disapproval. But the younger ones, many of whom had come in on the wave of the new administration, thrilled with excitement. Angie watched him nodding and smiling as hands reached out to touch him. She suddenly felt sorry for him and his family, the repository of the hopes and dreams of so many. He looked as if he would be far more comfortable at the tiller of a sailboat. She filed away the impression for another column.

He was quite close, and as she stared at him he looked up, caught her eye, and winked.

"Hi, young Angie," he called. "Does this beat standing out in the rain?"

People turned to stare at her and she felt herself blushing. But she managed to smile at him before moving back into the crowd.

She worked the room for half an hour, chatting with some and eavesdropping on others. She was inching closer to an undersecretary of state who was deep in conversation with a national columnist when she felt her arm clutched.

"Hi," he said again. "Talk to me for a minute, like we're real old friends. You know all about my reputation with blondes, so let's give 'em something they can gossip about."

"I'm not doing gossip anymore, sir," she said. "I'm starting on the serious stuff next week—my own page, or most of the page. A political column."

He shrugged and his blue eyes twinkled.

"You mean I'm going to get a new shadow?" he asked. "Damn. I bet they put some fat-bellied old police reporter on my case. Just when I was starting to enjoy you."

She laughed, feeling the magnetism and charm he radiated. He was a man who would be a winning friend and a dreaded enemy.

"Anyway," he said, handing her another glass of champagne and taking one himself, "if you're going all serious you'd better meet some serious people. I'll introduce you to our host." He dropped his voice slightly. "The guy himself is okay, but I can't stand the regime he represents. Fascists, but they've got oil. Someday oil is going to be in short supply, so we have to be nice to them. I just wish they'd realize they don't have to buy acceptability. This guy spreads gifts around like confetti. It's real tough on my sister-in-law when State tells her she can't keep all the baubles these people send to the White House." He grinned again. "Come meet him."

He steered her through the crowd, which parted for them, and into the tight little group surrounding the tall, bearded figure of Ambassador Lazenger Ardheri. The ambassador smiled broadly and waved the others away.

"Your Excellency," the envoy said, bowing to the attorney general, "I am so grateful you have honored our little party with your presence. I know how busy you are."

"It's a pleasure," he said. "But I'm going to have to run in a minute, so I wanted to say hello and introduce you to a friend of mine." He nudged Angie forward. "Ambassador Ardheri, let me present Miss Angie Waring."

The ambassador bowed, reached for her hand, and pressed it to his lips. His beard tickled and she willed herself to look serious.

"Thank you for coming, madam," he said. "Your youth and beauty enhance the evening, as does the dignity and bearing of your companion." The ambassador reached out and placed his hand on the attorney general's shoulder and Angie saw a flash of anger in the blue eyes. The ambassador didn't notice. He turned away and beckoned an aide to his side, whispered something to the man, then turned back to his guests.

"Please, Your Excellency," the ambassador said, "it is noisy and crowded here. Would you honor me by accompanying me to my private apartments? There are so many things I wish to discuss with you."

The attorney general shook his head abruptly but did manage a smile.

"No, Laz," he said. "I never mix business with pleasure, no matter what the rest of Washington does. We'll talk sometime. But now I've got to go. Miss Waring does too."

All eyes were on them as they swept out of the room and through the massive marble foyer to the top of the steps. Angie caught sight of a face in the crowd, someone staring at her with unconcealed malice: Mary Hickson.

Angie still hadn't said a word to her new friend, and soon they were in the limousine and gliding away from the embassy.

"Hope you didn't mind me whisking you off like that," he said. He chuckled. "Our departure will give 'em something to talk about. Where can I drop you?"

"I don't know," she said, bewildered. "Back at my apartment, I guess, if it's not out of your way. I haven't got a column to do tonight."

He gave the driver her address and they sped through the night, away from the imposing embassies and into the quiet suburbs. Suddenly he reached forward and slid open the glass partition.

"Joe," he said, "stop at the first small bar you come to. I feel like an honest-to-God beer with some ordinary people. And you, Fritz," he said to the Secret Service man who rode beside the driver, "just stay in the car. I'll wear my disguise."

They found a bar and the car stopped half a block away. He rummaged around in the car and found an old floppy hat and put it on. Thick horn-rimmed spectacles completed a convincing disguise and he and Angie strolled down the block to the bar.

It was a typical neighborhood place, half a dozen men and a couple of women sitting at the bar watching television. No one paid them any attention, and they slid into a booth.

"You'll have a beer?" he asked, and walked over to the bar to get them. She watched him chat with the bartender, crack a joke, and laugh loudly.

"Do you do this often?" she asked when he came back to the booth with two overflowing beer mugs.

"Not often enough," he said, serious for a moment. "It's sad, the way we Americans put walls around our leaders. You travel around in a limousine all the time, never get to pay for anything, never talk to anyone outside official circles. How in hell can you know what's going on in the country?" Then he grinned. "How could I get away like this often? I've always got people like you on my tail."

"I'm sorry, sir," she said. "I'm just doing my job. Right now, though, I feel quite ashamed."

"Don't be," he said. "Just do it as well as you can. And," he added, draining his beer, "you can call me Rick, not 'sir.' "

She sipped her beer, shook her head when he offered her another, and watched him stride back to the bar. She must not blow this, she told herself. It was the best connection she could ever make. Yet she almost wished she wasn't a reporter at all, that she could just enjoy him for the sake of his company.

"What you were talking about, the isolation of power," she said when he sat down across from her again. "I'd love to write a column from your perspective, show the people life at the top isn't all that wonderful. Do you think you could sit down for a piece like that?"

"I'd rather not," he said. "People don't want to hear about how tough it is at the top. Hell, any of them would gladly change places with me. And I can see that. Most people lead lives of hopeless frustration, scared of bosses, scared of losing a job they don't even like.

"I think people live vicariously through their leaders and their tycoons and their movie stars. That's why gossip's so popular. Look, I'd rather drive myself around and carry my own bags. But if we all started doing that, demonstrating that life at the top is just as humdrum as anybody's life, we'd be taking away people's dreams."

"I know," Angie said. "My mother writes me about the glamorous life I have up here. I can't bring myself to tell her how much I long for a quiet night curled up in front of the TV with a pizza."

"Yeah," he said, laughing. "Here you are stuck with America's second most glamorous politician, instead of watching reruns of 'Rawhide.' I know how tough this is for you, and I think I better get you home."

They started out of the bar and up the block to the limousine.

"I'll help you wherever I can," he said. "This is a tough town and we outsiders have to stick together. And the honeymoon's over for our administration now and we need all the friends we can get, especially friends in the press. I'll use you and you use me, okay?"

"Okay," Angie agreed. She remembered what Ken

Beckworth had said about using, and now this charming, powerful man was talking the same way.

"I'll let you in on one secret," he said as they neared the car, "strictly in confidence and not for publication. I don't play around. I love my family. But the reputation you people have given me, I encourage it. It draws attention away from some of the things we have to do. If our enemies think we're just a bunch of *nouveaux riches* Boston playboys and we don't have to be taken seriously, that helps us a lot." He helped her into the limousine. "So if you get tagged as Rick's latest lady friend, don't figure on me consummating it. It's all another disguise." He laughed again. "I like this situation! The gossip writer being gossiped *about*."

He dropped her outside her apartment, waved once from the window, and was driven off into the night.

From that point on, she had a dream run. It wasn't just the guidance Rick gave her, though that meant a lot. He passed on good tips, gave her exclusive press access to several family parties, even arranged a wonderful interview with the First Lady.

Angie had her own contacts, too, and she broke some big stories. She had developed a unique style—"bitchy" was the way some described it—and her column became essential reading for Washingtonians who wanted to know what was really going on. After six months, the column was even picked up for syndication. Americans far from the capitol liked to read an insider's view of Washington.

"You've killed 'em again, kid," Ken Beckworth said as he walked into his bedroom, the *Tribune* opened to her page. "Another Waring exclusive. You can thank me for this one.'' He dropped the paper on the bed and pulled open the draperies. The spring light flooded in and Angie groaned and tried to bury her head under his pillow. Too much wine last night at that awful party. When would she learn to take things easy? And she hated waking up in Ken's bed. She should have gotten dressed and gone home last night.

He pulled the pillow from her and she groaned again and opened her eyes.

''Put something on, will you?'' she said. ''I can't face all that rampant masculinity at this hour. I know you're proud of your body, Ken, but there's a time for everything and this isn't it.''

''That's not what you thought last night,'' he said, grinning. ''You were wild for me last night. You're coming along nicely, Angie. Not the frigid little Florida girl anymore.''

She scowled.

''Okay,'' he laughed. ''I'll fix coffee and you sleep. It's Saturday.''

She lay back on the pillows. Once he was gone she lifted the sheet and examined her nakedness. Her breasts were tender and it hurt to move her thighs. How had their affair come this far? They had just drifted into it, she supposed, the way so many liaisons were formed in this town. Two people, both ambitious, both putting success ahead of everything else, but still needing the comfort of a warm body. It wasn't love or anything close to it, but it was lots better than nothing.

''Yes, indeedy,'' Ken said, coming in with coffee and juice on a tray. He was still naked. ''Today's column will have them all talking. The way you described—''

"I know what I wrote, Ken," she snapped. "Give me the *Post.* I'm more interested in seeing what the opposition says."

"Here you are." He gave her the paper, still grinning. He never minded how grouchy she was in the morning. It was, she thought, as if Ken Beckworth could never conceive of anyone's being angry with him. Therefore her demeanor had nothing to do with him. Therefore he could ignore it.

He sat on the edge of the bed and slipped his hand under the covers and between her legs. She jerked away angrily, almost upsetting the tray.

"Don't do that!" she said. "I hurt like hell."

"It didn't hurt last night," he leered. "You couldn't get enough of me. And the noise! I had to put a pillow over your face. It wouldn't do for the neighbors to hear shrieks of ecstasy coming from the apartment of a vice-presidential contender."

"Go read your paper," she said, laughing despite herself. "And put a robe on. It also wouldn't do for a vice-presidential contender to be arrested for flashing."

She pulled the covers up over her breasts and flipped through the *Post* until she got to Mary Hickson's column. She began reading and, by the third paragraph, her mood had plummeted.

Under the headline "High-placed Sources," Mary Hickson had done the ultimate hatchet job on both Angie and the attorney general. Oh, she hadn't named either of them, but anyone who knew anything about Washington would know instantly who was meant. It was damaging stuff, accusing a "high administration official" of leaking state secrets and malicious gossip to "his favorite reporter." Hickson listed the times and places of many of their meetings and the stories that had flowed from those meetings into Angie's column. Worst of all, the story carried a heavy innuendo that theirs was a sexual relationship.

"Oh, God," Angie said. "This is terrible."

Ken put down his newspaper.

"What's the Dragon Lady done now?" he asked.

"She's crucified me. Which I can stand," Angie said bitterly. "But she's also carving up the attorney general, making it look like he trades secrets for sex. It's so tawdry and awful. What'll his kids think?"

"So Hickson finally got on to you and Ricky," Ken said, smirking. "You should have listened to me, Angie. I warned you people were keeping a real close eye on that guy. Hell, even I know all about your little meetings."

"But," she protested, "we're friends, that's all. He's helped me. There's nothing wrong with that."

"Doesn't matter, not in this town," Ken said. "Appearances are all that count. And if you go having clandestine meetings with a guy like that, you can't blame people for getting ideas." He looked at the Hickson column and shook his head. "She may be an old bag, but she sure isn't senile. She's got dates and places. She had real good sources."

She looked at him with loathing.

"Sometimes I wonder what you and I are doing together, Ken," she said. "This woman makes me out to be some kind of journalist-hooker, and all you do is admire her sources. Whose side are you on?"

"You and I are together because right now, we suit each other," he said. "Oh, there's a bit more to it than that, but our relationship is based on mutual needs. As for taking sides—I never do unless I absolutely have to. I can't risk being identified with the wrong side. You shouldn't risk it, either. Which is why I've warned you to stay away from that guy. He is going to take a big fall."

She retreated into the shower for as long as she could. She had no illusions about Ken's ambition or his selfishness. Was it possible, she asked herself viciously, that she was not comfortable with nice, normal people?

"You got tough fast," she said to herself savagely.

Ken was playing golf at Burning Tree and Angie left him as soon as she could, returning to her own apartment. The anger for herself cooled. She didn't really care what Hickson said about her. But she was very upset for Rick. She called him at his home late in the day.

"I'm sorry about all this," she said when he came on the phone. She could hear the shrieks of children playing in the background. "She's made it look so cheap."

"Yeah," he said guardedly. "I've been pictured in better lights. What I can't figure is where she got all the details from. It's as if she'd had someone tailing me."

"Look," Angie said, "are you sure you're not being followed or bugged or whatever?" How she wished she'd warned him before!

"Honey, I'm the attorney general. *I* tell *them* who to harass."

"It's just something I was told, by a contact," Angie said carefully. "He let it slip that the FBI was on your case, or something along those lines. But that doesn't make any sense, does it?"

"Shit!" he said. "Of course! That bastard, the director! He doesn't like us one bit. And he regards the bureau as his fiefdom. I just didn't give him credit for the balls to pull a stunt like this. I must be getting soft.

Okay, then, I'll fix his wagon. Thanks, Angie. I think we'll salvage something from this mess after all.''

But, as she hung up, she knew things would never be the same for them. It made her sad. He had been much more than a good source, more than one of the reasons for her staggering success. He had been her friend.

The doorbell jerked her out of her gloomy reverie. Trish Wright always cheered her up. They'd become close friends during the past year, drawn together by their ages, backgrounds, and ambivalent feelings about Washington.

Trish breezed into the apartment clutching a bag and radiating her usual warmth. She kissed Angie and set down the two bottles of white wine, then got glasses for them.

''I read all about you today,'' Trish said. ''And on the very slim chance that a scarlet woman would be home alone, I decided to come over.''

Angie watched her friend uncork the wine and fill their glasses. She admired Trish's brisk efficiency, her confidence, her unflagging vitality. She was a tall, striking, dark-haired young woman, a soft Texas drawl concealing the sharp mind and swift wit Angie had come to rely on. Trish was a real Washington veteran. She'd left her beloved San Antonio to work as one of the few female Senate pages, then gotten the ''Washington disease,'' as she called it, and stayed on as researcher of a powerful Senate subcommittee. She was now that subcommittee's administrative director.

''Is Rick still taking your calls?'' Trish asked. ''I guess not. You're an embarrassment to him now.''

''I just got off the phone with him,'' Angie said.

"He was okay. Not really happy, of course, but okay. I just feel damned sorry for him and his family."

"Oh, he'll survive," Trish said. "With his reputation enhanced, if anything. It's you I'm concerned about. How're you handling getting both barrels from Hickson?"

"It bothered me," Angie admitted. "And it made me see what we journalists do to people. I've been dishing it out for a long time now and I never understood what it was like to be on the receiving end. On the other hand, I kind of don't care."

"You're pretty tough, aren't you, Angie?" Trish said.

Angie winced. *Tough.*

"I'm as tough as I have to be," she said sharply. "You know the way it is. And you're a damn sight tougher than I am, the way you run your committee while letting the senators believe they're the ones in charge."

"Ah, but my toughness is a front," Trish laughed. "It hides a soft center. You are becoming the genuine article." She became serious all of a sudden. "And I worry about you because of it." She waited for a response, and when there was none, she went on, "Angie, even with me you put up a wall. Don't you trust anyone?"

Angie flushed. She was embarrassed and a little scared. She wanted to explain, to tell someone the truth, just once. But it was safer to keep on hiding.

"Leave it, will you?" she said tersely. "I'm just trying to get by as best I can. Give me some more wine and cheer me up. This has not been the greatest day in my life."

"Okay," Trish said. "I'll lay off. Except for one thing. This apartment. It's awful! No wonder you feel blue. Look at you, rich, young and infamous, and you live in a crummy walk-up on the wrong side of town. Why don't we pool our resources and move into something grand? You can afford it, even if I can't.''

"It's not much, is it?" Angie said, glancing around the gloomy old apartment. Ever since Greer had moved to Chicago she'd been meaning to do something about the place. But there was no one to spur her on, and no time. "But I can't face the hassle of moving and I've gotten used to living alone." She looked at her friend. "Wait until things settle down," she said. "Maybe it's a good idea. We get along well, when you're not lecturing me."

"From you, that's an incredible endorsement," Trish said. "I am truly flattered." She laughed. "What've you got planned for tonight? Want to order Chinese and pig out in front of the TV?"

They did, drinking the rest of the wine and some of the contents of Angie's meager bar. It was the first evening in months Angie was able to forget both the pressures of her life and the loneliness.

In the newsroom of the *Tribune* on Monday, Mary Hickson's attack on Angie passed unnoticed. The staff had something far more important to worry about. Suddenly, after years of struggle and loss, the paper's New York owner had had enough. The paper would close in a few months. It was a terrible blow to all of them—the old hands who had been through other newspaper deaths, and the younger ones, who thought newspapers went on forever.

Television was booming, taking away readers and advertising revenues. Washington was merely repeating a nationwide pattern of one newspaper becoming dominant and the others going under.

* * *

"I don't know what you're worrying about," Ken said to her as they lay on the sand at Rehoboth Beach, Delaware. It was early fall, and there was only one month of life left for the *Tribune*. "You can have just about any job you want in Washington. I hear Channel 2 offered you your own show."

"Television!" she snapped. "Television! Pretty faces, capped teeth, talking heads. I'm a newspaper journalist and it's all I want to be. But there's no newspaper for me to go to in Washington. There is only one other paper, you know."

"The *Post* would grab you," he insisted. "Sure, you wouldn't be such a big fish in a small pond, but it would be a living. And I love the thought of Mary Hickson having you looking over her shoulder."

"You don't understand, Ken," she said. "To you, it's just a newspaper closing. To me it's the end of a huge part of my life."

The sun had gone and she was shivering. She wished she were somewhere, anywhere. This stolen weekend in a borrowed beach house was a dreadful mistake.

"I'm sorry," he said. "I was just trying to cheer you up. But I think you'd be great on TV. More money, more power—isn't that what you want?"

"I tried TV once, Ken," she said, "and I don't want to do it ever again. Come one, let's go inside. Freezing to death is just making me more depressed."

He gathered their things and followed her across the dunes to the neat cottage. The wind was coming up hard now, cold from the vast stretches of the Chesapeake Bay, pushing dark storm clouds ahead of it. She lit the oil lamps while he built a driftwood fire. Soon the little living room was aglow with light and warmth and she felt a little better.

"Big drinks," Ken announced. "Big, big drinks to keep the storm outside." He handed her a massive rum and tonic and she nodded thanks and took a long swallow. She didn't really like rum, but it warmed her and she drank more. She didn't want to talk, just sit, pleasantly dazed, in front of the fire.

"Have another," he said, filling her glass to the top. "And just relax. I'll fix dinner. You're tired, so it's my turn to be the slave."

He messed around in the kitchen, always keeping her glass topped and the fire blazing. She drank a great deal. Once she glanced up and saw Ken staring at her, his blue eyes gleaming. Was it just firelight reflected in them?

By the time he placed food before her Angie was light-headed and heedless. It was as if she had retreated into a world of childhood where someone else did the worrying. Her only duty was to feel safe and snug and warm. Even the food he'd prepared, soup and hot dogs, echoed the nursery.

"Smoke a little of this," she heard him saying. "It will make you feel good."

She was relaxed enough but she did as she was told. After these years of being strong and brave and independent, she suddenly wasn't responsible for herself. Inhaling made her cough but she smoked enough to feel the marijuana working through her system. She had never used the drug before, but she had read enough to know what its effects were supposed to be, so she was not alarmed when it began taking hold of her.

Later, in front of the fire, they smoked some more. She was lucid, she thought, yet floating outside her body. Ken talked to her all the time, but she heard only a little of what he said. It was reassuring to have his deep, masculine voice crooning in her ear.

"You've been a naughty girl," she heard him say. "I think Daddy should spank you." She giggled. The childhood illusion was complete. She giggled again when he pulled her jeans down and forced her over his lap.

"Are you sorry for what you've done?" she heard his husky voice demand.

She shook her head and heard, rather than felt, his palm strike her bottom. He hit her a few more times, soft slaps that made her tingle a little. She kicked her legs, willing to play the game so as to bolster the illusion.

"I don't think you're learning your lesson," he whispered hoarsely. "We'll just get these panties off now and give you a real spanking."

She felt him pull the flimsy garment down around her thighs. The palm hitting her bare bottom stung and she was aware of her exposed nakedness. She struggled but he held her firmly and increased the rhythm of his spanking. It was still a game but she wanted it to end. She struggled harder and felt the hugeness of him pressed against her naked stomach. Desire mounted in her.

"Stop it," she gasped. "That's enough. Take me to bed."

"Yes," he said. "The bed. I'll make you apologize for being such a bad little girl."

He carried her into the bedroom, Angie giggling, yet filled with desire. He sat her on the edge of the bed and stripped off the rest of her clothing, handling her like a child, raising first one foot and then the other as he eased off her bunched jeans and panties.

He gently pushed her face down on the big four-poster. Her head was pleasantly swimming and she hardly noticed as he took her wrists and slipped soft cords around them and tied them to one of the posts. Then she turned her head on the pillow to look at him in the soft light. He was standing beside the bed, naked and huge, flexing a wide black leather strap.

"No," she whispered. "No, please don't."

He raised his arm, the broad belt with it, and she buried her face in the pillow. She heard the first blow, a resounding slap, and felt it a moment later. Before the pain could register he had struck again, then again. She started pulling at her bonds, and her movements excited him more. Again and again the strap lashed her bottom. She lifted her head and screamed for him to stop.

He saw the tears streaming down her face, dropped the strap, and knelt beside her.

"I'm sorry," he whispered. "I'm so sorry. I didn't mean to go so far. I didn't mean to hurt you." He fumbled with the cords, freeing her. "It's just a game. I thought you were enjoying it. It's just a soft old strap. It doesn't leave any marks." He climbed into bed beside her. "So many people like playing games like that," he murmured, his hand stroking her buttocks gently. "Even Mary Hickson. She likes to be bound with chains and caned."

Angie's senses were drifting again, and she could only just feel Ken entering her. Fancy Mary Hickson liking to be tied up and whipped with a cane. How strange people could be.

The next morning Ken was embarrassed and shy. He tried to apologize but she cut him off.

"It was partly my fault," she said. "I had too much to drink, and all that pot. I guess I gave you the impression I was into kinky scenes. Well, I'm not. What

I can remember of it was painful and humiliating. Don't ever try it again, okay?''

He nodded, but did she see that gleam in his eyes, just for a moment?

''I am sorry, Angie,'' he said. ''I guess I've been around twisted people so long I think everyone's twisted. I really do respect you. In fact, I think I love you. I don't want to upset you. Can you forgive me?''

''I'll try,'' she said, and forced a smile. He looked so contrite. He was a very flawed man; but so, she thought, was she flawed. She nodded to herself. Flawed.

The *Tribune* won a surprise stay of execution. A mystery suitor appeared and the *Tribune*'s owner gave it another month of life, then another. Negotiations went on. Slowly, hope rekindled in the staff and everyone, Angie especially, worked harder than ever.

''I can tell you who your new owner is,'' Ken said as he joined her at their lunch table in the National Press Club. ''My people in New York just called. The announcement's being made tonight.''

''Thank God! Something's going to happen at last,'' Angie said. ''We've been waiting so long. Who is it?''

He glanced around and dropped his voice to a whisper.

''Mansion,'' he said. ''Lyle Mansion.''

Her heart stopped but he noticed nothing and went right on talking.

''The Mansion take-over is all right for the staff, I guess,'' he said, ''but it means trouble for me. Lyle is a limousine liberal, nothing like his big brother. Lyle's paper hates our party and cuddles up to the current administration. If it were Richard Mansion buying the *Tribune,* I'd be thrilled. Still, they say Richard pretty much rules the family now, so maybe I don't have too much to worry about. I'll still have you on the paper to protect my interests."

"No, you won't," Angie said, quite fatalistic about it. "I'm not working for the Mansions. I did that once."

"Don't be stupid," Ken said sharply. "It doesn't matter who owns the paper. So the guy's a wimp—so what? As long as he signs your checks."

"You don't understand, Ken," she said. "All you think about is power and money. I try and put integrity in my life *some*where. I know enough about the Mansions to tell me there's no integrity anywhere."

"Don't preach," he snapped back. "You'd be worrying about money if you were smarter. You'd know how much it matters. I've never had any and I'm not likely to on a congressional salary. I exist only through the good graces of my backers—who may withdraw at any time. I'm way overdrawn at the bank. I can hardly meet my rent. I drive an old wreck. And I have to suffer insults from people like you who think I'm a fat cat. I tell you, Angie, if you were in my position, you'd be thinking only about having money, not whose money it is."

There was no point in trying to make him understand. And she wasn't about to tell him or anyone else what Richard had done to her. They finished lunch in strained silence and Angie made a show of signing the check.

Back in the newsroom there was jubilation over the advent of Lyle Mansion.

"He's a real good guy," Jack Newton told Angie.

"I know a lot of his people and they all say he's the ideal publisher. Liberal, noninterfering. Nothing like the rest of the Mansion family."

"I'm not going to work for him, Newt," she said. "I was mixed up with the Mansions down in Florida, and once is enough."

"Give him a chance, Angie," Newt said. "He's promised there'll be no editorial changes, the same executive staff, all of us will be asked to stay. And I know he thinks highly of your work. It was one of the factors in the take-over that we had developed a star who could sell papers for us. You'll be letting us all down if you go."

"Newt," she said wearily, "I don't want to let you down, but I'll be quitting before Mr. Mansion rides in on his white charger."

She turned and walked away before he could produce further argument.

Lyle Mansion called her at home a few nights later.

"Miss Waring," he said, "I'm sorry to disturb you at home. But Mr. Newton has told me about your . . . reluctance to work for me. I don't want to lose anyone from the *Tribune*, particularly you. If it's a matter of money—or anything else—I'm sure we can work it out."

She should have been flattered, the newspaper baron pleading with her to stay on. But all she could hear in that soft voice were the echoes of Richard Mansion. In their privileged family, they could all get anything they desired. Or so they believed.

"No, Mr. Mansion," she said. "It's nothing we can work out. It's time I made a change."

"Look," he pleaded, "just don't do anything for a few days. Please? As soon as the paperwork has been completed I'll be moving down to Washington to help get the *Tribune* on its feet. Just give me a little time."

"All right," Angie said. He was giving her no room for a refusal. "I can wait a few days." She would tell him no to his face.

Except, the next day came the dreadful news from Dallas. Angie fell apart, grief transcending everything else. She could not be like her colleagues who, no matter how shocked, went about their business, reporting the terrible events. She just wanted to be away from Washington and away from the person Washington had turned her into.

She fled the cold, mourning city and went the only place she could go.

Chapter
Seven

"I saw Jeff Tyrell at the store today," her mother said. "He asked after you. Said he'd heard you'd been here for months and months. I think he wanted me to ask him over. I told you before how well he's doing."

"Poor Jeff," Angie said. "All that seems so long ago. I don't know what I'd say to him if I saw him now. I wonder if he's changed as much as I have."

"Not so's you'd notice," her mother said. "You've certainly changed, though, Angie." She refreshed their drinks and sat down again in the deck chair inside the screened porch. It was a warm, still March afternoon. "You've grown very insular. I'm not sure it's a good thing. You don't see anyone, do you? It worries me."

"I'm sorry, Mom," she said. "I just haven't been able to face anything for a while. So much happened up there. I thought I was so tough, independent. Then things happened and I just crumpled."

"Well, so you did," her mother said, "but you can't go on like this forever. You're always welcome here, but I can't sit back and watch you mope your life away. It's been three months now, even a little more."

"I know, Mom," she said wearily.

She knew her mother was close to discerning the truth, that her daughter hated the career she'd chosen and knew of no way to stop her own forward momentum. She knew, too, that May couldn't bear it, that she had to believe Angie's career would bring her great happiness . . . somehow. Someday. Anything else was too awful for May to contemplate, so she hid her understanding from Angie and Angie protected her mother by helping her to pretend.

"Mother, there isn't anything else I want to do, really. I know I'll start over. I want to. It's just . . . I need some time, a few more weeks." She forced a smile. "I'll make you proud of me again."

"I am proud of you, Angie," her mother said fiercely. "Whether you're here recuperating or up in Washington being a famous columnist. And your father is, too. But he does worry for you. He was saying last night how sad it was you aren't seeing anyone. If only you had a little comfort in your life. It might make all the difference."

"Actually, I am seeing someone." Angie smiled. "Ted Buchanan's driving up from Miami this weekend. He called a few days ago and I suddenly realized how much I'd like to see him again. I thought we'd drive up the coast a ways."

"Great," her mother said. "He was so kind to you when you did the internship, and you seemed so fond of him." She sipped her drink and stole a glance at Angie. "And the congressman? Is he still in the picture?"

"Not for a while," Angie said, shrugging. "He

never calls. I guess he started to lose interest when I quit the paper. I don't blame him. Ken's got to hustle all the time if he's going to make it to the top." She had learned, in a letter from Trish Wright, that Ken had taken up again with Mary Hickson, but she wasn't about to tell her mother that. Down here, far away from the incestuous world of politics, Ken seemed a remote figure, and yet somehow menacing. If she went back to Washington would she be drawn to him again? She hoped not.

Her mother was talking. "Whenever I see his picture, he always looks like, well, a man looking out for number one."

"Everyone is, up there," Angie said. "That's what makes it so hard for me. I liked the power, the sense of being near the center. But it made me hard, I know it did. There just isn't time to really care about anyone else."

"Do you want to go back to it all, Angie? Maybe it's too ugly. Maybe you should stay away."

"I don't know," Angie said. "The trouble is, once you've had all that, nothing else seems enough. I don't think I could stand a job on a nice little paper in a nice little town."

"I know the feeling," her mother said drily, then patted Angie's hand. "This may not be typical motherly advice, but I think you should head back to Washington, or go to New York. Never leave with a bad feeling, Angie. It feels like failure."

Ted Buchanan said the same thing as they set out up the coast road that bright Saturday morning.

"I can't fathom you, Angie," he said. "One minute you're the hottest thing in Washington, the next you're hiding out with the old folks at home. I never figured you for a quitter."

"It got to be too much, Ted," she said. "But now I'm just about ready to go back. If anyone wants me."

"Jack Newton wants you," Ted said. "I've talked to him a few times. He was really pissed at you, but they need you. Lyle Mansion's pouring money into the paper and not getting any result. They need their star columnist."

She shook her head.

"Nothing doing. Me and Mansions don't get along. No, I'll have to find something else. And the *Post* won't do—they've already got their bitch-in-residence."

"What about television?" Ted said. "Channel 4 just lost their anchor to ABC. They're searching all over for a replacement. I know the people there. I could make a call."

"I don't know," she said. "There's a lot I hate about television. So trivial, after newspapers."

"Gee, thanks," he said. "A ringing endorsement of my chosen career." There was real bitterness in his voice. He pulled off the road and drove down a dirt track. "There's a clam shack I know here," he said. "Fresh seafood and cold beer."

The proprietor was a little old Indian man, dark and gnarled as a walnut. He greeted Ted like his oldest friend and managed to pat Angie on the fanny as he led them to a bare wooden table under the thatched roof.

"Hey, Ted," he wheezed. "No wonder you stay away so long. This gal, you give me someone like that, I ain't getting out of bed either." Angie laughed. She did feel a glow in her body today, a kind of abandon.

"Don't mind him," Ted said when the old man went to get their beers. "It's his only pleasure in life, looking down the fronts of his lady customers."

They had several beers, crisp and cold, and lunched on conch and cold poached pompano. She felt languid, sexy, and happy to be with Ted.

"It doesn't have to be trivial, you know."

Ted's remark snapped her out of her pleasant trance.

"Television. It doesn't have to be trivial. There are better and better people getting into the medium now. It's not enough anymore to be just a pretty face. You'd be great in TV. You were before."

"Okay, Ted," she said. "I appreciate what you're trying to do for me and I'll think it over. Seriously. But not today. Let's just have fun." She looked deep into his eyes and got the answer she wanted.

It got hotter and hotter as they drove on and the Mustang's air conditioning faltered. As they drove by an endless stretch of white beach, she asked him to stop.

The car bumped over palm roots and sandy ruts until they were at the edge of the beach, out of sight of the highway. The beach was deserted.

"You coming in?" she asked, springing out of the car and into the relentless heat.

"I didn't bring a bathing suit," he said. "I'll just lie in the shade and watch you."

"I don't have a suit, either," she said.

She unbuttoned her blue sundress without a second thought and let it fall around her feet. She felt him watching her and was glad for the glorious tan she had gotten in the last few months. The little white bra and bikini panties gleamed against her bronze skin.

Angie dashed across the beach and into the ocean. The surf crashed over her, gloriously cold, challenging. She plunged under the waves, striking out strongly until she was beyond the line of the breakers. She floated on her back gazing up into the stark blue sky. After a little while she heard him splashing through the water toward her.

"To hell with modesty," he said. "The water feels great. But I sure hope some fat-bellied sheriff doesn't come along and catch us. Make a great story for the opposing network."

She could see down through the crystal water. He was naked. And as he moved against her he was hard. She reached down and clutched him, laughing, enjoying the desire in his eyes. Ted clutched her shoulders and pulled her against him, forcing himself between her thighs. They went under a swell and came up spluttering and laughing. She broke away from him and swam for shore, catching a wave and bodysurfing to the beach. She ran from the water and stood on the sand, waiting for him, laughing.

Walking out of the surf, water shining on him, he looked glorious, slim and tall and manly. He made straight for her.

"You're lovely," he said.

She glanced down at herself, shy for a moment. Her nakedness showed right through her flimsy wet underwear.

"You're lovely, too," she said, taking his hand and leading him across the sand to the shade of a palm tree. He found a soft blanket in the trunk of his car and spread it out on the ground. They lay there, the warm air caressing and lulling them. Angie closed her eyes, drifting with the palm leaves.

She felt Ted move closer to her, his hand gently

brush across her breasts then trail down her body. She shivered. Murmuring, she parted her legs, and cried out softly as he entered her. There was a roaring in her ears, a great, pounding beat in her body.

"Oh, Christ!" he swore, and hastily withdrew from her. She opened her eyes. There was a roaring nearby, and Ted looked upset. The noise got louder. A pair of motorcycle riders, frightening in their heavy leather vests emblazoned with swastikas, were pulling into the clearing next to Ted's car. They gazed down at them.

Ted roughly pulled the blanket around Angie and urged her to her feet.

"Get yourself into the car and be ready to drive out of here," Ted whispered. "Go."

Angie walked to the car as fast as she could, clutching the blanket around her, trying not to seem too scared. The bikers watched her all the way, sitting astride their huge machines. The menace in them was real and ready to erupt. Her past suffering and terror flooded over her, sickening images of another time when she'd been naked and vulnerable. She fumbled with the door on the driver's side as the bikers cut their motors and carefully put the bikes on their stands.

Angie watched in the rearview mirror as the two figures walked slowly toward the car. Ted opened the passenger door and threw their clothes in the back of the car.

"Where are you going, pal?" one of the bikers demanded. "No need to run. We're friendly."

"Yeah," said his companion. "We liked what you were doing, and we want to see you do it some more."

They were standing at the side of the car, only a few feet from Ted, who was naked.

"Fellas," Ted said calmly, "we're on our way."

"No you're not." She heard the click before she saw the flash of sunlight on the knife blade. "We're going to teach you both a lesson. Bare-ass naked, fucking on a public beach. What if some little kid had come along and seen you? Disgusting!"

They laughed. They were in complete command and they were going to have some fun. And then . . . she knew what they would do to her. She feared even more for what would happen to Ted. There was nothing to hope for, so she took a chance.

"Ted!" she yelled. "Get in!"

The key was in the ignition and the engine roared into life instantly. She rammed the car into reverse and the car leapt backward as Ted jumped in. It all happened so fast that the two bikers had to leap away from the moving car. She turned the wheel and there was the scream of chrome against steel as the car smashed into their bikes. The bikes crashed against each other and fell into a tangled heap. She sent the Mustang on, over the bikes, and it shuddered for a moment. Then it wrenched itself free and she gunned it again and steered a crazy backward course through the trees and back to the road.

She glanced back. She had gambled right. Instead of pursuing them, the bikers had rushed to their machines and were desperately looking them over. They had forgotten all about their "fun." Their prized possessions had to be attended to before anything else.

"Jesus Christ!" Ted moaned as they sped down the road. "You fixed those bastards!"

But after a few miles the elation faded. Certain they were not being followed, she steered the car off the road into a stand of trees. They got out cautiously, made sure they were alone, and hurriedly dressed.

"Where to now?" Ted asked as he took the wheel. "I don't think they'll be mobile for a long time. You did a real job on their bikes. But maybe they got our number and they've got friends or something."

"I refuse to be afraid," Angie said. But she was shaking, the full impact hitting her. "But we should put as much distance between us and them as we can. Where were you planning to spend the night, anyway?"

"I booked us into a very nice inn at Vero Beach," Ted said. "About an hour up the road, I guess. That's far enough away."

There were no signs of pursuit, but when they reached the inn Ted parked the car as far from the highway as possible and behind the building. They grabbed their things and hurried into the lobby. She was beginning to relax and she smiled as Ted registered them: Mr. and Mrs. Buchanan.

"You're taking me for granted," she teased, when they were finally in their oceanfront room on the third floor. She opened the sliding door and stepped out onto the deck. "This is beautiful." The sun was going down and the worst heat was over for the day. The sand looked pink, and gentle waves lapped it. Evening breezes stirred the palms around her. She felt his hand on her back.

"You saved us, Angie," he said. "I don't think there's anything you can't do."

She turned into his arms and they kissed, long and deeply, until she broke away, her hands on his shoulders.

"I was scared, Ted, really scared," she said. "But I

think it was the fear itself that made me react. I'm not as strong as you think. Inside I'm Jell-O."

"You're great," he insisted, and she let it rest. But she wished someone understood.

They didn't move from the suite. Ted ordered a pitcher of piña coladas and they drank on the terrace as the tropical night enveloped them. Later there were steaks and red wine accompanied by chirping tree frogs and a full moon springing out of the Atlantic.

And later there was the huge bed, where she gave herself to him fully. His heat and masculinity throbbed through her, and Angie put the menace behind her. She felt wonderfully free as his lean body entwined with hers. She arched her hips and brought him even deeper inside her, until she crested and he flowed with her crest.

Later, as he lay sleeping beside her, Angie reached out in the moonglow and stroked his face. Dear Ted. It would be so easy to stay with him. But he was pushing her to go on, telling her not to give up. And he was right: if she gave up on herself, what would they have together anyway?

BOOK
TWO

Chapter
Eight

"Hold camera 3! Don't move away. This is where she nails him to the wall."

The director's command, whispered into his mike, was relayed to the floor crew. The loving close-up of Angie on camera 1 would be seen only on the control room monitor. Channel 4's vast audience was seeing the sweating senator waiting to be skewered.

"You say, then, Senator, all these campaign funds have been accounted for? None of them was diverted for your personal use, or for your family?"

"No, I've told you that three times already." He was going to tough it out if it killed him. There was so much to lose. A three-term senator, desperately wanting a fourth term. "I told the subcommittee the same thing and they accepted it. Why don't you?" He tried a joke. "I'm one of the few people on the Hill with a certified clean bill of health." Damn the bitch, she didn't even smile. "In fact," he said in his most masterful voice, "I don't know what I'm doing here, being subjected to this. I suggest we move on to more substantive things.''

"Take camera 1," the director snapped.

"More substantive," Angie echoed. She paused for a beat, gazing deeply into the camera lens. She was sharing an intimate moment with her audience, the moment they had come to expect, the moment just before some pompous figure was pricked. "How substantive, Senator, is the figure of four hundred and twenty-five thousand dollars?''

They cut to camera 3 to catch the victim's involuntary start, then back to Angie. She didn't wait for a reply.

"Because," she said, "that's the figure we found in an account in the Bank of Hamilton, in Bermuda—an account in your daughter's name.''

A photograph of the senator, beaming and holding a little girl, came on the screen.

"She's ten years old," Angie said in that deadly calm voice her audience knew so well. "What we can't understand is why three land developers in your home state would want to give four hundred and twenty-five thousand dollars to a ten-year-old girl.''

The senator was sweating freely and he ran a finger around his collar. He opened his mouth but no sound came out. He looked like he wanted to slip under the desk, but the camera, the red light above it accusing him, pinned him where he was.

"The money was paid first into the Popular Bank of Mexico City," Angie said as calmly as if reading a shopping list. "It was transferred to Costa Rica, withdrawn in cash, transferred to Dutch Antigua and, from there, deposited to your little girl's account in Bermuda. Can you explain?''

"Yes," he croaked, playing for time. "My opponents . . . a smear . . . someone will be sued . . ." Then he put his head in his hands and waited, just sat and waited for the ordeal to be over.

The floor manager gave Angie the windup sign and she said, "All the relevant documents have been turned over to the authorities." There was no hint of triumph in her voice, no gleam of victory in her eyes. "Thank you for being with us, Senator. And"—to the camera—"thank you all, on behalf of the 'Nationwide' team, for joining us tonight. We hope you'll be back next week."

The credits rolled while camera 2 pulled back to show all of the studio, the senator still slumped at his desk and Angie calmly gathering up the papers from hers. It was as if a wall stood between them.

They killed the bright lights and the floor crew began clearing away the props. The studio looked drab and empty as Angie waited impatiently for a technician to remove her lapel mike: she wanted out of the senator's presence. He might start crying, or attack her. It had happened before. She pitied the man. She pitied most of their victims. "The Dragon Lady," as she was called, wasn't really any tougher than ever.

She nodded thanks to the technicians and moved swiftly out of the studio and into the elevator.

Steve Franklin was lounging on a couch in the executive suite, drink in hand. He grinned at her.

"Powerful, Angie," he said. "The ego of these guys. We've been knocking them over for years and still they come on the show thinking they can bluff it out. Tonight's effort will get you another award, for sure."

Angie mixed herself a gin and tonic from the big chrome bar.

"It's getting harder," she said. "The crooks are getting smarter and the voters are even sometimes electing honest people. Maybe someday there won't be any need for a show like 'Nationwide.' " She flopped down in a chair. "For which I would say thank God and amen."

"Come off it," Steve laughed. "This show made you video's Brenda Starr. The first show ever out of Washington to get into the top ten. All your doing."

"Not me," she said quickly. "The team. George and Ian and Walter. The fearless 'Nationwide' team."

She had a staff of twenty. Well, they weren't hers, exactly, but belonged to the show. Whenever one of them got a tip—and they paid hefty bribes for any information leading to any break—the others were recruited. Angie's background and reputation had garnered them a lot of tips that had panned out, so whenever she was on to something, they all flew with it.

But she never had the feeling they were working for her. On the other hand, she never felt she was working for the show. It would have been fine if the whole team had been focused on one thing, or if she had been the spearhead of all their activities. But there was neither a feeling of teamwork nor the thrill of personal achievement. The staff of researchers were, like her, employees of a faceless and anonymous employer. How could they feel like crusaders when they all worked for something that had no identity, no personality? Everyone told her she was a crime-stopper: she felt like a piece of fiction.

She tried to talk to Trish about it, but Trish was as awed by television as anyone else, though she wouldn't admit it. Angie had even tried to talk to Steve Franklin about it, but stopped midsentence, knowing he would never begin to understand. Oh, Ted, she thought, you'd know what I mean, wouldn't you?

Steve sat down beside her. "The reason you sound like this is, you're tired. And bored. What you need, Angie, is a good lover. I'm available. Get rid of your boyfriend and give me a chance."

"Ken's okay," she said briskly. Why did he always think it was all right to get personal with her?

"You could do better," he insisted. She was getting ready to tell him off. "Hell, your guy's been passed over so many times. We all thought he was going on the big ticket, then they dumped him."

"He'll bounce back," she said. "He's still young and he's got seniority, some good committees." She finished her drink. "Politics is so depressing. But for us, that's all there is."

"I know," he said, the veneer falling away suddenly. "This decade started off so great. And then the killings and the end of our beliefs. Now we don't expect anything. So nothing is what we get." He fumbled for a cigarette. "You knew him pretty well, didn't you? I guess it hit you harder than the rest of us."

She refused to discuss Rick with anyone.

"You'd cry forever if you dwelled on it," she said. "Instead of crying I do our show, stirring up the pond, dragging people down. That's what I'm getting to loathe about the show, Steve. We always show everyone in a bad light."

"We cut down the tall poppies, Angie."

"That's the problem," Angie said. "Shouldn't journalism sometimes be about positive aspects of the world? Shouldn't we salute achievers instead of always tearing things down?"

"We do," he said. "The baby doctor on tonight's show. Astronauts. The heart transplants. Hey, 'Nationwide' is upbeat, a lot of the time." He shrugged. "But of course they'd rather see someone like the senator fall on his face in the mud. It makes 'em feel better. No matter how well we're doing, we always need to see somebody get his. You know . . . Oscar Wilde said it, I think. 'It is not enough that I succeed. My best friends must also fail.' "

The studio limousine drove her home and Roy, the chauffeur, saw her safely into the lobby of the Watergate. She didn't really like living in all that splendor but it went with the job. She was too famous to have a private life in a normal suburb. There were too many kooks out there. She needed this security.

She let herself into the large apartment and moved through the rooms turning on lights. She felt uncomfortable alone in the place. She checked her answering service: Ken had called from his apartment two floors down, to say he had a dinner date, and Trish had called.

She tried Trish.

"Hi," her friend answered. "I was just getting into the shower but hang on while I go in the kitchen and pour some coffee instead." She was back in a moment. "You were extra good tonight, Angie," she said. "You really nailed him. Almost made me sorry for the bastard."

"I did feel sorry for him," Angie said. "I mean, I know he took the money. He deserves to be drummed out. But . . . I don't feel like a crusader anymore. I feel terrible."

"It gets to all of us, especially when the big three-oh comes around." Trish laughed. "You wonder if you shouldn't be home with a good man making babies. Some nights, my own brilliant career doesn't seem enough to get me through to morning. But at least you've got the fame and rewards to make up for things. I may be stuck with my boring congressional committee for life. Although," she confided, "I did have a heavy date late night. This hotshot Wall Street lawyer, Sam Hardy, who came down here to set the committee straight? He stands for most of the things I hate, but Angie, he was fun. Oh, sure, there's a lot of macho bullshit about him, but when you get him away from his rich cronies he's a nice guy. He wants me to come to New York next week for the opening at the Met."

Angie said as many encouraging things as she could think of. She was worried about Trish, who seemed wedded to her committee, content with her pitiful salary and living in a cramped little apartment. She was wet-nursing a bunch of senators who weren't half as smart as she was. Angie knew what a strain it was on Trish, concealing her intelligence and playing the role of glorified *secretary* while actually running the whole thing. It exasperated Angie.

"Good," she repeated. "It's time you started having a life of your own. Go to New York, and stay a week, let them miss you here. Hell, I might even come with you. I need to get out of this town and talk to people who read something other than the Gallup poll."

"Why not?" Trish said, then added shyly, "He's sending his plane for me, so we can go in luxury." She warmed to the idea. "We'll have a week there together, Angie, and shop, see some shows. Sam's busy and I know I'll only see him a couple of nights. Would you come?" She paused. "I suppose you have to check with the congressman."

"Hell, no," Angie said. "I do as I please and Ken does as he pleases. We're not married, you know."

"Yeah, well, you've been together an awful long time," Trish said. "Quite the established couple, no matter how many times Mary Hickson writes that you've split up."

"You know how it is," Angie said. "We just drift along. One drink too many and we get all clucky and start talking marriage and family, but the next morning we face the real world. We're both too selfish to get married."

"*You're* not," Trish said firmly. "Him, yes. But you're the kind of person who's going to fall madly in love and turn her back on everything when the right man comes along."

Later, Angie fixed herself a sandwich. Restless, she prowled around the apartment, looking out at the lights of the city. All those people had places to go and she, the TV star, was alone.

She wanted to call someone, someone from home maybe. Ted was out of the question. He wouldn't be in on a Saturday night and, anyway, the last time she'd seen him, at the convention in Miami, he was with a feature writer, a long-standing affair. She felt hurt by their closeness but she knew she damned well had no right to feel that way about Ted.

She did what she always did when she felt like this: she called home.

"Hello, darling!" May Waring always sounded as though she hadn't talked to her child in a year. "We were just talking about tonight's show. Were you pleased?"

Angie knew her mother sensed her growing desperation, but she didn't want to get into a career discussion if her father was there. He'd been through enough on Angie's behalf and he couldn't stand to think she was unhappy. If his daughter-the-star was miserable in her crusading role, what did she think had happened to him during all those years at the *Clarion?*

"We were pleased, I guess. It was a good show," Angie said quickly. "But how is Dad taking retirement? Is he driving you over the brink?"

Her mother laughed. She was delighted to have Harley off the *Clarion* and said so several times every day.

"He's learning that golf isn't as easy as it looks, and he fishes and takes long walks. Yesterday he calculated the time he's put in cleaning the pool over the years. I think he wants payment for everything he does, now. He's becoming impossible."

Her mother sounded bright and gay and Angie thanked heaven she hadn't done any moaning about how unhappy she was. She had no right to be unhappy. At least she knew that much.

They had the usual conversation about when Angie might be coming to visit, and then she talked with her father, and then they hung up.

She was unsettled after the call. Maybe she did need a change of scene. A few days in New York with Trish might be fun, and she had a couple of pieces in the can. A little time off might be just what she needed.

They settled back in the Learjet and giggled like schoolgirls all the way to New York. Sam Hardy's limousine was waiting for them at the private jet apron at LaGuardia. They drank champagne on the drive into the Plaza where adjoining suites awaited them. Angie had insisted on picking up her own tab and the setup was bigger and more expensive than she would have chosen, but it was only for a few days and she was there to have fun.

Trish came into her suite as Angie was unpacking.

"Sam's picking us up at seven, drinks at 21, then on to the opera, supper after at a place uptown he's just discovered. Elaine's."

"I'm not coming along. I'd be in your way," Angie protested. "I'll take care of myself tonight, and tomorrow we'll do the stores."

"It's all taken care of," Trish said. "He's even arranged a date for you, so we're going to be a foursome. And don't bother arguing: when Sam Hardy fixes something it's fixed."

Hardy was waiting for them in the lobby. He was charming and handsome, a big, strong man with steel gray hair and a ruddy complexion that meant yachting and tennis. He exuded power as only very successful New Yorkers can: a certainty that doors will be opened, cars waiting, the best table reserved for them.

"I'm honored," Hardy said, taking Angie's hand. "And damn pleased I'm just a boring old lawyer instead of one of those politicians you train your guns on." He took their arms, one on each side, and they swept out of the ornate lobby and into his limousine. "My friend got tied up in a board meeting. He's meeting us at 21."

There was much deference at 21 as their coats were checked, and the owners came over to greet Hardy and be introduced to Angie. She was used to that in Washington, but hadn't expected even to be recognized in Manhattan.

"We'll just take a table in the bar, Walter," Hardy

said. "Has Mr. Mansion arrived yet? He'll be joining us."

She froze. Her evening bag fell from her hand and Sam retrieved it.

"Angie?" Trish whispered. "You're white."

Angie looked around for an escape.

"Come on," Trish urged her. "One of 21's famous martinis and you'll be okay."

There was no way out. What could she tell Sam? And she couldn't run forever, anyway. She would look Richard Mansion in the eye and let him feel her utter loathing and contempt. She would hold her head high.

She clung tightly to her bag to stop her hands trembling as she followed the others into the dimly lit bar area. She kept her eyes straight ahead so she wouldn't seem to be looking for him.

"Trish Wright, Angie Waring," Hardy said, "may I present Lyle Mansion."

Relief nearly overwhelmed her. She nodded to the tall, thin man who rose and held a chair for her.

"I've seen you in Washington, of course," she said. "Always from a distance. I'm pleased my old newspaper is doing well under your guidance."

"I thought you two would have a lot to talk about," Sam Hardy said, pleased with himself.

"Indeed we do," Mansion said. "I tried very hard to have Miss Waring stay on at the *Tribune* when I bought it. In the years since, I've watched her go from strength to strength. Our loss was television's gain. But it was still our loss."

She managed a smile. She studied him while their waiter took drink orders. Up close, he looked less like a Mansion, or at least less like his brother. He was in his forties, thinning sandy hair and pale blue eyes, a softer, gentler version of Richard. He was diffident, almost shy, ducking his head when he talked. How had his brother described him so long ago? A wimp. He probably was, she thought.

But as the evening progressed, she softened. It wasn't his fault he wasn't a forceful figure like his friend Hardy. Or his brother. She smiled grimly to herself. She had no reason to admire forceful men, yet there she was, comparing him unfavorably with those who were. She took hold of herself and tried to look at him without bias.

During the second intermission at the opera Sam took Trish off to meet some friends and Angie struggled to make conversation with Lyle. Finally, when she confessed she knew nothing about opera, he opened up. He explained *Il Trovatore* to her, all the grandeur, all the passion, and, he chuckled, all the melodrama of it. He talked of other performances he had seen and operas he loved, and as he talked she began to see that he was a passionate man. He loved art, music, books, and talked about them as though they were old friends. This gentle scholar, this classicist, seemed out of place running a chain of newspapers.

They went to Elaine's, a bright, noisy saloon uptown, and there Lyle took charge. Sam, for all his Wall Street power, seemed cowed by the place. The patrons were all casually dressed, all at ease, as if they were in an old friend's living room. Sam Hardy's brand of authority meant nothing. But Lyle was welcomed by Elaine herself, and he knew most of the patrons. They were mostly writers and directors and she recognized a lot of the names.

It was an easy evening from then on. They drank wine and worked through steaming bowls of pasta and spicy veal dishes. A stream of people stopped by their table to talk with Lyle. A few people knew Angie, or knew who she was, and she was glad to feel less alien. She saw Jim Stone, who'd been a part-time sports commentator at Channel 4 the year Angie joined.

"Hey," he cried, "Angie! You're a star! I love your show, but every time I watch I think back to the days when you were just starting out. You were so nervous."

"I still am, Jim," she said. "You were always the cool one." Indeed he had been—cool, tall, slim, cheerfully admitting to being Channel 4's token black. But he'd been much more than a token, a natural television performer with style and grace.

He was very glad to see her, and talked about himself with ease. "Why, I even get to anchor the local Sunday night news now. One of these days, who knows?"

She introduced him to her table. Trish smiled and Sam nodded brusquely. Lyle stood up and shook hands and asked him to sit with them.

"How long you here for, Angie?" Jim asked when he had settled beside her.

"Just a few days," she said.

"Well, if there's anything you need, tickets, restaurants, call me at the station," he said. "We're all working for the same people."

They all had more wine, and while it was being poured, Angie saw Sam watching Jim. There was something like hatred in his eyes. He would be a mean enemy.

She looked at Lyle and thought how unfair it was to compare him with the dashing young man beside him. Lyle was quiet and safe and ordinary-looking, a nice man with nice manners who seemed to find the world just a little too much for him. Jim, by contrast, breathed youth and vigor and mystery. He was as handsome a creature as she had ever seen, with glowing black skin and perfect teeth, slim yet muscled, his whole being exuding strength and grace.

"It's time we were going," Sam said suddenly, and snapped his fingers for the check.

As they gathered their things Jim handed her his card.

"Call me, Angie, you hear?" he said. "Good to meet you all and thanks for the wine."

In the car Sam asked if they'd like to come back to his place for a drink. Angie wanted to leave the field clear for Trish, so she asked if she could be dropped off at the Plaza. Lyle said he would get off at his house in the Fifties.

"I've enjoyed talking with you, Angie," he said quietly as they swept down nearly deserted Fifth Avenue. "I'd like to see you again while you're here. But—" There was his little smile again. It irritated her. "I guess you've got younger, livelier people to spend your time here with. Maybe you'll have dinner with me when I'm in Washington next? Tell me what I'm doing wrong with the paper."

She waved to her three companions as the car pulled away from the Plaza. Poor Lyle Mansion, she thought as she rode the elevator. Born into that family of toughs. They probably walked all over him.

Trish came into her suite at ten o'clock the next morning and helped herself to the last of the coffee.

"Quite a night!" she exclaimed, clearly excited. "Sam really knows how to live. He's got a penthouse on the river, and the ships go by the end of his bed."

Angie was very pleased for her friend. After all the years of hard work and no fun, something nice was happening for Trish.

They did all the stores and staggered back to the hotel laden with packages, tumbling them across the burgundy-carpeted floor of Trish's suite. Trish had bought the most: Sam had arranged for her to visit Halston's studio and she had selected six outfits, costing thousands. She tried them all on again as Angie watched, the brilliantly colored garments floating around the room like tropical butterflies.

"I'm crazy about them all," Trish said, standing among the wrappings, hands on hips, wearing her sensible panties and bra. "I could really get into being a kept woman." She poured them champagne and said, "Come on, Angie. I want to see all your stuff."

Angie felt shy as she slipped out of her plain tailored skirt and blouse, but when she carefully put on the Armani outfit and looked at herself in the full-length mirror, she was pleased.

"Now the rest of your stuff," Trish insisted. "All the sexy lingerie you got at Bloomingdale's. I want to see why some girls think it's important to spend a fortune on what they wear underneath." She giggled. "Down home in Texas, the boys don't care what underwear looks like as long as it comes off easily."

Angie picked up the sensuous wisps of French lace and retreated to the bathroom where she stripped naked and carefully put on the lacy bra and knickers, buckled the suspender belt, smoothed the stockings up over her thighs. She hadn't worn stockings since high school and then they had looked nothing like this. She thought she ought to feel peculiar, but she felt great. She walked slowly into the room, feeling more naked than she had ever felt.

"Good God!" Trish said softly. "You look ravishing."

Angie blushed and said, "I look like a . . . a centerfold."

Sam had flown to Chicago for a late-afternoon meeting and Trish and Angie were free to do as they pleased. After they had put away their shopping and changed for the evening, they went down to the Oak Room. It was rich, burnished, everything gleamed softly in subdued lighting. There were a great many men at the bar and the tables but instinctively they knew they wouldn't be hassled, so they relaxed.

Outside, limousines came and went in an endless stream punctuated by aggressive and battered yellow cabs.

"God, it's an exciting city," Trish said. "All the wealth and glamour and power. New Yorkers seem to know how to do things right."

"The rich ones do," Angie said soberly. "The ones who are at home in places like this. But step out of here and go into the neighborhoods. Derelicts living under bridges, muggers waiting. It's a glamorous city, but there's a cruel layer under the veneer."

"I know," Trish said. "But a person can be insulated against it." She drained her drink and nodded when the waiter came to their table. "I think this is what I want. And Sam asked me to marry him last night."

Angie choked.

"What?! You only met him about a week ago. And there's your career—everything you've achieved in Washington. Are you crazy, Trish?"

"Washington!" Trish exclaimed. "My achievements! The committee sees me as a secretary who gets their papers in order and makes sure witnesses arrive on time. Oh, sure, women are making a few advances, but not in Washington. Not yet. It'll be some time before women are taken seriously in politics. I'm better than almost every member of my committee but the truth doesn't mean a damn and you know it. As Mrs. Sam Hardy, I'll be a woman of real influence.''

''You can't know whether you love him!'' Angie vas aghast. What was happening to her friend?

''He's great,'' Trish said. ''Forceful, strong, handsome. And he thinks I'm the smartest lady he ever met.''

Angie just sat and stared at her.

''I'll decide after tomorrow night with him,'' Trish finished.

Angie spent the rest of the evening trying to keep her opinions to herself. Trish was happy. She had no business letting her friend know how shocked she was.

Chapter
Nine

Angie planned to see a brace of movies the next day; Trish had gone off with Sam and she was completely free. Free—until the phone rang in her suite as she was going out the door. Steve Franklin was calling from Washington.

"Angie," he said, "I'm glad I caught you. We just ran through Saturday's show and the tape's stretched on that old Pentagon item of yours we talked about. The picture's okay but the sound's useless."

"You want me to fly back and dub it?" she asked, weary but resigned.

"Hell, no," he said. "I wouldn't think of it. But could you go over to the studio on West Sixty-sixth Street and make a new audio tape? We already telexed the script there."

They were expecting her at the studio and everyone treated her with deference. A production assistant brought fresh coffee while another set up the mike for her to rerecord her four-minute segment. She flubbed it the first time, the telex copy unfamiliar to her a month after she had written it. But the second take was fine and soon she wandered out of the recording studio and into the reception area.

"You need a car, ma'am?" a soft voice inquired.

"No, thanks, I'll get a cab," she said, then looked up into warm, familiar, deep brown eyes.

"I heard you were coming over this morning," Jim Stone said. "Our network believes in working their stars to death. I've got to spend all day here putting together a bit on the maple syrup industry in Vermont. Exciting, huh?"

He walked her to the revolving doors.

"But I'm clear for the evening," he said, "and if you're free there's a Knicks game at the Garden. You really should see them play before us black folks take over the whole starting line."

"Hey, I'd love to," she said impulsively. "What time and where?"

"I'll come by your hotel about seven," he said, smiling that warm smile.

She loved the game. They sat courtside and the striving, steaming players seemed only a touch away. She got caught up in the excitement of the roaring crowd in the great arena and found herself screaming for the Knicks as though they'd been her team forever. When the home team finally eked out a three-point win she was as exhausted as any of the players.

"You're some fan," Jim said admiringly. "Pity D.C. doesn't have a decent team. You must get real frustrated."

"I never even watched a whole game before," she said, breathless. "Not even in college. I don't know what came over me tonight!"

They were pushing out through the happy crowd, and he asked, "You want to meet some of the guys?

They go for a beer at a little bar up the street. We can get something to eat there, too.''

The bar was very masculine and very crowded with fans and players, everyone talking over the game and watching highlights on television. Angie didn't feel out of place: her whole working life had been spent in a male-dominated industry. Jim introduced her to several of the young giants and it was a pleasant sensation to be among men who were all taller than she was. It was midnight by the time they sat down to huge steaks in a rear booth. She was so thoroughly at ease that she didn't even notice how she was feeling.

"If you like," he said shyly, after they had eaten, "we can go back to my place for a drink. I'm right near your hotel, on Central Park South. The view's nice."

She stood at the windowed wall, nineteen floors up, looking out over the park while he fixed them drinks. It was a cold, clear night and they agreed Central Park was a wonderland, a few lights marking out streets and paths, the rest greeny black, the whole park surrounded by the impressive spires of grand apartment houses and hotels.

"Yeah," he said, handing her a drink. "Times like this it looks pretty great. But I always remind myself when I'm standing here that the other end of that park, up where you can't see it, is Harlem. And that is not a wonderland."

They talked easily, first about the game and their jobs, then about themselves. He was from Georgia, and had gone to Duke on a basketball scholarship. He'd been premed, meaning to be a doctor like his father. But he'd gotten involved in campus media and television became his passion.

He showed her around the apartment. She grinned: a real Manhattan bachelor pad. A gleaming kitchen that looked like it didn't get used much, a vast black and white bathroom, and a bedroom with king-size water bed facing a wall of television, stereo, tape deck.

"You've made yourself comfortable," she said wryly. "What the New York male needs to survive. The eligible man's paradise."

"Am I eligible?" he asked, so softly she scarcely heard him.

"Very." She spoke emphatically. He looked at her for a moment, then came to her and kissed her. She returned the kiss, thrilling to the strong manly aura. She stepped back and slowly unbuttoned her blouse and unzipped her skirt and let them fall to the floor. He watched approvingly as she stood there in her exotic new lingerie, gazing up at him.

He undressed her, both of them moving slowly, enjoying the sensuous silk gliding over her skin. Everything felt good to Angie, the time and the place and the fact that this intimacy hadn't been anticipated. Out of her control, she could just relax and enjoy it.

He stripped quickly with the grace of the athlete, and stood naked before her. His body was magnificent, glowing brown and strong. She reached out and ran her fingers down his chest. He felt like warm velvet.

Hand in hand they moved onto the bed and slowly explored each other. She watched, dreamlike, his dark head between her white breasts and as he moved lower she began trembling deep inside. She parted her legs to greet his eager tongue and heard herself cry out in pleasure as he touched her core.

It was too much pleasure, too soon, and she

squirmed away from him and began her own odyssey down his straining body. It felt as if there were a surging dynamo inside him, pumping vibrant energy through him. She hesitated for an instant, her cheek on his downy stomach, then moved again and took all of him in her mouth. He was huge and hard and she felt both fear and longing as his muscular thighs pressed against her. He was growing even larger and moving, despite himself, faster and faster.

Angie felt his large, gentle hands moving her away and bringing her up beside him on the bed. He moved across her body like a great, dark, enveloping cloud blocking out the light in the room, replacing it with the light that burned inside her. The weapon thrusting into her should have been too much, but he was easy with her and she had time to savor every moment. At long last he quickened, then flooded inside her just as her own body arched to meet him.

They lay still for a while in each other's arms, then made love again, more slowly, but it was every bit as satisfying as the first time.

He brought wine to the bedside and they drank, sitting cross-legged and naked, then smoked a joint. Sometime after that, sensuality blocking out everything else, Angie pushed him back on the bed and mounted him. She rode him furiously, drained him, then rode him again until every nerve in her body surged with joy.

At last, exhausted and replete, she rolled away and lay beside him. They slept in each other's arms, neither waking for the rest of the night.

She called Trish at the hotel just after 9:00 A.M.

"I thought you might be worried," Angie said. "I, uh, didn't come home last night. I stayed with a friend."

"So did I," Trish said, laughing. "I just walked in here myself. I hope your friend was as much fun as mine was. When are you coming back? I've got some amazing news and I've got a hell of a lot to do and I need you."

They hung up and she found Jim in the kitchen making coffee. She took a cup from him and they smiled at each other, full-out, nothing to hide.

"I've got to go now," she said. "And the next couple of days are going to be busy. But I hope we'll see each other again, here or in Washington. We're on the same network, after all."

He saw her to the elevator and waved goodbye. She smiled all the way down and a businessman glanced at her sideways. She didn't care. It had been a wonderful, thoroughly satisfying experience, and she knew Jim had further freed her from the terrors she had lived with so long. She sent him a silent prayer of thanks.

"Friday?! You can't get married on Friday," Angie said. "This is crazy, Trish! What about the people you have to invite?"

"Who?" Trish said. "My father's too far away and too old to come all this way. You're here. And Sam's here. So we're getting married on Friday and I want you standing beside me."

"But—your job!" Angie wailed. "Your apartment! Your car!"

"Fuck the job," Trish said, and meant it. "And Sam'll have one of his people handle the car and the apartment. Come on, Angie, stop sputtering. We've got a lot to do before Friday."

The wedding was conducted by a judge in the vast living room of Sam's apartment. There were fourteen guests. They stood around, drinking champagne and trying to make conversation, after the anticlimax of a three-minute ceremony.

"It was quite nice, but too modern, too swift for me," Lyle Mansion said to Angie as they stood at the window looking down on the East River. He laughed. "Not that the traditional wedding I had guaranteed a happy marriage! Mine ended bitterly, so I guess formality doesn't ensure anything."

"I'm more concerned about the swiftness of the courtship," Angie said. "They hardly know each other."

"Oh, I wouldn't worry," Lyle said. "Sam's not the kind of man who makes mistakes. Not often, anyway. He sees something he wants, he goes after it. And from what I've seen of your friend, she can look after herself."

"I guess," Angie said. "I just don't understand why all the hurry."

"That's a young person talking," he said. "At your age, there's time for everything. For people like me, time is running out."

She looked at him closely. What a serious, melancholy man. She knew he was little more than forty, yet he talked like an old man.

They waved goodbye to the happy couple, who were going to Bermuda for the weekend. Sam had some papers to sign down there in connection with a reinsurance deal he was putting together.

"Are you going back to Washington tonight?" Lyle asked. "Because I'm taking the five-thirty shuttle."

On the flight to Washington they talked easily, mostly media and political gossip.

"I'm getting a new editor for the *Tribune*," he told her as they started their descent. "Newt's finally decided to retire and go fishing. So I'm hiring a fellow I think you know. Ted Buchanan. He's working in television, but I know he's still a newspaperman at heart, and he's a damned good one." He chuckled. "Ted just had the devil of a fight with my brother, which endears him to me. You worked for Richard there too, didn't you?"

"Just briefly. For a summer . . . a long time ago," Angie said carefully. "I was only a kid. It was an internship."

"Oh, then I guess you wouldn't know Richard," he said, sounding relieved. "My brother and I are not at all alike. He's the kind of man who will not be thwarted in anything he wants. He thinks I'm a ditherer. Richard is Dad's kind of man. They let me run the newspaper chain because they figure it's so broke I can't do any harm."

The Mansions were quite a family for telling their secrets to strangers, Angie thought. She really didn't want to hear any more. She was tired of being imposed on by Mansions and their confidences.

"Ted Buchanan's a good man," she said. "He's honest and tough and he shouldn't be wasting his time in television."

He smiled. "I'm *so* pleased to hear you say that," he said. "It confirms my own view of television. Maybe with Buchanan's help I can lure you back to the *Tribune*."

"Thanks," she said. "I'll always wish the *Tribune* well. But the way things have worked out, my career is in television now whether I like it or not. They pay me an awful lot of money and they give me power of sorts."

"But you're not really happy?" he said eagerly.

"Who's ever happy?" she replied tartly.

* * *

Ken had actually driven out to the airport to get her, an unheard-of gesture. He seemed pleased to see her and kissed her as she came through the gate. She introduced him to Mansion and he nodded curtly at her traveling companion.

"I hope you put in a good word for me," he said as they drove home. "In all the years he's owned the *Tribune* they've never found a nice thing to say about me. I need all the backing I can get, Angie. I've got another tough race this year. It doesn't get easier."

They had dinner in her apartment then went off to bed early and made love swiftly, almost impersonally. After, as Ken slept, she lay staring at the ceiling until she saw the first gray light of dawn.

Chapter
Ten

The New York trip shook something loose in Angie, something the toughness she'd cultivated so long didn't cover up. Did it have to do with Jim? With Trish's complete change of life? Whatever it was, she didn't like it: she couldn't bury herself in work and forget herself, not anymore. She got scared and lectured herself into a kind of hollow depression, desperate to cover feelings.

It might have been easier if Trish had been there to talk with, but Trish was always away, traveling with Sam. Angie grew infuriated. How could Trish just up and leave everything? She resented it terribly, and she used that resentment to cover her loneliness. There was always her work to save her, she told herself.

"The lawyers are crapping themselves," Steve Franklin said one afternoon, laughing nervously. "Great show, but they weren't quite expecting an exposé of the First Lady."

"She kept all the jewelry," Angie said firmly.

"Protocol and the law says foreign gifts have to be handed over to the government. My job is to lift the lid on corruption and that's what I do—no matter how pretty it is or who's involved. It's as simple as that."

"You're a tough lady," Steve said. "I wouldn't like to have you against me. I have to hand it to you, the way you come up with scandals week after week. What's in the pipeline?"

"I'm still working on the foreign bribery scam," she said. "It's bigger than we thought—almost everyone is swilling at that trough. I think we'll have to concentrate on the airplane manufacturers. There are hundreds of millions in secret commissions there alone. And an international fund is in it, dealing out low-interest loans in return for all kinds of favors."

"Just be careful," he said. "It's one thing shooting down a senator or two, or even taking on the First Lady. But the guys you're talking about are really big. And a lot of 'em are probably network sponsors, not incidentally."

"Don't worry," she said. "I won't do a show until I've got them nailed to the wall. And besides, the administration's going to have its hands full now with this Watergate thing anyhow. It's going to blow up in their faces."

"Watergate? Angie, no one's paying any attention to that."

"The *Post* is," she said, "and they're confident they're on to something big. Why are we just ignoring it?"

Steve laughed at her.

"The *Post* better be wrong," he said. "How would it look? The famous investigative reporter missing out on a big story that broke in her own apartment building?'' She didn't think it was funny.

Ted's arrival in Washington to take over as editor of the *Tribune* filled a huge void for Angie. She had a real friend again, someone who knew the real Angie. She met him once or twice a week in funky late-night newspaper bars, far removed from the world of power and influence that was her working environment.

"God, I love this life!" Ted said as he waved to the bartender for more beers. "I never realized how much I was missing newspapers until I came back."

It was just before midnight and, barring a major news break, the *Tribune* had been put to bed. Ted and a few of his staff were winding down the way they did every night—a few drinks, a lot of joshing, and scurrilous gossip that would never see print. There was an intense camaraderie that couldn't exist among Angie's jealous ratings-obsessed colleagues. She had been accepted into their newspapermen's world—she had been one of them, once—and she enjoyed their boozy bonhomie, envying them.

"You fit the newspaper crowd," Ted said as they walked to the parking lot. "And they all like you. It means a lot, you know, having somewhere you belong, being surrounded by people you trust and respect. I think you're living in the wrong world. It's time you came home."

She shook her head.

"I like being with newspapermen and I used to like newspaper work. But, hell, I've carved out quite a lot for myself in another field and I'm prepared to sacrifice friendships if that's what I have to do.''

"Even mine?" he said softly. He stood leaning against his car, long arms folded.

"Why should it ever come to that?" she asked. She opened the door of her own car and said, "Thanks for the evening, Ted. I'll talk to you in a couple of days.''

She ran a hot bath, stripped out of her clothes, and relaxed in the tub. What had Ted meant about losing his friendship? He didn't approve of her long association with Ken, and Ken had remained a barrier between them since Ted's arrival at the *Trib*. It was something they just didn't talk about: Ted was too straight a man to understand her relationship with Ken. She wasn't too sure she understood it herself.

"You need a break from this rotten town," Ken said. "It seems like winter's never going to end." He stared out the window of her apartment. Gray sleet lashed the glass. "Why don't you come on the committee junket with me?"

"I just might do that," Angie said. "On a day like this, the Caribbean looks like heaven."

"Sure," he said. "You can get a couple of weeks off. You said yourself the season's almost over for your show and you've got more than you can use already. Come with me. The hearings we're doing are just a joke. I'll have lots of free time and we can cut out from the rest of the members, maybe go to Antigua or someplace quiet like that."

"You guys really know how to rip off the taxpayer," she said. "I ought to do a show on *you*."

"Not funny," he snapped. "Anything I tell you is

in club, off the record. And anyway, it is legitimate business. There are a lot of very strange companies operating out of hole-in-the-wall offices in the Bahamas and the Caymans. If we flush out just a few of them the IRS will recover millions of dollars. So don't worry about the cost to the taxpayer. He'll come out ahead.''

''Well, if you're going to be doing some serious investigation, I might get something out of the trip for a future story,'' Angie said. But the truth was, she wanted to get away to some sunshine.

''Hey, this is supposed to be a vacation for you,'' Ken said. ''But if you insist on sleuthing, the committee will be real happy to help. We don't get enough exposure. If you like, I can have you included as a member of the official party—all expenses paid.''

''No thanks,'' she said hastily. ''I can pay my own way.''

''Okay then,'' he said. ''But at least let me get you the same perks the official party is getting. First class for tourist rates, suites at standard room prices, that kind of thing.''

He had it all arranged within two days and the station reluctantly approved her vacation. She was happy: two weeks of sunshine and rest on romantic islands was just what she needed.

''What about the tickets?'' she asked Ken as she was going through her closet, digging out bright summer clothes and bathing suits. ''Who do I pay?''

''If you still insist on paying, your share is twenty-four hundred dollars,'' he said. ''Even at the VIP rate, it's a lot. You sure you don't want to travel on the public purse?''

"No!" she said sharply. "I don't. And I can afford it."

"Okay," Ken said. "Make out a check to the committee and I'll pay it in for you. But I'm telling you, it's an unnecessary expenditure. Everyone loads up these junkets with friends and relatives."

Angie shook her head emphatically. "No."

It was snowing the day they flew out of Washington and Angie was glad to put the cold, gloomy city behind her. She was glad the committee didn't get any media farewell. She felt awkward being attached to the official group without really belonging.

Their party made up about a third of the complement of the 707 and the first-class section had been expanded to fit them all in. All the members had a wife or secretary along, which made Angie feel less awkward. There was a great deal of merriment as the plane broke out of the leaden skies and into the blue above the Carolinas, setting course for Miami.

"It's going to be great for us," Ken said, squeezing her hand. "We've had too little time together lately."

At Miami they transferred to a smaller plane for the short flight to the Caymans, and Ken filled her in on the scam they were investigating.

"Until recently the Caymans were a sleepy little British colony," he said. "Then they got into the offshore company racket. American companies do a series of paper deals—reinsurance, that kind of thing—to get money out of the U.S., untaxed. The Caymans ask no questions, just act as a clearing house for the money. The money vanishes into European dollars, or goes into Swiss accounts. Sometimes it finances dirty deals like massive drug buys in Thailand or Marseilles.''

''How much is involved, do you all think?''

''It's anyone's guess,'' Ken said, shrugging. ''Hundreds of millions, maybe. Some of the people using the offshore route are just ordinary crooks. But some of them are major companies who get greedy. That's what the committee aims to find out—just who is screwing us out of taxes, and for how much.''

The Caymans were a disappointment to Angie, flat and sandy, with a few artificial-looking palms scattered around. And ferocious sand flies.

''You'll like the Bahamas better,'' Ken apologized when they were settled in their suite. ''This place is strictly for business, and the people who do business here never have to spend any time here, so they haven't developed the place. But at least it's hot and sunny.''

She lay by the pool, her biggest decision each day which drink to order and her only worry whether she was getting too much sun. In the evenings, she and Ken dined with the rest of their party, then retired to their suite to make long and uncomplicated love. They had left their Washington lives behind them, and found a new vigor in their lovemaking. It was the most peaceful time she had ever spent with Ken, and she was sorry when they left for Nassau.

''Don't worry,'' Ken said as they stood in the lobby of their large, garish hotel. ''Two days of hearings, two nights in the casino, and then we'll get away by ourselves. I've borrowed a house on a private island for the last few days of our vacation. We'll be on our own in paradise.''

Again she spent her days by the pool. Sometimes

tourists recognized her and asked for her autograph. And there was a little knot of reporters and photographers hanging out at the hotel bar, all bored and restless.

"It's the Hughes stakeout," Angie told Ken when he asked about them. "The elusive Howard is supposed to be still occupying the penthouse, though no one's had a positive sighting in months. The reporters and photographers are all that's left of the big media pack. The poor guys thought this was going to be a great assignment, but now they're going stir crazy, their employers are cutting back on their expenses, and the whole thing has gone flat. But none of them's willing to go because Hughes may emerge the day after they leave." She smiled ruefully. "That's what most reporters' lives are like, Ken."

"Maybe you can talk your way in and meet Hughes," Ken said. "Be a real scoop."

"Forget it," she laughed. "I'm no foot-in-the-door reporter. These guys are professional stakeout merchants, and if they can't get him, no one can. Anyway, I'm not interested."

One of the photographers snapped her and Ken by the pool. It didn't bother them: they were an accepted couple in Washington and no one would care about their being together in the Bahamas. She found herself beside the cameraman at the bar, late in the afternoon.

"Hi," she said. "Will you send me a print if it comes out?"

"Sure," he said. "I'm Johnny Brennan, on assignment with the *London Globe*. Normally I freelance out of New York. Sorry about taking your picture without asking, but I figured it might be handy for my files. I

need to come out of this assignment with something."

"But they're paying you, aren't they?" she asked.

"Just a per diem and picking up the hotel tab,"
he said. "It's bloody maddening, stuck here while
your competition is back in the real world, getting
the good assignments. It can't last much longer.
They'll pull out soon. Bloody stakeouts! I hate
them."

"I know," Angie said. "I've been on a few myself."

"Come off it!" he laughed, his Irish blue eyes
mocking her. "Angie Waring, ace TV reporter, on a
stakeout?"

"This is not just a pretty TV face," she said force-
fully. "I paid my dues, did lots of time on a newspaper, got wet and cold huddled in the bushes of
Georgetown waiting for people who didn't appear.
At least you get to do your stakeout in a tropical paradise."

"You can keep your tropical paradise," he said,
shaking his long mop of blond hair. "I'll swap it for a
city. I'm going island crazy."

"It is a bit   flashy here," she said. "All these
people determined to have a good time. I'm looking forward to leaving after one big fling in the casino."

"Good luck," he said. "You'll need it. I already
lost any profit I could make on this trip at the tables."
He nodded at her empty glass and bought her another. "So, back to the mainland then?"

"No," she said. "We're slipping away to Eleuthera, to a private house. No one around. Miles and
miles of deserted beach."

"Half your luck," he said. "But I'd still settle for Central Park."

On this, their last night, she had agreed to accompany Ken to the casino. She dressed carefully in a white strapless dress that showed off her tan, put up her hair, and determined to have a good time. She and Ken made a handsome couple, and heads turned their way as they entered the casino. Ken headed straight for the crap table and cashed what looked like a big roll of bills.

"It's all right," he said, grinning. "I won quite a bit last night while you were sleeping." He handed her some chips. "Wander around and try your luck," he said. "Roulette's probably the easiest for a beginner."

"Can I just stay and watch you?"

"Sure, but you'll be bored," he said.

She didn't begin to understand craps, but Ken seemed to be winning. The pile of chips beside him more than doubled in an hour. He was drinking fast but playing with an icy calm. That calm broke only once, when the flashbulb went off. She was standing at his shoulder and looked up to see Johnny Brennan being hustled out of the casino, not gently.

"Damned photographers," Ken snarled. "They'll use that picture against me. But, hell, this is a legal casino and I'm entitled to a few hours off duty."

He played some more and Angie finally drifted away from the crap table. She found a large crowd around the roulette wheel and waited on the edge until a space became available. She understood the rudiments of the game but a handsome young man in a white tuxedo explained more to her. He had a system of riding one color and doubling his stake until the color came up. She followed his system and quickly won over a hundred dollars. She gathered the chips and dropped them in her evening bag.

"Don't go," the young man implored. "You're bringing me luck. I've won ten thousand since you joined me."

Shocked, she looked down at the green baize. The gold counters in front of him were indeed worth a thousand dollars each. She shook her head and slipped away from the table, her place taken immediately.

Ken had doubled his money yet again and there were gold tokens in his pile. He was winning thousands.

She touched him on the shoulder.

"I've had too much sun, Ken. I'm beat. I'm going to bed. I'd like to stay and watch you win, but I just can't."

"You go," he said, patting her hand. "I'm on a hot streak. Go on. Don't wait up."

She went to the bar for a final drink and no one tried to pick her up. That was gambling, she thought. Everyone in the casino had suspended his interest in everything except the roll of the dice, the turn of the cards, or the spin of the wheel.

In their suite Angie undressed, leaving her lovely things strewn over a chair. She stepped out, naked, onto the darkened terrace and let the warm night air caress her body. She hoped Ken wouldn't be too long: she wanted him.

She didn't know what time it was when he finally appeared. She had been between the cool sheets for hours. But she still wanted him.

"Hurry, darling," she whispered across the dark room.

"Oh," he mumbled. "I was trying not to wake you up."

"But I want to be awake," she said. "I want you."

"Sorry," he said. "I just came for my reserve stake. Only a few more hours and I'll win everything back. The dice are about to go my way again."

He slipped out of the room without another word and she lay there, awake and longing. Her nipples were erect. She let her hand stray across her thighs and rest on her mound. She caressed herself, slowly at first, then found her secret rhythm and brought herself to a climax. Not satisfactory, but it tipped her over the edge into sleep.

Ken was beside her when she woke, his lean handsome face pale, his fair skin gone dark under the eyes. He was breathing harshly and perspiration dampened his hair. He looked like he'd had a long, hard night. Angie tried not to wake him as she slid out from under the arm flung across her chest, but he stirred and opened bloodshot eyes.

"Christ!" he muttered, blinking in the bright morning sunlight. He surveyed Angie and the room, then moaned.

She brought him a glass of ice water and put her arm around his shoulders while he drank it.

"You should have taken me with you when you left the casino," he said. "I've never had a more unlucky run. The dice turned on me."

"But you were winning so much," Angie said, surprised.

"I was," he said. "But my luck turned."

She remembered his late-night visit to the suite and suddenly she was scared.

"How much did you lose?" she asked.

"A lot," he said quietly.

Then he managed a grin. It made him look like a naughty boy.

"It's only money," Angie laughed. "It's not the end of the world. And *I* won a hundred and ten dollars, so that makes up for some of it, doesn't it?"

He winced. "Every little bit helps."

They took their coffee onto the terrace and Ken pulled himself together. His gaiety was forced, but she was grateful to him for making the effort.

She left him with the coffee and went inside to pack. In the bathroom she knocked over his shaving kit and a clear plastic bag fell out, spilling a little white powder onto the glass shelf. She had been to enough chic parties to know it was cocaine. She carefully scraped the white powder back into its bag and carried it out to him.

"Where did you get this?" she asked. "There's so much of it." Indeed there was, quite a lot.

His face lit up.

"I'd forgotten about that!" he said, reaching for the bag. "A gift from one of the local power brokers." He hefted the package. "There must be a quarter of a pound here, at least. So this trip hasn't been a total loss." He reached into the bag and squeezed some of the powder between thumb and forefinger, then snorted it. He did it again. "Good stuff," he pronounced. He held out the bag to Angie. "Want some?" he asked. "The perfect cure for a hangover."

She shook her head. "I haven't got a hangover. And you know I'm not into coke."

"Suit yourself." He shrugged. "I've never understood people who'll do grass, but throw up their hands in horror at a little coke."

It was a brilliant day, and Angie felt vibrant during the boat trip to Eleuthera. Ken was bubbling with energy, but she figured that it was cocaine, not the sparkling sun.

The house was everything he had told her to expect, a long low white stone mansion, hidden in tropical bushes and trees, on a spit of land walled off from the rest of the island. There was a smiling housekeeper to meet them and show them around. The master suite was a vast, marble-floored room, cool, with a breeze coming through the green wooden shutters.

"It's glorious, Ken!" Angie began dancing around the room the moment the housekeeper left. "I could stay here forever. I don't want to go back."

"We'll enjoy it while we can," he said. He led her out across the terrace to the private beach, cut off from the world by a riotous jungle of colorful bushes and graceful palm trees. "I think I'll send the housekeeper away for a few days so we can be alone."

"Good." She smiled at him. "We'll play house, all by ourselves."

They found the house stocked with everything they could desire. The housekeeper proudly showed them the meat hanging in the cool room, and the vast kitchen, its three refrigerators packed with fish, vegetables, meats, and cheeses. The wine cellar held hundreds of bottles of good vintages.

"Are you sure you'll be all right on your own, sir?"

the housekeeper asked Ken anxiously. "I'm only too happy to fix your meals."

"No, no thanks," Ken said. "We'd really like to be alone here. But thank you." He gave her his best politician's smile.

"I understand," she said. She smiled coyly at them and Angie realized she thought them honeymooners. "I live just outside the compound, not a mile from here, so if you want me, just drive down the road in the Jeep."

Once they were alone they became children exploring a newfound paradise. They ran naked down the golden beach and splashed in the warm water. They lay naked in hammocks under the palms and let the hot sun dry them. They dined on the shady terrace, eating pâté and cold lobster, feeding crumbs of French bread to the brilliantly colored birds around them.

"You want to go out in the sailboat?" Ken asked when they had finished their second bottle of white wine. "Or snorkel on the reef? Water-ski?"

She shook her head. "I want to be lazy today," she said. "And I want to try out that bathtub. It's the greatest thing I ever saw."

Ken led her back into the house to the fantastic bathroom next to their bedroom. The roof and wall were one long curve of glass, making it totally open to the sky and the sea. A massive sunken tub of black marble dominated the room. The rest was stark white except for vivid green palms in alabaster pots around the room. It took forever to fill the tub with warm water and they laughed and caressed each other until it was ready. Angie poured bath oil into the tub until they were enveloped in tropical fragrances. Finally they slid into the welcoming water.

"I feel like something out of an old Hollywood musical," Angie said, floating on her back. "I love it. It's decadent."

"I'll show you decadence," Ken growled, affecting a leer and twirling an imaginary moustache. He stood up. "You are trapped. There is no escape. I shall have my way with you."

She giggled and pretended horror.

"Please, sir!" she begged. "Don't touch me! I am young and innocent."

He was huge. He moved across the tub to her, still playing the villain. There was a glint in his eyes and Angie felt a thrill of anticipation run through her. He reached out and put his hands around her head and pulled her down on him. She opened her mouth wide and took the massive weapon, felt the rock hardness beneath his silky, oiled skin. Clasping her head, he moved her to his rhythm, and she could feel every vein pulsating as he forced himself into her. There was no sensation of gagging or choking, then suddenly he exploded and she was engulfed in his hot tide.

She broke away and lay back against the tub, her arms stretched out along the marble. She felt . . . used. But she also felt it was right that he should take her that way—selfishly, brutally. He stared at her, gazing deep into her eyes as if he could see right through to her soul. She returned his stare. He nodded once; he knew her. Had she understood this all along?

Later he dried her with towels and led her into the bedroom and laid her gently on the cool sheets. He snorted some cocaine and soon he was huge again.

And then he did an amazing thing: he took some coke and rubbed it on the tip of his penis, then lay down on her and entered her. At first it was a feeling of numbness inside her, as if from a mild anesthetic, chilling but not unpleasant. Then she felt the drug entering her membranes, flashing through her, reaching every part of her. Her whole body tingled and glowed and she felt surges of energy as powerful as desire. Their lovemaking—no, it wasn't lovemaking, but a congress of uncomplicated lust—lasted perhaps half an hour. He owned her body . . . but she owned his, too. His weapon was her weapon, attached to her, driven by her. When they finally reached one last shuddering climax, Angie knew what it felt like to be a man.

During their stay on Elouthora there were quiet moments, times when one walked on the beach while the other swam or read. But these times didn't satisfy Ken. Always hyper anyway, the coke kept him on a constant, nervous high. Angie was uneasy. Their time alone in paradise was bringing to a head all the tensions of their relationship. She tried to talk to him about it one evening as they sat with drinks, watching the setting sun streak the pale blue sky with mauve and orange.

"You and I, Ken," she said, "haven't got much in common, outside of the bedroom. All the years we've been together, I still don't know you."

He shrugged. "What's to know? As long as the fucking is good, does it matter? We're the kind of people who live for number one all the time. There's no inclination toward hearth and home and companionship, if that's what you're talking about."

"But sometimes I think that's what I want," she said desperately. "I can't see a whole life of caring only about myself and fending off feeling." She swirled the wine in her glass, gazing down into the ruby depths. "I think I'm really a quiet little person who wants to love and be loved."

He laughed. She almost hated him. "Come off it! You're as tough a person as I've ever met, and I've met them all. It doesn't matter why you got tough: tough is what you are."

She said nothing more. Why should he want to understand her? She hadn't wanted to understand herself for a long time. For more than ten years she had buried herself in the dogged pursuit of ambition. Now she had it all and, of course, it wasn't enough. It also wasn't there to be pursued any longer.

Their last day on the island, they lay on the little beach trying to soak up enough sun to get them through the Washington-winter. Angie decided on one more swim over the reef with a snorkel, watching the tropical fish darting in and out of the coral. Finally she swam back to shore and strolled up the beach toward Ken. They were both naked, as they had been every day of their idyll, and Angie glanced down at herself, pleased with her all-over tan. As she looked up again, a flash of light from the encircling jungle caught her eye. She stopped and stared at the spot.

"Ken! Ken!" she yelled. "Someone's in the bushes, spying on us."

He jumped up and ran into the foliage. Angie saw the intruder break cover and spring away through the trees, back toward the entrance to the compound. He was fast, but not fast enough. The camera and telephoto lens might have been enough; the long blond hair clinched it.

Ken gave up the chase, hampered as he was by being naked and barefoot. He came back shaking his head.

"Fucking paparazzi," he said. "Why does he think you and I are worth chasing? Although," he added, "you're worth photographing anytime, looking like that."

She grabbed a towel and wrapped it around her. Now that their privacy had been invaded she was suddenly self-conscious.

"It wasn't just anyone, Ken," she said. "It was Johnny Brennan, a freelance from New York. He was the one who snuck a picture of us by the pool last week, and then that time in the casino. Now he's got us naked. Someone's trying to set us up. Why?"

"Who cares?" Ken said, shrugging. "We haven't done anything wrong. And my being pictured with you—well, it'll win me as many votes as it costs me."

The incident hung over them the rest of the day and all the way back to Washington. They were edgy with each other anyway, eager to end the enforced intimacy of the past two weeks.

They took the same elevator in the Watergate and Ken got off at his floor.

"I guess I'll be busy catching up for the next couple of days, Angie," he said. "I'll call you when things are back to normal."

Things never got back to normal.

A Mary Hickson exposé led the *Post* three days later. Alongside a picture of Angie leaning over Ken's shoulder at the crap table in the casino was a devastating account of how Ken had taken Angie on a congressional junket at taxpayers' expense. Hickson took great pleasure in recounting Angie's role in exposing similar frauds.

"It's not true!" Angie yelled at Steve Franklin. He was lounging back in his executive chair, looking at her almost as if he *wanted* it to be true. "That Hickson bitch," she said. "For years she's been trying to get me. Well, this time she's gone off half-cocked."

"So you'll sue her," said the station manager smoothly. "You want me to get our lawyers cracking now?"

Angie paused midflight in her anger, recalling the adage about reporter never suing reporter.

"I don't know. I just want her to set the record straight. Of course I went along on the trip, I made no secret of it. But I've got more than enough money to pay for that trip. I can prove it. I've got the . . ." Something told her to stop there, not to mention the check she'd given Ken.

"So you'll sue Hickson," Steve said. He stood up. "Because if you don't, I'm afraid I'll have to suspend you. The network . . . well, you know how it is. We have to be like Caesar's wife. And the job you do, nailing people for indiscretions, makes it impossible for us to ignore this. I'll arrange for you to have a meeting with our lawyers. Meantime, you better go home and await developments."

She left the building numb, went home, and called Ken's office. He was out of town, according to his staff.

She spent the rest of the day in her apartment waiting for something to happen. The phone rang all the time. A *Post* reporter called soliciting her comment and she hung up on him. Ted Buchanan called offering personal sympathy and a forum in the *Tribune* to tell her side of the story.

"Thanks, Ted," she told him. "But I don't want to get into a mudslinging match. I just want her to retract. What she said isn't true."

"Hell, I know it couldn't be," Ted said. "It's all just a mistake of some kind." He dropped his voice. "But you've got to be careful in situations like this, Angie. A lot of people owe you one. You've done your job real well and you've got a high profile. You've made a lot of enemies."

That was when she started to cry.

"Oh, Ted," she sobbed, "I never wanted to make enemies, to be feared. You know what I'm really like. I've just been trying to do my job."

"Cut it out!" he said. "Don't apologize for your career. You're one of the best investigative reporters in the business. But you've got to be prepared to take the heat when it's on you. You're a public figure, Angie. You have to expect to get the spotlight turned on you sometimes. This isn't a game we're playing, it's lives and careers at stake and you've done your bit to alter quite a few of them."

"Thanks, Ted," she said bitterly. "You sound just like my boss. Well, you can all go to hell. I didn't do anything wrong and I don't deserve to be crucified. I'm going to clear my name first and then I'm going to take a long look at what it is I do and what I want. And I'll tell you now—I want something very different from what I've got."

"Good," he said cheerfully. "I told you television wasn't enough for you. A shallow medium." Then his voice turned kind again. "Love, you are in big trouble. I guess the station wants you to sue the old bitch?''

"Yes," she said miserably. "I think I'm under suspension until I do."

"Well, be very careful," he said. "Don't let their lawyers steamroller you. I don't like Hickson, but she's seldom wrong because she's very cautious. Don't do anything, don't get into anything, unless you're sure you're going to win." He paused, as if considering his next remark. "Because that guy of yours, that Ken"—she heard the deep loathing in his voice—"is the snakiest son-of-a-bitch in Washington." He hung up.

It took her three calls to New York to track down Johnny Brennan. She finally got him in a reporters' bar on the East Side.

"I thought I'd be hearing from you," he sighed, his Irish accent deepened by an afternoon of drinking. "I'm sorry, but it was a job and I needed one. I'd rather not have done you harm. You seem a nice girl—nicer than on the telly—but there you are. You understand: a job to be done. And it got me off that goddamned island."

"Sure, Johnny," she said. "I'm not mad. I understand. A job. Although sneaking pictures of me naked on the beach was not the fairest thing you could have done." She put a hard edge in her voice. "What I do want to know is who assigned you to my case. Was it Mary Hickson? Your picture ran with her story. I just want to know who's trying to destroy me."

"Yes," he said, "that was the lady who assigned me to take pictures of you and the congressman. I had to take the job. I've not had an assignment from the *Post* before."

"Okay, Johnny," she said wearily. "We all have to make a living. No hard feelings."

"Thanks," he said gratefully. He paused and she waited, sensing more. "Angie? Look, I better tell you now. After the story broke today, every paper in the country called me to see if I had any more pictures of you and your fellow. I'm afraid I sold the beach pictures to the *Clarion*."

It should have been funny. The *Clarion*. She had nothing to hide, and with her naked body plastered all over the *Clarion* she'd have nothing *left* to hide. Sure, they'd put strips across her boobs and pubes so as not to offend their readers. Which would make her look even worse on the supermarket shelves of America. She remembered how proud she had been of her naked brown body just a week before and she smiled wryly.

She had to make another call. "Mom?" she said. "There's a story up here I think you should know about."

"You and that Ken?" her mother said. "It was on the six o'clock news. Your father almost threw something through the screen. He was so mad at them for picking on his little girl. But then he calmed down and agreed you wouldn't do anything that dumb."

"I didn't, Mom," she said, "but it's going to take a while to establish that. Look, Mom, there's another problem. The guy they put on our case, he got some other pictures, me with no clothes on." She waited. Her mother said nothing. "He's sold them to Dad's old paper. I don't think there's anything I can do about it. See, I'm a public figure according to the law. Libel, I mean, and invasion of privacy. There's nothing much I can do about it. What about Dad?"

"I'll handle him, darling," her mother said. "And

don't worry about side issues. I'm only concerned about this attack on you. You didn't do anything stupid, did you?''

''No, Mom,'' she said. ''I may be pretty stupid in my personal life, but professionally I'm as smart as they come. They can't lay a glove on me.'' And then she started to cry and it made it worse that her mother was trying to reach out to her, to hold her across all those miles.

He came knocking at her door around midnight, furtive as a man whose apartment has been dogged all day by blood-lusting reporters.

''I flew back as soon as I could,'' Ken said as she let him inside. ''I even canceled the meeting with the Hadassah.'' He threw off his coat and took the drink she gave him. ''Angie, we are in deep shit.''

She looked at him levelly. ''Why, Ken? Why are we in deep shit? Just because your old girlfriend has done a number on us, a patently false number?''

He tried to shrug it off. ''It's not good for me, this kind of thing being splashed around.''

''So,'' she said, icy calm overcoming her, ''we are not going to accept this. The station insists I sue Hickson and the *Post* because it's not true.''

He drained his drink and made himself another. She stood and watched him, waiting. Refueled, he sat down and stared at her. Finally he spoke.

''It is true, Angie,'' he said. ''The check you gave me, for your expenses, I meant to pay it in to the committee. But I'd already put a ghost down on the trip, figuring you wouldn't be so insistent about paying your own way. I was going to fix it all up when I got back here, but I lost so much money in the casino that I took your check and endorsed it to the casino so I could keep playing. I would have straightened it all out, but now it's too late."

She sat down slowly, carefully.

"You mean, Ken," she said, her voice flat, "that all the time we were on vacation I was on the committee's books as one more press aide? One more floosie paid for out of the public purse?"

"No, no," he said weakly. "It wasn't meant to be that way. Honestly, I would have paid your check in to the committee, really. It was just I lost all that money—more than twenty grand in one night—and your check was there so I signed it over to them."

"Well," she said, "you're going to have to go public and explain all this. Because you've put me in a spot I determined I'd never be in, where people are laughing at me. You get on the telephone in the morning and straighten this whole thing out."

"I can't, Angie," he said. He hung his head. "It's out of my hands. There's no trouble about putting a phantom press aide on the books—we can explain it as a simple clerical slipup. It's already arranged for one of my assistants to accept responsibility for that, as a mistake. I've spoken to some of the House leaders and they'll go along with it. At worst, I could be censured." He gulped down the last of his drink. "The thing is, though, I can't fix the matter of the endorsed check. I could be indicted for that because, technically, it was public money. I would be ruined, politically and every other way."

"And me?" she demanded. "I'm facing professional ruin too—through no fault of my own. It wasn't me who tried to cheat the government out of my fare; it wasn't me who went nuts at the gambling table. You've *got* to clear my name."

"I can't," he repeated. "If it comes out that you gave me the check, then I'm in big trouble and you won't be any better off, actually. Well, not much better. Please go along with me on this. We'll announce it was all a mistake, I'll give you the money back, and you'll pay for your trip. Everyone will be satisfied and the whole thing will blow over."

"Except my reputation will be ruined," she said. But she already knew there was no way out for her. Ken could get away with it, politically, in the name of expediency. She couldn't get out from under unless she could prove the Hickson story totally wrong. She was washed up. And Ken wasn't to be relied on.

"You bastard," she said softly. "You spoiled, selfish, cowardly bastard. With all your faults, I never thought you'd stoop so low. Get out of here. Get out of my life. Now."

He started backing toward the door, looking scared of her but still anxious to know.

"You'll go along with it?" he pleaded. "It's the only way, Angie, the only way not to destroy both of us."

She hurled her glass at him savagely, wanting to smash his smooth politician's features, wanting to hurt him as badly as he'd hurt her. But he dodged it and the glass shattered against the wall. Ken fumbled with the door and ran out.

She sat there for a long time, too weary and beaten to think. It was late and so much had happened to her. She couldn't sleep, and spent the night pacing. When first light appeared she knew what she had to do.

* * *

Steve Franklin was relieved by her decision: firing her would have been messy.

"You're doing the right thing," he said briskly. "After all this has died down you can always get another job. You've got a lot of talent, Angie; you just made a bad error in judgment, letting your personal life interfere with professional sense. I'm sorry."

The other visit was to Ted Buchanan. They met for lunch at an Italian restaurant near his office.

"You can't run away," he said. "You haven't done anything wrong. Have you?"

"I haven't, but it doesn't matter, Ted," she said. She was past arguing. "I can't clear myself of this without bringing others down too.

He protested some more but he was worldly-wise enough to know she was right.

"There's always a job at the *Tribune*," he told her firmly. "Sure, I understand, not just yet. But when things have quieted down, when you're ready to work again, there'll be a place for you. You're a top talent. Think of this as just a setback along the way."

"Thanks, Ted," she said. They stood on the sidewalk outside the restaurant and said goodbye. "Thanks for everything you've done for me. I wish I had something to give you." She hailed a cab. "Meantime, I'm going to do what I always do when I'm in trouble—go home to Mom. I'll write you." She left him standing there on the sidewalk.

BOOK
THREE

Chapter
Eleven

Lantana was a quiet little town, not very interested in the outside world. Her scandal was of no consequence there; the attitude was that people up north were all crazy, anyway, so their deeds meant little. She sometimes saw old friends from school but they were engrossed in children and mortgages and their marriages, and her life was just too alien for them to understand. They didn't try. So she was left to mend, slowly, from one month to two, then three. She confronted the bitterness that might have destroyed her and worked with it. She played tennis, swam, walked miles on the beaches, read a lot—and only occasionally wondered what she was going to do with the rest of her life. Ted wrote and called regularly and Trish flew down twice to visit her. But mostly she let herself drift, ignoring the future.

Where was the light? she kept asking herself. Where was there some feeling for another day? But all she had was the leaden hopelessness she'd been living in since leaving Washington. It was all very well to tell herself to snap out of it, and fine for dear Ted to cheer her over the phone. But there wasn't a tinge of anything around her but despair, and all she knew how to do anymore was look backward.

It was her mother, as always, who knew when to start applying some pressure.

"You've done enough penance," her mother pronounced as they loaded the car outside the supermarket. "The little storm has blown over and it's time you decided what you're going to do."

"You want to get rid of me, Mom?" she teased. "Most mothers would love to have their little girls at home. You're an unnatural mother."

"Cut out the little-girl nonsense," May said. "You can't waste your life in a backwater. Anyway, your father and I aren't getting any younger. After we're gone there'll be nothing here for you. I don't want you to be stranded."

"Don't be silly, Mom," she said, chilled suddenly. "You and Daddy will go on forever." But she knew they wouldn't and she knew a sudden fear of being left alone.

They drove to the Hawaiian, a little motel on the A1A which boasted a pleasant open bar overlooking the ocean. They ordered piña coladas and found a table away from the shrieking children of holiday-makers.

"It's time you went back," her mother said. "You'll do what you have to. It's only a matter of someone giving you a push out of the nest. Your father . . ."

"What about Daddy?" Angie demanded. "He can't talk to me anymore. He can't stand me, somehow. If we're alone in a room together he finds some excuse to leave."

"Darling, try and understand," her mother said gently. "He was so proud of you, the successful journalist who did classy work. It was like he was exorcising the *Clarion*. When all that nonsense happened, it was as if he had been cut off in his prime. And," she said, "the pictures didn't help. Having his beloved daughter featured naked in his old paper—well, that's hard for any father, especially someone as straight as Harley. Don't misunderstand," she added quickly. "He's still as proud of you as he can be. It's just, he's old and he feels by now that so much is out of his control. If you go back and get another job, a job that makes you happy, he'll know you're all right again and he'll be happy."

"I'd like to do that for him—and for you. But I'm not sure I can," Angie said honestly. "All the fight's gone out of me. I just want peace and quiet now."

"It still hurts that badly?" her mother asked.

"I guess," Angie said. "But the other thing is, I don't want to go around exposing people's mistakes anymore. I've made enough of my own to know nobody's perfect. I'm tired of looking for people's flaws."

May eyed her daughter carefully. "I see." She looked out over the ocean, taking herself far away. "Nothing's unflawed, Angie, not after you stop being a child. Don't go looking for perfection."

A couple of days later Trish called from New York, pleading and insistent: Angie must spend the summer with her in Newport, Rhode Island.

"Sam's involved with sponsoring a boat in the America's Cup race. We've got to spend months in Newport and I'm going to go mad. I need you to keep me company. Please, Angie, he's taken this big house and I don't know how I'm going to cope. You're not doing anything right now, so come and keep me company. We can lie on the beach, go to the fancy parties, play tennis. Please!''

At first she refused, and then Trish came clean.

''Angie,'' she said, ''I *need* you. Things aren't . . . things aren't going so well for me. Please do this for me.''

She liked Newport from the first day when they touched down in the seaplane on the choppy waters of Narragansett Bay and taxied up to the wharf. All along Thames Street the narrow Colonial shopfronts glowed in the setting sun; gulls wheeled over them, swooping and diving and fighting for scraps the fishermen left. It was an old town and it made Angie feel welcome immediately. She had left behind the world of neon and plastic. Two of Sam's staff were waiting for them as the plane edged up to the wharf, and their bags were whisked into the trunk of a long black Mercedes.

''So far, so good,'' Trish said as they settled into the plush rear of the car. ''I wouldn't have been surprised if we'd been met by a horse and cart. Hell, I'm a Texas girl. What do I know about a New England fishing village?''

Even Trish was silenced when the limousine pulled into the driveway of the house Sam had taken for the summer. It was one of the grandest of the Newport ''cottages'': a vast gray stone mansion, three stories spread in a U shape around acres of lawn spilling over the cliff edge to the surging surf way below. They stood in the echoing entrance hall under a gleaming chandelier, staff bustling around them.

''It's a palace,'' Angie breathed, lost in the space, listening to the clacking of the servants' heels on the old white marble. "Sam believes in the grand scale, huh?"

"He hasn't even seen this place," Trish said. "It belongs to someone he does business with. But I'll tell you something: when he arrives, next week or whenever, he won't even notice where he is. He'll settle into a room with telephones and a telex and a couple of secretaries and go on making money." She made a face. "Now I know how boring millionaires can be. They prob'ly build places like this to keep their wives off their backs, or show their competitors how well they're doing. I know it has nothing to do with caring about the finer things. Men like Sam don't notice the finer things."

They parted at the top of the grand staircase and Angie followed the man with her bags to the suite assigned her. It was a huge white room dominated by a Victorian four-poster bed. A deep colonnaded balcony opened off the bedroom, offering an unrestricted view out over the dark blue ocean. She thanked the servant when he had put her two bags on stands in the walk-in closet, and set out to explore. There was a bathroom as big as a bachelor apartment, dominated by a huge claw-footed tub on a pedestal. And in the bedroom a nest of chairs and couches, angled to the view, where Angie imagined herself taking afternoon tea. A long, sturdy mahogany cabinet opened to display crystal and silver and a bewildering array of bottles. She kicked off her shoes and let her feet sink into the deep white carpet, then fell back on the magnificent bed. She laughed. For a girl with no job at all and doubtful prospects, she was set up quite nicely.

Trish marched into Angie's room, a martini in one hand and a cigarette in the other.

"Will this do?" Trish said. "Not a bad little shack? It would even impress Dallas." She crossed the room and walked out onto the terrace. "Fix a drink and come sit out here," she ordered. "Enjoy the view before the light goes."

Angie made herself a gin and tonic and joined Trish. It was a different ocean out there, dark and forbidding, nothing like Florida or the Caribbean.

"A good swimmer who headed straight out would wash up in Europe," Trish said. "One day, that's what I'm going to do—walk into the ocean and see how far I can go."

There was a catch in her friend's voice and Angie glanced at her anxiously. The strain on Trish's face had been bothering her all day.

"What are you talking like that for?" Angie demanded. "Are you going to talk to me or not?"

Trish shrugged and pulled her sweater around her body.

"Don't mind me, Angie," she said. "I just get depressed sometimes."

"How can I not mind you? You're my closest friend, for heaven's sake. Trish, what's the matter?"

"Sam," Trish said honestly. "Things haven't worked out the way I imagined," she said. "Sure, I've got everything money can buy, but that's all I've got. Sam is . . . well . . . Sam's a very tough guy on Wall Street and he's the same at home. When he comes home at all. I hardly see him, maybe once a week. And when we're together, it's as if he doesn't like me very much. Some of his demands . . . look, I shouldn't talk about it, not even to you. But I can't thank you enough for coming up here. If things get too bad, I know I've got you on my side." She turned to go. "We better go dress for dinner," she said. "Forget what I was talking about, please."

Angie watched her friend carefully all evening, marking the faint lines of strain around her eyes, the general body tension. It wasn't that Trish had aged, but that something had taken away her vivacity. Was it Sam? What might he have done?

Dinner was casual by Newport standards. Sam had been delayed in New York but his guests were there: the chief of his America's Cup syndicate, Ed Barrow, and the skipper of the 12-meter yacht, Jim Davis, and three yachting couples from New York. The men were in yachting blazers and slacks and the women in short dresses. The staff did its best to conceal their disapproval. Neither Trish nor Angie knew anything about sailing, particularly the esoteric world of the America's Cup, so they nodded and smiled their way through dinner.

"No," the yacht club commodore on Angie's left said emphatically, "it would be unthinkable to lose. The trophy's been ours for one hundred twenty-nine years. It's going to stay with us. Right, Davis?" He glared at the skipper seated across the table from him.

"Whatever you say, Commodore," Davis said. "You guys have certainly bent the rules far enough to give us the edge. But," he winked at Angie, "one of these years some damned foreigner you wouldn't let in the doors of your club is going to come along and surprise us all."

"Not in my time, fella!" the commodore snapped. "Not in yours, either, I trust. It wouldn't be pleasant to be associated with a failure that dismal. And it wouldn't be pleasant to be the skipper who lost the cup." He glowered at Davis again.

"Yes, I feel the weight I'm carrying. I guess I'd have to emigrate or something if we lost."

She warmed to Davis. He seemed the only man in the room not in awe of the battered old cup. Yet he was the sailor charged with the task. She looked him over as he chatted with Trish. He was of medium height but his body looked all muscle. Like other top sportsmen she had met, Jim Davis gave the impression of being wound up tight, nervous energy waiting to be released. His features were sharp, but relieved by dazzling white teeth and flashing green eyes against the mahogany tan that came from months at sea. His hair was blond and close cropped, precise and purposeful, like the rest of him.

He caught her looking at him and raised his wineglass to her. She smiled back and their gazes held.

The company took coffee and brandy in the library where Ed Barrow produced a box of video cassettes and showed endless footage of previous America's Cup races. Angie watched for a while, bored to death. Finally she slid out of her chair and stepped through the French doors to the wide terrace. The cool summer night air revived her and she leaned against a white stone column, drinking in the night scents and welcoming the silence.

"They take it awfully seriously, don't they?" Jim Davis said softly, moving out of the dark to stand beside her. "Still, if it were my five million invested in the boat, I would, too. But I'm just the skipper and I only have to steer the damned thing." She said nothing, intent on watching his face. "All those old farts from the New York Yacht Club parading around in straw hats and carrying on like each Cup campaign was World War III. I have been known to act disrespectful, at times."

She believed him.

"Why do you do it?" she asked.

"I love to sail," he said, "and the Cup, for all the bullshit surrounding it, is still the greatest contest on the water. Besides, I love to win. I've never been a loser." He looked at her carefully. "I see something I want, I try to get it. Usually I succeed."

His brashness was not his most appealing quality. But it was an essential part of him, as was the way he moved on the balls of his feet, like a fighter, and the way he looked right into her eyes as he spoke, confident she understood all he meant.

"You're very confident, Mr. Davis," she said. "About your sailing. About yourself."

"Why not? And call me Jim, please. As for confidence, you look like you could use a little. What have you been doing since the fiasco in Washington?"

"None of your business," she said sharply. She did not like the scandal coming at her out of left field.

"I'm *in* the business," he said easily. "I own a little broadcast group out on the Coast. It hasn't done nearly so well since they fired you. I think they were crazy to do it. You're a natural."

The video session had broken up and the rest of the dinner party drifted out onto the terrace. There was a round of farewells and the guests moved down the broad steps to their waiting limousines. Davis left with the others.

"Sorry it was so boring," Trish said when they were back inside. "Sam had arranged it, so I had to go along with it. He badly wants to be the American defender in this race, and being nice to the yachting crowd is part of his campaign."

Sam Hardy arrived late the next day and with his arrival the atmosphere in the house changed. He was a generous host, but Angie felt he didn't care whether they were there or not. Hardy was all high-powered business. He spent most of his time on the phone, or dictating to his two secretaries. He might as well have stayed in New York.

And his coming brought a change in Trish. She seemed almost afraid of Sam, and glad to get out of the house. She was frankly avoiding him.

"Hey, try and relax," Angie said as she and Trish strolled down Thames Street in the warm afternoon sun. "You're all wound up, Trish."

"Sorry," her friend said. "It's just this summer is developing into a bigger production than I was expecting."

They walked out onto the wharf where the syndicate boat was slipped. The guards bowed them past and they stood under the sleek yellow hull of the yacht. It looked lovely and fast but it didn't look like several million dollars, not to Angie.

"It's a bit fragile to be carrying all the hopes of America's yachting world, isn't it?" Jim Davis was standing behind them, wearing tattered shorts and scuffed boating shoes. Sweat was running down his hairy brown chest. He looked like an untamed animal—lithe, challenging, dangerous.

"Hi, Jim," Trish said. "We just stopped by to keep an eye on Sam's investment. He's too busy making more money to come down to the docks."

"No need for him to," Davis said. "The boat's in good hands. Just so long as Sam keeps signing the checks." He turned to Angie. "Bored? I don't blame you. The preparations would put anyone to sleep. But wait till the racing begins. It'll really turn you on. Like making love. Hours and hours of preparation for fifteen minutes of ecstasy."

Angie flushed. It wasn't just his bold remark but the nearness of him, the musky maleness of his body. His eyes met hers, challenging. He could have her and they both knew it.

"Cut it out, you two," Trish muttered, half in jest. "People are watching."

Davis laughed. He didn't care what anyone thought.

"You want to have dinner tonight, Angie?" he asked. "I'll show you the other side of Newport, the side the rich don't see."

He picked her up at the house just before seven, and all the way into town, sitting beside him in the little red BMW, Angie wondered what she had let herself in for. But Jim Davis had taken charge of her and she was happy to abandon herself to him.

They drifted through a succession of waterfront bars, the ones the tourists didn't visit. Their fellow drinkers were fishermen and sailors and they all seemed to know and like Jim. In most of the places they visited she was the only woman. But she was accepted because of him, and if the talk of winds and tides and great races was beyond her, nobody cared.

"It's a good town, Newport, if you can get away from all the bullshit that goes on in the grand houses," he said. They were sitting under the stars at a table looking out over the harbor. The clam chowder and the pan-fried fish had been perfect. But Angie had scarcely tasted the food or even felt the effects of the wine: she was besotted by his company.

"Yes," he continued, "I could have lived here if I hadn't gotten myself caught up in the rat race. As it is, I have to work quite hard six months of the year, running the stations, so I can sail for the other six months." He glanced across her. "That's the arrangement I have with my wife. I give her and her family business half the year and the rest of the time is mine." He waited for a reaction.

So then, he was married. So what? She had known there'd be no future with him. What sort of reaction had he expected?

After dinner they strolled along the docks and he slipped an arm around her shoulders to ward off the chill of the fog. She felt him against her, all muscle, but warm. He steered her down one of the wharves and out over the water to a docklight glowing yellow in the shrouds of gray fog.

"Up here," he said softly, taking her hand and leading her along a narrow gangway of a huge motor cruiser tied to the wharf. He unlocked the door to the main cabin and they stepped inside. It was dry and warm. The cabin was lit only from the docklight, but she could see it was large and comfortable.

"It's one of the syndicate boats," he explained. "Sam doesn't believe in stinting on anything, thank God. You want a drink?"

"No," she said, and waited for him to direct her.

He took her hand and led her back through the boat to a cozy sleeping cabin. He turned on a soft lamp above a big V-shaped bed, looked at her steadily, then went to her and embraced her. His kiss was hard, as was his body against hers. She yielded to him, melting into his strength, and they stayed locked together for minutes, silently exploring each other, delighted. He broke away for a moment and turned off the light. She could still see him, dimly, as he slid out of his clothes. He came back to her, naked, and gently removed her clothes. When she was naked he dropped to his knees and put his strong arms around the back of her thighs and pulled her against him. She felt the stubble of his cropped hair against her belly, his cool, knowing lips on her thighs. She gasped as his tongue probed her and then she was pressing him on, harder and harder, moving faster and faster, until she came in a dizzying surge. She would have fallen but for the arms still gripping her; she had no sense of balance because all her senses were concentrated where his eager tongue caressed her. She slowly pulled him up to her and they embraced again, then he carried her to the bed.

She could see all his body, even in that dim light. Just beneath the smooth brown skin was a layer of rock-hard muscle, rippling as he moved. Her fingers played across his chest and she brushed his nipples before moving down over the flat belly to the tangle of tightly curled hair. He shuddered as her cool hand encircled him, straining against her as she stroked him. His weapon felt like a steel spring, rigid but giving slightly, coiled energy waiting to be released. She wanted that energy inside her but she also wanted to prolong the passion sweeping her. She released her grip on him and he lay down. She knelt over his body so her breasts were brushing his penis. He moved his hands down and took the twin globes and squeezed them together, entrapping himself so his huge member was moving within the soft pocket of flesh. The head was only inches from her lips, reaching out for her, imploring her, and she bent a little and took it, silky smooth, bursting with vitality, into her mouth. They were connected now and a current of sexual energy flowed between them. He reached around her and entered her with his rough sailor's fingers, and as she rocked back on his hand and forward on his weapon she felt herself come in a torrent of passion.

She felt him close to release, too, and was glad

when he gently pulled her up beside him and turned her on her back. He spread her legs wide and knelt between them, and she looked down and shuddered with anticipation. He was, it seemed impossible, even bigger now and she watched as he slowly entered her, filling her to the brim, bringing her instantly to the brink of ecstasy. He stayed like that, kneeling over her, playing her body, thrusting deep then withdrawing almost totally. At last he gave up all pretense of being in control and let his body lock with hers. They rocked and heaved against each other and came together in a crescendo, him so deep inside her she could feel their pubic bones against each other. At last they were finished and he collapsed, his damp brow resting on her shoulder.

"You're magnificent," he gasped. "I've almost never felt like that." She could feel him slipping out of her. "I didn't want it to end," he said. "I want it to go on forever."

Angie let her fingers run through her hair. It had been so good for her, too, but she didn't want to tell him in words: she let her body talk, instead, soft and pliant against him, giving everything, wanting to be taken again when he was ready.

As they lay there they heard giggling from the dock, then footsteps coming up the gangway.

"Oh, shit!" Jim whispered. "Visitors."

They lay still as the new arrivals entered the main cabin, listening carefully as the party moved around. There was the clink of bottles, laughter, mumbled speech.

Jim slipped away from her and padded silently across the cabin to lock their door. Then he came back to bed, his arm around her and his hand gently stroking her breast.

"We're stuck here until they go," he whispered. "I'm glad."

But the intrusion had broken the magic spell for Angie. She didn't like being trapped in their cabin and eavesdropping on the next-door party as well. She could hear every word through the bulkhead—a man and two girls, all the voices slurred with alcohol.

"Get your clothes off," the man ordered. She'd heard that voice before.

"It's bloody Sam!" Jim whispered. "Oh, God, if he's staging one of his orgies we could be here for hours."

"Hurry up," Sam Hardy commanded. "You, Trixie, go down on her. That's right, that's right. Now sixty-nine each other. Good, good."

Angie could hear the sound of flesh against flesh, the gasps and moans and—she imagined—even Sam's labored breathing. The sexual tableau played on, nobody talking for a while.

"Harder, harder," he said after the long silence. "You're both loving this, you sluts. Filthy little dykes, you deserve to be punished."

There was more scuffling and then Angie heard a loud slap, then another.

"Ow!" one of the girls cried, and there was a sound of something rushing through the air and another slap, louder than the other. Both girls seemed to be crying real tears.

"Shut up," Sam said hoarsely. "You know what I'm paying you for."

The blows came faster now and the girls were crying hysterically.

"What should we do?" she whispered. "He's really hurting them."

"Keep quiet," he whispered back. "Sam's into S

and M, that's all. They knew what he wanted when they came."

"Dirty girls, wicked little girls," Sam gasped between the rain of blows. "I'll beat all the bad out of you."

It went on and on, and Angie tried to shut out the sounds until she thought she, herself, was screaming.

At last there was quiet, then the sound of people dressing, stumbling around the cabin. Then a banging of doors and footsteps going back down the gangway.

"It's awful, Jim," she said. "He's married to my closest friend."

"A lot of people play strange games," Jim said. "Maybe the risk of discovery heightens their pleasure. I don't know. I've always been boringly straight myself. But don't worry about your girlfriend. If Sam's taking out his lusts on hired women he's not whipping Trish, is he?"

At breakfast, Angie felt awkward with both of them. Looking across the table at Sam—bluff, urbane, in control—she worried for Trish. She had, in the middle of the night, recalled her friend's unexpressed fears.

Sam folded the *Wall Street Journal* and bestowed a smile on them both. They were breakfasting on the terrace, the early sun warming them.

"You haven't forgotten the Mansions' ball tomorrow night?" he said. "I promised Lyle we'd lend him a little moral support. Poor bastard, his family terrifies him."

Trish glanced at Angie and said, "I don't think I told you about it. We'll enjoy ourselves, I'm sure. It's one of the important parties. All the old-money crowd will be there—none of the Cup racers, except us. The old crowd doesn't really approve of the America's Cup crowd in their exclusive resort. I almost think they'll be pleased if someone does win the Cup away from America!''

"I guess I have something to wear," Angie said slowly, trying to conceal her panic. Richard Mansion would be there. But she would have to face him sometime. Better to get it over with.

"I brought a closetful of ball gowns," Trish said cheerfully. "There'll be something for you. But what about an escort for Angie, Sam?"

"Well, you can't bring Jim Davis," he said, grinning. "I'm only barely acceptable because I'm a friend of the Mansion family and I own a yacht. But they wouldn't have a skipper in their house. No, if it's all right with you, Angie, Lyle's kinda expecting you to be his date. He was real pleased you're staying with us."

She forced a smile.

"That will be fine," she said. "At least I know the man, so it's not a blind date." Sam grinned at her.

The three of them drove the short distance to Atlantic House in Sam's black Rolls. The Mansion place was lit up like a great ocean liner and the sweeping drive was jammed with limousines edging slowly up to the massive portico. She could see couples moving up the portico and was glad she'd borrowed the blue silk gown from Trish. The crowd oozed wealth, good taste, old diamonds. A red-liveried footman helped them from the car. As she stepped out into the mild night air, walking with Sam and Trish across the gleaming marble, Angie steeled herself: this was *their* territory, the place of the clan she hated—but she was damned if she would be intimidated by the Mansions.

The sound of an orchestra greeted them as they entered the paneled reception area. Immediately she saw Lyle Mansion hurrying toward them.

"Welcome," he said, smiling shyly. "Sam, Trish." He bowed. "Angie. I'm so glad you could come. I hope it won't be boring for you." He led them into the great ballroom where fifty couples were dancing already, with more to arrive. "I can't stand these affairs myself," he confided to Angie, "but it's one of the things our family does." He steered them around the dancers and on to the next room, a large, vaulted conservatory with nests of tables and chairs scattered throughout. He selected a table for them and nodded to a waiter for champagne.

Angie tried to relax, concentrating on Lyle's amiable chatter about who was there and who was coming. And then he was there, looming over their table, casting his shadow over the four of them.

"The old man wants to see you," Richard Mansion said to his brother. He was about to turn away when his glance fell on Angie. She met his gaze steadily. Richard was almost unchanged; his hair had thinned and he'd put on a little weight, but that was all, and there was still the air of a man used to getting anything he desired.

"Well, hello," he said. "What a surprise. Angie Waring. My summer intern all grown up. I followed your television career with interest until it was . . . interrupted." He looked quickly around the rest of the table. "Sam, hi. Welcome to the family summer place. This must be your wife." He jerked his head at Lyle. "Move it. Don't keep Alex waiting. I'll sit with your friends until he's finished with you."

Richard Mansion settled in his brother's chair and surveyed them, the man in command of a great house, the host pleased to bestow on them the pleasure of his sought-after company.

"A big year, Sam," he said. "The one in which we win back control of this country and send that sniveling little peanut farmer back where he came from. Some of us are sorry you haven't been able to make your usual effort for the party. Too tied up with this damned boat race?"

"I've been steering clear of politics this time, Richard," Sam said. "I've been burned too many times. Anyway, I'm not sure I could be a Reagan man, not after the arguments your brother's newspapers have presented against him."

"Lyle and his crowd of limousine liberals haven't backed a winner since God knows when. You come back to the strength, Sam. We'll be running this country again, real soon. And we remember our friends."

Angie watched him with loathing tempered by wry amusement.

"And what are *you* going to do when the good times come back?" Mansion demanded of her. "Someone told me you dropped out after your Washington scandal. You can't hide forever, you know. You've paid the price. In fact, the way I hear it, we owe you. Quite a few people appreciate the way you took the rap for Beckworth. There are those who think he's still got a big future in the party, though I'm damned if I can see why."

She looked at him fully, without flinching.

"Anything I did for Ken wasn't meant as a sacrifice for your party," she said coolly.

"Well," he said, rising from the table, "when you're ready to come back into television, just let me know. I'm sure we can find a spot for you somewhere. You really were quite good."

Even Sam must have noticed something in Angie's face as she watched Mansion amble away from the table, through the crowd of backslappers and acolytes.

"A bit patronizing, our Richard," Sam said. "But he does run a damn fine network. The shares touched eighty-seven this week. Richard's problem is he can't see anyone else's point of view. Like, he thinks Lyle's an imbecile for sticking with the newspaper chain. But I respect Lyle for that."

"Do you, Sam?" Angie said. She tried to phrase the words carefully. "I would have thought Lyle wasn't your kind of guy. He seems so quiet and, oh, I don't know, unsure of himself."

"And I'm just another Wall Street bully," Sam laughed. "Yeah, we are different but I find Lyle's worth listening to, if you can get him talking at all. God knows, he's had a hard enough time getting his voice heard in this family. He'd probably have been happier—and done more good, by his lights—if he'd taken a safe Senate seat years ago."

"You never told me how you and Lyle got to be buddies," Trish said. "I'm intrigued by the friendship. Most of your friends are macho, macho, macho."

"You can cut that out," he said, scowling. "I like to know people right across the spectrum. But if you're really interested, someone referred him to me when he had a big problem with that whore of a wife. Luckily she OD'd before she dragged him down with her. Then came a few problems with the kids and I pulled a few strings to keep them out of the headlines, fixed some cops to drop charges. The poor bastard hasn't had it easy."

"Richard Mansion had a son, didn't he?" Angie

asked. "I recall something about him having trouble with his wife, too, and taking the boy away from her."

"Yeah," Sam said, glancing around to be sure they weren't being overheard. "He married some titled English broad and it was a disaster from the word go. One story has it she slipped away on their wedding night and screwed her first cousin. Whatever, the marriage was a disaster and Richard pulled in every political debt he was owed and grabbed the kid. Little Davey: Richard gave that kid everything, the best schools, travel. You know what happened? Davey Mansion is a raging faggot. He's on Christopher Street, working on some gay newspaper. He's about, oh, twenty-five, I'd say." Sam laughed bitterly. "So he's still in media, but not the kind his old man wanted for him."

"When I hear about your friends," Trish said, "I'm glad I'm a simple Texas girl. Hell, don't we know anybody who's happy and normal?"

"Happy? Normal?" He grunted. "We're all too busy making money, keeping it, and building power bases to be normal. Ordinary people can sit back and let life roll over them. Our kind can't. And you know something? We wouldn't have it any other way." He settled back and looked them both over. "It's a different world, where we operate. There's no time for niceties. But ladies like you two don't need to worry about any of it. Just leave it all to us."

Angie caught Trish's eye for a second. Did Sam really believe half the things he said?

"I'm sorry to have left you for so long," Lyle said quietly. "Father's at an age when he expects everyone to answer his demands instantly. I guess he feels time is running out." He smiled his soft little smile and sat down. "I hope Richard kept you company, Angie."

"Oh, sure," she said. "I think he offered me a job, too. Kind of suggested my time in the wilderness was over and the party owed me a favor, so why not come aboard the Mansion network."

Lyle frowned. "I wouldn't want to see you do that," he said. "Ted Buchanan particularly asked me to speak to you about coming back to the *Trib*. It's a real struggle, that newspaper. Ted and I need your talent. If you *are* preparing to work again, I want you to think of us first. Please."

She smiled at him then. His whole approach was so different. This was no wheeler and dealer, no buyer and seller of people. He seemed genuinely to want her and, more important, for her to want his organization. Among this crowd of ruthless men, he seemed like such a nice person.

"I think you've almost got me, Lyle," she said slowly. "It's time to come in from the cold. But am I thought of as a dumb broad who was just part of Ken Beckworth's baggage? Because if I am, there's no way I'll be of any use to you, not in Washington."

"You don't have to worry about that," Lyle said earnestly. "Everyone who matters has a good idea of what really happened. I think you're quite admired in some circles for not blowing the whistle."

"Your brother said something similar," she said. "It doesn't make me love Washington more, to think I'm beloved there because I covered up for someone."

"It's the way it is, though," he said. "No one wants to know the truth, either, not while Beckworth is still a man on the rise. All they care about is, you took your lumps and didn't take anyone down with you. It's not fair, but it's politics." He paused a moment. "I just want your by-line back in the *Tribune.*"

Angie felt she had made her decision. She had surprised herself, and her spirits rose. She danced with Lyle three times and they went in to supper together. She continued to like Lyle. He had one passion that burned right through his mild manner, a total belief in newspapers and their power. And she liked it that he didn't care if Richard dominated the ball, if Richard's stock soared while his own didn't. He was, simply, a nice gentle man trying to maintain his standards in a most ungentle world.

"I'm really enjoying myself," she said to him late in the evening, as they danced. "Thank you for inviting me. I didn't think it would be such a lot of fun."

"So far my family's been on its best behavior," Lyle said. "Newport seems to bring out our better side. But don't count on it. Either of my sisters is liable to do something terrible. And if father has a couple of drinks too many he'll come out here on the dance floor in his wheelchair, stop the music, and send everyone home because he's bored with them."

She didn't say anything. She wouldn't pretend with him, and she'd followed the exploits of the Mansion girls over the years. Ellen and Gloria Mansion, in their forties, were still changing husbands and lovers at a breathtaking pace, still highly visible on the international glitter circuit, still fine grist for the scandal sheets.

"We really are an awful family," Lyle said. "You'd be well advised not to get involved with us."

"It's only a job you're offering me," she said, smiling. "And anyway, every family has a few skeletons. I don't believe yours can be so different from other families."

"Come to lunch tomorrow and see for yourself," he urged.

Surprisingly, she agreed.

Lunch with the whole Mansion clan *was* something of an ordeal, but Angie managed to get through it by pretending she was there as a reporter. Thus protected, she was able to observe them with some detachment.

Richard was polite to her but distant, which suited her fine. To his younger brother he was downright rude. He talked over Lyle, derided the few comments Lyle made, and repeatedly demonstrated that he was in command there. He deferred only to his father.

Ellen and Gloria appeared desperate. But where the gossip columns had suggested a life in the fast lane, Angie saw only two unhappy, hardened women using gin and vicious gossip to keep the world at bay. They drank martinis right through lunch and sniped at each other, at the rest of the family, and at the people who had been at the ball.

There were about a dozen of the next generation of Mansions at lunch, all with good skin and fine teeth and an air of spoiled boredom. Angie spoke only with two of them, Lyle's children, Emily and Curtis. Emily was fourteen. She would have been pretty but for her dull eyes and sullen face. She just nodded when her father presented her to Angie, and rarely spoke during lunch. Curtis, a couple of years older, was a good-looking boy, already taller than his father, and amiable in conversation.

"You're staying with Mr. Hardy," he said, "so I guess you're involved in the America's Cup. It's so exciting, really livened up Newport, which needs it. I sailed in Mr. Hardy's yacht before the serious trials began. They're really fun—not like this crowd.'' He waved his hands around the loggia to include his family and the other guests sitting at sun-dappled tables. ''None of these people ever worked a day in their lives. Not real work, anyway. But the guys involved in the twelve-meters, they've got a real challenge, something worth doing.''

''Don't be too tough on all of us, Curt,'' his father protested. ''What about me? I work damned hard on the newspapers. And I'm proud of my work.''

''Oh, Dad,'' the boy said, ''you can't count that. It was handed to you on a silver platter.'' He grinned and Lyle smiled back. She was glad to see the easy affection between them. ''And anyway,'' he continued, ''your efforts don't make any money, which means you're letting down the Mansion tradition.'' He shook his head in mock despair.

The meal was a casual buffet and the guests moved from table to table, talking and laughing. Over dessert Lyle led Angie over to his father.

''Dad, I'd like you to meet Angie Waring,'' he said. ''Angie's spending the summer with Sam Hardy.''

The old man, anchored in his wheelchair, gave her a long stare. His eyes were dark blue and penetrating. He surveyed her with the arrogance of age and power before he spoke.

''Yes.'' He nodded, ''I used to see you on 'Nationwide.' Quite good, considering the network. They canned you. Why?''

She felt herself blushing and was furious. The rude old bastard, sitting there glowering and flexing his massive torso to demonstrate his authority over all of them.

''We had a falling-out,'' she said carefully. ''But it

had nothing to do with my work. I was the best thing on that show and everyone in the industry knows it."

He smiled then, a tortured smile, a split in the wrinkled brown face.

"Good for you," he said. "Don't let the bastards get you down, eh? It's a badge of honor to be fired by at least one network. They're all run by timid little people who watch only ratings instead of watching what goes on the screen. Even my network. A bunch of accountants! And that most certainly includes you, Richard," he snapped at his other son, who was just joining them.

"You're getting soft, Richard," Alex Mansion continued. "All the new shows are over budget. And the deals you're doing with sponsors—you're not going to get last year's profit, much less make the gains we need." Old Mansion was enjoying himself: it was far more fun, and more effective, to chew people out in public than to be discreet.

"Dad, I don't think this is the place . . ." Richard protested. Angie was happy to see him looking so disconcerted, the humble office boy being dressed down by the chairman.

"Just get with it, Richard," the old man snapped. "And listen to me. Have you met Miss Waring? She has some talent. Even those idiots at XYZ recognized that. She's worth having a look at."

"I do know Miss Waring, Dad," Richard said. "I gave her her first job, interning in Miami. And," he said proudly, "I offered her a job last night."

"So you're coming aboard," Alex Mansion said. "Good."

"I'm afraid not, Mr. Mansion," Angie said. "At least, not on television. Lyle also offered me a job, and that's the one I'm going to take, with the *Tribune*."

The old man nodded approvingly.

"So you're not one of those smart-aleck young people who think newspapers are finished," he said. "I like that. I've still got faith in them, although God knows I get little support from other people. And I get no profits at all," he added, frowning at Lyle. "But you just come up with the big stories and we'll take care of the numbers." The conversation was over. Alex Mansion signaled for his nurse and had himself wheeled indoors without saying goodbye to anyone.

She watched Richard's face as he stared after the old man. There was something close to hatred there. As he turned back to them, she saw it was indeed hatred—hatred for both his father and his brother. And, by association, for Angie. She almost flinched away from his gaze, but then she controlled herself. There was no reason, she realized at last, for her to be afraid of Richard Mansion. He had done the worst that could be done to her and she had lived through it.

Richard took a step toward them and she stood facing him, prepared for anything, even to hit him if she had to.

"You've made a big mistake, Angie," he said. "Two. The first was casting your lot with Lyle. He's a failure." He spoke as if his brother weren't there. "The second was rejecting my offer. You'll regret it forever."

"No," she said, icy-calm. "Television has nothing to offer me. And I agree with your father: the people who work in television leave a lot to be desired."

Richard turned abruptly and left. Lyle was pale but he tried to joke.

"My brother takes the world very seriously," he said. "He's not quite as bad as he seems, you know. It can't be easy, being the one Father has chosen to take over the empire." He smiled at her. "One good thing, though, is your decision to work with us. I'm thrilled and Ted Buchanan's going to be too. When do you want to see Ted and work things out? I'll fly him up here from Washington, if you like. A break would do him good."

"Whatever suits you," Angie said. "But I guess I can't start work until after the Cup race. I promised Trish I'd stick with her for the whole campaign. So let's leave it awhile."

"The end of September's fine," Lyle said. "I'll tell Ted."

The next two weeks suddenly turned into a real holiday for Angie because, at long last, she had something to look forward to. She and Trish spent their days on the beach and the tennis courts, or strolling the cobbled streets of the old town. There was great excitement in the air now, with the defense of the Cup only a week away. The house had become campaign headquarters, with Sam presiding over an army of people who worked day and night to reduce as far as possible the role luck could play in the racing. Sam even had two lawyers there full time, to handle any rule interpretations that might arise in the vicious match-racing series.

"Now I can see why Sam is such a success in business," Angie said one afternoon, standing in the gallery looking down on the ballroom where the operation headquarters were installed. "He was born to command."

"Yes. If you want to get along with Sam Hardy you learn to take orders," Trish said. "You do what you're told, blindly, even if it's something abhorrent to you.''

''What's wrong, Trish?'' Angie asked for the third time that month. ''Is it something we can talk about?'' For a moment she recalled the hookers. Surely he wasn't putting Trish through the same humiliation. She put her hand on Trish's arm. ''I know you're not very happy. Can't I help you?''

''Happy!'' Trish said. ''Who wouldn't be happy in my position? I'm rich, mistress of all I survey.'' She laughed a cold laugh that hung in the air between them. ''No, Angie, there's nothing to talk about. I'll get along. Come on, let's take a walk along the cliffs before it gets cold.''

They strolled arm in arm across the lawns to the gravel path that separated the neat turf of the huge cottages from the wind-bent scrub at the cliff edge.

''You don't seem to be seeing any more of Jim Davis,'' Trish said. ''I thought you two were going to be the big summer item. He's quite attractive.''

''He is,'' Angie said. ''We had our little fling and maybe we would have carried it on a few more times, but now he's so tied up with the race. I saw him the other morning and he mumbled something about would I meet him if he broke the team curfew. It all sounded childish, so I said no. Anyway, he's made it very clear there's no future with him. He's staying with his rich wife forever.''

''Why should that bother you? You're not in the marriage market. You never were. I thought a guy like Davis was exactly what you wanted—a lot of fun and no commitments.''

''So did I,'' Angie said. ''But some days I'm not so sure anymore. I wonder who's going to take care of me when I'm old, when I can't work. I know it's unliberated to talk that way, but sometimes I worry. Anyway, I'm not worrying now. Thank God I decided to accept the job on the *Trib*. I feel like I'm going home after drifting a long, long time."

"Back in Washington," Trish said. "Remember how we were then, so confident, so sure we were going to make it? Nothing seemed impossible in those days. Now, nothing seems worth achieving."

"Trish," Angie protested, "you can do anything you want. Politics, social work, public relations. Why don't you get into something?"

"Sam wouldn't like it," she said. "Sam has to know where I am every minute of the day. Not that he's possessive—he's just afraid I'll be in the wrong place with the wrong people and make him look bad. Sam doesn't like loose ends."

"Why don't you have a baby?" Angie asked suddenly. "You and Sam have so much to give a child."

"Forget it," Trish said. "Sam isn't interested in children. No, I'm trapped in a very rich cocoon and it's my own damn fault. You told me not to rush into this marriage but I wouldn't listen."

They turned around and walked back as the cold wind picked up from the Atlantic and ended the summer day. They were both shivering as they hurried into the entrance hall. There was a note for Angie on the message tray and she ripped it open as Trish stood waiting. The maid had scribbled the message from Angie's mother.

"Your father is very sick. Please call at once and be prepared to come home."

She found a telephone in one of the anterooms and dialed the old, familiar number. When her mother answered she sounded old and tired and sad.

"Daddy's very sick. He had a massive stroke on the

golf course and he's not responding well at all. They don't think he'll live much more than a few days."

"I'm coming right now, Mom," she said, her voice catching. "I should be able to get a plane from Providence to New York this evening, and then I'll take whatever's available to West Palm Beach tonight. I'll be there around midnight. I'll get a cab to the house. Will you be at the hospital, or where?"

"I'll wait for you at home, after I've stayed with him through the evening. I'll tell him you're coming. He understands what people are saying. The news will help him hang on awhile. Angie, we both love you."

Trish swung into action, helping her pack, phoning the airlines, driving her the one-hour trip to Providence.

"Hope for the best, Angie," Trish said as she kissed her goodbye. "Call me when you want to. Thank you for holding my hand all summer."

"Take care of yourself," Angie replied. "Try and be happy. Something's happened to you that's not good, I know." She looked at her friend, once so strong and self-sufficient, now so nervous and unhappy. She hated leaving her but she had to.

It was a rotten flight down the coast, first fog then turbulence, and she had to waste an hour in New York before her Florida connection. Even the Moonies gave up on the airport that late in the evening and Angie sat in a near-deserted bar nursing a gin and tonic and feeling about as terrible as she had ever felt. The worst thing was, she wasn't consumed by grief. Yes, she wished she had spent more time with her father, maybe understood him better. But it was only on television that children and parents were close: in real life everyone was too busy growing up, getting ahead, to be so close. She knew her father had always loved her; she hoped he knew she loved him.

She cried on the plane, her face pressed against the blank window. She cried for her father and for herself, for the way things might have been and never were. And then, before the plane began its descent into the familiar airport, she took herself to the bathroom, repaired her makeup, and told the person in the mirror to grow up.

Her mother was waiting at home and they embraced as the taxi headed back down the driveway. It felt good to hold each other, but different, too. Now they were standing together as adults brought there by a common grief. Angie was no longer a protected child, but someone living alone in the world.

"Thanks for coming so quickly, darling," her mother said. She seemed older, even smaller. Angie restrained an urge to pat her on the head. "There's no change. I don't think we should go back to the hospital tonight. Dr. Kitto says nothing will happen for a day or so. But there is no hope. There'll be a few minutes tomorrow when he'll be lucid and you can talk with him. He wants that very much, I can tell."

"So do I, Mom," she said. "There's so much I want to say to Daddy, about what he meant to me, to us. I feel like I've missed all the chances I ever had, chances to say these things over all the years. Now all I'm going to have is a few minutes at the end."

Her mother smiled gently.

"I had one good talk with him early today. I knew he could hear what I was saying, and I was reproaching myself for all the years I complained about being taken away from Boston and stuck down here. You know how I rattle on. Anyway, I was holding his hand and he squeezed it and I swear he winked at me. I think he always understood us, Angie."

They went to the hospital early, in bright fresh mocking sunshine. Everything around the neat white buildings was green and thriving and Angie thought of all the old people who came to Florida to die, people so out of place with the exuberant surroundings.

Her father lay very straight and spare in the high bed, his body hardly making a ridge in the starched sheet. He was white under his tan and his face had shrunk, leaving little folds of skin around his mouth and under his eyes. But the eyes saw, and he recognized her. She took the limp hand resting on top of the sheet and held it gently.

"Hello, Daddy," she said, her mouth close to his ear. "I came as soon as I could. Mom said she's going to need my help, getting you up and around again."

There was the faintest pressure on her hand and his eyes moved.

"But you'll have to hurry," Angie said. "Because, after all this time, I'm going back to work. Not television, 'cause I'm sick of that. I'm going back to the *Tribune*, Daddy, in Washington. They want me to be a columnist again."

This time the pressure on her hand was greater and the eyes were brighter. She looked across the bed to her mother and saw the joy in her face.

Her father settled farther down in the bed then and his hand slid from hers. The old eyes closed. Gentle, regular breating was the only sign that he was still with them.

"We'll sit awhile longer," her mother said quietly.

They stayed on opposite sides of the bed another hour, silent, watching, thinking about their lives with this man. The nurses came and went quietly, not meeting their eyes. They would not give false hope: it was a hospital more attuned to death than to recovery.

In midmorning they tiptoed from the room and moved silently out into the sun.

"Was that true?" May asked. "About going back to the *Tribune*. Because even if it wasn't, you couldn't have given him a greater gift. He's been so upset about your career. He was so proud of you being a columnist. Much more than when you were on television. He always thought his talent—and mine, too, he used to allow—had gone to you."

"It's true," Angie said. "I decided a little while ago. I was going to tell you but I hadn't gotten around to it. I start back there next month. It'll be like going home."

"I'm happy," her mother said firmly. "It's where you belong, on a newspaper. We were both so worried about you, worried about what would happen when we weren't here anymore. Now we know you're going to be all right."

They spent the afternoon at the bedside. He opened his eyes twice and seemed to know they were there. They each held a hand and tried to send their own life flowing through him but by then they knew it was themselves they were comforting. He died as the sun went down.

They drove home in the dusk, not speaking. Inside the house they embraced silently for several minutes.

"I'll miss him so much," her mother said finally. "God, it was only a week ago we were sitting on the porch and he said, 'May, it's been a good life together. Thanks.' He was right. Never mind all the complaining I did. It was a good life.''

They didn't go to bed that night because, if they slept, it would mean his last day was over. They stayed awake until the sun came up.

Chapter Twelve

Ted ran through the happy throng, lurching slightly, and threw his arms around her. Would the glass of sticky eggnog in his hand spill down her back? He kissed her, a big kiss.

"I saw you here, deliberately standing under the mistletoe," he said. "I figured, now there is a girl who wants to be kissed. Everyone else is scared of you, but not old Ted." He stood there swaying gently and smiling at her. She kissed him back, giggling. He always made her feel like twelve years old.

"I don't know why anyone at the *Trib* would be scared of me," she said. "Unless they think I'm the editor's favorite."

"You are, you are," he said happily. "Even if I didn't already love you, there's the sales figures. We're up to twenty-three thousand a day. An awful lot of those new buyers are coming in because you're just about the best writer in town."

"No," she laughed, "it's because we've got the best paper. And"—she waved her hand around the

Trib's cafeteria, decorated for Christmas—"we've got the happiest staff. Not just happy tonight, happy all the time. You've brought a terrific group together, Ted. This is a marvelous paper."

"It helps to have an owner like Lyle," he said. "Look at him. You'd think he was some little guy writing for the business section, not one of the Mansions."

They watched Lyle standing at the bar, deep in conversation with a group of reporters and rewritemen. He didn't look like a publisher in his battered old tweed jacket, his manner diffident, being lectured to by the younger reporters. He was enjoying letting them badger him.

"He's a nice man," Angie said. "Extraordinary, considering his family."

Ted peered at her.

"I never did figure out what happened in Miami. But I knew you wouldn't just walk out without a reason. It had something to do with Richard Mansion, didn't it? He put the make on you?"

"Water under the bridge, Ted," she said. "It doesn't matter now."

"Okay. He turned out to be a real son-of-a-bitch," Ted said. "Quitting on him was one of the most satisfying things I ever did."

"Lyle's okay, isn't he?" she asked. "The *Trib*'s doing well and has great prospects. I was talking to him in the city room the other night and he seemed full of confidence."

"Sure, we're doing well," Ted confided. "If you consider cutting our losses from fourteen million a year to six million doing well. But Richard doesn't like red ink and he's not used to it. He'd get rid of the newspaper division in a second, if he could. I only hope the old man lives forever, because he's on our side. Much as I like Lyle, I think, without his father's support, we're doomed. I can't see him standing up to a concerted attack by Richard."

"I think he's a lot stronger than he looks," she said. "He's certainly not scared of the administration. This paper has so much editorial freedom . . . the White House really hates us."

"Yeah, I love it," Ted said. "The moment the powers that be start liking you, you've failed as a newspaper." He looked for another drink. "Angie? What's going on? Are you seeing anyone? You and I never get together anymore. And it's not because of that creep Beckworth. He *is* past history, isn't he?"

"Sure," she said. "Oh, he calls from time to time. I'm writing again, so I could be valuable to him. Can you believe that? But, no, he's past history. I'm not even living at Watergate any longer."

"When are you going to invite me to see your new apartment?" he asked boldly. What had become of the quiet deferential Ted? Was it just the liquor?

"It wouldn't work just now, Ted," she said quietly. "Not with you being my editor. You know that. Come on, let's circulate before the party breaks up."

He shrugged. "Okay," he said, "we'll circulate. There's a new blonde in Features who doesn't share your scruples about dating the boss."

But then Lyle approached them.

"I wanted to ask you two if you were busy on New Year's," he said, prepared as ever for rejection. "With no paper the next day, I wondered if you'd care to come to the house in Virginia. It'll be very dull, I guess, just me and the kids, but we could have lunch, go riding if the snow stops, maybe talk a little shop. Could you come?"

They both said they'd love to.

Lyle Mansion's home was big and comfortable, surrounded by seventy-five acres of woods and fields. Around all that, tract houses were encroaching. But on the estate itself, nothing intruded. The snow glistened against a cold sun and the hot toddy awaiting them in front of the huge fire looked and tasted wonderful.

"It's nice of you to spare me the day," Lyle said when they were settled. "I love having people down to this house, though I don't do it often enough. This is the place I feel most at home. Even the children are quite relaxed here."

Emily and Curt joined them for lunch, and both made the effort to be friendly. Curt was quick and funny, almost hyperactive. His eyes were so bright, his energy bubbling.

Emily still had the dull eyes Angie had noted in Newport. The girl tried hard to be part of the lunch company, nodding politely when spoken to, smiling. But she seemed to drift in her own world.

"Em, you've got the attention span of a cocker spaniel," her father laughed. "Mr. Buchanan was asking you about the newspaper business. Are you interested in it?"

"Sorry, Daddy," the girl said softly. "Yes. When I'm older I'd like to work a summer at the paper, here or in New York, see what it's all about. I don't think I could be a reporter, though. My English grades are awful."

"None of the young reporters can spell or construct a decent sentence," Ted said. "I wouldn't worry about grades. Enthusiasm, caring about getting a story first and getting it right, those are the things that matter.'' He smiled at her but Emily still didn't loosen up.

The sun was shining after lunch and the temperature had climbed above freezing, so Lyle suggested they all go riding.

''The men will have cleared the bridle paths now,'' he said. ''It'll be easy, just a little cold.''

The children said they'd pass and Ted, laughing about being a New York city boy, declined in favor of brandy and a cigar in front of the fire. Angie and Lyle stepped out into the cold crisp air and walked down to the stables together, talking happily, glad to be out and doing.

''What kind of rider are you?'' he asked. ''I don't want to put you on anything too high-spirited.''

''I rode some at school, but hardly at all since then. They say you never forget it, though, so I'm willing to try if you're willing to risk a horse!''

He selected a big gentle gray for her and they stood outside in the sun while grooms saddled it and Lyle's own chestnut hunter. From the rise they rode to, they could see across rolling snow-covered country to the distant mountains. Wisps of smoke rose from hidden chimneys and hung still and low in the pale blue sky. The only sound in the world was the sliding snow from dark green branches and the horses' breathing.

''It's beautiful, Lyle,'' she said, watching her breath fog the air. ''So beautiful it makes everything else seem unimportant. I don't know how you can tear yourself away from here.''

''Come back in the spring,'' he said. ''Then it's the loveliest place in the world.'' Sitting high in the saddle, he was a new Lyle Mansion. The diffidence was gone: he was in command. Walking their horses, they started down the hill toward a copse of beech trees.

"Yes," he continued, as their mounts gently jostled each other for position on the trail, "it's hard to leave at the start of the week, but much as I'm tempted to live the life of a country squire, I want to keep the newspaper going. Apart from my father, I'm the only member of the family who cares about the papers. Maybe my children will. I hope to leave it to them."

The snowplow had cleared a broad path for them through the woods and fields, and they let the horses find their own pace, first a trot then a canter. Angie was pleased with herself: after the first few minutes she was sitting well and letting the horse do all the work. Lyle was a most accomplished rider, in his element guiding his high-spirited mount over the slippery ground.

The snow was banked up on either side of the path, creating a white-walled tunnel down which they raced, the horses caught up in the feeling of freedom, the new world all around them. Angie's confidence grew and then they were at full gallop, shoulder to shoulder, the horses' hooves drumming below them. Her long hair flowed out from under the riding helmet, the cold air on her pink cheeks accenting the red tones in her hair. She glanced across at Lyle and grinned, then dug her heels into the gray. Her horse began to draw ahead of his mount, who responded to the challenge at once. She was in a world where all that mattered were the wind and the air, and the power of the horse. She wanted to shout for joy.

She didn't see the deer until they were on it. If it had run away from them everything would have been all right. But the creature jumped sideways and fell across the path. Lyle's chestnut rose in the air as if the deer were one more fence and she saw, in suspended seconds, the pure joy on Lyle's face as he and the horse flew above her. But her horse stumbled trying to go around the deer and, in full flight, crashed into the banked snow. Angie flew through the air and landed: she seemed to be gliding painlessly through a cold, white world. But then she struck something painfully hard and visions of red exploded in her skull. After that, all black and deathly cold.

She came to, cradled in his arms. His thick riding jacket was around her and his arms held her close. She looked up into his face and saw only concern and love. How strange, she thought, as, slowly, she came back to consciousness: he was looking at her with love.

"Lie still," he whispered. "There's nothing broken but you've got a bump on your forehead." He continued to cradle her, pressing a silver flask to her lips. The brandy burned wonderfully inside her and in a moment she was able to sit up.

"The horse, the horse," she stammered. "Is it all right?"

"A bit sore, like you're going to be." He smiled, one arm still around her shoulders. "But no permanent damage. You gave me a terrible scare."

She accepted another sip of brandy and tried to stand.

"No," he said firmly. "Just take it easy. You could have a concussion."

"And I could get pneumonia, lying here in the snow," she muttered. After a moment he helped her up. They were standing very close and she looked into his eyes and saw love again. She released his hand and stepped carefully out of the snow onto the path. Her horse was standing, head down, a few yards away, and she moved on unsteady legs to pat it.

It raised its head a little and gazed at her, as if ashamed. She put her arms around its neck. "Poor us," she murmured. The horse nuzzled her.

"If you're okay here for a few minutes I'll ride back to the house and get a car," Lyle said.

"Why?" she asked. "If the horse is okay, I'll ride back. Isn't that what you're supposed to do after a fall—jump right back on? And the horse feels guilty," she said with a grin.

"If you can, all right," he said. He walked around the gray and knelt and ran his hands over its legs. "Yes, he's all right. Have a little more brandy and see how you feel."

She felt fine, exhilarated. Later she would have a headache but just then all that mattered was that she had survived a great danger.

"I've got something for you," Ken Beckworth said. "A big story, but I can't talk about it over the phone. Will you meet me somewhere?"

She leaned her head against her hand, filled with loathing. Beckworth. But she couldn't avoid him for ever, and a source was a source.

"Where?" she said.

He gave her an address, a bar out near the National Institutes of Health in Maryland.

"No one goes there," he said. "It's safe. I'll see you at one-thirty this afternoon."

She found him in a back booth behind a martini. He had lost a lot of that confident swagger and when he stood to greet her Angie thought he looked like a man on the run, shifty, watchful. He forced a smile and signaled the waiter.

"Mineral water," she said. "I have to work a lot harder at the *Trib* than I did on television, so no drinking during the day."

He winced at the reminder of her former career, but kept up the smile anyhow.

"I think what you're doing now is so much more . . . meaningful," he pronounced. "You're the talk of the town. I see you scooped the *New York Times* and the *Post* on the health and welfare cutbacks last week. Good stuff, Angie."

"Cut the crap, Ken," she said. "You got me here to give me a story. Which means there's something in it for you. So talk."

"That's what I always liked about you, Angie," he said. "Right to the point. We were good together, weren't we?"

"We were goddamned awful together," she said wearily. "I don't want to remember. Just tell me what you've got."

"Okay," he said. "I'll give it to you and then we'll eat." He finished his drink, looked wistfully at it, then followed Angie's example and called for mineral water.

"There is," he said, "a wonderful scam going on in one of the Senate Defense Department subcommittees. A few of the senators and some generals at the Pentagon are getting very rich."

"Not another Pentagon waste story, please," she said. "We've got them coming out our ears."

"Not waste. Real corruption," he said, trying to build suspense. "This is a big one. What's been happening, some of the subcommittee members have been buying up big tracts of land, all across the country. Worthless stuff: swamps, deserts, places miles away from transportation. What happens is, the senators—or rather, dummy companies acting for them—then announce that major industrial developments or housing developments are to be built on the lands. They get a little ink in the local paper, then sit back and do nothing for six months or a year. Then, just as they're supposedly all geared up to start the development, the Pentagon expresses interest in the land for an air base or a training facility or a missile silo. Eventully, after due deliveration in the subcommittee, the land is resumed for the military and compensation is paid the developers.''

''But surely the land is still worthless,'' she argued. ''So you only compensate them for the price they paid, plus the legal fees and paperwork.''

''No.'' He shook his head, smiling. ''That's the beauty of it. They get compensated for the *perceived* value of the land, and the perception is based on the stories about major new developments that never really existed. They make at least a hundred percent profit. See, the members of the subcommittee who aren't in on the racket don't know what's going on. They're not going to rush off and inspect some Florida swamp or a rocky outcrop in Arizona. If the military says they want it, and it's only going to cost a couple of million, well, why in hell not? And the locals get a military plant instead of an industrial park. Everyone's happy and no one's suspicious.''

''Except?''

''Except some of the good guys at the Pentagon, who are pissed because they're being saddled with land they don't want in places completely unsuitable for military facilities. That's where this gets into big money. The ten million or so the guys in on the racket have made, that's chicken feed. It's the billions in misplaced military spending because of this scam that makes your headline."

"It's not bad." She nodded. "I like it. How do I stand it up?"

"I've got an envelope here for you," he said. "It details the dummy companies, where the land is, and what the military has done with it. I think you need to establish the companies were just shells, with no money . . . and *no intent* to develop. Then you can track the companies back to the subcommittee, particularly the chairman. It's going to be harder to nail the generals, but once you start the ball rolling someone will crack." He looked at the mineral water with disdain. "To hell with this," he said, "I'm having another martini and a big bloody steak."

She watched him. He was attractive, smart, ambitious. And ruthless. Everything needed to go right to the top in politics.

"Why me?" she asked. "Why give this story to me when you could have given it to the *Post?* In fact, why blow the whistle at all? That committee is run by your own party people."

"I owe you, Angie, that's why," he said, putting on his sincere face. "After what you did for me, I'm always going to owe you. I came out of it all okay, thanks to you. My career is on the move again. They're going to run me for the Senate, if a couple of things can be arranged. That's one of the reasons I'm getting married," he confided. "We think it'll help my chances. And the woman in question has a very, very rich daddy. So my campaign worries will be over after all this time." He glanced at her. "We almost got to marriage, Angie. I wonder what would have happened if we had."

"We'd be divorced now, Ken," she said. She wasn't interested in memories. "You haven't answered my other question: Why blow the whistle on your own people?"

"Because I want the best for the military," he said firmly. "I believe in a strong America and we're not going to be strong if the military is forced onto unsuitable sites because a few politicians and land boomers want to get rich."

"Very noble of you," she said. "But I always need to know the *real* reason someone's giving me a story. That way I don't get used any more than I can afford to be." She stared at him. "Let's think. Ken's backers want him to run for the Senate but the senior senator from New York is firmly entrenched and you couldn't beat him in a primary. I could look it up when I go back to the office, but you tell me now. Peter Carette is the senior senator and, I think, chairman of the subcommittee we're talking about? Yes? Am I on to something?"

He nodded and shrugged.

"And when this scandal breaks," she continued, "Carette's party—your party—will offer him the choice of stepping down to make room for you or facing the wrath of the Congress and maybe even prosecution. Right?"

"Close enough," he said. "But what does it matter what I get out of it? You get a good story and justice is done."

"Sure," she said. "I'll go with the story. I just always like to know why I'm being used and who's using me." She stood up. "Thanks for lunch. Good luck in the Senate and good luck with your marriage. What's her name, by the way? I'll pass it on to the gossip column."

"Thanks, Angie," he said. "Let's keep in touch." He was paying the check when she left and he had to run outside to catch her as she was driving away.

"Look," he said, his face at the open window of her car, "I know what I did to you. I understand if you want to hurt me now. But I need to know. They're really going to start pushing me again. Am I safe with you? Or are you going to destroy me for what I did."

She put the car back in drive and turned to him with the biggest, sunniest, most insincere smile she could muster.

"You never can tell, Ken," she said brightly. "You never can tell." And she drove off leaving him standing in the street, a scowl on his face. She felt terrific.

In the months since the visit to Virginia, Angie had seen a lot of Lyle Mansion, and a friendship was developing out of shared interests. He was devoting most of his time to the *Tribune*—the New York paper was doing fine without him, he said—and on many occasions they were at the same party, or left the office at the same time and had a drink together. It was a nice, casual relationship, and he was content not to press her, not to attempt to follow up on their one moment of intimacy in the snow.

Work was again the dominant force in her life. The tip-off Ken had given her panned out; after a month of delving through records and after many secret meetings with disgruntled Pentagon officers, she produced a three-part series on the scam. The *Tribune* played it big, page one every day.

"But not a damned thing is happening about it," she complained to Ted and Lyle. They were sitting in

232

the publisher's office, waiting for the main edition to come up.

"No one's going to jail, no one's even getting fired," she said. "A couple of the generals will be quietly transferred to the boondocks and a couple of senators will decide not to seek another term. But where are the prosecutions? Why aren't the bad guys in court, facing prison?"

"You can feel very proud of the series," Ted said. "You exposed corruption. You can't expect heads on platters, too."

"But that's just it!" she exploded. "If some ordinary person does anything out of line, like a welfare mother who cashes a check she isn't entitled to, they come down on her like a ton of bricks. These guys steal millions and they're allowed to walk away with freedom and dignity intact. No wonder people don't trust the system."

"But these men will have been punished," Lyle said gently. "By their lights, at least. Two senior senators wiped out, some military brass stopped at the peak of their careers—it's quite a disaster for men like that."

"And a nice little bonus for Ken Beckworth," Ted said casually. "You know he's getting the Senate endorsement, unopposed? A big step for him, maybe enough to head him for the veep's job again. Yes, forcing Senator Carette out of the running really opened the way for Beckworth."

She decided to shut up then. She still felt awkward about letting Ken use her to squeeze out his rival.

The edition arrived and they all flipped through the smudgy pages. Ted penciled in a few corrections, talked to the news desk about a couple of late stories, and then the three of them went for a drink at the bar around the corner.

"You're still depressed," Lyle said quietly while Ted was getting their drinks. "It's the letdown after a big story. Don't worry, there'll be plenty more. Meanwhile, do you feel like a little break from the grind? A few days down in Virginia? I'd love you to see the place in the full flower of spring."

"Thanks, Lyle," she said slowly, thoughtfully. "But I don't think I should, not with you being my employer. It was okay when I came down with Ted, but it wouldn't look right if I came alone."

She was sorry he didn't argue with her. She would have loved to go.

She worked hard right through the summer, when everyone whose job allowed it fled the city. She broke some good stories and wrote some good columns, but she still felt she was headed nowhere. In August her mother came down from her new home in Boston. It was a relief to have someone to talk to.

"I guess I'm hard to please," Angie told her mother. "I've got the job I wanted, but it doesn't seem enough." She refilled their coffee cups and glanced around the apartment. "God, I've got to do something about this place. It's as bad as the dump I started out in. But I never seem to have the time or energy to fix things up."

"You can have the apartment fixed up for you, dear," her mother said firmly. "Hire a decorator. You can afford it. I don't think it's the apartment that's bothering you."

"No," Angie admitted, "it's everything. Nothing. I just feel . . . it's like I've done all the stories there are, and now I walk through it all. I don't get that thrill anymore, the fear and excitement of wondering whether I can do it. Journalism's becoming routine."

"It happens to all of us," her mother said. She smiled. "You forget, I've been through all this. You get jaded. It's not like other jobs where routine is so much a part of it, where it's satisfying to master it, keep on top. In newspapers, you're always looking for the challenge of the new, and when you find you've done it all and there are no more thrills, well, it's hard. The best way is to strive for a greater depth in what you do, and also to try and distance yourself from it a little. That's where it helps having someone in your life. You don't appear to have anyone. Do you?"

"No, Mom, there's no one just now," Angie said. "I seem to have drifted out of the relationships I was in. It doesn't matter. It's not important."

"It is so!" May said vehemently. "You can't live without love—or, at least, without a normal emotional life. You should be seeing lots of men. You should be, as they say, 'getting laid.' "

"Mom!" she cried, shocked. "You're my *mother*."

"I'm also a woman," her mother said firmly. "And no matter how old and out of it you may think I am, I know what we need. You've got to be emotionally involved with someone, and you're not. Angie, you're trying to live all on your own and that's not right."

"I can't just invent a man to make me happy, Mom," she said.

"No, but you can put yourself in a frame of mind where you'll be receptive if the right person *does* come along," her mother replied. "Angie, you're still on the defensive because of what happened to you. You were a child, and it was tragic. It seemed to have

235

clouded your mind. In some ways, it was good. It forced you out of a little town into the world you were meant for. Now you have to begin to look after your heart."

"I guess you're right, Mom," she said, itching to change the subject. "What are you going to do next? Are you glad to be in Boston?"

"Yes," her mother said, "but I'm about to move on. I'm going to Europe for a couple of months. With a friend."

"That's great!" Angie said. "Who is she? One of our relatives?"

"It's a he, not a she," said May. "Andrew Hedges. He's the op-ed page editor at the *Globe* and they're about to retire him. We were almost lovers years ago, but I met your father instead. So we've taken up where we left off and we're going to Europe together." She studied Angie, waiting for the reaction. "And I don't give a damn whether you approve or not."

"Oh, Mom," she said, "I think you're wonderful. Picking up with an old beau, taking off with him across the world . . ." She crossed the room and hugged her mother, tearful. "I'm so happy that you're happy," she whispered. "You're brave and strong and you deserve everything nice."

Her mother squeezed her tightly. "I can take care of me. It's you I worry about. You force yourself out of this shell, hear me? All kinds of wonderful things are in store for you if you do."

Indeed, after her mother's visit things did start to look up. She attacked her work with her old enthusiasm, filled with new hope. She worked seventeen-hour days, spending time on the phone at night, from her apartment, tracking down rumors. She worked without stopping, allowing the job to protect her from any invasion. When she had allowed herself to be overwhelmed by work for weeks at a time, going through meals or walks home as mechanical things, she would force herself to do something, anything, that wasn't her job. One time she took herself to the zoo. Like grabbing a child away from the Saturday cartoons, she told herself. She made herself get up before noon on a Saturday in late August, dress in jeans, and take a cab to the zoo. She hated it, hated the caged animals and the quarreling families on all sides of her and the food and the awful smells. But she'd expected to hate it. Forcing herself to take a break from her work had a refreshing effect: it made her feel terrific to remember that this wasn't normal. She had a job, an obsession, to return to whenever she chose.

She put off the act of going back until dark, hating every minute of her day at the zoo, keeping relief away as long as possible so as to savor it more.

One night she took herself to a singles bar, another place she'd never wanted to go, forcing herself into another break. She drank too much and she saw a young man who looked like Jeff. She began wondering how come Jeff still hadn't married. Her mother kept her abreast of everyone's comings and goings, and May reported that Jeff had a large tract of farmland a hundred miles away and came home often to see his parents. Angie knew why *she* hadn't married, but hadn't Jeff ever recovered from her betrayal? He ought to've found a good woman by now, she thought. Dear sweet Jeff.

Thinking about Jeff and what had caused the breakup was not, she reminded herself, what she'd come to a singles bar for. So she let a red-haired beefy man several years older pick her up. She listened to his complaints about selling cars, expensive ones, and about his children whom he saw rarely and about women in general, about which she was gracious, knowing she'd never see the man again. She suffered through a recitation of his virtues, which included sensitivity and honesty, and she even suffered through a fast feel before she told herself she'd seen enough of how real people lived and went home. The apartment was empty and stifling hot and the phone didn't ring, but there was nobody there to talk her to death.

She suffered through breaks like those about once a month. It was penance for being unhealthily bound to work and in love with pressure. It was also a form of prayer: thank God I'm obsessed; thank God I've got what I love best all around me, all the time. The fact was, she loved work and didn't want anything else.

"Don't put away your summer stuff," Ted said to her one afternoon in late September. "You're going to Hawaii the second week of next month with Lyle and me."

She pushed her chair back from the desk. "Hawaii?! Why?"

"Well, it's an editors' and publishers' convention," Ted said, "so Lyle and I were going anyway. But we just heard today you've been placed in the final ten for their new award: Reporter of the Year. They're going to try to make it bigger than the Pulitzer. You must have heard about it."

"I read about it in the Guild newsletter," Angie said. "But it didn't suggest there was a trip to Hawaii just for getting nominated. Who pays for the trip?'' she asked suspiciously.

''We do, dummy,'' he said. ''The *Trib*. It's not just that we nominated you. The judges have put you in the final ten, so we've got to fly you there on the chance you win.'' He leaned against the next desk. ''Angie, if we could get that award it would be another big boost for the *Trib*. It's not for one story, but for a body of work over the year. So it establishes the winning reporter's paper as a good place to be, a good newspaper.'' He started to walk away, then turned back. ''Angie, congratulations. You are now, officially, one of the ten best reporters in the country. I always said you had it in you.''

''Just be glad you don't have to attend any of the sessions,'' Ted said as they lay beside the pool at the hotel. ''These guys, most of them, are interested only in the technical side of newspaper production: computer setting, offset printing, facsimile. Jesus, they never talk about going out and getting stories. I don't know,'' he added gloomily. ''The way the business is going, I don't know if there's going to be a place for an old newsman like me. I'll have to buy a little weekly paper in some place with a population of ten unless I want to be an editor of video display units instead of what I am—an editor of words.'' He sighed.

She didn't answer. After thinking about it awhile, he picked up the bottle of oil and gently began smoothing it into her back. His strong hand felt good and Angie sighed contentedly and flexed her body, letting the sun and his massage work on her. After a few minutes, a spirit that hadn't flowed between them for a long while began taking hold. She looked into his eyes and saw the desire she'd seen before. "Let's go upstairs," she whispered.

They didn't talk in the elevator. There was an electric anticipation between them neither wished to violate with words.

Angie's room was cool and dim after the bright light outside. The sliding door to the terrace was open but the long white draperies, billowing gently, diffused the light, and they were too high up for noise to reach them. She stood in the center of the room. Ted came to her and kissed her. His hands moved up her back to the knot of her bikini. His touch was so smooth, softened by the oil on her skin. Then her breasts were free, pressed hard against his bare chest, the hairs tickling and arousing her. His hands strayed down her front and he moved her bikini bottom down and she kicked it off. She parted her legs as his fingers gently probed her. She opened her mouth wide and their tongues caressed. She put her hand on the waistband of his shorts and pushed them down, freeing the force of him against her thighs.

He broke off the kiss and quickly moved her to the bed. She glanced down at him, huge, rampant, and hugged him close. She lay back on the bed and he knelt beside her. The bottle of suntan oil was in his hand.

"Mustn't let you burn," he whispered as he poured oil into his cupped hand. He began gently to work the oil into her skin, starting at her neckline and moving ever so slowly down until he was massaging her breasts. She was warm and desperately ready for him but he was determined to spin out the moment: the oil soothed its way down her body, over her mound and between her thighs, making all of her one long, sensual river.

"*Now*, please. *Now*," she whimpered as his hand brushed closer and closer to her core. She raised her hips to meet him. But he still held back, loving the sensation he was producing in her and in himself.

She was moving urgently against the pressure of his hand between her legs, reaching out to him, forcing against him in a rhythm that would bring her to fulfillment no matter how long he wanted to wait. At last he swung himself over her, knelt poised between her yearning thighs for a moment, then eased himself forward and entered her. Angie gasped and took him, their bodies locked, oil lubricating them. It was afternoon love, stolen on a hot day in paradise.

The tremor started at her center, running up to her brain, coursing back through her body. She cried out, arched her hips again and again, and fell back on the rumpled sheets at last, replete and exhausted.

They lay a long time in each other's arms, content with the silence in the room and the strength between them. Once she turned and watched his face: there was gentleness there, and sadness. She suspected he wanted to make a declaration of love, but knew she wouldn't welcome it. She slept for a little while, dreaming she was a girl again in the Florida heat with a mystical lover beside her.

She stayed in her pleasant haze through the next day, soaking sun into her, moving slowly, thinking little, the languor of the island bewitching her. When Lyle and Ted came to find her late in the afternoon she was so mellow that Lyle looked at her anxiously.

"You *are* going to get dressed for the award?" he asked cautiously. "You've so totally dropped out these past couple of days I'm worried you're not going to make it to your moment of triumph." He seemed to care for her so much, as proud as the father of a talented child. She liked his protectiveness very much.

Ted was nervous for her and for himself and he'd skipped the afternoon sessions and spent the time with a long-lost buddy in a bar.

"I'll be ready in plenty of time," Angie said, getting out of her deck chair and stretching. "I wouldn't miss it for the world—two handsome escorts, the three of us representing the hated Eastern radical press. You guys be ready on time and I'll come tie your black ties and we'll have a martini before we go down to the ballroom." She slung her towel over her shoulder. "You know we're not going to win the award, but we'll put on a good act, show 'em what Easterners are all about." She linked arms with the pair of them, feeling good and friendly and easy.

She didn't take a long time dressing: the blue gown was simple and she decided on light makeup and her hair pulled straight back for classic beauty. She enjoyed doing the men's ties and checking them over. Their nervousness amused her, and they both looked so proper in their black tuxedos, so terribly earnest. She was proud of her men.

They were squeezed into a small table well toward the back of the room. The major newspapers, the ones making lots of money and wielding the great influence, had been given the good places up front. It didn't bother Lyle, who was used to the *Tribune* being treated as a poor relation to giants like the *New York Times.* But Ted made noisy comments about banishment to the boondocks.

"We beat all their asses on news coverage," he growled. "We're about the only paper in the country picking up circulation, but they look down their noses at us because we're tabloid. I don't know what we're doing here, Lyle. This is an exercise in jerking off.'' He glowered at the surrounding tables but no one, thankfully, took notice of him.

Dinner was the usual convention fare: fish cocktail, chicken smothered in coconut and pineapple, chocolate cake. And more to drink for everyone. The party was very boisterous by the time the prize-awarding ceremony started, and the chairman needed five minutes to quiet them down so he could be heard.

Angie listened to the ten names, a roll call of the best in American journalism, thrilled to hear her own name. *That's for you, Dad*, she thought.

The chairman went into a long-winded speech about the threat to press freedom posed by government actions, and after he cited several examples of government interference, the crowd got restless. He cut short his speech then and got to the point.

"Reporter of the Year," he intoned. "A most difficult selection, the judges tell me. All of us here— publishers, editors, writers—deserve an award for battling against rising costs, illiteracy, government interference. But," he said, taking an envelope from his pocket, "only one can win this inaugural award. And the winner . . .'' he paused for dramatic effect, holding up the slip of paper, ''. . . the winner is—Angie Waring, of the *Washington Tribune*.''

There was silence, just for a second as the stars of the more prestigious newspapers absorbed the shock. And then applause began to roll across the room, genuine applause, swelling in volume. They rose to their feet, turning toward the humble table at the back. Lyle and Ted stood, applauding hard, both gazing at Angie with pride and love. Lyle put his hand under her elbow and raised her to a standing position.

"Go get it," he whispered. "Go get your award."

She moved among the close-packed tables, smiling and nodding thanks as they applauded her, and climbed the three steps to the podium. The chairman held out his hand and drew her to the microphone.

"That our first award should be won by a young lady demonstrates, I think, the equality in our profession," he boomed. "I also think it's marvelous that the award has gone to a reporter from the *Tribune*, a newspaper that hasn't had an easy time of it over the past few years. I see you back there, Lyle. We're all pleased for you. I guess everyone's going to have to pay a lot more attention to the *Trib* from now on." He turned to the table behind the podium and produced a portable typewriter, a real typewriter with only one oddity: the body was made of solid silver. It gleamed in the spotlights as he handed it to Angie. "I hope it's not too heavy for you, honey," he said in a low voice. "We never figured on a girl winning." Then he found another envelope and made a great show of opening it. "The other part of the prize is this check for ten thousand dollars. Congratulations, Angie Waring."

She looked at the figures on the check, so many zeros. And the beautifully crafted typewriter, so handsome, so ridiculous. And she felt a surge of triumph and pride. She was the best: they'd said so. She put her prizes down and stepped to the microphone.

"Thank you," she said. Her voice was strong and clear, unwavering. "I'm stunned and happy, happy for all of us at the *Trib*. As you said, Mr. Chairman, it's been a long struggle. We've been up against one of the best papers in the nation, with resources far greater than ours, but we've produced a newspaper we are proud of and, more important, a paper people want to read. The *Trib* doesn't pay the highest salaries in the industry." That brought laughter. "But it has to be the best place to work. For that, I thank two people: Ted Buchanan, the finest editor I've ever known, and Lyle Mansion, a brave and dedicated publisher who isn't afraid of anyone—not even temperamental women journalists.''

There was more cheering as she worked her way back to their table carrying the typewriter and envelope. A procession came by to congratulate the three of them and admire the typewriter. Ted celebrated by starting on his own bottle of scotch and began to slip farther down in his chair.

She and Lyle had to help Ted up to his room. He was laughing about Angie's triumph, a very happy drunken editor.

''I've never seen him tie one on like this before,'' Angie said, as she found his room key in his pocket and swung open the door.

''We all have so much to celebrate,'' Lyle said. ''I certainly do. I'm so proud for you, Angie. You deserved that award, you know.''

They got Ted's jacket and shoes off and put him on his bed, where he lay grinning to himself. They cheerfully called good night to him and left. In the corridor, Lyle looked at her shyly. ''I . . . I don't want the evening to end. I could use something real to eat and maybe a glass of good champagne. What do you think?''

She brightened. She wasn't ready to end the evening either, not an evening of such excitement, such personal excitement.

''I'd love to!'' She smiled at him brightly.

''I'm a member of the Outrigger Club here,'' he said. ''It's out toward Diamond Head. They've got a good chef and they serve late.''

The club was rich and quiet, elegance in contrast

with the tourist glitter of Waikiki. They were given a table on the terrace looking out over the ocean. Somewhere inside the club a pianist played gentle melodies as they were served a late candlelight supper of crab and avocado. The champagne was crisp and cold and Angie felt herself glowing.

"The perfect place to end a perfect evening," she sighed, watching lights sparkle on the sea. "Sometimes I wonder why you go on working so hard, Lyle," she mused. "Why you settle for the hassle of a newsroom."

"I told you," he said, "I feel responsible for the newspapers and I won't give them up. It would be nice to drift around, live in one paradise after another, but who'd look after the papers?"

"We're lucky you feel that way," she said. "The *Trib* would have gone under if not for you."

"Let's take a walk on the beach," he said then. He didn't want to talk about newspapers and the real world. "Just leave your shoes and bag here. They'll be all right."

They stepped over the low wall dividing the terrace from the beach and strolled slowly along the edge of the surf. A three-quarter moon lit the water. Tiny crabs scuttled out of their path, leaving faint tracks in the sand. Angie suddenly wanted to feel the sand between her toes.

"Turn your back a moment, Lyle?" she asked. "I've got to get rid of these pantyhose."

He stared solemnly out to sea as Angie shucked off the stockings and rolled them into a ball.

"Okay," she said, clenching the stockings in her fist. The sand felt good, warm and electric, and she danced on ahead of him. "I love this place," she cried, raising her arms to the night sky. Just offshore a ship hooted, as if in reply, and she laughed again.

He reached out his hand and she took it without thinking. Gently, he pulled her to him and kissed her. It felt good, natural, and Angie responded, snuggling into him. She waited for him to go further. He was such a nice man, a good friend. She pressed herself against him, conscious of her nakedness under the silk gown, wanting him to take her. Then she felt him break away and step back. He was still clutching her hand, but he was suddenly shy, even embarrassed over his own impulsiveness.

"I'm sorry, Angie," he mumbled. "I didn't mean to . . . to take advantage."

This was something she'd never dealt with before! The poor man was so serious, so proper.

"You didn't take advantage, Lyle," she said easily, hoping to loosen him up. "It made me happy when you kissed me. You can kiss me again, if you want to."

He gripped her hand more firmly.

"Angie," he said, the words tumbling out, "I have to ask you now. I've tried to conceal it for some time, but I can't do it anymore. I love you. I have since that first night in New York. I want you to know that. Please think about it, because I'm going to ask you to marry me." He dropped her hand and turned away, walking a few steps back down the beach. "I know I'm not much of a catch. Someone as beautiful and talented as you can have anyone. But I'll love you and take care of you and share my world with you. You'd join me in running the newspapers, in everything I do. Please, don't answer now. I'm afraid now. Give yourself time. I've waited a long while and I can wait a while longer. I just wanted you to know."

They walked back to the club in silence. His head was bowed. He was a fine man and he loved her. Could she grow to love him? No one would be hurt if she said yes to Lyle. And Lyle would be hurt if she said no.

He was quiet in the taxi and escorting her through the lobby and up to her room—without, of course, suggesting he spend the night. He didn't even kiss her again.

The waves washing onto the beach lulled her to sleep and she thought it had been quite an evening: Reporter of the Year and a proposal of marriage. She was confused, but she was happy.

As their cab headed for the airport early the next morning Angie looked out the window at daytime Honolulu. It was in such contrast to the previous night's scene on the beach: there were jerry-built stores and low-rise apartment buildings, women hanging out laundry, old men on bicycles, chickens pecking in dusty yards. What was truth and what was illusion: Lyle's moonlight proposal or the ordinary business of the city? She glanced at Lyle next to her but he stared straight ahead.

Ted, in the front seat, turned to talk to them. He had just about recovered; his eyes were warm and sparkling again and he winked at Angie.

"How do you want to play our success, Lyle?" he asked. "A picture and story on Angie—where? The lead to the second section? Maybe a pointer on page one."

"The whole thing on page one, Ted," Lyle said. "It's worth shouting about, and you damn well know the *Post*'s not going to do the shouting for us. Let's play it up big. After all," he said, smiling, "Angie's not exactly a homely picture for the front."

"Good," Ted said, "I'll call the desk from the airport and tell them to give it a good run."

"I, ah, already did, Ted," Lyle said gently. "I called them this morning, and unless war breaks out, she's got the first two columns tomorrow."

The flight back was fun, sitting in first class on a nonstop to New York. They talked easily together about the paper and stories they planned. After three hours, Angie dozed. The drone of the engines and the overlay of quiet conversation washed across her. Drifting in and out of sleep, she found the clarity she needed. Lyle, beside her, and Ted, across the aisle, were still talking when she came fully awake. She put her hand on Lyle's sleeve and whispered his name. He turned to her. "I've made up my mind." She felt him tense. "If the offer still stands, the answer is yes."

He looked full into her eyes and there was disbelief, and then joy and love.

"You're going to marry me?"

"Yes, Lyle," she whispered. "That's what I want."

All his New England reserve fell away; all the lines of care and worry and responsibility disappeared from his thin face.

"Whooee!" he yelled, and blushed as the other passengers turned to look at them. He hunched down in his seat, embarrassed. He took her hand proudly and looked across the aisle at Ted.

"You're the first to know," Lyle said, "and there's no one I'd rather tell. Angie and I are going to be married," he said, searching Ted's face.

She met Ted's eyes. He was hurt. Or did she imagine that? Because instantly his face broke into a big grin and then he was standing up, pumping Lyle's hand and bending over him to kiss her. He waved to the steward. "A bottle of your best champagne," he said. "I just lost my best reporter and the boss got himself a wife. Let's celebrate."

She wanted to tell him it wasn't quite like that. He wasn't losing a writer. She'd go on working. She was proud of her profession and she loved to work. But even as she took the glass of champagne she realized it could never be the same. She was about to take on a husband and his children and his famous name. His famous, hated name. For an instant she thought she'd made a terrible mistake. But then she looked up into Lyle's eyes and saw all the happiness there and knew it couldn't be wrong to bring somebody so much joy.

A limo took them to the Plaza where they'd spend the night before their early flight to Washington. She was very tired and wanted only to fall into bed. She unpacked just what she had to and was about to undress when there was a knock.

"Yes?" she called, and when she heard the reply she ran to open the door to him.

Ted said, "I won't come in. I just wanted to tell you, Angie, I'm happy for you. You couldn't have picked a nicer guy. You've done the right thing." He suddenly opened his arms and she fell into them and let him hold her. "Don't be afraid, baby," he mumbled into her hair. "You're moving on, but I'll always be there if you ever need me." He released her quickly and stepped back into the corridor. He raised a hand to her and started down the corridor, and as Angie watched him go she felt a dreadful sense of loss, of telling him goodbye forever.

There was a message for Lyle and her the next morning: Mr. Buchanan was staying on in New York for the day and would see them in Washington that night.

"That's not like Ted," Lyle said as they rode to the airport. "He's always so eager to get back behind his desk. What do you think could have possessed him to just vanish like that?" he asked carefully, avoiding her eyes.

"I guess he just wanted a day to himself," she said just as carefully. Lyle nodded.

"I kind of sprang it on him about us getting married, and I know how he feels about you, how close you've been."

"Ted will be all right," she said firmly. So Lyle knew about them. That was good. "He's very happy for us, Lyle," she said.

Chapter
Thirteen

Alex Mansion insisted on a party, so Angie could meet the whole clan. Delighted by the news of their wedding, he took personal control of all details. Lyle shrugged helplessly.

"You're marrying into an important family," the old man told her. "You'll be part of it once you adopt the name, so you better find out what it's like to be a Mansion." He was talking to her in the book-lined study of his Fifth Avenue penthouse the day before the big family gathering. "None of my children has made out well in the marriage stakes, not so far," he said. "Maybe I raised them wrong and they're not fit to live with, I don't know. But their mother's been gone so long, and I was always so busy, they were raised by nannies and housekeepers and tutors. They're not normal. And they had the name to bear. It's not easy, being the children of one of the richest, most public families in the country." He looked around for a light for his cigar and she produced her own lighter. He nodded thanks.

"I think," he confided, "you may have picked the best. Lyle's not tough but he's decent. His kids are a handful, been in all kinds of trouble. But mostly I blame their whore of a mother for that. You'll be a good influence on them. I don't think Lyle knows how to talk to them, but I expect you can get through to them." He blew cigar smoke and grinned at her through the cloud.

"How do you like me spelling out what I expect of you?" he asked. "I'll be giving you orders next, won't I?"

"I, ah, appreciate your guidance," Angie said. "But I don't know if I'll be able to achieve what you're hoping for. All I can promise is I'll do my best to make Lyle happy."

"Oh, you'll do more than that," he said confidently. "I summed you up the first time we met, in Newport. You're tough, like me, and you expect to succeed at whatever you take on. I had a check done on you. Don't look so shocked," he said, seeing the angry flush on her cheeks, "it's like you were being given a big job in the company. Of course we're going to run a check on you. You've been around, and everything you've tackled you've done well. Anyway, I know all I need to know about you."

"Which is more than I can say about you—and your family," she snapped. "Look, I'm just marrying Lyle. I'm not running for president."

"Ask me anything you like," he said cheerfully. "Better still, ask Johnny Howard. He's our family lawyer, a member of the family himself, and he knows all our nasty secrets. He can give you a good unbiased view of us." He picked up the telephone and spoke a few words. "Johnny'll sit down with you as soon as you and I have finished. Ask him anything.

"Meanwhile, I get to ask you some questions. Why, after waiting so long and apparently getting along fine alone, have you decided to get married now?"

"I'm not quite sure," Angie said. "Lyle just kind of snuck up on me." She laughed. "I'd always been too busy with work to get deeply involved, but then I was working with Lyle, sharing his love of newspapers, and he was such a decent man. It happened, that's all."

"You don't love him, do you." It was a statement, not a question, and similar to her mother's reaction when Angie had told her. Her mother hadn't been so blunt but, while pleased for Angie, had said she didn't think of it as a love match.

"Love?" Angie asked. "I don't think I know what that means and I'm not sure anyone does. What I do feel for Lyle is friendship, empathy, loyalty. I want to share my life with him."

"Good," Alex Mansion said. "A far better foundation to build on than falling in love." He smiled at her. "I'm pleased you're coming into our family, Angie. God knows, we need new blood." He spun the wheelchair out from behind the desk. "You're going to have your hands full, so I assume you'll be quitting your job."

She had taken a few weeks off to prepare for the wedding and all the events leading up to it, but that was just time off.

"Oh, no," she said. "I want to go on working. I realize it'll be different, being married to the publisher, but I'm still worth my space as a columnist."

"Look," he said patiently, "there's a much bigger job for you taking care of Lyle and propping up those children. Just do me one big favor: Forget about work for a while, just a couple of years, and take care of the family. Then, if you want to go back, we'll give you a paper of your own to run.''

"But I want to make it on my own—I *have* made it on my own," she said sharply. "I don't need things handed to me because of who I married."

"You'll have to get used to it," he said. "Because once your name has changed to Mansion, you'll be seen as a Mansion and judged as a Mansion. You might as well enjoy the benefits, too." He held the door for her. "Johnny's waiting for you in the sitting room. Have a good talk with him. He'll show you the whole picture."

She found Howard talking on the telephone, his back to the sweeping view of Central Park and the West Side. He nodded to her, indicated the silver coffee pot on a tray near the fireplace, and went on talking into the phone. She poured coffee for herself and stood by the window, gazing at the park. What was she letting herself in for? she wondered all over again. She didn't want to marry a whole clan, only one man, sweet, gentle Lyle. But that wasn't the way it was to be.

"Sorry," Johnny Howard said, hanging up at last. "Despite the domestic surroundings, work goes on all the time. Don't ever think this family is resting: there's always something to be done or signed or undone." He poured himself coffee. "I'm very glad it's all worked out for Lyle. And for you."

"Thank you," she said. "Mr. Mansion said I should ask you for a rundown on the family. Where do you fit in, exactly?"

"Remember *The Godfather*? Well, I'm the Robert Duvall character," he laughed. "In the family, but not of it." He laughed again and she liked him. The shock of curly fair hair, the dancing blue eyes belied the conservative attorney's blue suit. He was in his early forties, trim and tall and carrying a sense of vitality.

"My father and Alex were partners in a couple of enterprises not mentioned in the official company history," he continued. "My father was killed while I was in law school and Alex had begun his amazing construction of this multimedia empire. He took me in and later offered me a job. I've never regretted accepting. I'm a member of the board, I won a large block of shares in the company, and I'm encouraged to say exactly what I think. I'm treated as a member of the family. No," he said, "actually, I'm treated better. Alex can't ride me quite as hard as he rides Richard and Lyle."

They talked for an hour, about the family and the business, and then she left the penthouse and started down Fifth Avenue, going nowhere in particular, just walking in the crisp winter afternoon, thinking.

The more she thought, the more agitated she got. Sure, she respected Lyle and cared for him deeply. And, sure, he needed her. But shouldn't there be a soaring sensation inside her when she thought of him, the certainty that what she was about to do was inevitable? Oh, but that was kid stuff and she was an adult. She should be content with what she had.

She had given herself very little time for thinking. She was busy with wedding plans, though she bowed to Alex's wishes in every instance, and she was worried about how Curt and Emily would like having a stepmother. In the little time she allowed herself for thinking, she found herself wondering why she wasn't marrying Ted. The moment she asked herself that, she forced the thought from her mind. She was a career woman and she hadn't expected a cottage and roses and bliss. She was lucky to be marrying a man who understood her work and she was lucky that Lyle was so gentle, so undemanding. She was lucky, she reminded herself, lucky.

She was in the upper Thirties by then and she was suddenly tired and confused; the afternoon had grown cold and the crowds around her on the sidewalk were sullen and aggressive. Angie gave up pushing against the crowd and slipped into a coffee shop. Apart from a couple of tired gray men reading afternoon papers, she was the only customer.

She slid onto a stool and ordered coffee from the plump, cheerful woman behind the counter. She thought about how many meals in how many diners she'd ordered since the days when, as a child, it had been a grown-up treat to be taken into one of these places. She started crying, silent tears flowing down her cheeks, crying for all the things that had once been new and exciting and were now just ways of passing time.

"Cheer up, honey, and have a slice of pie on the house," the woman said. She was resting her body on her red-raw elbows and gazing out through the plate-glass window at the workers hurrying home. She slid a plate in beside Angie's coffee cup and discreetly placed a napkin beside it so Angie could blot her eyes.

"It's a hard city for a woman," the woman said, still staring out into the dusk. "Hard for a man, too. But we survive and come back the next day and do it all again. You prob'ly haven't got too much to be heartbroken about. Whoever he is, don't cry about him. There'll be another one, the right one, coming along soon. Now eat your pie and get out of here and go somewhere you'll meet someone nice.''

Angie did as she was told. She ate her pie, finished her coffee, smiled at the woman, and left a dollar tip. And she walked out into the night, hailed a cab for the Plaza, and accepted that she was going to become a Mansion. Because there wasn't anything else for her to be and no one would understand if she turned away from her destiny.

Trish was matron of honor and they shared cigarettes and a bottle of champagne in Angie's dressing room before the ceremony.

"It wasn't exactly what I had in mind," Angie said, indicating the Mansion guest suite. "I always thought, somehow, I'd be married out of my own home. But of course I don't have a home anymore."

"Yeah, I know," Trish said. "Getting married in Sam's living room—it's kind of like they've taken you over, like a company merger." She smiled. "Still, the family's doing it's best. The dreadful sisters were even sober last time I looked, and old Alex is positively beaming."

Angie drained her glass and fetched the dress from the closet. It was white. Lyle had said Alex wouldn't settle for anything else. But at least it was short and Angie didn't feel too much like a ridiculous blushing bride. She faced herself in the mirror for a moment, then pulled the dress over her head, the stamp on the contract.

Most of the faces were a blur but she saw her mother smiling sweetly at her, and she saw Ted, doleful but managing a wink. She let her gaze pass over Richard Mansion, pretending, as she was doing, that he was nothing more than an in-law.

The reception was lavish, formal, and brief. Angie moved among the guests, accepting congratulations and smiling to herself as she watched them all summing her up and betting on the future of the marriage.

Alex Mansion kissed her on both cheeks and held her hands in his rock-hard grip.

"Welcome to the family, Angie," he said, looking up at her from his chair. His dark blue eyes burned into her: there was a kindness in those eyes, and hope. "You've made me very happy," he said, "almost as happy as Lyle is today."

They both looked across the room to where Richard stood with his arm nonchalantly draped over Lyle's shoulder. It was Richard's signal to the rest of the room, his demonstration of power over his brother. He leaned down and said something to Lyle and she saw her husband jerk away, champagne spilling from his glass, his face flushed.

"Richard does ride him so," Alex said. "If Lyle would only toughen up, fight back, he'd be able to beat Richard in most things. But he's a timid soul. Takes after his mother." He squeezed her hand. "I look to you to put some fire in his belly."

She and Lyle left a few minutes later to catch a 7:00 P.M. flight to Barbados. No confetti or rice punctuated their departure, just genteel murmurs of good wishes.

"It didn't feel like a wedding," Angie said when they were in the limousine. "No one got drunk, or cried, or made a long, boring speech."

"No," Lyle said, "my family is very correct. On the surface, anyway." He had been quiet all the way down in the elevator, pale and tense. She guessed the ceremony had been an ordeal for him.

"Did your brother give you a hard time?" she asked. "I noticed you two talking . . ."

"It was nothing," he said abruptly. "Just Richard being a son-of-a-bitch as usual. I think I'll have a drink. We're going to be stuck in this traffic for hours. I knew we should have had the damned wedding in the morning." He folded down the cocktail cabinet and fixed himself a scotch and ice, a big one, and a gin and tonic for Angie. They drank, sitting in the crawling, snarled traffic. Angie was glad the smoked windows prevented the tide of weary drivers around them from seeing inside.

She placed her hand in his and felt the tension in him, more extreme than it had ever been. She studied his profile, the hard set of his jaw.

"I think you really need this vacation, Lyle," she said. "Two weeks of tropical bliss with nothing to do but swim and be together. I'm looking forward to it so much."

"I shouldn't have done it," he said, suddenly hoarse. "I shouldn't have brought you into my dreadful family. All we do is destroy each other. Now they've got you to destroy."

"I'll handle them," she said, keeping her voice light, stroking his hand. He sounded so desperate, so hopeless. "You and I will handle them together, Lyle," she said. "There's nothing to worry about."

He was silent during the plane ride, but brightened a little when they arrived in Barbados. The hotel manager showed them to their cottage. They followed him through the dark night, across a fragrant tropical garden, around a glowing pool, to their hidden bungalow, once a sugar mill.

"It's beautiful!" Angie gasped when the manager proudly threw open the heavy wooden doors. There was a large sitting room dotted with rattan furniture, facing a flagstone terrace. The section they stood in was modern, but blended easily with the far end of the room where the roughhewn stone tower of the sugar mill rose away from them.

Their bedroom and bathrooms were at the top of the sugar mill tower, gleaming wooden stairs leading up. The stone walls were bright with splashes of local art. From big windows set in the stone walls Angie could see boat lights in the harbor below.

"It's the most beautiful view in all Barbados," the manager said. "But it is also very private. No one will disturb you here. If you ring the bell, staff will come. If not, you will be left alone."

They went downstairs again, to a small, gleaming kitchen off the living room.

"I took the liberty of stocking it for you for tonight," the manager told them. "I thought you might like a late supper." He opened the refrigerator. "If there is anything else you desire . . . ?"

Inside was a bowl of caviar, a pair of cooked lobsters, a side of pink salmon, tropical fruits, and a board of French cheeses. On the lower level were bottles of champagne and white wine.

"The bar is here," he said, opening a teak cabinet to reveal dozens of bottles of liquors and mixers. "We have tried to anticipate your every wish, but of course our staff, and our wonderful kitchen, as well, are standing by to serve you."

"It's all wonderful," Angie laughed. "I'm sure there's nothing you've forgotten. Thank you for being so thorough."

"Yes, thank you for everything," Lyle echoed.

"Good night, good night," he said, bowing.

She closed the door on the eager-to-please manager, and grinned at Lyle.

"They really have tried hard," she said. "It would disappoint them if we didn't have a romantic moonlight supper." She ruffled his hair and kissed him on the forehead. "Poor baby, you're exhausted, aren't you?" she said. "I'll open some champagne and lay out something for us on the terrace." He smiled back at last and she began to relax.

He was dozing in his chair when she finished on the terrace, so she left him there and went upstairs to the bedroom. She unpacked a few things, and took out her toiletries and the sheer white peignoir her mother had bought for her. She touched it softly, thinking of her mother. She showered quickly, splashed on a little perfume, then slipped into the peignoir. She looked at herself in the mirror and smiled with delight: When had she last worn something so frivolous? Then she hurried back down to Lyle. He was waiting for her on the terrace, where the soft light from the living room threw a glow on her midnight feast.

He poured them champagne. She scooped baby lobster from its shell and hand-fed him portions, realizing she hadn't seen him eat all day. At last he really smiled at her, reviving.

"You look so lovely," he said gently. "Like a dream, floating in the night. No matter what happens to us, I'll never forget this sight."

"Nothing but good will happen to us," she said. What was making him so morose? She moved to him and put her arms around him, pressing his head against her body. Desire rose in her, and love, too. At last she knew she did love him. She wanted him. She stroked his head, beginning to move gently, involuntarily against him.

He moved away. "I'm sorry," he muttered. "It's no good. I can't . . ."

"Don't worry," she soothed. "We have all the time in the world." But she felt silly, standing there in the ridiculous gown, and she turned and poured herself another glass of champagne. "Eat something, Lyle," she urged. "Then we'll go upstairs. It's so lovely. The view in the morning is going to be beautiful."

He followed her up the stairs, stumbling like a sleepy child, and sat on the bed while she handed him his robe and gently pushed him in the direction of his bathroom. She listened to the water running and moved around, turning off most of the lights and leaving the room bathed in a soft rosy glow from the headboard lights. The bed had been turned back and she smiled at the sprig of hibiscus and tiny wrapped chocolate on their pillows. The shower stopped and the only sound was the peep-peep of tree frogs outside their tower. She drew the peignoir from her shoulders and stood there, proudly naked in the soft light, as he came into the bedroom.

He walked to her, his eyes devouring her. But then he hung his head and whispered, "Sorry, sorry. I shouldn't have done it," he said. "My fucking family, we are all so screwed up. I'm sorry, Angie. You're the most beautiful creature I've ever seen. You never should have gotten mixed up with us." He dropped his robe. Just as he turned away from her she let her eyes run over his slim body. There was a beaten look about him and he was not aroused.

She suppressed a sigh as Lyle slid into bed. She turned off the last lights and crept in beside him. He was feigning sleep but she took him in her arms and held him. There was no desire in her, just the wish to sooth away the torments that wracked Lyle.

Thunder woke her, rolling in across the sea. Jagged lightning flashes lit the room. Lyle was standing at the window, staring out at the storm. She called out to him, but thunder drowned her voice. She threw back the sheets and moved across the room to him, her hands gripping his shoulders.

"The storm woke you up," she said, kissing him on the cheek. He stood still, gazing out. She could see the whitecaps on the waves, the palm trees bending and thrashing. It was still warm but she felt goose bumps on her naked flesh. "Come on back to bed and let me hold you," she whispered. Then she felt movement in him, a heaving motion starting at his shoulders and traveling in spasms all down his body. She forced him around to face her and saw the tears coursing down his face.

She held him a long time, his face buried in her shoulder while he gasped out his sorrow. It was hard to hear him because of the storm and his choking, tearful, ragged voice.

"All my life," he gasped, "I've been in my brother's shadow. He was bigger, smarter, more handsome than I was. He was always the heir, Dad's great hope, the golden boy, the chosen one. I tried not to care too much and for a while I succeeded. I had my newspapers, and even if Richard despised them, they *were* mine. I made them work. Maybe I was lucky Richard didn't want them, or he might have taken them away." He took a long, shuddering breath. "And then you came, someone I didn't dare love, not at first. But you liked me, and maybe someday you would have grown to love me. It didn't matter: it was enough that you were willing to be with me." He paused.

"I had something of my own, something greater than I'd ever hoped for, in you," he said. "Something my family couldn't corrupt, couldn't buy, couldn't take away from me." He shuddered and she held him closer.

"Today, at the wedding," he said, "for the first time in my life I felt whole and strong and on my own. And today, Richard came to me and said . . ." He was crying harder.

"What?" she demanded. "What did he tell you about me? It was about me, wasn't it?"

"He said"—Lyle was racing now, trying to get it all out—"he said 'Good luck, little brother. I hope she's a better fuck now than she was at twenty. She wasn't much good then. But she'll probably satisfy you.' And he laughed and clapped me on the back and went off to drink more of the wine of my wedding."

The tears stopped. His body was still and resigned, all hope and strength gone. He slumped against the window as her arms dropped away from his body. He stared fiercely out to sea as if searching for a vessel lost in the storm.

"Do you want me to tell you what really happened?" she whispered.

"I don't want to hear about it," he said.

She led him back to bed and they lay there, apart, while the storm passed away to the west and the first light of the sun came up on the far horizon.

The day was beautiful and Lyle seemed to recover because of it. There was still a great sadness in his eyes but he chatted with her happily enough as the maid served them breakfast on the terrace and he went along with her plans to take out a sailboat and have a picnic.

Lyle was a good sailor. He sent the little skiff racing across the bay in the light breezes, weaving in and out of the other boats until they were around the headland and abeam of a tiny island topped by palms. He let the boat run up on the sand of the deserted beach.

They carried their things up the beach and found a shaded spot where Angie spread a couple of towels. They didn't say much, but it was a companionable quiet between them.

"Come on in for a swim," she said after a while, standing up and brushing sand off her legs.

He followed her into the warm blue water and they swam out, stopping to float on their backs. From that position the surrounding islands rose and fell, green jewels flung around the horizon.

When she began to get hungry, she called, "I'll race you to the beach." They swam stroke for stroke through the water and hit the beach together, laughing and sputtering, then ran up the sand.

The Chablis was very cold and he opened it and filled the glasses while Angie investigated the other treasures the hotel had packed. A soup of chilled consommé with fat fresh shrimps in it; a delicate fillet of beef stuffed with walnuts; two halves of guava filled with marinated fruits.

"Hey," she said as they touched glasses, "I *love* living as the rich live."

He laughed.

The sun was full on them when they'd finished lunch and they stretched out. Angie removed her bikini top and felt the warmth, the stirring in her nipples. She murmured in sleepy pleasure as she felt his hand move gently to her breast. Her hand brushed the cotton of his swimsuit: he was hard. She slowly turned to face him and they kissed, first their lips moving together, then tongues seeking each other out.

She slipped her hand inside the waistband of his shorts and his breathing grew faster as she found him, erect and straining at the fabric. Lyle's hand moved up the inside of her thigh and she parted her legs as his fingers found their way past the elastic of her bikini. She was moist, ready for him, and she moved swiftly against the probing fingers, arching her hips.

She tugged at his shorts and forced them down over his hips, then closed her hand on him again. His lips took her nipple, gentle at first, then his tongue swept around the erection and she moaned. With her free hand she shucked off the bikini bottom and fell back on the sand.

"Now! Now!" she cried, holding him tightly. "Come inside me, Lyle."

Lyle's body blotted out the sun as he swung over her. She was on fire, straining for him, wanting him to fill her. But even as she guided him into her, even as she felt the silky-hard pressure of his member entering her, he went soft. There was nothing to satisfy her or release her.

They tried hard, Lyle sweating in the frustration of the effort until finally he flopped away from her and lay on his back, an arm thrown over his eyes. There were no words to console him so she remained silent.

They dressed, Lyle pulling up his shorts with his back to her, ashamed. Then she reached out and touched him.

"Tonight," she whispered. "It will be fine tonight."

* * *

That evening everything was perfect. A marvelous meal under the stars, a final brandy in the round bedroom at the top of their tower, flowers scenting the air.

They approached it slowly, gently exploring each other's bodies, stroking and touching, finding their rhythm.

Her nightgown was hiked up around her breasts and he was full against her, his pajama bottoms a lost tangle somewhere down in the bed. She stroked him faster and faster and he continued to grow; she welcomed his hand. At last it was time and she felt his body on top of hers. But again he collapsed, flaccid between her thighs. The rest of him was still tense with desire, and anger, and shame.

Angie worked her way down his body. She took him between her lips and gently moved on him, searching for response. She sought more of him, probing and swirling her tongue around him, bringing her hands into play between his legs, over his buttocks, beyond.

He pulled her up and slumped back on the bed.

"It's no good," he said, his voice thick. "It's no damn good. I can't, I just can't." There was silence for a moment. "I guess I was never much good," he whispered. "And maybe this is a cop-out. But when we get to the point, just when . . . I think of . . . you and Richard." He turned away. "I'm sorry. It's my problem, not yours."

She sat up in bed and waited for her emotions to subside.

"It *is* my problem, Lyle," she said quietly. "We can't start our marriage with the ghost of Richard in our bed. You said you didn't want to know what happened. I'm going to have to tell you whether you want to hear it or not." She found a cigarette and lit it. The flame was very bright in the dark room and she could see him beside her, his arm shielding his face.

"I was twenty, a kid," she began, no emotion in her voice. She told him about the internship, then went to the point. "He took me as if I wasn't there. I suppose I could have cried rape but no one would have believed me, a stupid little girl going out on a boat with a man like Richard Mansion. Anyway, all I wanted to do was blot the whole ugly scene out of my mind. I ran home to hide. And then, as if fate was making sure I could never forget, I found I was pregnant. I had an abortion. The result was that I could never have a child."

She put out the cigarette.

"So that is what your brother meant when he told you he had me first. He has nothing to boast about. He didn't *have* me at all. He *took* me—a child in a stupor. He got nothing. So you don't need to feel his presence in our bed." She heard herself crying, tears of hurt and anger for herself, and pity for the man beside her. His arms were around her and he was trying to console her, to console himself, but she knew nothing had changed for them.

Book
Four

Chapter
Fourteen

Mary Hickson had aged well. She was still sleekly confident of her power and her position as doyenne of columnists. She would always be in the center of things, no matter what administration was in power. No matter who fell from grace, Mary would be queen.

Surveying the small gathering at the White House reception, she saw many new faces and chuckled, knowing how nervous most of them were. It was always a strain for first-time visitors, even the rich and powerful. She watched the tall, lovely, titian-haired woman standing at the center of a little group of publishers and writers. Angie Waring had done well for herself, Mary conceded. She'd been playing wife and mother to Lyle Mansion and his kids, keeping out of politics and the newspaper business, seen only at occasions like this one. A well-liked couple, the Lyle Mansions, although Mary had heard rumors. Lyle, whom Mary considered a wimp, was visibly loaded much of the time. Her spies at the *Tribune* said he sometimes had to be helped to bed on the nights he stayed over in the publisher's suite at the newspaper. And sometimes, she'd heard, he didn't stay overnight alone. Still, Mary could afford to be magnanimous about her old enemy: Angie Waring Mansion was no longer a competitor, no more the bright young girl all Mary's enemies hoped would dethrone Mary. She crossed the room and joined Angie's group.

"My dear girl!" Mary said, cutting in on the conversation. "How lovely you look. We don't see nearly enough of you, now that you've tucked yourself away in boring old Virginia."

"Hello, Mary," Angie said, putting on her nicest smile. "No, when I come to Washington at all it's usually just for one of these parties, then straight back home. But I do spend quite a bit of time in New York when Lyle's looking after the paper there."

"But it's not the same, is it?" Mary said smoothly. "You're not *involved* anymore. I think it was a great loss, the way Lyle took you away." She glanced up. "And here he is. Come here, Lyle. We're talking about you."

"Hi, Mary," he said. "Great evening, isn't it? Nice of the president to bring us all together. Even you couldn't find anything nasty to say about this."

"Oh, I can always find *something*, Lyle," she said, showing her claws for an instant. "But you're looking so tired," Mary said. "You must be working too hard. I know you're spending a great deal of time at the *Tribune*, even nights. It must be paying off, though. You've finally got it in the black. Good for you." She turned to Angie. "You should be very proud of your husband. Buying those newsprint mills in Canada was a master stroke. Everyone thought he was crazy. But now, while the rest of us are held up for ransom by the newsprint producers, the Mansion press has its own supply. And getting the Export-Import loan for the purchase at only eight percent—well, that showed real foresight.''

Lyle did look tired—and old—Angie thought. It had been a while since she'd looked at him carefully. They spent little time together, only short formal visits. They maintained a mutual respect for each other and put on a loving facade for the sake of the children, but that was all. Angie's life revolved around the house in Virginia, the children, and her friends in New York. Lyle . . . well, she didn't want to know how Lyle spent his time away from her. She knew he drank too much but there was nothing she could do about that; she supposed he had women. In bouts of drunken self-reproach, he sometimes urged her to take a lover. She never had, never in all the barren months of their marriage. She had chosen to be a Mansion and no matter how much of a sham the marriage was, she would honor her promise.

''Yes,'' Mary Hickson was saying, ''money's so tight. I guess they really wanted to do you a favor at the Ex-Im. Why, I even heard the administration might be looking for a return favor next year. The president really needs control of the Senate.'' She smiled brightly at them. ''Anyway, we mustn't talk politics in the White House, must we?'' She surveyed the room, preparing to move on to something more interesting. ''Oh, look, Angie,'' she said. ''Our mutual friend, Ken Beckworth. Hasn't he turned into the perfect senatorial figure! Who'd have expected it, years ago when you and I knew him? Now he's riding herd over those dreary people at the FCC who keep trying to regulate us. So we must all be nice to Senator Beckworth.'' She fluttered a hand at them and moved away.

Angie had already exchanged greetings with Ken. He was indeed a substantial figure, sure of himself among all these communications tycoons, the man with the favors to distribute. But, face-to-face with Angie for a few moments, there was still that look of apprehension in his sharp eyes, the fear she could undo him. She'd been pleased to see that.

"God, she's a bitch," Lyle said as they watched Mary Hickson walk away. "But she's the best. No one can dish it like Mary Hickson."

"I don't know," Angie said, suddenly irritated. In this group she was just an appendate to Lyle, just the publisher's wife. "There was a time when people thought I could beat her. I was pretty damn good once, Lyle."

"Until I took you away," he said quietly. "I know. You miss it all terribly and I'm sorry for the way things turned out. Maybe when the children are on an even keel, you'll want to come back. You're still the first person Ted and I would hire."

"It will be a while before the kids can supervise themselves, Lyle," she said. "I wish you'd spend more time with them. Curt seems to be calmer, but we had another note from Emily's school last week. Her grades are way off and she won't even—"

"I'm sorry," he said. "But you know I can't get through to them. You're the only one they talk to." He reached for another drink from a passing waiter. "Thank God for your influence on them. Dad's very pleased with you, by the way. He says you're a good influence on us all. He sees quite a lot of you, I gather. More than I do."

"You're never at home, Lyle," she answered hotly before she could stop herself. But she didn't want to fight. Lyle withdrew into his shell at the merest breath of dissension. She tried another approach, knowing he wouldn't talk about the children. He was so defensive about both Emily and Curt, he just wouldn't talk to her about them honestly.

"I see your father a good deal in New York. For all Alex's money and power, he hasn't made much happiness for himself that I can see."

Lyle gave her a sour look.

"He hasn't got any friends—or, if he does, they sure aren't people he confides in. Whenever I spend an afternoon in his study, I feel I'm hearing everything he couldn't say to anyone else since the last time I was there."

"Is this a burden, Angie?" he asked nastily. What was wrong with Lyle? It wasn't just the drinking, though he did enough of that. This simply wasn't the Lyle she had worked for on the newspaper. What was eating away at him?

"No, Lyle. I love Alex. You know that. And I love you."

He looked away, pretending to study a painting on the wall to his left. He wasn't going to reply, but she knew he'd heard. For what it was worth to him.

"What's your brother up to?" Angie asked after a silence. "I haven't seen him in months."

"He's the same," Lyle said, his voice taking on its particular Richard timbre. "He's come up with some scheme that's going to make billions. I don't understand it, but Dad's very excited. Richard's going to put up a satellite linked to private ground stations. That's why he's so tight with Beckworth right now. He has to have an exclusive deal in order to make it pay, and the FCC is going to have its arm twisted to give him the exclusivity. The figures scare me—something like five hundred million dollars' initial investment. At least half of it will be lost outright if we don't get the exclusive license."

"Richard always did think big," she said. "But this project means he'll be going head to head with the major networks *and* all the cable networks."

"He seems very sure he can make it work," Lyle said. "Richard always believed he could buy anything, including a political party. And with these people in power now, maybe he can."

"Is that what Hickson was talking about?" she demanded. "Saying the party was about to demand a favor from you for the newsprint loan?"

"It's just talk," he said vaguely. "There's nothing they can do to pressure me. I'm in the clear."

Angie was still worried the next day, though, and she called Ted at the *Trib.*

"Can you have lunch?" she asked. "I haven't seen you in ages and I need someone to bring me up to date on what's going on."

They met at the current in place for movers and shakers. As she walked to Ted's table she watched him untangle himself from his chair and rise to greet her. Dear Ted. She smiled as she approached him. He was still the same rumpled, cheerful man she had known all these years. Everyone else had changed so much, but Ted just went on, loyal and hardworking, honest and brilliant. There was a little gray in his hair but his eyes were as bright as ever and his smile as charming.

"You look great," he said as she sat down. "Life in the country agrees with you."

"One of these days I'll give it up and come back to work," she said. "I was sparring with Hickson last night. I'd still like to beat her."

"You could," he said, and she appreciated the assessment of her value from someone at the top. "But you'd be more valuable taking over the whole enterprise. As publisher."

She looked at him sharply.

"What do you mean? That's Lyle's job you're talking about."

He ordered martinis.

"It's something you should think over," he said. Ted wasn't beating about the bush. There was no deviousness in him. "I don't think Lyle's going to stand the heat much longer. The strain is getting to him and if he buckles we could all be in a lot of trouble. He's a nice man, but the way the pressure is now, well, it's not enough to be a good guy. The job needs someone tough. Someone like you."

She laughed.

"It's a while since anyone described me as tough, Ted. I'm just a respectable wife and mother tucked away in the country."

"Yeah, well, you and I both know better than that," he said, dismissing the idea. "And I think you should be preparing to come back into the business. Come back at the top. The New York paper's got big problems, editorially. The reader profile is awful. Lyle made a pitch to the chairman of Garfinkle's for advertising last week and the guy told him no, 'because your readers are my shoplifters.' The paper has to get some integrity back into it. You could do it."

"How about you taking over New York?" she asked. "Lyle would go along with it. He thinks you're the best."

"No," Ted said. "My job is here. We're not out of the woods yet and someone's got to keep the bastards honest. I feel like part of the *Trib*. Anyway, I'm not cut out to be a publisher. I'm a newsman and that's the way I want to stay."

Over steaks Angie asked him what she had come to find out.

"Hickson hinted last night the administration was preparing to lean on us because of some favors owed them. The Export-Import loan. Did we get a favor, and do we owe them one? And if so what do they want?"

"Oh, we got a favor, all right," he said. "It was a sweetheart loan, thirty million bucks on fixed interest. At the time we got it, last year, there wasn't much fuss about it. Interest rates hadn't really taken off yet. And, besides, who could oppose our buying our own source of newsprint to stop the Canucks screwing us? Some of the radical magazines hinted at a deal, but nothing much was said beyond that. Now, though, I think the politicians will be coming around asking for their turn."

"What can we do for this administration?" she asked. "They're riding high. They've got a big majority in the House and they own most of the statehouses."

"But they need the Senate, badly," Ted said, "and they're not going to get it, not if the early polls are right. There's the usual off-year backlash against the party in power. On the figures, they'll actually lose three or four Senate seats."

"So what do they think we can do?"

"It's early days yet and it may not happen," Ted said. "But from what I hear, they'll be looking to tie up the whole Mansion empire, to get everyone on the team and endorse every Senate candidate early and often. It sounds heavy-handed but that's the way these guys are. Beckworth's masterminding the strategy for them, seeing as he's not facing an election this time."

"I still don't see how that would help," she argued. "A series of biased endorsements would turn people off."

"It would be more than just endorsements," he explained. "There would be 'investigative reporting' of the opposition candidates—your basic hatchet jobs. Flattering coverage of the good guys. A communications network as big as the Mansion one could play one hell of a role if the whole coverage was orchestrated. It hasn't been tried since the bad old days—remember Chicago?—but it worked then, so imagine how much better it would work now, with television and radio besides the newspapers."

"Well, it's an interesting scenario but it isn't going to play," she said carefully, considering. "I don't care what the television network does—we've no control over Richard's domain—but it would destroy all the credibility our newspapers have earned. If the administration thinks they can do this, they're pretty naïve."

"I hope it comes to nothing," Ted said. "But we don't know about Lyle. As I said, I don't know how much pressure he can take, and I don't really know what kind of deal he made with them when he got that loan. Just remember what a sneaky son-of-a-bitch Beckworth is: he does not play by accepted rules."

"If he starts to play rough with us, just let me know," Angie said. "I wouldn't at all mind having a showdown with Ken and I think I know who'd come out on top."

"I'll keep you in on things," Ted promised. "But you keep an eye on Lyle. He's jittery."

* * *

Lyle was staring moodily into the burning logs in the big stone fireplace. It was a crisp, beautiful late afternoon and she had tried to interest him in a ride through the fall countryside, but he was so lethargic all the time.

Angie wished there was something she could do for him. He didn't seem to be part of his children's lives anymore, or hers. He was morose most of the time. The only thing still alive in him was determination to make the newspapers successful. And that, she reflected sadly, was fueled only by his obsession with Richard.

"I was thinking of going up to New York next weekend," Angie said. "Do you want to come with me? Maybe we could have a look at what's going wrong with the paper."

"Next weekend?" he said vaguely. "No, I'm going on a . . . hunting trip. With some people. Not for pleasure. Strictly business. People from the Hill."

"Okay," she said. "The kids are staying in school for the rest of the semester—or until they get their grades up, so they won't be here. You go shoot bears and I'll have a girls-only visit with Trish. I haven't spoken to her in ages."

"Trish?" he said, finally looking up from the fire. "Trish won't be in New York. Sam kicked her out. I heard about it, oh, a couple of weeks ago. I assumed you knew."

"What are you talking about?" she demanded. "Trish and Sam? No, she would have called me."

He hated gossip and was uneasy with what he remembered being told.

"It came from, uh, Ken Beckworth," he said. "He's thick with Sam these days. Ken said the whole thing was hushed up. Trish would have lost the little boy if she'd made a fuss. She got custody, and she got child support—peanuts—and nothing else. Ken said she'd done the smart thing and left town, gone home to Texas.''

''What do you mean? Trish is a fighter. She wouldn't give up everything. And I know some things about Sam Hardy—'' She stopped.

''Just leave it, Angie,'' he said. ''Sam Hardy is a very powerful man and when he's crossed he can be spiteful and frightening. She wouldn't have stood a chance in the divorce courts against Sam, even if she *hadn't* been guilty. I think she was damned lucky to get custody. Although knowing Sam, he prob'ly only saw the kid as a bargaining chip anyhow. Just let it rest.''

It took a while. The only number she had for Trish was the Manhattan penthouse. Finally, on Sunday evening, she called the *Tribune*'s library and had them go through the library clips on Trish. From what she learned, she got a number outside San Antonio. An old man answered the phone.

''Mizz Wright?'' he wheezed. ''Mizz Wright passed on some time ago.''

''Is that Mr. Wright?'' she said, raising her voice. ''Trish's father?''

''You mean Patricia? Yes, that's me, her father.''

''Is Trish there?'' she asked. ''I've got to speak to her.''

''She's in New York,'' the old man said carefully.

''Please,'' Angie begged. ''I'm her oldest friend. I've got to get in touch with her. You must have some idea where she it.''

''What did you say your name was?'' he asked. ''I'm not supposed to tell anyone she's here.''

She felt a surge of relief.

She told him her name and waited, listening to the

lonely whistling of space between her and Texas. And then Trish was there.

"Hi, Angie." Her voice was washed out, tired. "I guess you're going to scream at me for not calling. But it was all such a goddamned mess, I just packed my bags, grabbed Ben, and caught the first plane." She was trying not to cry.

"Calm down, honey, I'm not going to yell," Angie said. "I love you and I just want to do anything I can to help. But I got such a shock when Lyle told me about . . . about it. Are you all right? And Ben?"

"We're fine, Angie, fine," Trish said. "I just thought we'd come out here and be with Daddy while I decided what I'm going to do."

"Do you want me to come visit? Or you come stay here in Virginia for a while?"

"No, don't come here," Trish said. "There's nothing here for you. But maybe, when things settle down, we'll come visit with you in Virginia."

"What happened?" Angie demanded abruptly.

"I don't wank to talk about it, Angie," she said. "I'm just happy to be out of it. I've got my child, which is all I wanted from Sam Hardy. I guess sooner or later I'll go back east and take a job, something *I* want to do for a change. I've still got plenty of connections, people who aren't terrified of Sam. We'll be all right, Ben and I."

"What can I do for you now?" Angie asked.

"You've done it, just by calling. I'm fine, really. Soon as I've straightened up a few things, I'll call you. Maybe we'll come visit, too."

Angie made her trip to New York that weekend, her mind filled with memories of the weekend at the Plaza, with Trish. Oh, why had Trish married Sam?

A limo was waiting for Angie at LaGuardia and whisked her to Lyle's Beekman Place house where the smiling staff welcomed her. It was, she thought, the way everyone should live. She wondered how much she would miss all of it, when the break with Lyle finally came.

She fixed herself a drink in the big front sitting room, enjoying the late-afternoon light on the trees lining the quaint street. Idly, she wondered what she would do that evening. She was deciding on a play when Mrs. Sommers, the housekeeper, came in.

"Telephone, Mrs. Mansion," she said. "It's young Mr. David Mansion. Will you take it in here?"

Angie nodded, frowning. She had met Richard's son only two or three times, at her wedding and family parties. He had seemed polite and intense, a young man of the Mansion mold. They had never had time to talk. She picked up the telephone.

"Angie?" he said. "David Mansion. Uncle Lyle said you were going to be in town on your own tonight, and I need a date for a very special Broadway opening. Would you like to come with me?"

"Well, I . . ." she stammered.

"It's a new play, *Torch Song Trilogy*. It's supposed to be great."

"Why, sure, David. What do you want me to wear?"

"Anything," he said. "People don't dress for Broadway openings anymore. I'll pick you up at the house around seven, maybe a quick drink there. Have you got the limo? Good, we'll use that. My Honda died last week."

David arrived on time, bringing a breath of life into the stiff, formal house. He was wearing jeans and black leather boots and a black velvet jacket over an open cream shirt. She was glad she'd chosen the short gray dress, so they wouldn't look odd together. And she was glad to be spending the evening with him. He was the one Mansion, apart from old Alex, who had any vitality about him. He looked somewhat like his father had looked when Richard was young, but he had none of Richard's crude aggressiveness. His Mansion eyes were dark blue and fiery, but their light came from enthusiasm, not rapacious greed.

"You're looking great," he said, smiling at her. "I thought by now our awful family would have turned you into a bitter old lady, but no." He took the champagne she offered and prowled around the handsome living room, looking. "Nothing much wrong with this place a good decorator couldn't fix," he said. "All it really needs is living in. But that's our clan: we collect houses and people and then don't know what to do with them. So we leave them empty." He chuckled. "The family sure doesn't know what to do with *me*. Here I am, staring thirty in the eye, and I'm still 'different.' Dad won't admit I'm gay, thinks it's just some passing kid thing. Hell, Mansions have been and done everything else you can think of, so why wouldn't one of us be a faggot?"

"As long as you're happy . . ." she said lamely.

"Happy! Being a Mansion means you're never going to be happy," he said. "Happy is too plebian. No, being a Mansion is about doing your duty in public, and destroying the competition in private. We're like Sicilians: anything's excused in the name of the family. That's what I like about Grandad. He's honest about what we are. But an asshole like my father—and Uncle Lyle, too—people who pretend we're really doing good, well, that's what I can't take."

"I think you're being harsh," she protested. "Yes, they're rich and powerful, but they have feelings like everyone else."

He laughed. "Feelings don't come with our family. Look at my aunts, rich bitches destroying everyone they touch. Same with my father. And Lyle." He stopped suddenly, as if he might have gone too far.

She said nothing. She was unnerved by this young man: he seemed to know all the family secrets and take the worst for granted. "I don't think the situation with your family is nearly as bad as you paint it," she began weakly.

He smiled, a genuine smile.

"You're probably right," he said. "Whatever, I think you're one of the few nice things to have happened to us. I'm pleased you're one of us." He fished an ancient fob watch from a pocket. "But if we don't move now we're going to miss the first act. As arts editor of the *Christopher Street Argus*, I can't afford to do that."

As they moved through the lobby Angie's heart sank. It was not a typical Broadway opening: the gay crowd was dominant, and she recalled what she'd heard about the play. All she needed, a night of homosexual *angst*.

"Don't worry," David said, squeezing her elbow. "It's a great play. You'll love it."

And she did. From the first act, as the brave and funny character of Arnold Beckoff battled to be himself while still fitting into a world he was not in step with, she lost herself in the play. There were so many different ways of being and loving and living. They stood in the foyer after the performance as the crowd flowed around them and she put her hand on David's arm.

"Thanks," she said, "for showing me something I needed to see. We're all minorities, aren't we? Trying to conform on one level and be ourselves on another."

"Oh, it's just a play," he said, "a little soapish in the third act. But," he gave her that smile again, tender and real, "I love anyone who likes it. Without the fireworks, it's close to being my story. And yours, I suspect. And a lot of other people's, straight or any-which-way." He moved her through the crowd. "There's a party, if you like, but I hate waiting around for the *New York Times* review. For once, that review won't matter. *Trilogy* will get this season's Tony."

They found her limo and went back uptown to Beekman Place and she asked him in for a drink and supper. She wanted to spend more time with this one young Mansion who had defied all conventions and was so sparkling. Maybe he had the answer to surviving the clan.

She watched him over the rim of her glass: only the best of the Mansions was in him, none of the cruelty. Maybe Alex would have something in his lineage to be proud of. But he was gay, and his grandfather would never understand that. She watched him, wondering. How gay was he, really? She drained her glass and he refilled it. Her body and mind, freed by the play, cried out for stimulation. And a part of her considered the ultimate revenge—taking Richard Mansion's son inside her and conquering him and turning him around to achieve with him what none of them had been able to. She laughed aloud. She was getting high on the joint he had passed her in the limo, and the champagne and the excitement of the evening were all working together.

"You're a good lady, Angie," he said, gently. He was standing by her chair and holding her hand, his touch silky-soft, his tall young body leaning over her. "You can count me on your side in anything. Anything."

She wondered whether to touch him, take his slim body down to hers. She put her glass down carefully on the table beside her and began to rise and face him.

The telephone rang. Now that the staff was in bed, it had been plugged in.

"Angie?" Ted Buchanan's voice was anxious. "Thank God I found you. We've got a big problem. Young Emily's in trouble. She walked out of school yesterday and tonight the Baltimore cops picked her up on The Strip." He paused. "The thing is, they found some heroin—not much—on her. They're holding her for possession." When she didn't speak, he went on. "See, she's over sixteen so they can't keep it out of the courts. The whole thing is one goddamned mess. I've been trying to find Lyle all evening but no one knows where he is, off with Beckworth somewhere, I was told. I've sent a lawyer to Baltimore and we'll have her out of jail within an hour or so. I've arranged to have her brought back here. After that, I don't know what to do with her."

"Oh my God." Angie found her voice. "The poor little kid. It's a mistake. Not little Emily. Not heroin."

"Yes, little Emily," he said, his voice suddenly harsh. "I spoke with one of the cops in Baltimore. The kid's been a user for a while, he said, at least some months. How the hell didn't either of you know?"

"I'm sorry," she said. "But I haven't any experience with that. I wouldn't know what to look *for*. And Lyle . . . he's even more naïve than I am." She started crying.

289

"Okay," he said gently. "We'll untangle this. Once I get her up here, I'll take care of her until you arrive. I think you better get yourself down here as soon as you can."

She looked at her watch: it was almost midnight.

"I've got the limo," she said, "but the driver's gone home. I guess I'll try and handle the car myself."

David shook his head and pointed to himself.

"I'll make it some way, Ted," she said hurriedly. "Expect me in three or four hours. Take care of her, please, Ted. And Ted? Thanks."

She hung up and sat by the telephone for a moment, slumped in shock. She looked at David, despair in her eyes.

"Emily," she said. "The police say she's been using heroin."

"It figures," he said, not at all surprised. "A lot of the kids are looking for new highs right now. Particularly rich kids. Okay, so you've got to race down there and unscramble it all. I'll drive you. We can set some kind of record in the limo. You better go get your things together while I fix us a thermos of coffee. There won't be anything open on the highway, not at this hour."

Later she remembered little of the journey, just the huge car sliding through the night, her sitting up front with David, smoking endless cigarettes and feeling despair go deeper and deeper. David was everything she needed him to be: cool and calm and unshocked. All Angie could think about was the girl, her fair young skin pockmarked with needles, huddled in some filthy cold prison cell.

The reality, when she found Emily in Lyle's suite at the *Tribune* office, was as bad. The child was deathly pale and dead-eyed, her body wracked by shuddering fits. Ted had found her a doctor, but Emily still looked deathly ill and strung out. Angie ran across the room and flung herself down, cradling the girl in her arms. There was no response at all.

"Oh God, Ted," she said, turning to him, "is she going to be all right?"

"Yes, Mrs. Mansion," the young doctor answered for Ted. "I've checked her over and I don't think she's been fooling around with the stuff for too long. It'll take a day or two to detoxify her. I doubt there's much physical dependence yet. But psychologically, you're going to have to do some searching. Why is she taking heroin? Who is she trying to punish?"

"Punish?" Angie said. "Why should she want to punish anyone? She has everything."

"They're often the ones who do this," he said, as kindly as he could. He was so young and matter-of-fact, as if he'd seen hundreds of cases just like this one. And she supposed he had. "She should be all right now, Mrs. Mansion," he said. "So I'll leave you all. Ted, good night. Glad I could help."

"What are we going to do?" she asked Ted after the doctor had gone. Emily was asleep and she wasn't worried about being overheard.

"It's a mess," Ted sighed. "You don't have to worry about charges. We can fix that. But I can't get her name off the booking sheet, and some police reporter is sure to see it. That's why we've got to find Lyle as soon as we can. He's the only one who can call other publishers and get her name kept out of the papers. Do you know where he is, Angie?"

"He said he was going hunting with some people from the Hill," she said helplessly. "I wasn't really listening. I don't know where to look."

"Okay," Ted said, "I'm going back down to the newsroom. A couple of guys I trust are trying to track him down. We need him back by tomorrow if we're going to keep the lid on this. Will you be all right, bedded down here with Emily?"

"Sure," she said. "I'll stay with her. But what if she wakes up and needs something? I don't know what to do."

"It's okay, Angie," David said softly from the corner where he was sitting, "I'll be here, and I know exactly what to do in cases like this. I've been there myself."

Perhaps Lyle could have kept it out of the papers. Perhaps the brotherhood of publishers might have swung together and protected one of its own. But Lyle was still out of touch on Monday morning, and the story broke everywhere. A Philadelphia paper gave it a great play, reminding readers of all the rich children who had fallen afoul of drugs.

And a gossip column made the unkindest cut of all, under the heading "Where's Poppa?" It revealed that Lyle, Senator Ken Beckworth, and "two blondes, whom park guards described as 'stacked' and who did not appear to be carrying tools of the secretarial trade" had spent the weekend in the palatial hunting lodge of the Mannaheim Corporation, a major supplier of communications hardware.

Ted relayed all this to her in Virginia, where she and Emily had gone on Sunday morning. Lyle himself called at noon Monday saying he was on his way and would be at the house late that afternoon.

"I'm sorry I wasn't there," he said before he hung up. "I guess I've never been there for the children—or for you. I'm sorry. I do love you and I love Emily and

Curt. I've just never been good at loving. Tell Emily everything is going to be all right." He sounded desolate, absolutely defeated. Any other time Angie would have tried to comfort him, but she was exhausted and furious.

"You come home whenever it suits you, Lyle," she said, her voice shaking. "The crisis will be over by the time you get here. There'll be nothing to disturb your comfortable existence. David and Ted and your lawyers have cleaned up the mess. Your father's coping with it all reasonably well. Emily's going to be fine. Really, it's just another chapter in the adventures of the Mighty Mansions. Don't let it disturb you in any way."

He wasn't there by four, or six. It was full dark before she began to wonder what had happened. He had probably, she thought bitterly, gone on drinking with his Washington cronies, unable to face the responsibilities at home.

The state police captain came to the house just before ten o'clock that night, as Angie was checking to see that Emily was safe in her sedated sleep. David answered the door and called Angie down to the entrance hall. He came to her as she ran down the stairs and put his arm around her shoulders. The gesture, and the tall uniformed man standing in the hall, told her what to expect.

"Angie," David said gently. "An accident. Lyle, in his car, driving down here."

She nodded. "He's dead, Angie," David said, and the officer bowed his head in confirmation. She nodded again. "It may have happened a couple of hours ago. But there's so little traffic on the back roads, no one drove by until recently."

"Can we get you something, Captain?" she asked,

slowly and deliberately. "Coffee? A drink? David, please see to our guest." She ran a hand through her hair. She was having trouble focusing on them. She saw the two men start toward her as she fell. David caught her just before she crashed to the marble floor.

In a strange way her father's death was what saved Emily. The tragedy bound her and Angie and Curtis together. Curt took a few weeks out from college to stay with them in Virginia, and the three spent long days and nights together, bound by their grief and confusion. They realized they had nobody except one another to hold on to. They had squandered love and friendship and trust, and now they were all they had left.

Alex Mansion came down and stayed. The death of his son reduced him: suddenly he was an old man, clinging desperately to life and to the people who would live on after he was gone. He got to know the children, bit by bit, and they warmed to him. Late in the evenings he would talk with Angie about the future of the clan. She was touched, even during the worst of her grief, by Alex's unwavering inclusion of her in everything.

"No," he said, one night when she had protested that she was not a member of the family. "You are a Mansion now and you are the best hope for the survival of the line. I don't know what I did wrong, but I accept all the blame. The girls—well, you know how the girls turned out. Richard is as tough as I could have made him but Richard doesn't know how to use strength. He's a killer, but for all the wrong reasons. He'll soar to great heights, but when he crashes it will be all the way.

"I thought Lyle would have matured and been the

good one. And you almost got him there. But it was too late. Lyle was too damaged already.'' He slumped forward in his wheelchair and made a choking sound, and she jumped up and ran to him. But when she knelt before him she saw his strong old face was ravaged by tears. The heaving in his shoulders was caused by grief. She put out a hand to console him, but withdrew it. Alex Mansion, builder of empires, could not be consoled by Angie Waring, who could not console herself.

She went back to her chair and waited until he was calmer.

''Alex,'' she said finally, ''I want out. I'm not a Mansion and I never will be. You and all your family react to things in a certain way: you believe in some divine right to run things. I'm just an ordinary person who does the best she can and I'm way out of my league with you. But I love the children and, for the few more years they're going to need someone, I want to take care of them. After that, I'm going back to civilian life.''

He raised his huge old head, not bothering to wipe away his tears, gazed at her, and nodded slowly.

''You *are* a Mansion, though,'' he said. ''I decided that a long while ago. You more than paid your dues to become one.'' He smiled a bitter smile. ''God knows why anyone would want to be a Mansion, but what we have to do now is face the future. The newspaper chain needs a publisher and I want you to be that person. I'll protect you from my dreadful family as long as I can. You can run the chain; you're better qualified then anyone in the family. I shall give you my total support. If, at the same time, you can continue to counsel Emily and Curtis, then you will have made me very happy. I know you haven't gotten anything but grief out of being a Mansion, not so far. Please stay with us. I'll try my best to see you properly rewarded.''

"Alex," she said, "the fight has all gone out of me. I don't want to take on causes anymore, I don't want the responsibility.''

"Ah, but you have it," he said gently. "You're stuck with it. Do this, please—not just for me but for yourself. Go ahead and be the publisher of great newspapers. Make our name a name to be proud of again.''

"But there have been too many deals done already, too much sold out for the sake of other Mansion interests," she protested. "Even Lyle made deals to get what he wanted. There was pressure on him for blanket endorsements of party candidates; they were going to call in the loan if he didn't play ball. I couldn't go along with that kind of thing.''

"Don't then," he said. "Take over the newspapers and cancel all obligations. Run your own race. I'll back you to the hilt, Angie." He watched her closely. "I don't know what happened long ago between you and Richard, but I figure it was bad. It's all water under the bridge now, anyway. I have told you I will back you and that's all you have to be concerned about. I'm asking you to run the newspapers and take care of my grandchildren. Will you do that much for me?''

Suddenly, for the first time in weeks, Angie heard herself laugh. A laugh from deep inside her, laughter of frustration and joy. Because old Alex Mansion had backed her into a corner and she didn't mind.

"Okay, Alex," she said. "If you're supporting me I'll do it. But it's going to be a bloody affair. Because you're right about Richard. He and I have some major scores to settle."

"One other thing I want to impose on you, Angie," he said. Alex Mansion was not used to having to ask for favors; he mumbled now and she had to strain to hear him. "Could I stay on here, in Virginia? I'd keep out of your way, and while you're off running the papers I could look out for Emily, at least until she goes away to college. Living here I could get to know her and Curtis properly. I didn't spend enough time with my own children and I want to make up for it with them. And," he added humbly, "there's no place else I can be of any use. Richard's running things now. It only annoys him to have me bobbing up in the boardroom."

"I'd love it!" Angie said, smiling at the old man. "And so would the children. They've become very attached to you. And Emily so badly needs someone to talk with. She's only now beginning to understand what she did to herself; next she has to understand why."

"How about Curtis?" he asked. "He seems a fine young man in every respect. No trouble there, is there?"

She debated telling him about Curt. The boy had come to her in tears after his father's death to tell her he had been messing with coke. A five-hundred-dollar-a-week cocaine habit, paid for out of the generous allowance Lyle had given him. Now he wanted to quit fooling around with any kind of dope, Curt had told her. He said he wanted to "be a man" and said he would appreciate her help. She hadn't let him see how disturbed she was by all the drug use. She felt such despair; young lives twisted so early.

"No, Alex," she said. "There's no trouble with Curt."

She edged into her new role slowly, terrified that she couldn't handle it and concerned about upsetting Ted, who had been running the chain since Lyle's death.

Ted sensed the problem.

"Look, Angie," he said one afternoon, pacing the floor of her publisher's office, "cut out this diffident crap. I told you before that you should be the publisher, that you'd be great at it. I also said I didn't want the job. Now I'm happy on both scores, so for Christ's sake, will you start acting like a boss so we can all get on with our tasks?"

"Thanks, Ted," she laughed. "Okay, I'll do it your way. But please, if I ever get out of line, or try and do something really stupid, save me, will you? You and I have been through too much together to risk it over some office clash."

One of the bigger problems facing her was what to do about the group's editorial stance on the midterm elections: the pressure was being stepped up, Ted said.

"I've just stalled them," he said. "But make no mistake—these guys play hard ball. Beckworth's turned it into a personal crusade to win big for his party. I guess he'll get the vice-presidential slot if he quarterbacks this election right. If you renege on Lyle's deal, the least they'll do is pull in the Canadian loan. Can the Mansions stand that?"

"They'll have to, won't they?" Angie said. "Alex says he'll back me in anything, and all agreements about political deals are off. I don't know what Richard will do, though. Lyle's cozy arrangement with the administration was all part of Richard's strategy to rule the communications world. I guess old Alex can handle Richard, though." She lit a cigarette; she was smoking too heavily again and she would give it up, just as soon as everything got back to normal. "I think I better have Ken Beckworth up here and tell him what the new rules are. If we're going to have a battle we might as well do it now."

Before she set up the meeting with Beckworth, Angie flew to New York to huddle with Johnny Howard. The family lawyer had been wonderful to her during the past dreadful months and they had formed a close bond, two outsiders taken into the bosom of the Mansion family.

"We don't need to talk in the office," he told her when she phoned. "I'll play hookey for the day, take you around New York, show you some of the places the tycoons don't go."

He picked her up in his limousine from the Beekman Place house. He wasn't wearing his lawyer's suit. In tweed jacket and jeans he looked young and appealing. They drove down the crumbling East River Drive and crossed over to the Village.

"Let's walk awhile," he said and they strolled through the narrow streets, the car inching along behind them. She hadn't been in the area in years and was impressed by the bustle of activity there, the bright little shops and restaurants, the trees defying the gritty air and reaching for the weak sunshine.

"The city really has made a comeback," he said happily. "There's a lot of optimism in the air. Real estate is booming and the Dow is set to go way past the thousand." They walked some more, shaking off too much work and too many worries. "When you consider the *Sentinel*'s problems, you might think about it in terms of what's happening in Manhattan," he said. "The paper is like the *Daily News* twenty years ago—still shock, horror, crime. But there's a far more sophisticated audience here now. I think you could take the *Sentinel* up market a little and do very well. Bloomie's and Saks and the rest would love another place to advertise; they get nervous being locked into the *Times*."

They rode over to Chinatown for lunch, to a Cantonese seafood place he liked. It was packed but the owner, beaming at him, found them a table.

"21 it's not," he said, ordering Kirin beer, "but the food is as good as anything in Hong Kong. You might not think so," he added, waving his hand around the crowded, noisy room, "but this place is one of New York's best-kept secrets. All the downtown people use it like a club."

As if on cue, a tall bald man pushed through the tables and stood over them.

"Johnny," he said, "it's always good to see you but I had to come by and meet your companion. The kind of new face we need around here."

"Mr. Mayor," Johnny said, rising, "I'd like you to meet Angie Mansion. Angie . . ."

"I know who she is, dummy," the mayor said. A chair appeared for him and he sat down with them. "I hear you're going to be putting some life into the *Sentinel*. God knows, it needs it. If there's anything City Hall can do for you, pick up the phone and ask. The *Sentinel* has never endorsed me and, frankly, the way the paper's been in the past I could do without it. But I care about this city and we need all the strong voices we can get. So I mean it: I'll do anything I can for you just as long as you're running an honest, positive newspaper."

They talked awhile and she liked his breezy, funny manner. He felt like an instant old friend and she was caught up in his enthusiasm for the city. She was beginning to look forward to the time she would be spending in New York.

The mayor left them, and they ordered food and Angie got around to the subject she had to discuss.

"The Canadian newsprint mill loan," she said. "I take it you know all about that."

"I know the figures," he said. "A sweetheart deal. I never wanted to know what the bottom line was: some promises must've been made."

"Yes," she said, "and I'm about to break them. I need to know what it means to us all if the Ex-Im bank loan is suddenly called in."

He frowned, studying her face to see if she was aware of the enormity of the problem. "It would be a goddamned disaster," he said. "Interest rates are heading over twenty percent and won't get better for years. I wouldn't like to go out and find thirty million bucks to pay those bastards back, not right now. And I wouldn't like to try and sell the mills on the present market. Newsprint price is actually coming down now. Lyle's scheme was a good one when he did it, and it has paid off for the newspaper division, but it's a dreadful time to be thinking about restructuring the debt. Do you have to?"

"Yes," she said. "If I went along with Lyle's promises, the newspaper group's credibility would be ruined. So what are we going to do?"

"Well," he said carefully, "there is one prospect. I haven't bothered you about this. It's a sensitive issue. But Lyle was carrying a 'key-man' life policy, purchased by the company. It's worth twenty million bucks. Richard's already got it earmarked to go into his satellite scheme, but if you've got Alex on your side, I don't see why the money shouldn't be used to repay most of the Canadian debt. Then we could finance the rest on the open market and be no worse off than we are now."

She couldn't believe how good this news was. "It would be appropriate, too, if his death can save the newsprint mills, Lyle's great dream and his one real achievement. I'm sure Alex will go for it."

"There's just one problem," he said, toying with his chopsticks. "The insurance company is balking at paying. They don't like the facts of the accident at all. The police say Lyle must have been traveling at more than a hundred and forty miles an hour to do that kind of damage to the car."

"So? He wasn't drunk or anything, was he?"

"No," Johnny said. "Negligible blood alcohol. No, they can't wriggle out of it that way." He looked embarrassed. "What they're trying to prove is suicide. That Lyle was so distraught over everything that had happened to him, he revved the Maserati up and ran it into a tree. They'd have one hell of a job proving that, but there's a lot of money at stake and they're hoping we'll settle for, say, half of it rather than take them to court."

She went pale and her hands trembled.

"They *couldn't* prove suicide, could they, Angie?" he asked gently. "If it goes to trial they'll dredge up anything they can on Lyle, you, the kids. They'll go to former servants, friends, enemies . . . anyone who might be prepared to say Lyle was a likely suicide because of personal or business reasons."

"It would all come out, wouldn't it?" she asked. "Unless we forgo a lot of money, they'll try and smear him and the family?"

"Yes," he said, "and I wouldn't want to put you through that. Perhaps a settlement . . ."

"No! To hell with them!" she said. "You tell the company we're not settling. I don't care what they dredge up. The money is owed and we won't be bullied. And tell them one other thing: I'll see to it this case gets page-one play every single day. That's going to be real good for future insurance business, isn't it—a widow fighting for the insurance her husband left to protect his family."

"I like you," Johnny said, grinning. "You're a real fighter. Leave this to me. I think, once they know you're prepared to go all the way, they'll fold up. But I had to know your reaction before I could take them on. Most people would have preferred to settle and avoid a fight."

"I've avoided too many fights, Johnny," she said. "Now, if I'm going to do my job right, I'm not going to let the bastards wear me down. Any bastards."

"Oh, I can see some fun times during family councils." He grinned. "Thank God you've got Alex on your side. You keep him down there in Virginia, where the others can't get at him. That's the best strategy."

"That's the other thing I wanted to talk about," she said. "With Lyle gone, what happens to the balance of power in the family? Who lines up with whom?"

"It's always hard to tell," he said. "The wicked sisters can jump either way on any issue, but they hate each other so they usually vote on opposite sides, which cancels them out. Richard and Lyle had equal blocks and Lyle's shares have been left to the children. I'm the executor and under the will you get to vote their shares until they're twenty-one. I have a percentage of my own. So, Alex and you voting the kids' share and me voting mine should just carry the day.''

''And I can rely on you about the insurance money?'' she asked. ''In spite of Richard?''

''Sure,'' he said. ''Why not? Richard's been getting his own way too much lately. And I love a good battle.''

After lunch they strolled across Mulberry Street and had coffee in Little Italy. She felt nervous but strong, knowing what she had to do. If Johnny Howard was prepared to support her, she need not be afraid. But the prospect of facing Richard down did not give her the thrill she had anticipated. Sure, she still wanted revenge, but more than that she wanted some peace.

''Thanks for a wonderful day,'' she told Johnny when he dropped her back at Beekman Place. ''You've given me a lot of confidence. I needed it badly.''

''You'll be okay,'' he said. ''And you can always call on me.''

Angie was having dinner with Trish that night and she was both happy and relieved. Trish had never come to Virginia: she had called during Angie's awful times, but had not wanted to impose on her friend. Trish was living in New York, holding down a high-profile job as director of the Manhattan borough president's task force on housing.

Angie was shocked by the change in her appearance. Trish was still a handsome woman but there was a strange remoteness in her face, the look of someone who had been badly hurt and wouldn't be hurt again. They embraced at Angie's door and Angie led her inside the house.

''It's been too long,'' Angie said when they were

sitting in the living room. "I know we've both been awfully busy but it's crazy not to see each other. We need each other."

Trish nodded and smiled.

"I've thought about you all the time," she said, "but there's been so much going on . . ." She sipped her drink. "Nothing worked out at all the way we planned, did it? All those hopes and all those dreams," she said bitterly.

Trish had obviously had it very hard.

"You were right, of course," Trish continued without prompting. "I never should have rushed into marriage. But I wanted something to get me out of Washington and Sam Hardy looked like a good way. I guess, going into it with that attitude, I deserved what happened to me." She thought for a moment. "No I didn't. No one deserves that."

"You want to tell me?" Angie asked quietly.

"No." She shook her head sharply. "No. I just want to bury the whole thing. I'm making out. The job is good. I like it and I feel I'm achieving something after all this time. It's amazing they hired me: Hardy has so much clout in this town not many people would go against him. I was lucky."

"You'd never have trouble getting a big job," Angie insisted. "You were always brilliant. The way you ran your committee in Washington—I think *they're* damn lucky to have *you*."

"Yeah," Trish said wearily, passing a hand over her eyes. "And I'm damn lucky to be surviving. Now what about you? You're devoting yourself to the New York newspaper, I know that much."

"It's a challenge, that's for sure." Angie laughed ruefully.

"You'll get lots of cooperation," Trish said cynically. "Even more than Washington, New York is obsessed with power. And a newspaper in New York is real power. Everyone's going to want to help you. I hope you survive all their help."

Chapter
Fifteen

As old Alex slipped deeply into decline, scarcely stirring from Angie's Virginia home, Richard dominated Mansion family affairs more than ever. Angie could win most of the battles she needed to win, because they all knew the patriarch supported her, but the strain of fighting Richard and dealing with the strange sisters was getting to her.

"If they'd only let me get on with my job," she said to Ted on one of her rare visits to the Washington newspaper. "Hell, they know they can't sabotage the newspaper division as long as Alex is alive. And we're turning the *Sentinel* into a decent paper. We might even make a little money one of these years. But Richard fights me over every point. It's only Johnny Howard who stops the board meetings from ending in real bloodshed. I'm so sick of it, Ted."

"Now you see why I don't want to be a publisher," Ted said cheerfully. "Who needs the hassle?"

"But it *could* be fun," she said. "The *Sentinel* is looking good already. Sales are up a little and the advertising linage is the best in four years. We've got a pretty good staff. Industrial relations are fine, thanks to Johnny Howard. He's got the unions eating out of his hand. I think we're on a winner. If it weren't for the awful family scenes, I'd be very happy."

"I see you're pushing your pal Trish in the news columns," Ted Said. "What are you trying to do, run her for Congress?"

"I just might try and head her in that direction," Angie said confidently. "She's a damn sight more qualified than a lot of the hacks they elect and she sure as hell knows the ropes in Washington. But mostly I push her and a few other women who are doing big jobs in the city because they haven't been given enough recognition."

"I never thought of you as a feminist," he joked. "You always just wanted to get on with the job."

"I still do," she said. "But sixty percent of our readers are women, so it makes sense to profile a few once in a while."

"You get much trouble from pulling out of the newsprint loan? I sure as hell did."

"There have been a few veiled threats from the party chiefs," she said. "But we paid them back their loan and it didn't really end up costing the family that much. The only person who's still livid about it is Richard. He wants every cent the family can raise to be put into his satellite project. He claims I've not only used 'his' money to pay back the newsprint loan, I've also alienated the people who will decide who gets the satellite. The trouble is, his arguments make a lot of sense when you listen to them during family councils. You forget about ethics and journalism and get entranced by the numbers. He talks grosses of three and four hundred million a year if he can get the exclusive rights. And I'm arguing to the family that, if they stick with me, I'll turn a loss of ten million or so into a profit of three or four million. With lots of luck.''

''Thank God for old Alex, then,'' Ted said. ''How is the old man? And what happens when he goes?''

''Don't even think about it.'' She shuddered. ''Alex is very old and subdued but he seems as strong as ever. I pray he lasts for many more years. Apart from the fact that I genuinely like the old devil, I don't know what will happen to all of us when he dies. The family will just become warring factions with no one strong enough—or rational enough—to pull anything together. I don't want to be around when it happens.''

''How's your personal life?'' he asked casually. ''New York can be a pretty lonely place when you're on your own.''

She laughed.

''I haven't got a personal life. The paper takes sixteen hours a day, minimum. I have the children up a lot of the time, or I fly down to see them and Alex. I eat lunch at my desk and go to three or four evening things I'm expected to show the flag at. In my free time I watch over my shoulder to see what Richard's going to pull on me next.''

After they'd talked a little longer, he glanced at his watch. ''I better go see how the first edition's shaping up. Later on,'' he said, very casually to let her know he would't be offended if she refused, ''I wondered if you might like to have dinner with me. If you haven't got anything else on.''

''Actually, I'm driving straight down to Virginia,'' she said. ''I thought I'd see the kids and Alex tonight, then fly back to the city tomorrow.'' She watched him watching her, and she made her decision. "But I can easily put everything back a few hours," she said. "I'd love us to have dinner together."

Before they met for dinner, she called her mother, just back in Boston from her tour of Europe. May and the beau had decided to move to California and live in the sunshine.

"He actually suggested Florida, if you can believe that! But I pointed out I'd lived there," her mother said drily. "The only thing is, I'll be a long way away from you. And I do miss you so much, Angie. I'm so proud of you, being a publisher, but those Mansions—don't trust any of them! I worry about who you've got to fall back on."

Angie laughed.

"Mom, you're a card," she said. "Here you are, flying all over the world, heading for California with an old boyfriend whom, you say, you can't see any point in marrying, and *you're* worried about *me* not having security!"

"It's what a mother is supposed to say," her mother replied. She laughed. "I know you'll be all right, Angie. Just watch those Mansions."

"I will, Mom. I won't let 'em out of my sight," she laughed.

Dinner with Ted was fun. They went to one of his comfortable haunts, Italian food, generous drinks, and a convivial crowd of newspaper people. Over coffee and cognac he asked her what she'd known he was going to ask.

"Will you stay with me tonight?"

She nodded. Of course she'd stay with him. She loved him. Didn't he know that?

It was, for Angie, stolen minutes of peace and real happiness. When Ted kissed her and brought a gentle hand to her breast, she was ready for him. Their bodies fitted together in harmony, and they made smooth gentle love until passion took over. She could feel the whole of him deep inside her. The first time she came it was a ripple; the second time it was a full flood, which rocked her, spasm after spasm, and made her cry out. The third time was when Ted rose on his knees and made one last mighty thrust into her. He came then, in a tide of passion flowing into her to meet her own tide.

He sank down and laid his head between her damp breasts. She stroked his rumpled hair and her fingers traced the outline of his backbone. Somewhere out in the dark night a police siren wailed, reminding her of how safe she was with this man.

"Ted," she whispered, gazing up into the darkness, "thank you. All these years. Thank you." Smiling in the dark, she went on holding him long after she fell asleep. He didn't sleep until much later.

Adam Carleton was pacing up and down in front of her desk, arguing loudly with Gerry Brand, the *Sentinel*'s city editor, and occasionally turning to Angie for support. She let the fight go on, back and forth, saying little. Carleton was always battling with someone over real or imagined infringements on the integrity of his gossip column. Today it was that Brand wanted to use Adam's lead item up front; the columnist insisted it stay right where it was.

"I got that story because the people involved want to see it in my column," he thundered. "They don't want it beaten up and butchered by you city desk hacks. Just because you haven't got a reporter worth a damn on your staff, don't plunder *my* column for something to fill your news hole. Right, Angie?"

She shrugged. She knew by now to just let these battles between her volatile staff play themselves out. If she intervened one side or the other felt slighted. She smiled to herself: all the turmoil was wearying, but it was what was making the *Sentinel* a success. What had *Newsweek* said about her publishing style? "Creative tension." Well, there was certainly plenty of creativity and tension at the *Sentinel*, and Adam Carleton was usually at the center of it.

He was handsome, arrogant, brilliant. The young man had come to Angie from the *Chicago Tribune* where, he said in disgust, he'd been confined to writing about show business. He was meant for much bigger things, he told her, and the *Sentinel* would be very lucky to get him. All he wanted was a daily column where he could break news, real news about the people who mattered in New York City. No sacred cows, no favors to anyone, no censorship: his demands began there. In return, he would put her paper on the map. She had listened to all this while trying not to smile. He was so sure of himself, tossing his mane of curly black hair, flashing his green eyes at her, giving her the benefit of his fine-chiseled profile. Adam was a huckster, selling only himself, and he was twenty-three years old. She had, possibly to the young man's surprise, agreed to take him on. She did so, moreover, on his terms. She regretted almost nothing about her decision. In six months at the *Sentinel* he had delivered the goods day after day. He got sensational inside stories about the biggest names in the city, stories the other papers would have killed for. There was a vicious twist to his column, which made it popular from the start. The people wanted blood and Adam Carleton was a killer.

The one thing she was uncomfortable about was

knowing that he was totally amoral in what he wrote. And if she ever tried to rein him in he would walk away from the *Sentinel* without a backward glance, straight into the waiting arms of her competitors, she was sure of that.

"All right," she said, "that's enough. What we'll do, Gerry, is a big type pointer off page one to Steve's column. With a picture of the subject. Okay?"

"I've got to approve the wording of the pointer," Steve said. "I don't trust—"

"Steve, quit while you're ahead," Angie snapped, and he nodded and subsided. She could still control him, just. "Now both of you go. I've got work to do and you've got an edition to get out."

After they had gone she crossed to a big leather chair by the window and gave herself a few minutes of peace, staring out on to the East River and the traffic on the Brooklyn Bridge. The view always soothed her. The river was so New York, busy, grubby, changing with every minute. Each day at sunset it repaired itself and became a creature of mystery and glamour.

At four o'clock her guest arrived and she looked up, a genuine smile on her face. The mayor had become one of her favorite people: what critics called his abrasiveness she considered blunt honesty.

"It's so good to see you," she said as he loped across the wide expanse of the room. "Come sit here beside me. Mary, if you'll bring in tea now, please, then hold all calls for the next half hour."

They talked easily about the affairs of the city and he tested her reaction to several programs he had in mind. Angie had learned fast that New York was even more intensely political than Washington. But

New York politics were more personal, the political battles like family vendettas.

"I hear you're going to run Trish Hardy for Congress," he said abruptly. "Not a bad idea. She's one of the most popular women in the city—with people on my side of the fence, anyway. But you might strike some problems."

"I can't see many," Angie said. "Trish is smart, attractive, high-profile. The man she'd be running against is an idiot."

"All true," he said. "But they're not going to give up that district without a fight and they'd see her as a very big danger to them. So if she is nominated, they'd try hard to destroy her *before* the poll."

"Well, that's politics," Angie said. "Trish will be able to handle it."

"I'm not so sure," he said. "I paid a courtesy call on our beloved junior senator when I was in the capital the other day, and he went out of his way to warn me against Trish Hardy running."

"Ken Beckworth?" she said, instantly alerted to danger. "Surely he's not concerning himself with one little congressional district?"

"He's still the party quarterback," the mayor reminded her, "but I guess, even so, he wouldn't normally bother with a race like that. I think he's concerned because Sam Hardy wants him to be. Hardy has an enormous amount of power here and in D.C., and he's also given a fortune to Beckworth's party. The message I got from Beckworth was Hardy didn't want his ex-wife running for public office. He'll do just about anything to stop her, too."

"Beckworth is a creep," Angie said angrily, "and Sam Hardy is just another power broker. Hell, all I want to do is help some decent candidates into Congress. If we have to buck the system to do it, so what?"

"Okay, Angie." He smiled. "I just thought I'd pass it along. It goes without saying that if your friend does get the nomination, I'll be proud to endorse her."

"Adam Carleton wants to see you before you go," Angie's secretary told her as she took the last of the day's documents from the publisher's desk. "He said he didn't mind how late it was and he also wouldn't mind if you asked him to have a drink. He's an insufferable pain in the ass."

"That he is, Mary," Angie said. "But he sells papers. I'd love to put him in his place but I need his column every day and he knows it." She brushed her hair back. It had been another tiring day and what she wanted to do was go home to Beekman Place and go to bed. It was one of the rare evenings without commitments. "Tell him to come up now. Tell him I haven't very much time. And you take off now, please. Your husband must really hate the hours you have to work with me."

"He doesn't complain too much." The young woman smiled. "Just so long as I'm happy. And I am. I love this job. I think you're an incredible woman, the way you've turned the *Sentinel* around."

They smiled at each other and Angie waved good night. How lucky Mary was to be going home to a husband who was proud of her, a man she could talk with about the day's events. Angie was finding it harder and harder to fight the loneliness. The more she worked the more she needed company, but there was no one in New York she wanted to be with. Johnny Howard, maybe. But the two of them were so tied together by the tentacles of the Mansion empire, she couldn't very well have Johnny as an intimate friend.

There was a knock on her door and she pressed the button under her desk to unlock it and let her caller in.

"Hi, Angie!" Adam Carleton bounced into the room. "I just thought I'd stop by and cheer my boss lady up. I've got some news for you, too, but it can wait."

She didn't smile. Of all her key staff who called her by her first name, only the cocky Carleton managed to make something insidious of it. Only Carleton dared treat her with thinly veiled male condescension.

"You can cut out the 'boss lady' crap," she said sharply. "Unless you want to be known as 'the boy columnist.' "

"I don't mind," he said, giving her his flashing smile. "I don't see my youth as a handicap."

"Nor I my gender," she snapped. "What do you want to see me about? I'm due uptown in a little while."

"Okay," he said. "I'm sorry. I didn't mean to offend you. Just trying to be friendly." He grinned again. "Could I fix us a drink? It's been one helluva day for me."

"I'll fix the drinks," she said firmly, rising from behind the desk and moving to the cabinet in front of the large window. "Martini?"

"Please. Very dry, straight up with a twist."

She calmed herself as she mixed the drinks. He was just brash, the way so many kids were brash these days. And he was brilliant. She carried the drinks over to where he had sprawled in a chair and managed a smile.

"Another good column today, Adam," she said. "I loved the bit about Senator Dunhill shoving his hand down Bitsy Amphora's dress. And the quote: 'What we need is more separation here and less in the party.' The senator must have been livid you picked it up."

"He was," Carleton said. "He had his flack call me and demand a retraction, an apology, the works. I told him to go fuck himself, that if he really wanted to make something of it I just happened to have a picture of the senator in the act with skinny Bitsy. I threatened to run it tomorrow. In the end the *flack* was apologizing to *me.*"

"Thank God you had the picture," Angie said. "I'm sure Bitsy would have denied everything."

"There is no picture," he said, beaming in self-congratulation. "But they don't know that." He got up and fetched the martini shaker and refilled their glasses.

The first drink had lifted her and despite herself Angie was enjoying Adam. She remembered her own time as a gossip columnist, the risks she'd had to take. It was a rough way to make a name and she couldn't blame the kid for boasting.

"Well, thank God they didn't call your bluff," she said, laughing. "I tried something like that myself once and I sweated for days thinking I was going to get sued and wouldn't have anything to back up the story with."

"Yeah, you were quite a columnist in your day," he said, and he didn't really mean to be condescending. "Washington wasn't used to the stuff you were doing. You were a pioneer, really. I looked it all up before I came to see you for a job. I figured you for the kind of lady—sorry, the kind of journalist—who'd dig what I was all about.'' He stood up, the shaker in his large hand. ''Let me fix the next one, will you? That wasn't quite dry enough. Just a mist of vermouth is all it needs. I'm quite good at this.''

She knew she shouldn't have another, but the drinks were working nicely, the view of the dark river and the traffic beside it was lovely. And there was no one waiting for her at home.

He brought the fresh drinks and as the big office slowly darkened they sat and talked, telling newspaper stories, laughing over the legends of their profession. She hardly noticed when he sat down beside her on the couch, but then his arm was draped along the back and suddenly he was trying to kiss her. As Angie moved away from him, his other hand went up her skirt and for a second he touched her there. She pushed him away and stood up, shocked, outraged and—strangely—amused. She moved quickly to her desk and turned on the lights.

''I'm sorry,'' he said. He looked bewildered. ''I thought you'd like me. You're a lovely woman, on your own and all. I thought—''

''Just forget it, Adam,'' she said briskly. ''A case of mistaken signals.'' But she wondered. Perhaps if he hadn't moved so fast, if the whole thing hadn't seemed like a teenage grope at the drive-in . . . Anyway, he was an employee—and just a kid. It was good that nothing had happened. She sat down at her desk and picked up the phone to order her car brought to the main entrance.

''Hey, wait a minute,'' he said. ''I haven't told you about the big story I'm on to. You'll want to know, believe me you will.''

''Okay, then,'' she said, putting down the phone. ''But just give me the facts, ma'am.''

He looked bewildered again, too young to remember the television cliché.

"It'll lead the paper for days and everyone will pick up on it," he said, his enthusiasm overcoming his embarrassment.

"There's this woman, whose name I'll tell you in a minute. She's very rich and very famous. She's into her fourth marriage and she wants out. But the current husband, one of those polo-playing jerks from an old family with no money, doesn't want to lose his meal ticket.

"If he can just stay married to her until she dies, he gets rich. But she's in good health and doesn't want to stay married to him. So what the polo player does is, he goes to the family chauffeur and offers him ten grand to seduce his wife. Since the wife has already slept with most of the servants and made plays for all her daughters' boyfriends, it's not going to be hard for the chauffeur to score.

"He has a real wild scene with the lady of the house, kinky stuff, whips, chains, even a dog. The chauffeur knows they're being secretly photographed by the husband but he doesn't care. He figures the polo player needs divorce evidence and he's got his ten grand, so everything's fine.

"But the polo player already knows that under their prenuptial agreement his wife can fuck King Kong if she wants and he still won't get a cent if they divorce. He really just wants to get the chauffeur close to his wife. Later, he goes to the chauffeur again and offers him a million bucks if he'll off his wife. Murder her, or run her into the bay in the Rolls and let her drown."

His glee was building with every revelation.

"At first the chauffeur agrees but then he loses his

nerve and decides to subcontract. But the guy he approaches to do the job, one of them's an undercover FBI agent. So the chauffeur is indicted for conspiracy to murder and so will the polo player be in due course.

"The chauffeur has come to me with the full story, even pictures. He wants to plead guilty, turn state's evidence in return for leniency. And we can have it all, weeks before it would surface otherwise. It's your super page-one series, and I've got it all on a platter."

Angie sat, fascinated. Sure, it was more like the old *Sentinel* than the new, but people would go for it like mad. She would have to remember to run some very serious feature articles while Adam's scarlet story was splashed up front.

"Why has he come to us, the chauffeur?" she asked. "What does he want?"

"He came to *me*," Adam said, his arrogance surfacing. "He's one of my fans. What he wants is the best legal representation money can buy, which he figures a big newspaper will be able to get him. Plus ten thousand dollars for himself." He raised a hand to still her protest. "I know you're going to say it's checkbook journalism but I tell you, Angie, if we don't pick him up the *News* or the *Post* or one of the national weeklies will. It's just too good a story."

"Okay," she said. "I'll take it, provided the lawyers clear it all." She laughed. "We'll get back all the old *Sentinel* readers we lost when we went upscale."

"Good," he said. "I need a couple of days to put it all together. You can kick it off Friday, I figure." He stood up and stretched. "There is one other thing, though. I'm sure it won't change your decision in any way. But the woman in question, the wife who made it with the boys, girls, and dogs, is Gloria Mansion."

320

"Gloria!" Angie cried. "Oh, Christ. You really sucked me in, didn't you, Adam?" She put her head in her hands. "I can't do it, not to the family. I can't have her plastered all over her own family's newspapers. There's got to be some loyalty, even among a clan like the Mansions."

"That's a natural reaction," he said smoothly, "but work it out: you admit it's a great story and it's going to break in court in a few weeks anyway, so why shouldn't we get it? And as a side benefit, we'll put to rest the popular view that the media always protects its own."

"I just don't know," she said, despairing. "I've got to think about it, Adam, talk to some people."

"Would you let me know your decision by tomorrow night, please?" he said, moving to the door. "Because if you refuse to run the best scandal of the decade, I'll have to reconsider my position with the *Sentinel.*" He smiled at her. "The *News* has offered me an open check to take my column there. If I also took the Gloria Mansion story, I figure they'd give me the sky."

She watched him go, wishing she'd never see him again. But people like Adam Carleton, no matter how disloyal, ambitious, corrupt they might be, were still what the *Sentinel* needed. She wished she were the *New York Times,* where the lofty heights of journalism could be scaled with grace, but she was only the *Sentinel* and her paper had to be sold every day to at least one million New Yorkers. She knew what they wanted to read.

She arranged for the Lear to take her to Virginia, and it was midnight when she walked through the great hall of the house. Alex, alerted by her message, was waiting for her in the study. He had had the staff leave coffee and sandwiches and cognac, and he was slumped in his chair, the steely eyes alert as ever but the rest of his body frail and old and beaten. She looked at the tired old frame of this once-stupendous man and wished she did not have to trouble him. But he was the only Mansion she could turn to for advice, and his was the only Mansion advice she would accept. She crossed to the cumbersome wheelchair and kissed him on his mottled bald forehead. He smiled up at her, holding her hand for an instant, and she knew she had been right to come to him.

"Alex," she said, sitting on a stool at his feet and taking his hand again, "you have been good to me, honest with me always, and I trust you and admire you. I have a problem now I want to put in your lap because you are the strongest of any of us and the problem affects you most of all. I've rarely asked your guidance before because I wanted to do all this on my own. It was you who told me to do it on my own. You told me I was capable of doing it." She paused and looked at the old man. He nodded slowly for her to continue.

"I've been handed a story, one that brings great disgrace on your family. I don't know how to handle it. When I came into your family, I had no feeling for any of you except Lyle. But you have shown me things, taught me things I didn't think possible." She was crying now, and the old eyes watched her gently. She let the story of Gloria and the polo-playing husband and the murder plot and the sheer sordidness of it all flow from her without censoring anything. She told him all of it, even the way the paper would play it, right down to the photos folks would slobber over. He heard her out without comment, without changing his expression.

"Well?" she asked, finally spent. "Well, what do I do? It's a sick, sad story and it'll sell papers. But it's about your family, and the empire you built. I don't want to be the one to do that to you."

He just looked at her. When at last he spoke, his voice was soft.

"Angie, my dear, would you please fetch me a cigar from the humidor over there? The doctors tell me not to smoke, but life without a few pleasures is not worth extending." He made a great show of preparing the Havana, rolling it in his fingers, lighting it carefully. Finally, when the clean gray smoke was drifting toward the ceiling, he spoke.

"When you came into the family, I welcomed you. I said we needed new blood and I told you bluntly what bitter disappointments my children were to me. Since then I have exulted in your progress, your strength of character, the example you are for the rest of my family, especially Lyle's children." He puffed on the cigar and smiled to himself at the pleasure of defying his team of specialists. "In these past sad months my one joy has been to live in your home and talk with the children you have made your own. At last I know there is a new generation of Mansions, young people who will make our name a proud one." He stared at her through the smoke. "I am reconciled with David, thanks to you. I no longer think of his life as an abomination. Before you came into our lives, that would have been impossible for me. My only regret is that I did not meet you when I was a young man. Together, you and I would have done things far more important than anything the Mansion empire has achieved." He paused again. "Would you pour me a brandy? I think I shall indulge all my vices tonight. Thank you," he said, taking the delicate glass and holding it up to the light before putting it to his lips. When he spoke again there was a harshness in his voice.

"Do your story. You have no choice. You are a newspaperwoman and this is news—salacious, yes, but with a moral to it. The moral, told and retold, is that money does not bring happiness. No one knows that better than I. Don't worry about the family's reaction. They will accuse you of betrayal but you and I will know that what you've printed is only a fraction of the sins my family has committed." He drained his brandy and tried to go on. "My family has been nothing but . . ." And then Alex Mansion couldn't talk about it anymore. He sat staring through the window into the darkness, his gaze remote, a king without a kingdom worthy of the name.

The tears welled from his eyes and she went to him and put her arms around the proud old shoulders, holding him to her bosom.

"I'll never let you down," she whispered. "No matter how tough it gets, I'll never let you down."

The story began running in Friday's *Sentinel* and the paper picked up seventy-five thousand that day and twice as much the next. The *Tribune* did almost as well in Washington. The wire services and television networks picked it up and ran with it gleefully. It was, in a recession year, the tonic everyone needed: as Alex Mansion had said, money didn't bring happiness. The scandals of the wealthy Mansion woman were reassuring.

Alex Mansion died in his sleep just before midnight as the *Sentinel*'s early Saturday editions went to the streets with the second installment. This one featured

a discreetly cropped picture of Gloria Mansion entwined with the chauffeur.

The obituary of Alex Mansion, running two and a
half columns, was on page 15 of the late editions of
the *Sentinel:* many appreciated the irony.

They met on Tuesday morning in the boardroom of
Mansion Communications, Inc., high above Park Avenue. Angie waited until the last possible moment before going in to face the family. There was dead
silence when she entered the boardroom. She stood
in the doorway for a moment, looking around at the
bright sunlight streaming through the big windows
and across the gleaming board table. A crystal vase of
pink roses stood in the center surrounded by pads,
pens, and carafes of water. Richard Mansion sat at the
head of the table. He did not look up. Ellen Mansion
was to his right, and appeared to be half-crocked already, her eyes slightly out of focus. Beside her were
two nonexecutive directors, Ronald Lawn and Bryce
Jenkins, and Johnny Howard was next to them.

And finally there was Gloria Mansion, slumped
down in her chair, toying with her pen. As Angie
moved to the one vacant place, Gloria looked up. Her
eyes were red from weeping but the hatred shone
through clearly. "Cunt!"

Richard looked up, annoyed. "Shut up, Gloria,"
he said. "Control yourself, at least until formal business is over and Ronald and Bryce have departed.
Your story is family business."

He began to read a formal notion of mourning, the
wording of a memorial notice to run in the group's
newspapers and be read over the group's television
and radio stations, and the notice of another board

meeting to elect a new chairman. They all mumbled assent.

"All right," he said in his firm executive's voice, in perfect control. "That completes the formal business. Bryce, Ronald, would you mind withdrawing? The rest is strictly family. Thank you."

The two gray-suited men hastily assembled their papers and hurried from the room, glad to be leaving the battlefield. As the door closed behind them, Gloria Mansion began to talk.

"If it's strictly family, Richard," she said, venom making her voice tremble, "what is this slut doing here? I can't bear to be in the same room with this traitor."

"Okay, Gloria," Richard snapped, "that's enough. We all share your feelings but keep them to yourself until later. What is vital now, in our time of grief, is this: we must demonstrate that Mansion Communications will grow stronger from this point on." He studied his papers, studiously avoiding looking at Angie. "The best way to inspire confidence, I think, is to announce what I have long planned for the company. It is a major change and involves selling off all our newspaper interests and employing the proceeds in the exciting new satellite television area. You all know the work I have already carried out toward this objective. It's now possible to move to the next step. I have good reason to believe we will be granted exclusive use of the new satellite and I have negotiated the patents for a new, cheap ground receiver. This venture is the costliest ever embarked on by our family company, but the rewards will outstrip anything that's gone before." He paused. This time he looked right at Angie. "We shall sell the newspaper division for several reasons. One, it's barely profitable. Two, I have a fair offer from the Kirkbride chain. Three, the newspaper division has been nothing but a tragic, humiliating embarrassment to those of us who believe in responsible media.''

He had thrown the challenge but Angie remained silent.

''We will have a vote on this,'' Richard continued, ''but, of course, a vote is only a formality. In the absence of anyone voting our father's block, Ellen and Gloria and I hold a clear majority. And,'' he said, glancing sharply across the table, ''I expect you, Johnny, to vote with us. It would be an act of decency if my brother's widow would make the vote unanimous, but I don't think any of us really cares what she does.'' He leaned back in his chair and looked around the table, satisfied.

Johnny Howard coughed. Everyone looked at him.

''Richard,'' he said gently, ''there's something all of you should know. As executor of your father's estate I had several meetings with him over the past few months. He added several codicils to his will—quite explicit ones—and he also told me what he expected me to do with my own vote in this particular matter. He knew you'd make this move, Richard, as soon as he was gone.''

''So?'' Richard snapped. ''If you want to turn traitor, I can't stop you. But even if she used Lyle's shares in combination with yours, you're still way short of a majority.''

''No, Richard,'' Johnny said, still gently. ''There'll be a formal reading of the will in due course but the provisions about voting powers are these: Alex has decreed that, as long as Angie is a Mansion, she will vote his shares. Assuming she will vote to keep the papers—and that was your father's wish, you know—

and I vote with her, your motion will be defeated. In which case, for the sake of public harmony, I think it would be better if you didn't put it before this meeting."

There was silence. Angie didn't really understand what Johnny had told them. It was enough that the papers were safe, for a while. She was weary of the whole thing and almost wished Richard had gotten his way. What did a temporary respite matter? Richard would beat her in the end. *Oh, Alex, I miss you,* she thought.

"You're as bad as he is!" Gloria screamed at Johnny. "You got to the old man when he was senile, drunk. You fucking pair of interlopers, sneaking into our family. It was fine until you two came along. We'll fight this, won't we, Richard? We won't let our inheritance be stolen by a couple of . . . carpetbaggers!" She was out of her seat and suddenly she lunged across the table, slapping Angie hard across the face. "You bitch! What you did to me last week, that's what killed my father! Just like you killed poor Lyle!" She sank back and burst into tears as Angie sat, stunned, a vicious red welt on her fair skin.

"I'm sorry it's come to this," Johnny said loudly, stepping into the angry silence, "but since it has, I think you had all better listen to a few home truths. Gloria, your accusations against me I find distasteful but I guess I can understand. True, I wasn't born to the Mansion blood. Alex envisaged a scene like this over that act. You see, when Alex took me under his wing he also took me into the family: he formally adopted me before I turned twenty-one. He wanted to be sure I had every legal and moral right to act as one of his sons."

"He wouldn't do that!" Gloria shouted. "You're

making it all up. Daddy was so proud of his blood-line, he wouldn't take in an outsider. He would have told us, anyhow."

"It was his secret," Johnny said. "He could be a very secretive man. But the papers are all on file and you'll have it confirmed in the reading of the will." He was pale, but he plunged on, wanting to get it all out. "Your other accusations, Gloria, made with the unspoken support of Ellen and Richard, are unworthy.

"Alex called me on Thursday after Angie had sought his counsel on the sad story of your predicament. He told me he had instructed her to publish the story. He wanted me to be sure that you, Gloria, had the best possible representation in what is going to be a humiliating and dangerous series of court appearances. The *story* didn't kill Alex, but perhaps the deeds portrayed in it hastened his end. As for Lyle . . . Richard, could you help your sister understand some of the things that might have contributed to your brother's death?"

They all stared at Richard, hunched over his papers. He gave an angry shrug and refused to answer. His knuckles were white. He was not beaten, just cornered for a moment, and doubly dangerous. At last he looked up. The eyes were hard as steel. His voice was pitched very low.

"It seems this is not the appropriate time to put my motion," he said quietly. "I declare this meeting of Mansion Communications, Inc., over." He stood up and walked out of the room. The sisters, clutching their bags to their chests as if to stanch wounds, were close behind him.

Johnny and Angie sat in the boardroom. He took a cigarette, pushed the pack over to her, and held a light. The cigarette trembled in her hand. She was close to tears. The hand he placed on her shoulder felt wonderful.

"Angie," he said finally, "you've just come through a hell of a thing and you've come through well. Don't worry about the past: you've got it all ahead of you."

"Why?" she asked. "Why did you go to bat for me like that? I thought all you Mansions stuck together in the end."

"The old man," he said simply and honestly. "I did it for the old man. It's a tragic commentary on the family but the fact was, he liked you and me best of all. One adopted into the family, the other married into it. Anyway, both of us know that Alex wanted to keep the newspapers going. I think it's our duty to do that as long as possible."

"I'm not sure I want to anymore," she said. "This family has drained all the fight out of me. While Alex was still here it made sense to fight them, but now I just don't care anymore."

"That's how you feel today," he said, "but it will be a little better tomorrow and a little better the day after. Just hang in for a while longer. I'm in your corner and so are the kids. We can still make the Mansion name something to be proud of."

"The name! That's been the whole problem with this family," she said despairingly. "They think the mighty Mansion name excuses all their excesses, compensates for whatever they do. These days, all you have to be is rich and famous enough and you can trample the ordinary, decent people."

"Honey," he said, standing up and putting a hand under her elbow, "it was always that way and it always will be. At least you've had a close-up view of what it's like inside one of these families. Sure, they've got power and privilege, but sure as hell they aren't happy."

"Who is?" she asked, and they laughed and walked out of the boardroom.

When they reached the sidewalk, he gently asked if she wanted to come home to his apartment and rest. She shook her head.

"No, Johnny," she said. "If we get involved like that it will only make everything even messier. What I am going to do now is get back to running the *Sentinel*." He held the limo door for her and she saw the yearning in his eyes. "Goodbye and thanks," she said. "You went out on a limb for me today. I'd like to believe I'll have the courage to do something like that for you someday."

"You will, Angie," he said, kissing her lightly on the cheek. "You will."

Chapter
Sixteen

What surprised her most of all was that Ted filled the void left by Alex's death. Ted had always been so much to her, but he became even more: the father role Alex had played Ted adopted easily; as a confidant he was honest and challenging; and as a lover he was an exhilarating mixture of passion and compassion. Through Ted she was, as near as she had ever been, satisfied. It helped that the *Sentinel* was doing so well. Even Richard seemed to have dropped his vendetta against her and the newspaper division.

"I finally feel like I've grown into myself, or something," she told Trish. "I wish it hadn't taken so long. So much time being unhappy." They were sitting in her office, drinking coffee in the quiet afternoon before the rush of putting the newspaper together began.

"We both wasted a lot of time, Angie," Trish sighed. "Not on purpose, not for fun, like the kids do now. We just didn't know what to expect."

"We do now," Angie said firmly. "That's one reason why it's time you and I settled this thing about you running. I want to endorse you, the mayor wants to endorse you—you're the best candidate for the office. I know being a congressman isn't the greatest job in the world, but you would be great at it. With your Washington background you won't have to waste a whole year discovering how the system works; you know already how to cut all the corners and you always did have the bureaucrats eating out of your hand. Trish, please run. You'll be doing a lot of us a big favor."

"It's not as simple as all that, Angie," she said. "You keep forgetting Sam Hardy, hovering like a buzzard. Sam released me on the understanding that I'd keep a real low profile. Already he thinks I breached that by taking the job in the borough president's office." She lit a cigarette. "And, Angie, there's stuff you don't know about, nasty stuff. It'll come out in any kind of tough campaign, and this would be a nasty campaign. The opposition doesn't want to lose that district."

"You and I can cope with any mud they sling," Angie said confidently. "After all, you'll have the *Sentinel* going to bat for you. How bad can it be?"

"I don't know," Trish said slowly, considering. "'The divorce papers were marked 'Sealed, never to be opened,' so I guess none of that will come out, but . . .'"

"No buts," Angie said. "We need you to run."

"Oh, hell, you'll never let up on me, will you? All right, we'll give it a shot."

On the day the *Sentinel* endorsed Trish, Senator Beckworth came to see Angie. He was no longer ill at ease with her: he was now the smooth, established

Senate power broker. Nothing in his past could harm him and he let her know that.

"It's been too long, Angie," he said, moving to kiss her cheek. She stuck out her hand instead. "You look as lovely as ever," he continued smoothly, "despite working in this grubby business."

"You'd know about grubbiness, Ken," she said without rancor. "The way your party's trying to steal this election—Tammany Hall was never like this. I guess this is your one big test. Win big for them and you get the vice-presidential nod in two years. Right?"

"That's what I've been working for all these years," he said, flashing his candidate's smile. "I gave up an awful lot to get where I am. I even gave you up, Angie."

"Nonsense!" she snapped. "We weren't going anywhere, Ken." She looked at her watch pointedly. "What is it you wanted to see me about?"

He nodded. "We'll get right down to business. You double-crossed us with the newsprint loan. Just because you paid it back doesn't mean the debt Lyle incurred is canceled. We let him have that money cheap for a long time and it got his paper out of a big hole." He looked at her levelly. "So, what's it going to be? Will you honor the obligation to come out for the party and get behind all the key candidates? Or . . . ?"

"Or what, Ken?" she snapped. "Don't bullshit me. As soon as we paid back the loan you lost all your leverage. There's nothing you can do to the newspaper now. I hardly think the president would appreciate a statement from you that you had a dirty deal with my late husband and now the deal's fallen through."

"You don't think there's anything we can do to you?" He was so calm it sent a shiver down her back. She told herself to be careful; she knew how ruthless this man was. "If that's your final word, Angie, I'm sorry. Because over the next few weeks I'm going to have to show you just how rough we can play."

"Give it your best shot, Ken," she said. He turned to leave. "I'm in the mood for a damn good fight, Ken, and I'll give you as good as I get."

Except it was a lot rougher, a lot dirtier, than she could have known. The weapon they used to fire the first shot was Adam Carleton.

"I've got a big one," the columnist said when they were alone in her office. "But it's also going to be very embarrassing for you, so I wanted to tell you first." He was tense with excitement, riding on the high of another big exclusive. "I've been given the sealed papers in the Sam Hardy divorce. Some of it's too dirty even for us, but the stuff we can run will rock the town." He opened his briefcase and took out a manila folder of six-by-four glossies. "Look." He pushed a photograph across the desk at her.

She recoiled with shock. The picture was grainy, hastily shot in bad light, but enough was clear. Trish was on a wide bed, spread-eagled naked, a skinny blond girl kneeling between her thighs. There were four more pictures in the sequence and he pushed each of them across the desk, relentlessly.

"There's more, too," Carleton said, "affidavits from a score of women who slept with her in the matrimonial home; details of the kinkiest sex games you ever dreamed of. She even did it with—"

"Stop!" Angie screamed. "Stop it! Christ, what

kind of journalist are you, to think we'd handle trash like this?''

"That wasn't your reaction when I gave you the goods on your sister-in-law," he said viciously. "What's different now?''

Angie was shaken. She needed time to regain some ground.

"This stuff can't be used, anyway," she said, thinking wildly. "It was sealed by the court. We'd be in contempt.''

"Contempt, shit!" he said. "We might get a rap over the knuckles for it, but Trish Hardy, by the act of running for Congress, has established herself as a public figure. By exposing what kind of private figure she is, we're just doing our duty to the voters. Anyway, the people I scored these from assure me there won't be a whimper from the judge. He's fixed. And San Hardy won't mind, either. They tell me he thinks it's time he took custody of his son, so this gives him grounds.''

"You don't care, do you?" she said. "You don't care who gets destroyed, just so long as you get an exclusive.''

He shook his head slowly.

"Angie," he said, "sometimes you amaze me. Getting exclusives is what you pay me to do for you.'' He gathered the photographs and stood up. "I realize, us having endorsed the dyke, you'll need a day or two to get the paper off the hook before we break the story. That's okay, but don't keep me on hold too long.''

She phoned Trish, trying to control her voice, and asked her friend to come to the Beekman Place house at once. Then Angie hurried out of the office, leaving the editors and writers and reporters to get out the paper without her.

Before Trish arrived Angie left orders with the housekeeper that she and Trish not be disturbed.

"I guess the worst has happened," Trish said. She was standing, framed in the long window, looking down at the river. She was deathly pale. "I don't know why I thought for an instant I could go public like this and get away with it. You gave me the confidence with your bullying." She smiled at Angie, a quick tight smile to show she didn't really hold her friend responsible. "And now they're going to spread the word I'm a lesbian. I guess that puts me out of the race. I'm sorry I wasted your time, Angie."

"It's worse than that," Angie said gently. "They've got the sealed records of your divorce case, everything. There are pictures and statements . . . oh, God, Trish, what happened to you?" She stopped. Trish was swaying, about to faint. She ran across the room and grabbed her friend and led her to a chair. She fetched brandy and held it to Trish's lips. It revived her.

"I didn't think they'd go that far," Trish said at last, hysteria near the surface. "The lesbian rumor alone would have been enough. Sam always did believe in overkill." She drank some more brandy. "Angie, I'm finally going to tell you the whole story of my wonderful marriage. You're probably the only one who will ever hear my side of it. And I do owe it to you."

Angie said nothing.

"When I first married Sam," she began, "it was mostly okay. Hell, we lived in a world of private jets and grand houses, wall-to-wall servants, always zipping off to the best places with the best people.

Sam indulged in some games I thought were pretty weird but, what did I know? Soon, though, the games got rougher. He liked to beat me, humiliate me. He'd try and arrange it so the servants walked in on me naked, or when we were screwing, that kind of thing. After a while I got my dignity back and said that kind of thing wasn't going to happen anymore. It seemed to work, too. I guess he just got his rocks off with other people. And there were plenty of sickies in our crowd, I promise you. His big-shot friend in Detroit, for one. He forced his wife to lie down for the family guard dog and he shot a video of it. That's why *their* divorce didn't cost him a cent. Another case of sealing the court records.

"Anyway, for a year or so Sam left me alone. He didn't care what I spent or what I did, just as long as there was never another guy around me. He was intensely jealous, even though he had no use for me. There was always a private eye following me around. I don't know why we didn't just get divorced then. I wouldn't have taken him for money, but I guess he didn't believe that. Also, he's got this thing about his public image. I guess he thought a divorce would make him look like a loser.

"Then something bad happened to him. I've never known the details, just some gossip I picked up from the wife of another heavy hitter. Remember all those stories a few years back about how they were making 'snuff' films, actually killing young girls in front of the camera? Most people thought it was just sensational newspapers making it up, but I kept hearing these rumors that maybe Sam and his crowd had set up a snuff movie and it got out of hand and the girl who wasn't really supposed to die did. The wife I knew told me she heard a million dollars changed hands to hush it all up.

"Whatever the reason, Sam suddenly needed to look like a model husband, so he needed me. He got me pregnant with Ben—which is the only wonderful thing that's happened to me in all these years. For a while we were the epitome of your happy upper-class couple. And then I guess the heat was off, he and his friends were out of danger, because he started using me again, worse than ever. And by then he'd learned he had Ben as a weapon. If I didn't do exactly as he told me I'd never see my baby again, was the threat." She looked at Angie. "I never doubted his power. I'd have had no chance against Sam Hardy in a battle for Ben.

"I went through a year of total degradation. I started taking drugs, anything to get me through. I was spaced out almost all the time, coming down just often enough to spend time with Ben. But it was nursemaids who really raised him. I just wanted the time to pass in a blur. I hardly remember who used my body during that time, but I guess that's where all the pictures came from. You see, even while Sam was getting his rocks off, he was also taking out insurance for when he got tired of me.

"It's funny," she said grimly, "but I actually do have a clear recall of the incident that ended it all and got me my freedom from Sam. I guess he'd done everything he could to me, anyway, and he was getting bored. He had never felt anything for Ben, so we were just in his way. We made this one big trip around Asia, fixing up a bunch of big deals. He needed me along for respectability.

"The trip wasn't all business, though, oh no. Toward the end we were staying in the presidential palace and Sam was getting all nervous and excited, like he knew there was going to be some action. The weird-sex scene was like a drug to him. So this first night in the palace there's just Sam and me and the president and his wife, eating pheasant off solid gold plates and waited on by half a hundred servants. The president made himself scarce right after dinner. I'm sure he knew what went on, but his wife was the real dictator in that family. The three of us end up in her bedchamber, Sam almost drooling by this time. There's cocaine by the pound—I think that's how she keeps so thin—and champagne. And two huge eunuch guards who are right there in the room with us.

"I did a fair amount of coke. I was doing anything in those days, to get me through. Sam and the First Lady stripped me, and then one of the eunuchs undressed her. She was your real bull dyke—Sam might just as well not have been there—and she attacked me on this huge gold-encrusted bed. I just lay there and let her do whatever she wanted to. I didn't care. After a while I raised my arm to do some more coke and I snagged my ring in her hair. She jerked back and her wig came off. She's bald! The glamorous First Lady is bald as a billiard ball!

"I was so high already, I started laughing, laughing till I cried, and all the time there's this deathly silence in the room, the eunuchs staring straight ahead as if nothing's going on, Sam looking like he wants the floor to swallow him up. Then she started screaming at me and ordered us to get out of the palace. The guards threw my clothes after me and I got dressed in the corridor, still laughing. I couldn't stop. Sam slapped me around, got our stuff from the guest suite, and we went to a hotel. We flew back to the U.S. the next day.

"After that he just wanted me out of his life. He said I'd humiliated him! Humiliated! He spent years degrading me, but I'd humiliated him! I could have the kid—he said he wasn't even sure Ben was his—but no money. If I ever made any trouble for him, he'd see the pictures of me were released." She slumped back in her chair. "I think I'd like another brandy, please, Angie," she said. "I never thought I'd tell that story to anyone. I'm sorry it had to be you."

Angie moved slowly to the bar, wondering what she should say. The whole story was almost beyond her comprehension but she did realize she had put Trish in great danger.

"Do you think Sam may try and get Ben back?" she asked as calmly as she could. "Something I was told today . . ."

"You never know what the bastard might do," Trish said. "I didn't believe he'd ever release the divorce details. I don't know why he's doing this."

"Actually," Angie said guiltily, "I think it's more of a warning to me than to you. There's some political pressure being applied. I'm going to have to bend to it, if we're going to protect you."

"But it's too late, isn't it?" Trish said. "If you've seen the papers . . . I guess they're being hawked around everywhere."

"No," Angie said. "I don't think so. There is a way I can stop this. Part of the price is you'll have to pull out of the race. I hate that, but they've got us over a barrel."

"I never should have been in the race," Trish said. "I was worried that they'd expose me as a lesbian." She laughed lightly. "Because I am one. After those years of horror with Sam I turned off men forever.

341

And you know something? I'm not in the least ashamed."

"As long as you're happy," Angie said. It was trite but it was all she could think of. "I'll fly to Washington this evening and try and unscramble this mess," she said finally. "I'll call you as soon as I know something. Anything."

Senator Beckworth didn't keep her waiting. And he didn't gloat. He sat her down on an old leather couch in his office and pulled up a chair opposite her.

"I'm sorry we had to go so far, Angie," he said. "But I had to show you how serious we are. It may be just one more congressional district to you, but to me it's part of the whole game plan for this election and beyond. I can't have one part of it unraveled. I'm sorry to be so brutal but that's the way it has to be."

"I understand, Ken," she said quietly. "You people have turned politics into a business, and in business you try and eliminate risk."

"Good," he said, smiling. "So now you're ready to have your newspapers play ball with us?"

"No," she said. "But now I understand the game you're playing. I brought along my own ball, so I could play, too." She opened her purse and took out a slip of paper. She handed it to him. "You'll remember that, Ken. It's a photostat of the check I wrote to the subcommittee before we took the Caribbean junket. That's your handwriting, endorsing it over to the casino in the Bahamas." She watched him closely and was reassured to see his hand trembling. "You got away then with just a rap on the knuckles for taking your lover along at public expense. You wouldn't have gotten away if they'd known I *paid* for the trip and you *stole* the money. I haven't studied the statute of limitations, but the original of that check would at least have you out of the Senate. And maybe in court." She lit a cigarette and continued to watch him closely. "I don't know why I kept the check when it finally came back from my bank. Certainly not as a souvenir, and not with a view toward using it against you. I'd lost my job anyway, and nailing you wasn't going to make me feel better. I did keep it, and now I have a use for that check. I promise you I'll use it if you don't get off my back and if you don't put a stop to this campaign against Trish."

He crumpled the paper in his hand and let it drop to the floor. It lay there on the crimson carpet like a white blossom, reminding her, oddly, of their vacation on a private island. Had it really seemed they had a future together, once? She was incredulous.

"I guess you've fixed me," he said. "I never should have underestimated you, Angie." He stood up. "Let's have a drink. No point in being a sore loser." He went over to his bar and fixed gin and tonic for them both, without asking. He brought them back and settled across from her again. "If we forget about the blanket party endorsements," he said, "will that be the end of the check? You wouldn't use it against me again?"

"No, Ken," she said. "We'll trust each other to keep that bargain."

"Okay. I have no choice in the matter," he said. "I guess it won't do too much harm. We've got Richard and the network tied up, anyway, and television's worth more to us than newspapers." He looked at her over his glass. "I take it you don't care who your brother-in-law endorses?"

"No," she said. "I don't give a damn what he

does, but I do think you'll find newspapers more important than you suppose."

He shook his head. "Television will swing it for us, with nice little easy-to-digest segments on all our fellows," he said smugly.

"All your 'fellows'!" she snapped. "When is your party going to move into the real world and start giving women a chance for office? That's the main reason I pushed Trish into the race, because she's so goddamned good. It's a damned shame she's dropping out."

He suddenly looked very worried, more so than when she'd presented him with the photostat. He drained his drink and looked around helplessly for someone to fetch him another one.

"Angie," he said, "I just realized something: you don't understand what's going on. Okay, you've defeated me on the endorsement thing and you won't get any more pressure from our side about that. But the thing with Trish, well, it's too late to stop it, Angie. Her pulling out of the race won't make any difference there. When I unleashed your charming boy columnist I knew there'd be no stopping him. You don't think Trish's pulling out of the race will kill the story? Not with Adam Carleton. Look, I'm sorry, but that's the way the game is played. I wasn't saying 'Get Trish out of the race or we'll smear her.' I was saying we *have* smeared her and think about how many others we'll smear if you don't play ball. We can't *un*smear her, Angie."

"But I'm not going to run that garbage in the *Sentinel*," Angie said confidently. "Carleton will have to forget it."

"Forget it? He'll take it to one of your competitors," Ken said. "That's why we picked him. If you refused to run it, we knew he'd take it somewhere else. That guy would kill for a good story."

"Oh, Christ," she said. "You and me, playing power games. You know what we've done? We've destroyed her. Trish will kill herself if all that filth comes out on the papers. You've got to stop it, Ken."

"Hey, I said I'm sorry. There's nothing I can do," he said. "I warned you it would be tough if you went against us, and then you did anyhow and I let the dog off his chain." He got up and refilled his drink. "I'm sorry," he said again, "but Adam Carleton isn't going to stop. He's off and running with a story. The only person who could stop him . . . no, he wouldn't do it. Forget that."

"What person, Ken?"

"Sam Hardy," he said. "But Sam gave me the papers in the first place. Sam doesn't like his ex-wife running around being the toast of New York liberals. He wants to hurt her. So even if I tell Sam it's no longer in the party's interest to destroy Trish, he won't have the story stopped."

"How could he have it stopped?" she asked. "How could Sam Hardy put a muzzle on Carleton?"

"Several ways," Ken sighed. "He could have it pointed out to Carleton the sealed documents are stolen—which, as far as we're concerned, they are. He could say that they invade his privacy and he's not a public figure in the accepted sense, not a movie star or a candidate for office. He could also use his corporate muscle with any newspaper that considered publishing the stuff. Sam's companies carry a lot of weight with advertising directors." He shrugged. "But Sam's not going to do any of that. He *wants* to hurt her. I think her running against us for Congress was just an excuse. He's got some kind of strange hard-on about Trish and the kid."

She stood up, gathered her things, and nodded to him in the fading light.

"What I like about you, Ken," she said, "is you're a crook and you're not ashamed. What I don't like about me is I'm a do-gooder and all I manage is to land good people in the shit." She started for the door. "You and I have our understanding now. But, as an old friend, please see what you can do to save Trish. Because, Ken."

She hurried out of the Senate building and went straight to Ted. He was in his office on the newsroom floor, sleeves rolled up, staring into the video display unit as if it were his enemy.

He jumped up and hugged her. He grinned. "You didn't say you were coming," he said, "but I'm so glad to see you. I'm trying to get the right slant on the lead editorial and then we can have a drink. These goddamned machines. It was supposed to be faster and better this way! Ha! Give me a typewriter any day."

"I'll be upstairs in my office, Ted," she said. "Come up as soon as you can. It's important."

As she sketched the story for him, he looked increasingly solemn.

"Carleton's a tough little bastard," he said at last. "He won't give up on the story easily. I think Beckworth's right—Hardy's the key to stopping him." He was silent for a while, thinking. "First thing is, Trish doesn't pull out of the race. It's her one bargaining chip with Hardy. She's got to tell him if all this crap about her runs, she'll use any forum she can find to tell her side of the story."

"She's not strong enough for that kind of game,

Ted," Angie said. "She won't take on a man like
Hardy if she's being held up to the public as a de-
praved woman, unfit to have custody of her child.
She just wants out. She doesn't want to fight."

"Yes," he said patiently, "but you've already established that just getting her out of the race won't
stop the shit from hitting the fan anyway. So we have
to force Hardy into a position where it's in his interests to kill the story. We need something to threaten
him with. If she drops out, where's your leverage?"

"There *is* one thing," Angie said. "Only a rumor,
something Trish told me." She detailed the snuff
movie gossip. "But if it happened, they put the fix in
long ago," she said. "There's nothing we can use,
not now."

"Don't you believe it," he said, grinning. "It's
something to work on. You forget I was once a tough
reporter on a very good newspaper. We were better
than cops at forcing confessions out of people."

"It's dangerous, Ted," she said. "Sam Hardy is a
powerful man with connections everywhere."

"All the better. He's got so much more to lose than
most do. Listen, this isn't the kind of matter for a lady
publisher to soil her hands with. I'll fly back with you
tonight. Tomorrow I'll put my old reporter's hat on
and go see Mr. Sam Hardy."

She ignored the "lady publisher" remark. She
stood up and went to him. "Oh, God, Ted, I'll love
you for anything you can do. I'm way out of my
depth. I'm scared of what it's going to do to Trish. I
was so confident, I just steamrollered her when she
said she didn't want to run. I pushed her into this and
it's going to destroy her."

"We won't let it," he said. Standing, he put his
arm around her shoulders and patted her gently.

"We'll fly back to New York now, have dinner in the city, and I'll work out tactics for tomorrow." He paused. "It's late to get a hotel. Do you suppose I could stay over at your place? It would save the company expense money."

"Yes, Ted," she said, fighting back tears of worry and exhaustion. "I think I can find you a bed at my house. I think I'd like to do that."

They didn't make love. Ted slept in her bed and held her close, protecting her against the night and her dread. It felt right to her, being in his strong arms, listening to the whoosh of traffic on the wet East River Drive below their window, drifting off to sleep beside him.

"I like this," she murmured, snuggling close to him. "Why can't it be this way always?" And then she answered herself, not knowing whether he heard. "It can."

Ted was already on the telephone when she came out of the bathroom. He waved to her and went on talking, his voice low and confidential. She went back into the bedroom where the maid had left coffee and juice and got on the other line to Trish.

"It's going to be all right, honey," she said. "It's going to be taken care of. Please trust me. And don't think about getting out of the race, not yet."

She left Ted on the telephone and rode down to the *Sentinel*, rehearsing what he had told her to do. Her secretary chided her for taking off so suddenly the day before, waving a stack of letters and memos in front of her.

"I'll look at them later," Angie said. "Get Adam Carleton up here at once."

He swaggered into her office and plopped into a

chair without being asked. He was, she thought again, a truly obnoxious young man. What a pity he had so much talent.

"Adam," she said, "this is about the Trish Hardy story. We're not going to run it." She put up her hand to silence him before he started. "Not because we have endorsed her and not because she is my oldest friend. We're not running that garbage because I've found out the truth of the matter. She's been through hell, through no fault of her own. If we run that stuff, she can rebut it—but it would finish her. Let's drop it. Okay?"

"Okay?" he snapped. "It's not okay! This is a major story, and it's legitimate. It's about a candidate you've put forward as the epitome of the new woman. Well, it turns out that she's a sex-crazed deviate and you want to say it doesn't matter. Well, it fucking well does matter." He stood up. "I am going to tell the truth about this wonderful new woman and I don't need the columns of the *Sentinel* to do it. I'm walking of here right now and taking an offer I should have accepted a long time ago. And I'm taking the Trish Hardy story with me."

"Fine, Adam," she said. "But before you go, allow me a second or two to talk to you about truth. I gave you an awful lot of leeway when you were starting out and you did well for yourself and the paper because of that leeway. It's as much my fault as yours, but somewhere along the way we began to separate truth from public benefit. Now, late in the day, I realize they can't be separated. For example, we shouldn't have run all the details we did on my poor sister-in-law. Sure, it sold papers, but we didn't need to be quite so salacious. I don't know anymore where the dividing line is between right to know and what's right to know. It's something I'm going to have to think about. And I apologize for the leeway. It did you no good, Adam. In the meantime, we're not running the Hardy divorce papers. If you can accept that, please go back down to the newsroom and we'll continue our mutually profitable relationship. If you can't—"

He was glaring at her, laughing mockingly.

"Of course!" he crowed. "It all falls into place now. No wonder you got so upset when I made a pass at you in this office. You're a dyke, just like her! Jesus, you women make me sick." He strode to the door and yanked it open. "Read me in a day or two, Mrs. Mansion, when I've found my new forum. Public right to know—ha! You're a dyke!"

She called Ted.

"Feisty little bastard, isn't he?" Ted chuckled. "It's just what I figured on. Pity we have to lose him, but he was getting carried away with himself. All right, Angie, leave it with me. I'm about set to roll now, and I'll keep you posted."

Sam Hardy wasn't interested in seeing Ted Buchanan. He wasn't one of those high-profile tycoons who got his kicks from being quoted in the press.

"He's very insistent, sir," his harassed secretary said. "He says it's to do with your former wife's campaign and you will be more interested in some material he's brought you."

Sam thought about it for a moment. "Oh, all right, send him in. But you come in and interrupt us after three or four minutes. I don't want to be stuck with some hack reporter. I've got a busy day." When Ted was shown into his office, he was all charm and grace.

"Ted Buchanan! Of course! We met at Angie's

wedding," he said warmly, striding around the desk and holding out his hand. "My secretary didn't explain who you were. She said it was some reporter. Hell, if I'd known it was the boss man I wouldn't have kept you waiting. How's Angie doing? That's one tough lady, I think."

"She's fine, Sam," Ted said. "Running some good papers, breaking some good stories. And, yes, I'm still her boss man. But today I'm playing at being reporter again, so don't feel bad about making me wait in the outer office. We reporters are used to waiting for major figures like you."

"You want coffee or something?" Hardy asked congenially.

Ted shook his head.

"No, Sam," he said, "I don't want to waste any more of your time than is really necessary. And anyway, I'm due downtown for a session with the D.A. in half an hour."

Hardy sat down in his executive chair and leaned back, hands behind his large head, not a gray hair out of place. He looked interested and slightly amused as he eyed Ted from across the desk.

"My girl said you wanted to see me about my ex-wife running for Congress," he said. "That's not the kind of story I'd have thought was important enough to bring you out of your office. And anyway, I hear she's going to pull out of the race."

"That's the funny thing, Sam," Ted said, pushing back his chair and spreading himself into a comfortable position. "We were just putting together a story about Trish's campaign, her being a prominent former staffer in Washington and all, and then we started turning up some stuff that was so hot, well, I just had to take over the story myself."

"Come on, Ted, we both know what you're on to," Hardy said, putting on his serious face. "Your people have gotten hold of the court papers. They were supposed to be sealed forever, but we both know the court system—and every other system—leaks like a sieve. But surely you don't want to run the story of what a whore my wife was. Is. Who's it going to help?"

"If she's out of the race, no one," Ted said. "But the bad thing is, the guy your people gave the papers to is like a mad bull elephant. Even though Trish is willing to pull out of the race and forget it all, Adam Carleton is going ahead with the story. We can't talk him out of it."

"Well, it may hurt, but that's freedom of the press," Hardy said. "And by the way, 'my people' didn't give anyone anything. If some enterprising journalist—"

The door opened and his secretary bustled in brandishing a sheaf of papers.

"These have to be signed, Mr. Hardy."

"Not now, Marcia," he snapped. "I told you I wasn't to be disturbed." He smiled an apology at Ted. They never give me a minute's peace," said Sam. "Where were we? If some journalist has breeched the confidentiality of court records, well, I deplore it but there's not much I can do about it. I guess my ex-wife should have just kept a low profile. Anyhow, Ted, you're here to . . . what? Do a story about a story? I don't understand."

"No, Sam, you wouldn't," Ted said. "What happened was, when we heard about the smear campaign against Trish we started going back over all the leads, you know, trying to find out how a sweet girl—I knew her years ago—could get mixed up in such weird things. And you know what we found, Sam? We found it was *you* who was the weirdo, not Trish.''

There was utter silence.

"You shouldn't toss terms like that around too loosely, feller," he said. "One man's weirdness is another's routine. Hey, this isn't on the record, but sure I've . . . experimented. I mean, we're all supposed to be liberated now. So maybe my sex life wouldn't get me elected church deacon. Would yours?''

"We're not talking about mine, Sam," Ted said. He gave him a big warm smile. "We're not talking about anybody 'experimenting.' What we're talking about is a bunch of rich, sick thrill-killers who got together in a downtown loft and watched as a girl, some illegal alien from Haiti or thereabouts, was tortured and mutilated and murdered while the cameras rolled." He paused because he felt himself shaking and feared his voice would break. "What I want to know, *Mr. Hardy*, is what finally killed the kid. Was it the heroin you'd stuffed her with, or the things she had shoved up her, or the red satin cord around her throat?''

Hardy had gone white. He knew he had to say something, anything.

"You can't prove . . .," he began.

"Yes we can, Sam," Ted said. "One of your associates isn't as tough as you. We lean on him a little more, he'll turn State's evidence. And some of the police you bought: I don't think they'd all stand firm before a grand jury. No," he said, and smiled benignly at Hardy, "we could put together a story about you that would stand up in court. And even if the charge weren't proved, even if you found some patsy to take the rap for you, you'd still be ruined. But what good would all that do? It wouldn't bring back the poor girl you hired and murdered, would it?''

"What is this, then, blackmail? I'll pay," he said quickly.

"Blackmail? Yes, I guess it is, sort of," Ted said. "But not for money. I want that story about Trish, the sealed court papers, stopped. You are the man to stop it. You've got so much muscle in this city, let's see you use it. Go to Carleton's new employers and tell 'em you don't want it run, that the papers are stolen property, and if it does get published you will deny all the allegations you made about Trish during the divorce. Tell them the pictures were faked and you'll say so publicly. Tell them a good story, Sam, and I'm sure they'll drop the whole sordid thing. And if Adam Carleton tries to take the story elsewhere, I'm sure you've got some people who'll talk with Mr. Carleton, show him the error of his ways." He stood up. "Do you understand?"

"Yes," Hardy said. He seemed calm, but Ted didn't miss the angry glint in his eyes: Sam Hardy was not used to being dictated to. "This is a once-only thing, right? I do this, you forget what you think you know about me? Because, Mr. Buchanan, if you were to come back to me, attempt to bleed me, I would have to do something about that. I would not lie down and beg for mercy. See?"

"I believe you," Ted said sincerely. "You'd have nothing to lose. You won't hear from me again *if* you get the story about Trish killed once and for all.''

Ted was sweating as he left the office. He'd played a dangerous game. He was sure Hardy knew a lot of Ted's claims were shots in the dark. He had calculated that Hardy wouldn't risk calling any bluffs, but he didn't like playing rough games with Sam Hardy.

He went to Angie's office. "Will she still run?" Ted asked. "After a scare like this I wouldn't blame her if she never wanted public life again."

"I think so," Angie said. "Every day she doesn't withdraw from the race she will grow a little stronger. I think I can prop her up long enough for the shock to pass. I want her to run, Ted, and to win big. She needs something great in her life after all the hell she's been through, and I know she's going to be great in Congress."

"Hey, we make a good team." Ted smiled. "In twenty-four hours we've fixed a senator and a tycoon. We're batting a thousand right now."

"I know," she said, "which is why I think we should quit while we're ahead. From now on I'm going to be a lot more careful about pushing people into things."

"Angie," he said casually, "now that this is resolved, how about we take a few days off? Some friends have offered me their place in East Hampton for a week. It's quiet out there this time of the year and—oh, hell, I'd just like us to have some time away together. The papers can get by without us for a few days."

She gazed at him across the desk. Dear Ted, the only constant force in her life, and the most welcome spirit. So familiar, so comfortable, and yet romantically handsome in his rumpled manner, the tousled hair just graying a little, the eyes still bright and eager. She had been taking him for granted for so long. She felt a pang of guilt, and of something else, but she didn't stop to analyze it.

"That's the best suggestion I've heard in weeks,"

she said, smiling. "Let's do that, just run away for a while."

In the rented car she watched him in the twilight, studying his lean profile and his long hands on the wheel. Perhaps it was the sense of being isolated in the car, of having skipped out on all her responsibilities, but she suddenly felt terribly close to Ted. A welling tenderness for him and a certain knowledge that he would always protect her surged up from deep inside her. She reached out and squeezed his arm and he took his eyes off the road long enough to smile at her.

Rain began to spatter the car and she pulled her jacket around her and huddled deep in the seat.

"I'm glad," she said. "There's nothing I'd like better than to be holed up in a cottage in a storm, with good food and wine . . . and you."

They found the cottage, grateful for good directions. It was pitch dark and an angry wind off the ocean was battering at the trees and flinging sheets of rain everywhere. By the time they had the car unloaded they were drenched and shivering. It was a small, comfortable old cottage that creaked like a ship. While Angie unpacked and put away their supplies Ted built a fire. She poured them whiskey and came to him, shivering, in front of the dancing flames.

"Thanks," he said, glad for the warmth of the drink. His hair had crinkled in the rain and he looked more than ever like a kid. She came close to him, and he put his arms around her.

"I guess we should have run off to some Caribbean island," he said. "I thought the rustic charm of East Hampton would be romantic in the spring. Instead we'll both catch cold."

"We'll just have to keep each other warm," she murmured, snuggling closer to him. It felt so good, being in his arms, the storm beating at their door. Ted wouldn't let the storm in.

They made love right there, shedding their clothes as the fire reached them. They lay naked together on the rough wool rug, and he entered her with all the strength and gentleness he possessed. Again, there was the feeling of its being so right, giving him her body and accepting his. They came together and relaxed together, so familiar by now, so knowing. Ted moved off her and they lay on their backs listening to the storm and feeling the fire's warmth on them. He sat up and found the cigarettes and lit one for each of them. He drew deeply on his, staring into the fire, his knees drawn up to his chest.

"Angie," he said finally, his voice deeper than usual, "I'm sick of waiting in the wings for you. I've loved you forever. You know that. And I've wanted to marry you almost as long. I've never pushed you because you always signaled the time was wrong, there were more pressing things you had to do. It broke my heart when you married Lyle. I had intended to propose to you there in Honolulu and then I woke up with a hangover and the realization that you were marrying another man." He drew on his cigarette again. "This is the last time. Will you marry me?" He stared defiantly into the blaze, shoulders hunched, prepared for a blow.

She just watched him, so strong but so vulnerable, and as she watched she felt tears rushing to her eyes. When she did speak her voice was choked.

"Yes, Ted," she said. "Yes, please, I want to be married to you." She moved forward and cradled his head against her bare breasts and felt the love coursing from his body to hers. "I don't know," she murmured, crying, "what took me so long. I love you, Ted."

They stayed at the cottage four days, walking in the woods and on the beach once the storm passed, making love in the afternoons and evenings, exploring each other, learning more than they'd thought possible. They were supremely happy: Angie realized she was, for the first time in her life, thoroughly at ease, without a single doubt or fear.

In one of the newspapers Ted picked up in the village they read a gossip column item about how a columnist on the *Telegraph*, Adam Carleton, had been beaten up by three men outside an East Side Manhattan bar. The item said Carleton had so many enemies the police didn't know where to start looking for the thugs.

The *Times* business section had a long interview with Richard Mansion about his plans to put a satellite receiving dish in the backyard of every American home. Richard came across very confident and the figures he quoted were staggering.

Ted read the interview, shaking his head mournfully.

"What none of these interviews mention," he said, "is the sheer naked power it'll give him, or anyone else who gets a monopoly on that kind of system. He'll have millions of homes plugged in directly to his transmission. It makes the present network and cable systems look benign. But the people who interview Richard are just dazzled by the figures. They don't think about the social implications." He glanced at her. "I don't think your brother-in-law is the kind of man to be given such a dangerous monopoly. This is too sinister."

"Neither do I," she said cheerfully. "And maybe we'll have to do something about it. But not now, not until we're back in the city. For now, come kiss me again."

Chapter
Seventeen

Johnny Howard was aghast. He dropped his head in his hands and groaned.

"Married! What in hell do you think you're doing, Angie?" He sighed. "Alex's will gives you control of your shares 'as long as she remains a Mansion.' What that means, Angie, is if you marry someone outside the family, you don't get to vote the stock. If you don't vote the stock, Richard's going to kick your ass right out of Mansion Communications, Inc. And he'll sell the newspaper division ten minutes after that."

"Well, the children are very happy for me, Johnny," she said, smiling at him. She was on such a high. She loved everyone. And the children *had* been so thrilled. They already loved Ted and they wanted Angie to be happy. "I want you to be happy, too. I don't care about the shares."

"But why get married?" he demanded, truly quite bewildered. "You never gave me a hint you were thinking of marrying again. Hell, if I'd known I'd have been in there myself, pressing my suit. I thought you were only interested in being the best publisher in the business. If you'd given me a chance . . . because, the odd thing is, you could marry *me* and still keep control of the stock. I'm a Mansion as far as the will's concerned.'' He stood up and came around the desk and stood next to her chair. ''There isn't a chance for me, is there?'' He shook his head, answering his own question. ''Well, I'll try and be a good loser. But why in hell get married? Just live together. Then you can keep both you and Ted in your jobs.''

''I have to marry him, Johnny,'' she said. ''There've been two or three times in my life when I've been so close to Ted, and each time I couldn't see what he was offering me. Now I can. It's my last chance for happiness.'' She stood up and kissed him on the cheek. ''You've been so good to me. I'm worried you'll feel I'm letting everyone down by doing this. But I want to be happy, Johnny.''

''You're entitled,'' he said grudgingly. ''But no one's going to be happier than Richard. He needs to sell off the newspaper division and he wants you out anyhow. You're giving him yourself and the papers on a silver platter.''

''I just don't care about him anymore,'' she said. ''There was a time when my hatred of Richard Mansion consumed me. That's all over now.''

''Richard won't see it that way,'' Johnny said. ''He hates you. Or he's afraid of you—which is worse. He won't let you walk away quietly. You won't come out of this very well anyway. You've got the Beekman Place house to yourself, so that's a nice piece of change. But Virginia was left to the children and you've no shares in the company in your own right. If you insist on marrying, you'll be left with nothing.''

361

"It doesn't bother me, Johnny," she said. "I'll do a column for someone, or a TV show. And Ted's about the best editor in the business. Oh, I *will* miss seeing the newspapers run as well as they can be. We were getting there, Ted and I. What I won't miss is fighting with Richard all the time."

"But you're playing right into his hands, doing this," he protested hotly. "He gets rid of you and the papers in one stroke. You've let him beat you."

"I can't help that," she answered. "I'll just be glad to have Richard Mansion out of my life."

"This doesn't sound like you," Johnny argued, refusing to give up.

"So I've changed," she said. "Or maybe the fighter in me was just a facade. I do care about the papers, though, and I'm going to keep control of them until the last possible minute. A lot of effort by a lot of good people has gone into those newspapers."

"They're yours just as long as your name stays Mansion," he said. "Forever, if you'll just be sensible." He looked at her solemnly. "Think about it, Angie."

Think about it? Did he believe her lighthearted dismissal of the newspapers? Didn't he see through her act? She'd thought of nothing but those newspapers for so long. And now, she realized, she was going to have to shove them away from her . . . the way she'd once shoved away her feelings for Ted. She couldn't hold on to the newspaper division as a part-time thing, anyway. It was be publisher or get out, and if she meant to have any life for herself, getting out was all that was left. She wished it could be otherwise: it couldn't.

She stopped off in Washington on her way to Virginia, where she was meeting Emily and Curt. She could only spare an hour at the *Tribune* office, so she had to get Ted out of his editorial meeting.

"Enjoy those meetings while you can," she told him, "because there aren't going to be many more of them." She filled him in quickly. "So you see, when I marry you we're both going to be without jobs."

He looked at her across the space between them.

"It doesn't matter to me," he said carefully. "There are other jobs. But I didn't know about Alex's will. Are you sure you want the marriage if this is what it costs you?"

She moved into his arms.

"Yes, Ted," she said, her voice muffled against his chest. "Yes, it's what I want."

Then she had to tell the children the papers were finished. Like Ted and like Johnny, they were amazed she would give the papers up.

"Are you sure there's nothing we can do to keep control of the papers for you?" Curt insisted. "Between Emily and me and David we've got a decent-size block of shares. And Johnny Howard would vote with us."

"You'd still be short of a majority," she said. "Richard gets to vote *all* his father's stock once I'm out of the boardroom."

"But what about Grandfather's wishes?" Emily demanded. "He wanted the newspapers to go on forever, you know that. He cared more about them than he did for Uncle Richard's television network. Why didn't he leave a will to that effect?"

"I don't know, dear," Angie said. "But he's gone now and there's nothing we can do. Maybe there was no other way to write the will. I'm sorry, I know it looks like I'm just walking away from the whole thing for selfish reasons, but even if I didn't desperately want to marry Ted, I don't think I could have kept up those battles with Richard—it hasn't been fun."

She assumed her capitulation would calm Richard. He'd hardly have to put up with her at all now. But when she returned to New York, Johnny Howard warned her the situation had gotten worse.

"He wants you out well before the election," Johnny said. "He wants to be able to deliver the whole group endorsement to the party, to clinch his satellite deal. He even," Johnny added wryly, "concedes that the newspaper endorsement might make a small difference in a tight race. Of course, if Richard's party loses, the satellite deal dies."

"Hell, I'm not moving out of the publisher's chair until I'm good and ready," Angie said angrily. "And that will be after the election. We've made something good out of those newspapers and I'm not letting Richard corrupt them."

"Why go on fighting?" he asked. He seemed weary of the whole matter. "You're getting out soon, so let Richard have his victory now. I might be able to negotiate you a better settlement if you're gracious."

"No, Johnny." She shook her head emphatically. "I'm staying to the end. You can tell Richard I said so, if you like."

Richard arrived unannounced at Beekman Place a couple of nights later. At first he was urbane and polite, in extraordinary contrast to his usual conduct.

"I think it's silly for us to still be fighting over what is now just a matter of time," he said. "You're going anyhow, so what's it matter who the papers endorse? I could make it worth your while—"

"No, Richard," she said, "you haven't bought me

yet and you're not going to buy me now. What are you worried about? Ken Beckworth told me the newspaper endorsements didn't matter."

"Yeah, Beckworth suddenly retreated," Richard said. "I can't figure why. But his masters still want across-the-board endorsements. They're starting to run scared."

"Good," she said.

He scowled at her, then forced his expression into as much of a smile as he could manage.

"Can I appeal to your family loyalty?" he asked. "We *need* the satellite deal to generate the kind of profits that'll keep us on top of the industry." He began pacing her drawing room. "Angie, I'm scared of what's going to happen in the television business," he said. Again there was that forced smile. "Already the cream is off the networks. Owning a network used to be a license to print money. But pay TV, cable, and those goddamned videotape players are hurting us badly. I want to lead the Mansion network into satellite broadcasting so we can keep up our growth. I want to leave something wonderful to the next generation. The Mansion children. Think of Curt and Emily," he wheedled. "And think of my father. You claimed to be so close to him. What would he have said in this situation?"

"He would have said, Richard—as he did say on many occasions—that you are a devious, dangerous, unprincipled son-of-a-bitch and not to be trusted," she said.

He reddened.

"Don't speak about my father like that!" he shouted. "You . . . cheap little fortune hunter. You set your cap for us a long time ago. You'd have done anything to become a Mansion! You seduced me years ago, thinking I'd marry you. But I was too smart for you so you turned your charm on my poor dumb little brother. And he fell for you and it was the death of him. Jesus, I'll be glad when you can no longer use our name. My poor father, he was senile when he fell under your spell."

He was ranting, in full flight, dropping any pretense of civility.

"How dare *you* tell *me* what you're going to print in newspapers owned by *my* family?" he stormed. "I won't stand for it. I should have fought you long ago, and exposed you for what you are. But I stood back, like a fool, and let you seduce this family. Lyle's poor children, looking up to you! Ha! And even my own son. He should have seen through you, but he's a degenerate, too."

Angie didn't want to say any more. She was afraid of this raving figure. She just wanted him to leave. If he did, she would give up. He could have his papers, endorse anyone he chose, right now. She just wanted out.

"Richard," she said softly, "there's no point in going on . . ."

"No point!" he shouted, murderous hatred in his eyes. I'll show you what happens when you take on someone like me. I'm going to grind you into the mud. When I'm finished with you, you'll wish you'd never heard the name Mansion." He took a step toward her, his hand upraised.

She moved away, really fearful. But anger was growing in her, too. "I *do* wish it! I wished I'd never heard that name from the night you drugged and raped me on your boat," she cried. "That night you robbed me of so much—my self-respect, even the chance to ever have my own child. I never wanted to know a Mansion again after that. And years later, when I met poor, sweet Lyle, I held it against him for being the same blood as you. But *he* was a good man. And the new generations of Mansions are fine people." He stood stock-still, listening, his face blank. "You could have just left us alone, Richard, but you couldn't bear to see your brother happy. On his own wedding day you told him—what was it, exactly?— about our night on your boat. You started his death then, Richard." She was crying hard. The tears wouldn't stop.

"You think what I told Lyle hurt him!" he sneered. "Wait till you see the job I'm going to do on you. We'll see how much support you have from the children when I tell them you fucked me first, then married their father because *I* wasn't available. And all the other people you fucked like that black bastard on television. And you and your best friend, the lesbian. I'll tell them all about the pair of you! I'll even tell Ted Buchanan, the poor schmuck, the kind of whore he's marrying."

"You do that, Richard," she said in an utterly calm voice, the tears wiped out by sheer fury. "Tell the children lies and peddle filth to Ted. I'd like that because, unlike poor Lyle who just let his heart be broken by your lies, Ted knows the truth. Ted would dearly love to beat you to within an inch of your life."

He lashed out at her, catching her a glancing blow across the face, knocking her against the curtained windows. She lay on the floor, stunned, and watched him advance on her. His eyes were glazed. His hands stretched out to seize her, and he fell on her and closed a hand around her throat.

"You bitch!" he hissed. "I had you before and I'll have you again. And then I'll throw you into the street." His other hand was tearing at her clothing as she clawed at the hand on her throat. Her blouse parted under the onslaught and her skirt rode up around her hips. He was gripping her throat even tighter now and she was beginning to black out.

A strong hand grabbed Richard Mansion by the back of his collar and savagely jerked his head up, freeing her throat. David Mansion pulled his father to his feet and began punching him, short, hard blows that doubled the older man over, then wrenched him up again. The beating went on forever, the silence broken only by gasps from Richard.

Dizzy, Angie adjusted her clothes and crawled away from the men. Richard Mansion finally fell to the floor, facedown, and his son stood over him, lean and strong, shaking with terrible rage. With a single contemptuous flick of his booted foot he turned his father over.

"Get the fuck out of here while I'm still in control of myself," he growled. "Quick!" he snapped, and Mansion rose to his knees. David said nothing as his father dragged himself out of the room. When they heard him being ushered out, David went to Angie and helped her up.

They sat facing each other in the formal room in the grand town house, silent, sickened. Finally, white-faced, his voice straining, David Mansion spoke.

"I knew what a shit he was," he said, "always. From the time I was a little kid. But when I listened to him tonight—I'm sorry, I came by, was let in, and couldn't help eavesdropping on you—I realized he was much worse than any of us believed. Sure, Mansions are supposed to be tough, but my father is sick. I should have killed him."

"Thanks, David," she whispered, her voice husky,

her neck throbbing. "You were just in time. This can't
. . . can't be easy for you."

"I'm sorry for everything," he said. "You must
hate us all so much."

"Now, David," she said, "don't take your father's
sins on yourself. None of it is your fault. And I don't
hate your family." She got up. "We both need a
drink. It's been an awful night. Did I say thank you?
Thank you, David."

He nodded, mute and miserable.

She called Ted after David left, having decided absolutely not to tell Ted what had happened.

"I'm going to quit in two weeks," she said. "I can't
take it anymore. But there's one last big assignment
we're going to do together. I'll fly down tomorrow.
We'll need our best reporters on standby."

"Sure," he said, his voice so soothing. "But what
happened? I thought you were staying on to the
end."

"Nothing, Ted," she said, "nothing I want to talk
about."

It took a week to put all the material together without any errors, to do it right. It was their last gesture.
All they left out were Ken Beckworth's theft of her
check and the vicious campaign designed to destroy
Trish Hardy. But the rest was all there, all the details
of the newsprint loan to Lyle Mansion and the *quid pro
quo* demanded by the administration. Also, chapter
and verse of the deal struck between Richard Mansion and party fixers to give him exclusive satellite access.

It was compiled with great secrecy. Dummy stories
were set up to lead the front pages of the *Tribune* and
the *Sentinel*. At the last moment, the Mansion exposés

were inserted in place of the dummies and the presses began to roll in Washington and New York. There was no time for anyone to stop them.

The phones started to ring in the *Tribune* publisher's office as soon as the first edition reached the streets. They ignored the clamor and sat together quietly. There was no celebration between Angie and Ted, just a sense of having done what needed to be done.

"It's all over," Angie sighed. "I guess I'll finish cleaning out my desk. We can go home now."

"To a nice long vacation before the wedding," Ted laughed. "Because you and I aren't going to be employable after what we just did." He laughed again. "I guess it's Arizona, here we come."

Epilogue

It was as she had planned it, a quiet wedding in a garden. The California sun warmed them gently, far from the freezing Washington January. She stole a look around the little group who were listening to the minister as he led her and Ted through their vows.

Her mother, tears in her eyes, looked sprightly and well, tanned, ageless. The old beau holding May's hand was a charming, intelligent man. Angie smiled as she thought of them, so happy out here, writing magazine pieces and tending their orange grove.

There was Trish, tall and lovely and proud, the freshman congressman from New York, glowing with vigor she hadn't had in years. Trish was the only politician they'd invited: Angie and Ted were still a major embarrassment to both sides of Congress.

It would be a long while before politicians believed they had the measure of Angie or Ted.

On the other side of her were the children. Not children anymore, of course. Emily was a pretty, confident woman, Curt a serious, upright young man. Laconic David had a wry half-smile on his face. Johnny Howard was risking a great deal by being there. She was deeply touched that he cared for her enough to venture into enemy territory.

She spoke her responses and Ted put the ring on her finger and they kissed. Happiness and love welled up inside her, and something else—a wonderful sense of certainty, that she had done the right thing at last. All those years hadn't been wasted, they had been preparation for this moment.

They were all drinking champagne in a happy hum of conversation and congratulations when the Mansion contingent edged Angie and Ted away into a corner of the garden.

"We thought we'd better speak to both you before you went away on a long vacation," David said. "Things have been happening."

"Yes," Emily said, laughing. "There have been fireworks in the family councils."

"We voted with the others to sell off the newspaper division," Curt said solemnly. "What with the Mansion interests being refused access to the satellite, the television network badly needs the money from the newspaper sale."

"So," said Johnny, "there's a chain of newspapers on the market now at a reasonable price. A new company—Wall Street still hasn't figured out who they are—tendered for the newspapers last week. The offer was accepted two days ago. Richard doesn't care who bought them, so he made no effort to find out."

"I'm sorry they had to go," Angie said, real hurt in her voice. "It doesn't seem right, the Mansion family out of the newspaper business."

"We're not out of the newspaper business," Curt said. "We four pooled our stock and some money. We are the mystery buyers. Our problem now is finding a publisher and an editor-in-chief for the newly created Mansion Press. We wondered if you two would take those jobs. Do you think you would?''

She glanced at Ted, got no reaction from him, and looked back at Curt, then slowly at Emily and David and Johnny. They were all looking at her with barely contained expressions of glee. The big bad wolf was dead, though no one was going to put it quite that way.

''Uh,'' she stammered, ''I hadn't planned on going back to work this soon, but . . .''

Ted was looking at her now, mock exasperation on his face.

''Well, I'm game, Angie. I mean, how long can a guy lie around on the beach?''

''I see,'' she said sweetly. ''But do you think you can cope with working for my children *and* me?''

He sighed and scratched his head. ''If not, I figure there's always Arizona.''